T0150655

BETA-LIFE

Stories from an
A-Life Future

Edited by
Martyn Amos
& Ra Page

First published in Great Britain in 2014 by Comma Press.
www.commapress.co.uk

Copyright © 2014 remains with the authors.
This collection copyright © Comma Press.
All rights reserved.

The right of the authors to be identified has been asserted in accordance with the
Copyright Designs and Patent Act 1988.

A CIP catalogue record of this book is available from the British Library.

This collection is entirely a work of fiction. The characters and incidents portrayed
in it are entirely the work of the authors' imagination, although some stories are
based loosely on certain documented events. The opinions of the authors, scientists
and historians are not those of the publisher.

ISBN   1905583656
ISBN-13   978 1905583652

Supported by
**ARTS COUNCIL
ENGLAND**

The publisher gratefully acknowledges the assistance of Arts Council England,
and the support of Literature Northwest.
This project has been supported by the European Commission Future and
Emerging Technologies programme, via the TRUCE (Training and Research in
Unconventional Computation in Europe) project.

TRUCE
Training and Research in Unconventional Computation in Europ

Set in Bembo 11/13 by David Eckersall.
Printed and bound in England by Berforts Information Press Ltd.

Contents

CONTENTS

Introduction:
How the Future Used to Look

COMPLEXITY AND LITERARY FUTURISM don't mix. We prefer our prophecies – whether utopian or dystopian – to be simple, pure; to select one emergent facet of society and project it, in its barest logic, stripped of any pragmatic compromises, onto the white screen of the future. It's what makes for the best stories: a backdrop that is itself an enemy for the protagonist to rail against, an inbuilt lack.

This rather ignores a fundamental law of the cosmos. The second law of thermodynamics dictates that as time moves forward, disorder increases... everywhere, in all directions, ineffably. Entropy rules and the universe is doomed to dissipation. The future and simplification are anathema. This perhaps explains why the golden era of futurist SF is so far behind us. Whilst we are right to admire the great masterworks of dystopia – Zamyatin's *We*, Huxley's *Brave New World*, Orwell's *1984* – it is well to remember that whatever 'emergent facets' these books picked out and distilled from their part of the 20th century, according to the second law they must be far, far less complicated than equivalent factors today. To 'futurize' our present concerns in a dystopian or utopian way would be far too great a simplification – they're too entangled for that now. In terms of cinematic and literary narratives, the whole project of prophesying and predicting, second-guessing the future, has become a little passé. Any attempt to paint the future dates even faster than our attempts to paint the present (old sci-fi TV shows look more 'of their time', than contemporary dramas of the day). Indeed if literary authors write about the future at all these days, it's usually just the near-future. Never a bold half-century away.

Beta-Life isn't going to be deterred by this. Its challenge for authors is to pitch new fictions way off, in the rather arbitrarily chosen year of 2070[1]. Growing from an initial meeting between authors and researchers at the *European Conference on Artificial Life* in September 2013, the project has paired 19 authors with scientists working in a range of artificial life and unconventional computing disciplines, from facial recognition to pattern recognition, brain-interfacing to crowd modelling. The authors' mission: to follow the research itself into the future, rather than reflect purely on current concerns; to regard the scientists as guides, cicerones into the great labyrinth of the future.

Complexity can't be avoided, of course. Indeed, the study of it sits at the heart of artificial life (A-Life) as a discipline. In many cases, A-Life cedes to the ultimate engineer of complexity, evolution, and either simulates naturally-evolved systems, or runs a version of evolution itself to design, solve or explore. In either case, complexity is the motor, the way forward – both in the natural unfolding of things, and in the way our technology must keep pace with that unfolding. So it should be for authors, wanting to keep pace with that keeping pace.

To put it another way, soon man-made technology will no longer stand apart from the natural world; the division between artificial and organic will blur, as the name 'A-Life' suggests. Instead technology will start to learn from life, model it, merge with it. We're being a little dramatic here, perhaps, but consider the other driving technology in this progress – unconventional computing – which itself plays a key part in the stories that follow.

Computation forms the nervous system of our modern society. *Unconventional* computing is an emerging research

---

1. Happily for us, exactly 250 years after Charles Xavier Thomas's first calculating machine, the Arithometer, was patented.

area that concerns 'non-standard' methods for performing computations. Researchers in the field are exploring new territory in the space of computational possibilities offered by materials such as DNA molecules, living cells and quantum chips. The very notion of a 'computer' is itself evolving, as models emerge that transcend von Neumann and Turing.

This image of the natural and the man-made merging and interbreeding is borne out by many of the stories here. Adam Marek's 'Gardening Skyscrapers' considers how synthetic biology might be put to use in the construction of that most ambitious and thrusting of man-made structures. Sarah Schofield's 'The Bactogarden' imagines similar technologies being used to heighten the gourmet's culinary experience. Other stories show science and technology exploiting naturally evolved complexity for its own benefit – either as a model to study, such as in Margaret Wilkinson's 'Quivering Woods' and Sean O'Brien's 'Certain Measures', or as a ready-made problem solver, an unconventional computer, as we see in Julian Gough's 'Blurred Lines' and Joanna Quinn's 'The War of All Against All'.

This metaphor of interbreeding or cross-contaminating is useful when considering how futurist writing might embrace complexity and navigate through its ever-deepening waters. Whereas classic dystopia writers like Zamyatin and Huxley saw their 'emergent facets' as simply diametrically opposing ideologies or conflicting systems of government – top-down authoritarianism (Zamyatin's *We*) versus bottom-up consumerism (Huxley's *Brave New World*) – a 'complex futurist' might do better to consider these opposing ideologies rather as expressions of a global symbiosis – top-down predators controlling whole ecosystems in the East, versus bottom-up bacteria colonizing their own niches in the West. The dystopian simplifiers would no doubt claim that the fall of the Iron Curtain marked a simple victory for one system over the other. But in our model, it wasn't a victory but the beginning of an interbreeding or cross-contaminating: the financial collapse of 2008 bringing an end to the gestation period, when suddenly, so-called capitalist states had to renationalize banks (albeit temporarily), and the remaining so-called communist superpower, China, effectively financed the West's ideological inversion with the proceeds of a system that had become, at heart, capitalist in all but name. Each side suddenly found the DNA of its rival emerging like an infestation in its nucleus, whilst externally maintaining the shell of its former ideology.

How are writers supposed to pick through this complexity? Let alone prophesy about a future 55 years into further interbreeding between already-hybrid systems?

Maybe, in the end, they're not. Maybe science fiction was never any more than just an allegory for the present dressed up in the technology of the future. Perhaps *1984* was just 1948, nothing more. Some of the stories produced by this project square up to this possibility, unflinchingly. Robin Yassin-Kassab's 'Swarm' holds the mirror of nanotechnology up to a very current world crisis, and invites us to rethink it. Frank Cottrell-Boyce's 'Bruno Wins!' allows for the possibility that taking future predictions too seriously could actually hinder progress.

But in commissioning these stories we are suggesting there might be a way for forward for futurist SF. At the start of this introduction we implied that complexity and futurism were wholly incompatible. As with any half-decent story-arc, the set-up was pure misdirection. It was a false opposition. Complexity and disorder (that which increases with time, according to the second law) are not the same thing. Complexity has very humble, mathematically simple origins; it can be grasped, harnessed, characterised. It relies on simple interactions occurring time and again, and it carries that simple iterative idea along with it, just as evolution carries the notion of the individual (even if each individual's DNA is different) along with it. This abiding 'I' is what saves futurist literature. The protagonist travailing against his or her context (which is often just a manifestation of the 'collective') is the central building block – the chronotope – of all stories. It is how writers are able to pitch their characters in the future, the past, or anywhere else. The individual will always have a collective to fight against – the clash of 'protagonist versus society' that defines the *bildungsroman*. Only, in our current futures (as opposed to Huxley's and Zamyatin's), the collective is closer to hand. It might be the homestead's swarm of 'robjects', as Adam Roberts suggests. It may be the family unit, as in Zoe Lambert's 'Keynote'. It may even be conflicting components of the protagonist's subconscious. The future has shrunk, it seems. The collective is no longer the epic backdrop of the state or the prevailing ideology; it has been miniaturised and now wants to nestle up close to us, become intimate, interface and network with the 'I'. Perhaps, in this respect, we can see why the novel, with its epic, sky-blue backdrops, may not be so compatible with the current version of the future. Perhaps only the short story is compact and cellular enough to infest it.

Martyn Amos & Ra Page

The Sayer of the Sooth

Martyn Bedford

LOGAN STANDS AT the basin in the en suite bathroom and raises his eyes to his reflection. All day, he stares at faces. Studies the data that leak from them. Compiles the analyses. Composes his reports. But those are others' faces. His own, he can hardly bear to look at anymore. Tonight, though, he makes himself linger before the lightly tinted glass, holding the gaze that holds his.

On one of the early dates with Mia he stood at the mirror in a pub restroom and looked himself in the face, just as he is doing now.

'Why would she be interested in you, you sad, old, ugly bastard?' he said out loud.

He was 44, she was 31. He's 56 now. They've been together the same length of time that his first marriage lasted. Which goes to show. Logan doesn't know what it goes to show, exactly. He doesn't know anything these days. Those features in the mirror belong to a stranger.

Through the closed door, he hears Mia in the bedroom. A drawer opens, the dressing-table stool creaks. She'll be stripping away her day-face and applying her night-face. He pictures her: the raised eyebrows, the widened eyes, the flared nostrils, the elongated O of her mouth as she stretches the skin across the bones of her skull. Her dark hair, scraped into a ponytail.

In his head, Logan rehearses the conversation they'll have when he leaves the bathroom. The trick will be to slip the key question in as if it carries no more weight than anything else.

How was Kirsten?

He has to make sure they're looking directly at one another when he asks it.

1

Logan removes a small case and a bottle of fluid from his dressing-gown pocket and places them on the ledge of the basin. He draws the dropper from the bottle. Tilts his head back and squeezes a couple of drips into his left eye, then two more into his right.

Mia is humming. He can't make out the tune through the bathroom door.

How was Kirsten?

There's a metallic taste in his mouth. His fingers tremble as he stows the bottle back in his pocket. Logan composes himself. Once his hands are steady again, he clicks open the case and lifts out the first of the lenses on the tip of his little finger.

Thats how the story begins.

My greatgrandfather wrote it far back in 2014 – 35 years before I was born – and here it is in a science fiction anthology. Granny Josephine sent it me.

A literal paper book in the literal mail. Hugely old and creased and yellowy.

The note tucked inside said 'Jack, I came across this when I was sorting out some boxes of my dad's stuff and thought you might be interested. The stories are all set in 2070! I don't recall ever reading his, however I do vaguely remember him promising to make me and your Great-Aunt Polly characters in it. As you'll see, he didn't. Granny J xx'

I never knew greatgrandad (long passed by the time I turned up) although I have read one of his novels – Granny J gifted it me when I started e-uni. Didnt rate it. But then I dont like any of the late Second Elizabethans. To be honest if it hadnt been for the 2070 coincidence I doubt Id have bothered to read this short story.

Youd never know it was set in 2070 from the opening scene though.

Maybe he couldnt imagine what a bathroom would be like 56 years into the future so decided to play safe and keep it neutral. Im guessing the lenses are mind reading devices. And its obvious the woman – Mia (is that a name?) – has told

Logan she was out with this friend Kirsten when shes actually been cheating on him.

Ha! Just tried to use voice-activation to turn the page! Glad Dex wasnt here to see me do *that*.

Looks like we leave the bathroom scene now to fill in some backstory. Yawnsome.

Logan had worked at TruTell for nine years before applying to transfer to the NPD section. Not that he was authorised to know which new products were in development at that stage. First there was the interview, psychometrics, induction. Only once he'd passed and had thumbed a confidentiality agreement

He thinks we use *thumbprints* to sign documents in 2070?!

was he granted access to the part of the complex known as 'the bunker'. Mia had no idea. He couldn't tell anyone outside the company the true nature of his job. He explained away the salary increase and longer hours as the result of a promotion within the data-rationalising section.

The paradox of lying about a job in the lie-detection business wasn't lost on Logan.

Skimming down the text I see it goes on like this for another half page or so: Whole place is buzzing with rumours about the latest R&D... after so long working on TruTells traditional progs and apps Logans excited to be at the cutting edge... Blardyblardyblardy.

Im already getting eye strain from reading on-paper. And all that *punctuation*.

Out of curiosity I search TruTell (on Mi-fi after tapping the word on the page a couple of times before I figured out why nothing was happening). No such company. Pity. It wouldve been good and spooky if the old boy had invented a business that had literally come into existence. Not that greatgrandad was all that old when he wrote this. 54. Two years younger than Logan. He didnt even have the imagination to create a lead who wasnt his own gender and roughly the same age.

Its too easy to see where the lie detection angle is headed when we eventually get Logan from the bathroom to the bedroom. The cheating wife. The questions he plans to ask her while he's wearing those hitech lenses.

I could write the rest of the story myself.

Logan settled into a seat across the desk from the project manager. Jaswinder Kaur. Please call me Jazz. Late 30s. Bright-eyed, intelligent-looking. Her bare forearms ought to have been hirsute but were smooth and hairless. Only the lower half of her face smiled.

'Welcome to the bunker, Jack.'

Hey Logan has the same first name as me! Good one greatgrandad.

As they talk Im not picturing Jazz too well. Which gives me an idea.

'Mi-screen' I say and the wall across the room blooms into light. Dont know why I didnt think of it before. I hold up the book at the scene Im reading. 'Scan text and play.'

2D or 3D? Mi-screen asks.

'2D.' Dex thinks Im weird but I cant be doing with immersive. Makes me queasy.

The wallcam gives a single bright-white blink and there they are — Jaswinder Kaur and Jack Logan — chatting across a desk. The avatars are defaults. Her voice is too cheerful but at least she has dark hair and skin. As for Logan he looks like that guy who massacred all those people last month at the climate refugee camp.

I v/a the story to pause while I customise them. Hugely better.

'Resume.'

Shes briefing Logan about the project and Im tempted to overnarrate and have them fuck right there on the desk. I don't though. This is my greatgrandads story after all.

4

She placed a small transparent case and a bottle of eye-drops on the desk in front of him.

'Contact lenses?' Logan asked.

'Go on, try them.' Jazz Kaur smirked, like a conjuror about to name the mystery playing card a member of the audience had picked from a deck.

Once the lenses were in, he let his gaze roam: the unpatterned grey floor-covering, the spiky leaves of a yucca, the reflection of a ceiling light-panel on the desk's glossy surface. Finally, Jazz's face. Everything looked exactly as it had before.

'Ask me a question,' she said. 'Anything you like.'

With so much choice, his mind went blank. He shrugged. 'Why am I wearing them?'

'Because I want you to see for yourself what the prototype does.' As she finished speaking, Logan could have sworn there was a brief flash of green light before his eyes. 'Ask me something else,' she said. 'Ask me my name.'

'Okay, what's your name?'

'My name is Jack Logan,' the woman said.

This time the flash was red. Logan laughed.

'I know.' Jazz was smiling with the whole of her face now. 'Tell me if I'm getting too technical for you, here, but in NPD this is what we call fucking incredible.'

A flash of amber this time.

Pointing to his eyes, Logan said, 'So, this is—'

'Silent Talker in a pair of contact lenses. Yes, that's exactly what it is.' Green light.

'But the colours—'

'Visible only to the wearer. Same as with the glasses.' Green.

'There have been Silent Talker glasses?'

'Yes. But you're not authorised to know that.' Green. 'I'm afraid I'll have to kill you now, Jack.' Red.

Logan laughed again. He took out both lenses and held one of them between thumb and middle finger, studying it, raising it to the light. 'The software?' he asked. 'Camera, mic?'

'Integrated into the lenses,' Jazz said. 'The size of the transistors wasn't too much of an issue. It was quite some job, though, to produce conductive paths narrow enough to connect it all up but wide enough to carry an electron. And to make everything transparent, of course.'

'Of course.'

She must have picked up on Logan's tone. 'Oh, same here – I'm just quoting what the guys and gals in Materials told me.'

'What about power?' Logan asked. 'I mean, are we talking about... what, an invisible battery tiny enough to fit into a contact lens? And with enough capacity to actually work?'

'Who was it who said that any advanced technology is indistinguishable from magic?'

'Arthur C. Clarke. And it was 'sufficiently advanced'.'

'Sufficiently. Yes.' Jazz indicated the lens Logan was holding. 'The battery converts energy from blinking and eye-movement into electricity to maintain the charge while you're wearing them. The lenses are powered by your eyes – isn't that some way north of phenomenal?'

'Don't they heat up, though?'

'What do I have to do to impress you?'

'You could tell me they won't burn holes in people's eyes,' Logan said.

'Look, I can't even pronounce the stuff these lenses are made of but, with the eye-drops, they test to 60-minute pre-discomfort endurance. No corneal damage. No allergenic issues. No holes. Gesturing for him to pass her the lenses, she said, 'Here, let me show you the upload.'

Jazz produced a thicker than usual mem-stick from a drawer and pressed each lens into an aperture in its side, then inserted the stick in a port in the drive panel on her desk. On the screen along one side of her work station, the plain grey floor pulled into focus, then the yucca plant, and so on, until the picture settled on the project manager's face. Her voice rang out sharp and clear. Ask me a question. Anything you like.

The glasses I mightve believed. But lie detection contact lenses with invisible miniaturised components? From a writer who cant even imagine the details of a 2070 bathroom. What next: Logan flies home from work in his jetpack to be greeted at the door by the automated yapping of a pet robo-dog?

Indistinguishable from magic. Thats an easy out for an SF writer isnt it?

I pause the story. 'Search for Silent Talker' I say.

A block of text appears in front of Jazzs freezed face. Yawnsome. I v/a audio.

Silent Talker was a computerized, non-invasive psychological profiling system for the collection and analysis of non-verbal behaviour. By means of Artificial Neural Networks, the system used multiple channels of micro-observations of a filmed subject to determine his or her psychological state when speaking. Its primary application was the detection of, and distinguishing between, truthful and deceptive non-verbal signal patterns.

'Simplify for fucks sake.'

'"For fuck's sake" is an exclamation which indicates–'

'No. Simplify Silent Tal–'

It hits me that Mi-fi *deliberately* misunderstood me. This is Dexs doing – overwriting the program to enable Randomised Disambiguation Failure. It passes for humour in the IT realm she inhabits. I fall for it every time.

'Very funny' I say.

Is it my imagination or does Mi-fi sound just a little pleased with itself as it gives me the proper answer?

Silent Talker used computer analysis of faces to tell whether people were lying.

'More. History.'

Silent Talker was invented and patented in the first decade of the 21st Century by a team of computing scientists at Manchester Metropolitan University. After successful trials and further refinements, yielding an accuracy rate of >90%, Silent Talker attracted interest from investors. Rebranded as F.A.C.E. (Facial Analysis and Classification Evaluator) – or the 'lying eye', as it became popularly known – the system entered commercial production in 2020 and by the end of that decade was in widespread use in the UK – for example, among police, security, intelligence and border control agencies, as well as in legal proceedings and in the prevention of *welfare fraud. Other markets soon opened up and by the 2040s F.A.C.E. had established itself as the leading international brand in anti-deception technology (ADT).*

Oh well everyones heard of the lying eye. Never mind writing a short story about it – greatgrandad shouldve bought shares.

'More history' I say. 'Anything on lie detection glasses or contact lenses?'

'F.A.C.E. Inc. launched a glasses version in 2055 but the prohibitive cost and media 'scare' stories about the risk of eye damage and brain tumours resulted in poor sales and the product was discontinued in 2058. No historical information on ADT contact lenses.'

So. Poor old Jack Logan – a cheating wife a dud plot and a pair of hitech lenses that are approximately 100% fairy dust. I should put the book down. But with Dex at her job interview and no virtual lectures today Ive nothing better to do.

'TruLens is the holy grail,' Jazz told Logan. 'Non-detectable lie-detection.'

He waited for her to continue.

'Using Silent Talker on traditional devices – cameras, cams, phones, droids and so on – there's little or no chance to hide the fact that the viewee is being filmed,' she said. 'Even with TruSpecs, the problem was–'

'Their high cost and the fear of blindness and brain cancer' I say.

'–that, once their existence was public knowledge, no matter how carefully we designed them to look like regular glasses, they ran the risk of viewees suspecting they were being lie-detected.'

'Not to mention the cost. Or the fear of blindness and brain cancer.'

Logan nodded. 'And if the viewer didn't usually wear glasses—'

'Exactly. With TruLens, though… imagine it, Jack — one day, anyone who can afford a pair of the little cuties will never be deceived again.'

'But, surely,' Logan said, 'if TruLens becomes popular then there's always the possibility of being lie-detected. In every conversation, by everyone we meet. And if other people can wear them without us ever being sure of it, the whole world is going to be clamouring for a pair.'

Jazz grinned. 'Do you want to break the bad news to Sales and Marketing?'

Logan loved working on TruLens.

In those early months, the prototype was trialled in-house, with members of the team as viewer and viewee. His task was to analyze the footage and compile his reports. Any hardware or software glitches would be fixed ahead of the lenses being tested 'out there', as Jazz called the world beyond the perimeter fence of TruTell HQ.

After the cancellation of TruSpecs, this new project — this holy grail — electrified the team in the bunker and Logan couldn't help being caught up in it all. For a time, at least.

'Logans avatar.' And there he is gazing out at me from the wall-screen.

Hes dressed in smart-casual office clothes from the early 2060s to show hes out of date compared to his younger colleagues. Ive made him look like greatgrandad I realise — what Ive seen of him in old photos. Tall thinning on top and round shouldered. Ive given him (Logan) the big nose that he (greatgrandad) gave dad and me.

'Edit expression. Edit posture. Logan dislikes himself. Logan thinks hes unattractive and old. Logan suspects his wife of cheating on him. Logans afraid of losing her.'

As I speak the avatar reconfigures. He looks like a man impersonating a dog that thinks its about to be whacked with a stick for pooping on the carpet.

Forget about the plot and the technology – Logans the point here Ive realised.

What happened between him starting in NPD full of excitement at working on TruLens and the scene in the bathroom? The man who can hardly bear to look at himself in mirror. Who doesnt know anything anymore. Whos sure his wife is screwing around.

Text message from Dex, Comms says.

'Convert to audio.'

Lo Jacko. Presentation ok-ish. Interview in 10m. Eeek! XX

Audio always turns her into a 5 year old with a cold. As for the kisses they sound like something off Pornflix. The *eeek* surprises me. Dex didnt seem hugely nervous this morning considering. 'I wont get the job is why' she said.

'Go lady!' I say. 'Send.'

Reply from Dex: You doing?

'Reading.'

Hahahaha

I send an X and shut off Comms.

Logans still there on the wall. I undo the edit to make him look how he did before, then scan and play the next couple of pages.

He opened the next file. A young man appeared, visible from the chest up, freeze-framed. Logan stared at the screen, hunched at a desk as though his head was too heavy for him to hold upright. When he finally spoke, his voice sounded flat, dull.

'TL-0127. Caucasian male, 25-30; interior of train compartment. Blond fringe covers most of forehead but sufficient observable channels in rest of face. Average profile exposure, 91.55% full frontal. Distance, viewer to viewee, 124cm. Both seated. Viewer I.D.: NPD 03TL – McCormack, R. Time and date of contact: 13.27 – 09/24/2070. Duration of contact, 8m 40s.'

Logan raised both hands to his face and rubbed his eyes. Eventually, he lowered them again. Refocused on the screen.

He pressed play.

It was evident that the NPD undercover operative and the viewee were unknown to one another and that McCormack had initiated the conversation by commenting on the weather. As they talked, Logan recorded his observations, pausing the film at each flash of red, amber or green. These responses, Logan replayed, logged, time-coded and classified.

In eight minutes and forty seconds, the blond man lied seventeen times. He lied about:

his shoes letting in water;

an online documentary he claimed to have seen;

the end-point of his journey;

the nature of his job;

his attitude towards migrant workers;

not having a pen the viewer could borrow...

One lie after another. Logan logged them all. When the footage ended, he compiled his stats report and analysis then stored them in the TruLens cache along with the film itself.

After a moment, he called up the next file. Opened it. Closed it. Opened it. Closed it.

'That function seems to be operating normally,' a voice behind him said.

Logan started, swivelled round in his seat. 'Hey, Jazz. Sorry, I didn't—'

'You must be due a break, aren't you?' Then, without waiting for him to reply, 'Me too. Let's grab a drink and a couple of slices of fresh air.'

In the octagonal garden behind 'the bunker', Jaswinder Kaur set her juice down on a picnic table but remained standing. Her black hair had a bluey sheen in the daylight. Logan stood beside her, drink in hand. They gazed at the fountain, its loud splashes competing with the traffic's relentless electric whine on the freeway beyond the perimeter fence. Droplets of water had settled like dew on the vibrantly green synthetic lawn.

'You seem unhappy, Jack.'

'Me?' He sipped his drink. 'Long morning, that's all.'

'Not just today. This week. Last week.'

Logan didn't respond.

'A hundred files so far,' Jazz said. 'That's a lot of reports.'

'A hundred and twenty-seven.' The breeze strengthened and a fine mist from the fountain settled on Logan's skin. He shuddered. 'It's not the workload, it's the—'

'Work itself. I know.'

They stood in silence for a moment.

'Before I switched to NPD I didn't think anything of it,' Logan said. 'The lying. Crime suspects, benefits claimants, asylum seekers. It goes with—'

'The territory. Yes.'

He gave a dry laugh. 'We used to call them the Red-Light Districts.'

'You didn't expect it from ordinary people in everyday contexts?' Jazz nodded as if in response to her own question. 'People with no apparent reason to lie or anything to gain by it.'

'Not so much of it, no. But the red-amber-green ratios on this project are more or less the same as they've been on all the others.'

'We are a species of liars, Jack.'

He turned to look at her. 'You sound very matter-of-fact about it.'

'Yesterday,' she said, returning his gaze with that half-smiling face, 'my son showed me a picture he'd done at school. It was awful, even for a six-year-old. I told him it was really good.'

'That's different.'

'Okay, what about when I say you don't seem happy and you tell me it's just been a long morning. If I'd been wearing lenses, would that have scored a green light. Or a red?'

He took a moment to reply. 'I know we all lie. I know it's part of the rich, complex fabric of human interaction and social cohesion – *Christ, you had me jump through enough psychometric hoops to get this job.' Logan shook his head. 'It's just that–'*

'You don't like witnessing hundreds of lies a day every day by people just like you.'

'Thanks for finishing another of my sentences for me, Jazz.'

The project manager laughed. 'Sorry, I do that, don't I?' Then, serious again, 'But the thing is – if you hate the smell of shit, don't become a pig farmer.'

'Overnarrate: Logan says *Fuck you.*'

On the wall Logans avatar turns to Jazzs avatar and says 'Fuck you.'

Back at his work station, he opened the next file in the queue. It was another from McCormack. This time she was at home, in the kitchen, talking to her boyfriend.

Logan closed it and opened a different one instead.

'Pause.'

I wonder if he was already suspicious of Mia at this point. Or maybe hed *always* suspected he would lose her one day. It was just a question of when and who to. Right from that early date when he saw his ugly old reflection in a restroom and prepared himself for rejection. Okay so shed stuck with him all this time. Proved him wrong. But if you have a set of scales with a 12 year relationship on one side and a lifetime of insecurities on the other – which weighs the most?

What do I know? Dex and me havent been together 12 *months.*

Theyre fictional characters. I realise that. Theres no Mia. No Jack Logan. But I really hope when he steps out into that bedroom and asks 'How was Kirsten?' Mia will say 'Yeah fine she was in good form − it was lovely to see her' or something like that... and Logans lenses will flash green.

'Resume.'

But the scene only plays for a few seconds more before reaching the end of the part Id scanned. I pick up the book again and skim down the next page.

Greatgrandad obviously wanted to make sure the reader understood just how hugely Logans job was messing with his head. As the weeks go by and he watches the lies pile up his mood sinks lower... barely talks to the rest of the team... outside work he distrusts everyone he meets... cant stand to look people in the face... irritable... sleeping badly... drinking too much... Blardyblardy.

Oh here this is more like it. Hes at home with Mia.

Logan pretended not to notice Mia's look as he pulled a bottle of red from the rack, unscrewed the cap and filled most of a glass.

'You sure?' he asked gesturing at the bottle.

'No. I'm good, thanks.' Her smile resembled Jaswinder Kaur's.

I pause to adjust Mia. For one thing she has a blonde bob even though she was described at the start of the story as having dark hair long enough for a ponytail. But I didnt scan that scene so how could Mi-screen know? I change the blue dress for a plain yellow short sleeve top and white cords and give her a wrist tattoo (like Dexs) in the style of a plaited rainbow.

I make her less pretty. If shes not so attractive maybe shell be less likely to cheat on Logan. It doesn't work like that I know but its the least I can do for him.

'Smells interesting,' Logan said.

'Quinoa tabbouleh.'

'There's no need for that kind of language.'

Mia didn't laugh. Logan didn't expect her to.

She told him dinner would be ready in ten minutes. He swallowed some wine. When neither of them said anything else, he raised the glass to his lips again. He watched her fetch salad things and set them on the counter. Watched her shred lettuce into a bowl. As she sliced cucumber, pepper, tomatoes, he went on watching her. Watching her face the whole time, not her hands. All the while, sipping his drink.

Mia stopped. Placed both hands against the edge of the worktop, the knife still clasped in her fingers. She looked like she was trying to push the counter across the kitchen towards him.

Without raising her gaze from the chopping board, she said, 'Don't stare at me.'

'I'm not staring.'

'Please, Jack. Just don't.'

'I like watching you.'

'You could lay the table.' She looked up at him now. 'That would be good.'

'Right. I'll do that. I'll lay the table.'

Logan remained where he was. Took another mouthful of wine.

'Or you could just stay sober till we're the other side of dinner.'

'Which is it: lay the table or stay sober? I can't do both.'

Mia held his gaze a moment then, without speaking, went back to preparing the salad.

Jack. JackJackJack. You might as well drive her straight round to the other feller's flat.

As for people in 2070 making salad that way.

At the end of the meal, most of the food remained uneaten. Logan went to replenish his glass but the wine was done. He set the bottle back down. Mia had already begun to clear the table.

'Oh — a guy at work offered me two tickets for one of the Korsakov recitals,' Logan said, his voice stilted with the effort required not to slur the words. 'If you fancy it.'

'When is it?'

'Friday.'

'We can't, then, can we?' Making her way to the waste-disposal, Mia said, 'That's the night I'm meeting up with Kirsten.'

'Right. Yeah, I'd forgotten about that.' His eyes trailed her across the room. 'Maybe you and Kirsten could use the tickets?'

She didn't think Korsakov would be Kirsten's thing.

Okay so were heading into endgame. Finally. I upload the last few pages and away we go.

The next scene is like something out of a spydram. The problem is the TruLens kits will be security tagged and greatgrandad has to come up with a plausible way for Logan to smuggle one out of 'the bunker' without authorisation. A *whole page* though? Anyway we already know he gets away with it because the story began with him at home about to put the lenses in his eyes. So wheres the tension the suspense the drama?

I fastforward.

Were back in that bathroom. The narrative reverts to present tense. In goes the first lens. Then the second. Logan stands in front of the mirror staring at his reflection.

Logan stands in front of the mirror, staring at his reflection. Steadies his breathing. From the bedroom come sounds of Mia slipping into bed.

She didn't take a shower when she returned from her evening out. That proves nothing, though. She could have showered there, with him. Wherever 'there' was. Whoever 'he' might be. They didn't kiss when she came home and so Logan never got close enough to tell whether she smelled of soap, or sex, or no different to when she'd gone out.

None of it matters now.

The answer is the other side of that door. He only has to ask the question.

'Pause.'

What occurs to me here is that nowhere in the story has there been any evidence of Mia cheating on him. No hints or clues or suspicious behaviour. Apart from the dinner scene shes been out of shot the whole time. Their relationship too – all off camera. If we read anything into the things Mia says and does in that kitchen – her *manner* towards Logan – its only because weve been primed by his belief that shes seeing another guy.

Thats all we have to go on: Logans distrust.

So one of two things is happening – there have been plenty of hints and clues and suspicious behaviour over the weeks leading up to the bathroom scene but greatgrandad

a) forgot to tell us about them or

b) deliberately left them out.

Now okay he wasnt the greatest writer of his generation but he turned out enough novels and short stories to make me pretty sure were not talking 'a' here.

Why leave out all that stuff on purpose though?

Unless 'b' is meant to lead us to a third alternative:

c) there have been no hints clues or suspicious behaviour whatsoever.

Logan goes to the bathroom door. Rests his forehead against it, each breath coating the sleek surface with a film of condensation.

He only has to touch the panel and the door-lock will release.

'Overnarrate.'

'Logan cant go through with it' I say. 'Cant open that door cant step into that bedroom cant ask Mia that question. Cant go on being the kind of man he has become: eaten up by jealousy suspicion insecurity and paranoia – hating Mia because of an affair that exists entirely in his imagination. Hating himself for hating her.'

On the screen he remains at the door. Blinking. Breathing.

'Logan takes a step back.'

Logan takes a step back.

'He removes one of the lenses. Then the other.'

He removes one of the lenses then the other.

'He goes over to the WC.'

He goes over to the WC.

'He shakes the lenses like dice in the palm of his hand and releases them into the bowl. They barely make a sound as they hit the water.'

He shakes the lenses and releases them into the water with barely a sound.

'Logan stares down into the bowl. He activates the flush.'

On the screen his avatar does the same, gazing down into the swirl of water.

If I say 'save overnarration' my ending becomes the way the story ends. Easy as that.

Greatgrandads ending will still be right there in the book of course but I dont have to read it. I can just put it on a shelf and forget about it. I dont ever need to find out how the original version of the story ends or what happens to Logan and Mia or any of that.

Those words he wrote in 2014 belong to me now and I can do what I like with them.

And yet, and yet... I must know his ending. I can't not know it.

'Undo overnarration. Play.'

When Logan steps into the bedroom, Mia says, 'I thought you'd drowned in there.'

'Dodgy tummy,' he tells her. It's not untrue; he feels as if he might be sick right now.

Mia is sitting up in bed, browsing her slate. Flicking through messages by the look of it. In the haze from the bedside lightstick, her freshly cleansed face is unnaturally pale, her brown eyes glinting with amber. They track from left to right as she reads.

He stands at the foot of the bed, facing her.

'How was your evening?' Mia asks, without glancing up.

'I haven't had anything to drink, if that's what you're asking.'

This is a lie. But it has the intended effect of dragging Mia's attention from the screen.

'In fact,' she says, 'it wasn't what I was asking.' Red light.

Logan returns her stare. 'How about you?'

'Have I been drinking?' Is she smiling at him, or to herself? 'Yes.' Green light.

He thinks she's going to lower her gaze again. She doesn't. Her expression is unreadable and he almost wonders whether Mia knows about the lenses and is offering her face up to him.

This is his moment.

'I meant, how was your evening?' He keeps his voice even.

'How was Kirsten?'

Here? He ends the story *here*!?

So were supposed to figure out for ourselves whether she... I throw the book across the room and it hits the wallscreen and flaps to the floor like a dying bird.

Its my fault for being drawn in. Christ I was even starting to feel sorry for Logan.

I scrapped *my* version for *this*?

Its not just the cop-out ending its the whole fucking thing really. A *love story*. My greatgrandfather is handed an amazing piece of technology and the chance to play soothsayer − to imagine any kind of future he cares to and write whatever he likes − and he comes up with a story about a feller whose wife is (or isnt) cheating on him. Oldest most unoriginal tale in the world. He doesn't even do the SF properly. Take away the lenses and it could be 2014 2070 or any year you like since Darwin invented apes.

Call that speculative fiction? Call yourself a futurologist?

The rest of the morning Im pissed off with Greatgrandad. With myself too for letting it burrow under my skin. The story. Logan. Mia. Even after an hour of Mi-Chi I still catch myself wondering how she answered his question. Whether the lenses flashed green or red.

I take a shower to rinse off the sweat from the workout.

And as I step out the bathroom I picture Logan stepping out of his.

Im eating lunch when Comms says *Text message from Dex*.

I check the time. I was expecting her back before now. 'Convert to audio.'

Lo Jacko. Interview over. That nasal childlike voice Comms gives her.

'Howd it go?'

If badly is zero and good is 10 I reckon 4.

I send a sadface. Shell have done better than she says. Shell get the job. 'You on your way home?'

Its a moment before the next message pings.

Thing is I just bumped into an old schoolfriend on the way to the Trans stop. Havent seen her for years. So she says do I want to have lunch over this side of town and maybe take in a gallery after?

I think about this. 'Convert to visual.'

Comms says *Visual blocked by sender. Text or Audio only.*

Jacko?

'Why no vis Dex?'

Sorry. Its this stupid phone.

'Yeah?'

So anyway Ill be back this evening. Okay?

'Which old schoolfriend?'

Oh you dont know her.

'Whats her name?'

There's another delay. Then a ping and even before Dex speaks I know — I just *know* — what shes going to say.

Kirsten.

Afterword:

No More Secrets

Dr James O'Shea
Manchester Metropolitan University

IN MARTYN BEDFORD'S short story – lovingly grounded in
the British Pessimism School of science fiction – the future-
tech featured in the 'inner story', TruLens, is fictional. Silent
Talker, however, is quite real. You can find it using google
patents searching for 'Methods and apparatus for analysing
the behaviour of a subject' – not quite as snappy as 'Silent
Talker', but that's the way patent titles go.

Silent Talker was developed by the MMU Intelligent
Systems Group, a team that includes Dr Zuhair Bandar,
myself, Dr. David McLean and Dr Janet Rothwell, and
patented in the UK in 2002 (the intellectual property
remaining with MMU). The technology has been evaluated
in a laboratory setting using a well-established lie detection
experiment from the field of psychology, including the 'theft
of money from a box' scenario. Its peer-reviewed results have
shown accuracies of between 75% and 87% depending on the
experimental scenario. So reliable is it, in fact, that we have
been encouraged to conduct further research to demonstrate
that the basic idea can also be used to identify human
comprehension in giving informed consent in clinical trials.

So how does it work?

Silent Talker essentially monitors lots of very fine-
grained non-verbal behaviours simultaneously, and looks for
relationships between them, over time, that indicate deception.
For example, one behaviour could be the left eye moving
from fully-open to half-open. The underlying technology of
Silent Talker is the Artificial Neural Network: many banks of
these tiny 'artificial brains' extract features, pre-process them

and finally make the classification required (truthful or deceptive). Although ANNs have been in development for many decades, only recently has the computing power to support the parallel processing required been readily available (or indeed the specialised accelerator hardware boards). The breakthrough with Silent Talker lies in its cross-application of these technologies, and the architectural approach of having many AI components working together to mine subtle patterns of interaction between the many input channels over a sustained time period.

It's important to clarify that Silent Talker is not a facial recognition technology; it does not need to know who it is looking at to classify whether they are behaving truthfully or deceptively.

In principle the technology is all there. There are no more obstacles standing in the way of its development as a practical, working system. There are a number of incremental 'usability' improvements, of course, for example tweaking the system to get better classification accuracy and automatically recognising when the interviewee starts to answer a question. But these are just fine-tunes.

Likewise, there is also some interesting work to do in customising Silent Talker for specific applications. One example is that applications such as border control will require dealing with people from different ethnicities (and cultures). It is generally accepted by psychologists that there is likely to be variation in patterns of non-verbal behaviour in this case. The philosopher John Searle has discussed the concept of 'the background', a core of universal behaviours grounded in our common physiology supplemented by a subset of behaviours specific to a particular ethnic group. Our findings are that a general Silent Talker will work with a diverse group, but specific systems trained for particular ethnic groups obtain higher classification accuracies. Part of the future of Silent Talker research is to build these specific systems and then use image processing technology (which may be influenced by facial recognition systems) to direct people from particular ethnic groups to specifically trained Silent Talker interviewing stations.

What is important to recognise is this technology does not operate with 100% accuracy and that careful human judgment must be applied before acting on its classifications. We get asked all sorts of questions about Silent Talker and one good illustration is 'Can you use it to detect and shoot suicide bombers approaching a target?' The answer is, of course, no – on purely ethical grounds. No human life should ever be taken by an automatic system on its own initiative (going back to science fiction this application would be the complete flouting of Asimov's first law of robotics!). Having established that, there are also purely practical reasons for not doing so. Suppose you build a Silent Talker system that is 97% accurate. That means that overall, 3 out of every 100 cases will be classified incorrectly. Some of these would be innocents and the resulting bad publicity would swell the ranks of future suicide bombers. Some of course would be guilty and the hubris of relying on a purely automatic system would wave them on unhindered to their targets.

Nevertheless, there are many applications in security and policing where a combination of Silent Talker's objective and deep scrutiny with human wisdom will lead to better interviewing outcomes than we have at present. One example is the Yorkshire Ripper, who was interviewed nine times by the police before being arrested. This must be put in the context of the magnitude of the task in which 30,000 statements were recorded from a pool of 250,000 individuals of interest. If a Silent Talker system had supported the officers interviewing the Ripper, they may have been a much swifter outcome.

Maybe we should also be asking ourselves more mundane questions. Logan is appalled by the ubiquity of lying amongst ordinary people in the story. How would we cope if we could not tell the white lies that oil the social machine? Will we control the use of Silent Talker outside of very careful defined security situations, or will we have to develop new social *mores* in which a white lie (as clearly detectable as a barefaced lie) is politely accepted as the truth? More seriously, how would people be able to organise to overthrow an oppressive regime (what would the impact have been on the resistance forces in occupied countries during World War II)?

On the technical side – could Silent Talker eventually end up embedded in the TruLenses? I had a brainstorming session about this with Martyn and he covered the bases (on a fictional basis) very effectively. Having begun my academic career as a chemist, my view is that the solutions to the problems, which must be solved to produce TruLenses at some time in the future, do not lie in computer science, but in Chemistry and Physics. There are periodic revolutions in these disciplines which work their way through to Materials Science and Engineering. For instance, organometallic chemistry (1970s) and the Buckminsterfullerene (1980s) were very much chemistry developments, whereas Graphene (2000s) is attributable to physicists. On this timeline we have potential for another three or so material leaps between now and 2070. Combine these with maturation of the existing breakthroughs since 1980 and there is definite potential for TruLenses to be feasible.

Part of being a scientist is that the scientific method of investigation will continue to progress in producing new and wonderful knowledge. Whether that progress will produce Silent Talker on a contact lens (and the consequences) remains to be seen.

Swarm

Robin Yassin-Kassab

'Historical events illustrate more clearly than anything the injunction against eating of the Tree of Knowledge. The only activity that bears any fruit is subconscious activity, and no one who takes part in any historical drama can ever understand its significance. If he so much as tries to understand it, his efforts are fruitless.' Tolstoy

HE'S WOKEN BY the drone of a mosquito, mechanical yet malicious. He must have dropped off, only for a few minutes.

He rises from the bed, scratches his thighs, rubs his eye sockets, then tells the system to play. It plays 'I've Got You Under my Skin', the old, old Neneh Cherry version of something even older than that.

He pulls on a cloak, then turns back to look at the woman on the bed, a long loving look.

He orders the system to give ten percent more volume. It doesn't matter. He can't disturb her now. She's already asleep, her face already as crumpled as the pillow. She won't wake up.

I've got you deep in the heart of me
So deep in my heart you're really a part of me

He sways for some moments, giving himself away to the music, the emptied body, his brain still vacant, nothing stirring in there. Then something revives and stirs an intention towards serious things, to work, at least to check that the work continues. But first, before he surveys the screens, he'll allow himself a moment in the courtyard, a lungful of jasmine, the balminess of the night air.

He shuffles his stark feet into slippers and walks out through the curtain. He wheels his head on his neck to gaze upwards at a swarm of ignorant stars, each indifferent to the others but constellating nonetheless, making some kind of order. And, if he gazes more keenly, clouding and blurring too. Confusing the eye.

He has a moment of vertigo, swimming under that roof, losing his bearings. He crunches his lids, his fists rub his brow and, focussing again, he picks up a glass from the courtyard table. Cloudy *araq*. He swigs and gasps.

I've got you... under my skin

He turns back to what is manageable. Taking the glass with him through the curtain.

Her.

She doesn't know. One day he will tell her, and she will (he imagines it) throw her hands to her mouth, that fine wet entrance, puzzling for an instant before she reaches for his face. She'll be very surprised but also very grateful. He feels sure of that.

'I carry you in my heart,' she says when she expresses her love. And sometimes, in her breathy passion, she rasps: 'I want you inside me all the time.' Well, now he is. He's inside her all the time.

★

People say the president's second son has more swarm in his veins than blood, that he relies on the insects to stop him hyperventilating, to prevent his teeth from chattering, to control his salivations, to unknock his knees, to keep him continent on public occasions, and to make his cock stand up. But people say all sorts of things.

What's certain is that the privileged have obtained still greater privilege since the nanobots became available. The beautiful people have become yet more beautiful. The swarms are what breast enhancement was to our mothers' generation, what hair dye was to our fathers'. A panacea for personal problems, psychological and emotional as well as physical, because everything's physical at the end of the day. This is what we call progress and development.

As for her, his Rosetta pinned there on the bed, she suffered from claustrophobia. That was her flaw. Enclosed spaces made her sweat. In a lift, even in the lobby of a restaurant, this was very unpleasantly apparent. It was embarrassing, not at all the image he aimed to project through a mistress. It put him in bad odour, so bad he thought he might have to give up on her. But during a morning's scanning he saw an article about the nanobot cure, not only for diaphoresis but for phobia itself. That's when he started dabbling in private use. It was a technology too expensive for the generality to take advantage of, but it was available to him, for occupational purposes.

Yes, everyone who was anyone was doing it, and his profession had long taken up position at the vanguard. His own area of expertise is the old bedrock of state: surveillance and social control – but the new technology's ramifications spread far beyond that. The insects revolutionised intelligence work on an international level. Soon agents everywhere were pouring swarms in statesmen's ears, not only to assassinate them (how crude!), but to change their mood, to alter their responses to stimuli, whatever stimulus was targetted, from a voluptuous ambassador in a red dress to a file containing incontrovertible evidence of gas attacks. As a result of all this activity, who-did-what-as-a result-of-what became an even more complex question than it had been before (in-the-name-of-what was always far less interesting). In their courtroom defences, fallen leaders have more than once claimed insect penetration to mitigate their bloody glories. (Ok, the terrorists didn't get hold of the sarin supplies; but they got hold of my tongue when it gave the order, because they'd shot me full of their insects.) Should their pleas bear weight? When swarms are located within their anatomies, then certainly, yes. But the media squabbles over it, and the definitive story is told by the loudest voice, as ever. But in terms of raw truth, away from the chattering mandibles of the history-writers, we are left with what is either a problem or an opportunity, depending on where you stand. Namely, an infinite refraction of responsibility.

*

He'd had himself injected, like everyone of his grade. First with sweeper swarms to check he was clear of penetration, and then a package of anti-aging extras. What else keeps his hair full and black? How else does he perform so well in bed? He's eighty four years old.

Ha! He taps his belly, peers down through the open cloak to his tired penis, which is curled like a snail in its slick shell of hair.

He injected her too. Unbeknownst to her. A nanoswarm of units 0.5 micrometres in size.

What effects does it have? Only benign ones. Now it's keeping her sleeping soundly. It smoothes away her tensions. It manipulates the serotonin feed so that when she wakes up there'll be a smile on her lips. (For her own good, these things; he wishes someone would do it for him. He could arrange that, he could be his own therapist. But he holds himself to a higher standard. Difficulty, adversity, is what makes a man. It's what's made him.) What else? It repairs cell damage, puffs out her wrinkles, helps preserve her hair as this thick curtain of night. It intensifies her metabolism so she doesn't run to fat. It shortens and eases her menstrual period. It flushes her with oxytocin when she's in his presence. It swells her breasts. It sexualises her.

He grins at the thought, a collection of thoughts. He wishes he could tell her. One day he will.

His groin is damp and itchy. He should shower. But first he's driven by that screen compulsion which once, decades ago before he became busy, made him check his Facebook and Twitter accounts every ten minutes. Things his grandchildren have never heard of. Simple things. He chuckles. First he will survey the work, then he'll have a shower.

*

An angry crowd between crumbling buildings. Piles of rubbish smouldering at the edges. One screen depicts the participants in silhouette, contains a flickering number count, and marks up points of density. Another shows the mass in thermal imaging. Others pick corners of the crowd to amplify. The demonstrators focus on the speaker at the centre of their circle – some radical fool waving his arms, begging for death.

In his private rooms, glass in hand, the intelligence man speaks a command and red dots superimpose on the information. These are the insects active in the crowd. So many of the things; redundancy is essential to the system. We used to do this with men. Sometimes we still do, but only as a step towards resolving the underemployment issue.

The number count is flickering around 1450. That's just in one small suburban square. So many more bodies in the country since he was young. Bodies teeming, crawling, brimming over. Are these numbers a signal of prosperity? – Even if they're poor, do their numbers not show the health of the larger organism, the state? Are they a sign of success? Or are there too many of them? They're difficult to keep an eye on, in any case. So many skittering cockroaches, spinning under tables, down drains, into the shadows. They'd be entirely untab-able without the technology.

For years we've had the nanobot science to administer either health or illness, according to our orders; the mechanical means of delivery also existed. But in the beginning this lacked effectiveness, and continued to, until our allies finally perfected miniaturisation, equipping the delivery machines with sufficient hardware to navigate intelligently. We used the first clumsy, painfully visible models to neutralise a space, that is to eliminate those gathered, like drones but slightly more discreet. But there are some things you don't want done discreetly, you want to make a point – and this made use of the first swarms quite pointless; they did nothing that couldn't have been done more cheaply and effectively the old way, with machine guns. We used them too for general surveillance (but we'd always done that traditionally, with eyes in the crowd). We used the robots for modernity's sake, and to please our allies.

But they grew more and more perceptive, learning to distinguish a subject's skin tone, the symbols he bore, the significance of his clothing. Still they were a clumsy tool until the robots shrank to the point where they could be disguised as flies, small enough to blend into the insectival background but large enough to fly without being set off course by wind or other unpredictable factors. Then what had been a hammer became a scalpel. Now, by some miracle of algorhythmic perfection, our insects are able to pick an individual out from a crowd, unerringly, in a mosque, on a street corner, in a market place, and to deliver their load. They can kill soundlessly, without spilling a drop of blood. If the crowd is dense enough, nobody even notices the death. And they don't have to kill immediately – a dose of death can be administered through a nostril, into an ear, through an air vent into the lungs, to slowly, persistently work its way towards the centre. The victim dies later in his bare lodging, or in the café drinking tea, or with his children in the park.

Then we can set the insects off – obviating the need for legwork – to follow the forensic traces of those our victim has been breathed upon or touched by in the previous hours. These new candidates, his social network, become victims of our victim. And the invisible assassins? They swarm away unseen, they buzz into the shadows, they disappear.

But perhaps it isn't 'we' who set them off. Perhaps these are the speech patterns of a previous age. No – if programmed properly they set themselves off, as if by their own intelligence. They are very nearly autonomous of us; we are very nearly not responsible. We trust them to do what's right.

He doesn't hear himself chuckling. Nice things, he thinks. The nanobots. The clever insects. He'd like to hold them in his hand, to stroke their alien heads with his fingertip. A massive fingertip, whorls like mountain strata, pores the size of craters.

What else can they do? There's no end to their ingenuity. In a crowd, for instance, or in a neighbourhood or school, they can kill, as it were, statistically, proportionately, destroying one body per every X metres squared. Naturally this creates a panic, a general demoralisation. But better than that, the swarm can calibrate the demoralisation into very specific modes by varying the victim ratios, the symptoms of death, the type of environment. It can select victims by age, gender, or apparent social status. It can choose a particular season or time of day. And so it can produce a riot, or a wave of empathy, or a street battle, or a petrified silence. A machine to make the human weather.

He wants to say 'we have psychologists working on these permutations', but again, that's the old tongue talking. True, there are dedicated psychological teams, a small one here, bigger ones in the laboratories of our allies. But once the basic programme is loaded, the swarm adapts it to the variables. You could say it does its own psychology. It observes and analyses. It learns from itself. Psychologists may soon be redundant.

And there's no point psychologising the insects. The individuals among them don't know what the collective mind knows. Their concerns are tremendously limited. They have no awareness of their larger function, of the logic of the superorganism. And even 'collective mind' and 'logic' are superstitious terms. The swarm works by interaction and randomness. By a species of magic, but a magic which is very normal. Like the cells which collaborate to build an organ – how much do they know? How much does the organ know? Or the men and women who cohere to build a state?

He swigs down the remaining *araq* and refills the glass, neat not cloudy, from a bottle on the console in front of the screens.

The very small controlling the very big. The ant animating the elephant. If the elephant is the lumbering state, the ant is him, him and his colleagues. He likes the analogy. It makes him very proud.

But it is not me, he thinks, meaning the whole structure now, insect and human. It is not even us. It's a system, a web. If it comes down from us it also comes up from them. It's a nest we all live in, our common home. No, not us. Is it God who makes the system or the repulsive human swarm? Or does it just exist, *a priori*, magically?

He doesn't even try for an answer. Answers are irrelevant. He's old enough to know that now.

He drinks back the *araq*. He's sweating. He needs to replenish the store.

As for this crowd here, he's tending towards the order to eliminate it entirely.

More and more demonstrations. It happens with each new generation; each time they need a stronger lesson. At a certain stage, spying on them, trying to find them out, loses its effect. That process works if they're actually trying to hide, as they always did in the old days, before the year eleven. After eleven, if they find a camera they shove their faces into the screen. Men with bare chests walking open-armed into our fire. Defected soldiers waving their ID cards at the internet audience. It's a mockery of all order. They are mocking us.

But there's no point getting angry. They don't understand their function either, no more than Lenin or Mao understood they were paving the way towards untrammelled capitalism when they modernised their countries. No more than the idealists of our own movement, decades ago when we were young, when we were as unruly as these ants are now, understood they were working towards the absolute rule of the Leader.

We put words in our heads to motivate ourselves, but we don't know where we're heading. By 'we' he means the intellectuals. And it's true in private life too.

He thinks brusquely of his wife, of a chain of lovers, and of this one he met in a cell. Currently pinned to the bed. Rosetta.

This one, he thought the first time he saw her, with this one I really could do something.

She'd been in her cell for a very long time, that cell and others, in communal coops and solitary confinement. This one he met her in was solitary.

She was naked but for a stinking towel. Her hair was grey and tattered, dank, and she was bald in patches. Her grey-green skin bulged with sores. Insects crawled all over her.

He thought he could really do something with her. With Rosetta. Blankly she told him her name.

★

By controlling the world we make it our own. By truly inhabiting it we shape it. Like a farmer who knows every inch of his land, and shapes by knowing. When we have shaped the world it reflects our image back to us. And so I recognise myself in this country, he thinks, the same way I recognise myself in her: my tastes, my preferences, my sensitive observations.

Conversely, if we didn't control the world we wouldn't possess it, and we couldn't shape it, and we wouldn't recognise ourselves. Meaning would be lost. Nothing would exist.

He's a little bit drunk now. He clenches a fist and stares hard at it, the silvered hairs, the pores. Gradually his gaze of vacancy or awe transforms to a fat, complacent grin. It all comes down to the fist, he thinks.

He looks round fast. A movement from the bed has startled him. She's stirring. She shouldn't be.

She rubs her face and stretches. Then she sees him watching her.

'What are you doing?' she asks.

He shakes himself. What dark depths has he plunged to? What's the *araq* doing? Why is she awake? Is she awake? If she's awake something has gone very wrong. Or is she talking in her sleep? Fifteen dark paces are between them.

He steps forward, four paces, five. Then he stops, his nose twitching, his cheeks squirming. Back at the console he could reorder this chaos. But it's too late now. She would see and understand. She'd hear the commands his voice made. He can't move in any case. She transfixes him with her eyes.

He recognises her look, even if he can't name it. But what is it he's recognising? Who? What does the face mean? Its referent has somehow shifted.

'What are you doing?' she asks again.

He opens and closes his mouth.

'O, you're worried because I found out.' She shakes her hair into its usual perfect shape and kneels up on the bed.

There's a noise behind him, in the air or at the screen. He thinks he hears the demonstrators pushing up against the perspex, crawling through the pixillations, the soft clickings of their legs, the pinprick tappings of exoskeletons on the plastic console.

She's speaking again, entirely awake now. 'I had migraines,' she says. 'So I went to Doctor Rami's clinic. He said to put in a spy swarm at the same time, why not. That's how I found out. When Rami told me what the insects were doing for me, I knew it had to be you.'

Blood buzzes in his ears. Behind him the screens overflow. The swelling human swarm has breached the square and all the monitors. It pours into his private rooms.

'Are you worried, darling?' she says. 'Don't be worried. Because I don't think I mind.' She steps off the bed and stands twirling her hands at her bare sides, bewildered, screwing up her eyes in the effort to see within. 'No, I don't mind. I find I don't mind.'

'Why should you?' His voice collapses from relieved to avuncular, and the noise behind him eases.

'I don't know. I feel perhaps I should.'

She's stirring him. The insects awaken his groin.

'Come to me,' she says.

He goes.

Afterword:

Rise of the Machines

Lenka Pitonakova
University of Southampton

WILL ROBOTS SAVE or destroy the world? The question has been with us since we first conceived of a thinking machine, and for a long time it remained just a fantasy; for decades the reality of robotics lagged woefully behind our first utopian visions of a robot-assisted future. Recently, though, things have started to speed up. A lot of research money is currently being spent on autonomous robotic navigation, path planning, flight control, as well as improvements in sensors, batteries and processors ('the brains'). Indeed our earliest aspirations for robotics – to take care of all our menial and domestic tasks – may soon, *finally*, be within reach. How great will it be when house-cleaning can be left entirely to the machines? When machines deliver shopping to our front door? When humanoids arrive capable of looking after the old and disabled, not just offering physical help, but behavioural and emotional support?

While private companies and universities race towards these goals, a different side to robotics has also been leaking into the popular consciousness. Movies like 'The Matrix' or 'I, Robot', show robots originally designed to serve humans suddenly turn on them, in pursuit of their own liberation and the punishment of the creators and slave-masters. Other movies like 'Terminator' or 'Transformers' imagine the sole purpose of robots to be military and destructive. These aren't just Hollywood concerns. Deep anxieties about the potential 'malfunction' of artificial intelligence prompted the University of Cambridge to create the Centre for the Study of Existential Risk in 2013, a facility designed to assess whether current or future technology will pose a threat to the human race.

Before we start a world-wide panic about machines going berserk, it is useful to look at how A.I. actually works. A program designed by humans for a specific purpose is loaded into a processor that then executes it. Most of the program's instructions are optimized solutions to a specific problem, because the most cost effective way of creating a product is to minimise the risk of it malfunctioning or behaving unpredictably. As a part of my PhD in swarm intelligence, I am looking into how control can be imposed on seemingly uncontrollable biologically inspired robot behaviour. In particular, I try to create programs for robots that not only adapt to their environment, but that can do so reliably and repeatedly. Without reliability, there is no guaranteed return of academic or commercial investment. Without a guaranteed return, there is often no money to sponsor development and more importantly, no real reason to use such a system at all.

It is also worth pointing out that no form of intelligence or autonomy can suddenly come into being out of thin air. Even when robots are designed to be autonomous (for example, knowing how to avoid obstacles, or how to find a patch of floor that needs cleaning), this 'autonomy' is entirely limited to the purpose of the task (or set of tasks). Robots cannot think in the same sense than we understand thinking in animals, let alone feel emotions. Nor will they, whilst we know so little about the animal (or human) brain and how that works. If we don't understand our own brains, how can we be expected to design and build fully functioning, artificial versions of them? The latter is perhaps decades behind the former, if it's possible at all. For the conceivable future, then, a *simulation* of emotion and a *simulation* of thought is the best we can hope for.

But maybe, further down the line, if we can crack the biological brain, it will ultimately be possible. Would these thinking, feeling machines really be allowed to roam wild and uncontrolled? Or would governments make sure they serve the public good, and safeguards against malfunction are in place? A good example of how carefully new technology is treated is drone technology. Amazon recently claimed that their flying drones would revolutionise product delivery by cutting its time to 30 minutes. Other drones could be used in agriculture to cultivate and protect crops, in search and rescue operations, in home security, etc, etc. The technology is great in theory, but society quickly becomes aware of its problems (e.g. how to ensure the safety of humans, animals, and other machines like planes and helicopters using the airspace). In the US, laws to regulate how drones can be operated in public spaces are currently being put in place. It seems that these laws, coming into effect in 2015, will ensure that a drone cannot move low enough to cause any damage or to invade privacy. In addition, a licence will be needed in both the US and the EU to remotely operate a drone or to let it fly autonomously.

However, one might ask what is to stop developing countries, or countries where democracy and the right laws aren't in place, from creating potentially dangerous robots. What stops a terrorist organisation or a ruthless dictatorship from weaponising technology or artificial intelligence? Robin's story presents one such scenario. The technology itself is not very far ahead. We can already build machines capable of flying over someone's house, taking pictures and recording conversations. Thanks to Facebook and the general public's poor awareness of internet privacy issues, anyone willing to pay enough money can potentially pin-point you based on your social status, education, religion, sexual orientation or even music preferences. The machines are currently too big and too loud to remain undetected. However, as we have seen in the mobile phone industry, things can get rapidly smaller and much more effective if there is a market to support the development. Remember your phone from ten or even five years ago and then look at your current phone. Could anybody have imagined the processing power that is now possible to put into such a small device?

While regulations are not in place, but the technology exists, it is indeed possible for a government or an organisation to build machines that not only spy on people but also kill them silently. Unfortunately, this scenario could be closer to home than we might be willing to admit. We all know the recent scandal about US intelligence agencies spying on the majority of our internet traffic and communications. There are indications that other countries, including the UK are involved as well. Yes, laws are in place that should theoretically prohibit this. It seems however that some countries think that they are above international law. What will happen when robots are the size of insects or of nano-particles? Will privacy be completely destroyed? Will it be a practice to have politically dangerous people executed silently and without a trace? Based on the current events, it seems fairly likely. Whether it can be stopped is a question for politicians. The threat that, at first glance appeared to come from the robots and their artificial intelligence, is in fact a human threat.

While technology marches forward at an unstoppable pace, it brings many dangers alongside its advantages. Should we try to stop the research? Or should we try to improve our democracies, our politics, our own societal morality?

Growing Skyscrapers

Adam Marek

LOOPIE LAY ON her nest of blankets plucking hairs from the bottom of the wall. As she pulled out each glass-like filament, it left in the curved surface a wounded pore from which a bead of dark liquid arose.

Since she and her mother had moved into this pod three weeks ago, the walls had thickened, losing some of their translucency, but they were still thin enough to allow the morning sun to penetrate the room as a green glow.

At this juvenile stage in the pod's growth, the windows were mere pinpricks – an orderly star-field in the low, domed ceiling. If she and Mumma stayed in this pod for long enough – and she wished that this time they would be able to – she might get to see these windows swell as the room expanded into a cavern around her, the material inside the windows transforming from a milky eye, to a mother of pearl disk, to the transparency of a dragonfly's wing.

The pore of the first wall hair Loopie had plucked when she'd awoken had now matured into a black scab. She dug her fingernail under its edge and gently picked it from the wall. It was plump and squishy, the size of a raisin and almost as sweet. She clamped it between her front teeth, disintegrating it against the back of her teeth with the tip of her tongue.

Just before the last of the sweet treat was gone, the silhouette of a person approaching the side of Loopie's pod appeared, and she froze.

The taste of salt found its way into Jean's smile. She hadn't been on a boat since she was a child, and with the wind buffeting her bangs and the spray spattering her face, this experience transported her back to that simpler time.

Jean's boss, Dr Cal Gallagher, had the steering wheel and was showing off somewhat, turning needless curves that caused the boat to tilt, pushing Jean deep into the padded foam of her seat. Jean's assistant, Morian, sat with his elbow on the boat's edge, his face propped in his palm, watching The Jetty approach.

Cal had suggested they wait until the early evening low tide to visit. Then, the full length of the supporting roots would be exposed and they would have a good couple of hours to investigate the underside before dark.

It had come to be called 'The Jetty' when, against expectations, the illegally planted tower had projected out into the ocean and thrust its support roots down into the ocean bed. When it was first spotted during one of the drones' flyovers, The Jetty was only a few metres across at the base, tapering to a point 10 metres out into the ocean. But then it had lengthened and thickened at a rate that could be seen when comparing satellite photos taken only a day apart, so that now, 'The Jetty' was almost 500 metres wide at its base and stretched 2.1 km out into the ocean. Growing without the guidance of a trellis or an architect, The Jetty had grown horizontally, and chaotically.

Along the top, Jean could see the outermost buildings silhouetted against the yellowing sky. Some of these pods were only two or three months old, and yet there were already signs of habitation – territorial flags flapping in the breeze and columns of smoke.

'How many people do you reckon are living in there now?' Jean asked.

'Aerial did a sweep two days ago and counted more than 10,000 signatures,' Cal said.

'Zowee,' Morian said. He screwed up his face and scratched his chin. 'A lot of people to move.'

'It won't be our job,' Cal said.

'It might not be anyone's job,' Jean said.

'Maybe,' Cal said.

Every now and then, when the breeze blew towards the boat, it brought with it a wave of overlapping sounds from the busy heart of The Jetty – music, tradespeople calling out their wares, arguments, combustion engines, the everyday percussion of thousands of people.

As the boat came closer, the full scale of the supporting roots was revealed: each as vivid green as a fresh pea shoot, but thick, like a gnarled tree trunk, twisting up over 10 metres from the ocean's surface to The Jetty's glorious underside. A titanic mangrove.

Jean hadn't expected the luminous photophores to be present beneath The Jetty, and yet here they were. And every degree darker the sky became, the brighter they burned. The combination of the setting sun through the translucent roots, and the photophores igniting within the long shadows of the support roots made a glowing palace of this structure.

'It looks like Oz,' Jean said.

'You mean the Emerald City,' Cal said.

'Not up top it doesn't,' Morian said.

The silhouette of the person outside Loopie's pod moved about in a restless, excited way. It was Balpa. His footsteps squelched in the soft ground outside. He didn't immediately thump on the wall of the pod, which suggested he was planning something. Again.

Loopie shuffled back from the wall. Last time, he had poked through a piece of thick wire he'd cut from the perimeter fence and jabbed her shoulder with it while she slept. He could have popped her eye. Since then, she'd slept on the other side, against the internal wall that backed onto Mumma's cell.

Balpa placed something against the side of her pod and then moved away. The thing's silhouette was small, about the size of a thumb. Loopie immediately thought 'firework'.

'Bal,' she called out. 'Don't you dare!'

The sound of her voice startled him. His shadow

sharpened as he came back to retrieve whatever he'd put against the wall, tutting to himself.

'What are you doing?' Loopie said.

'I'm just trying to... uh... come and see. I found something.'

Loopie's bare feet left prints in the spongy floor, which faded behind her after a few seconds. In this juvenile state, the front door was still too soft to take any kind of lock, so every night before bed, she and Mumma shoved a heavy chest of drawers they'd scavenged up against it, just in case. The blockaded door was enough to deter browsing thieves, and this far out on the growth fringe of The Jetty, those were the only kind of thieves to be found.

The sound of Loopie heaving the chest of drawers away from the door awoke Mumma.

'Where are you going?' Mumma called out from her room.

'Just outside for a minute.'

'Wait till I'm up.' Her voice was croaky.

'I'll be just outside.'

A pause.

'Who are you going with?'

'No one.'

'Not Balpa?'

'No.'

'Can you just wait. Give me another hour.'

'I'm gone already.'

'Please Loo.'

'Loopie's already left,' Loopie said.

There was the sound of something, maybe a thrown shoe, hitting the wall of Mumma's room.

Loopie squeezed herself through the small gap in the open door. If Mumma really didn't want her to go, she would have got out of bed to stop her.

Jean stood on the edge of the boat, supporting herself against one of The Jetty's thick roots. Morian stood further along the boat's edge, swinging the weighted end of the girdle round the back of the root. For the fourth time, Jean failed to catch it.

'It's still falling a good half-metre short,' she said.

'I'm worried about hitting you with the end,' Morian said.

Cal had dropped the boat's anchor, but this wasn't enough to keep it moored in a stationary enough position against the side of the root, and he had to keep correcting the boat's position with engine thrusts. Jean could feel these second-long thrums from the engine against the soles of her bare feet. She was sweating, the backs of her legs already aching from maintaining her balance in this precarious position.

On the ninth attempt, Jean finally managed to catch the end of the girdle. She clipped the buckle in place and tightened the strap.

They'd picked one of the outermost roots from which to take measurements first. The roots grew thicker the closer they were to the shore – the point of initial growth. Further in, Jean estimated that they could be as much as five times the width. But she wondered now how much further in they would be able to get. It had taken 15 minutes to get the girdle secured round the first root, and even though the photophores lit the vaulted underside of The Jetty, outside the sky was darkening so rapidly that the lights of far away cruise-liners were visible.

'You know,' Cal said, 'It might be easier next time to drive the boat in a circle around the root.' He demonstrated the action unnecessarily with his finger.

Morian hit the button to begin the vibration test. Jean leaned with her hand against the root, feeling the fabric of the girdle beneath her palm and watching the white froth of the waves slapping against the root.

'You won't be able to swing your strap round the wider posts,' Cal said. 'I think there's a box of cutlery in the hold. We could jab a fork through that loop there to hold it in place. The surface looks soft enough.'

The vibration levels of the girdle increased in strength by a factor of two every few seconds, quickly building to a rumble so strong that Jean had to remove her hand. A moment later the trembling in the root was visible.

'How's it looking, Mor?' she said.

Morian looked up from his screen. 'If the biomass estimates of The Jetty were correct, then the load-bearing capabilities should be just about adequate.'

'Told you so,' Jean smiled at Cal.

'We can't depend on *just about*,' Cal said.

'And this is one of the thinner roots as well…' Morian added.

'It'll be my call,' Cal said, and then, when he saw Jean's expression, checked himself and smiled. 'But this is just the first one. Let's take a look further in.'

Balpa was kneeling a little way away from the pod, beside one of the many pools in the growth fringe, which became treacherous holes when the tide was out. He was curled over, his elbows by his knees, nose close to the ground, gazing into a plastic ice cream tub.

Off the end of the jetty, gulls squabbled in the air above dozens of Midtown fishermen in coracles.

'So what is it?' Loopie asked.

He turned and waved for her to come over.

'It's amazing,' he said.

Inside the box was a bug. It looked a bit like a grasshopper, but thicker, armour plated, bristling at the elbows and neck with thin spines.

'Ewww,' Loopie said. She'd never seen anything like it before. 'Where'd you find it?'

'Just over there.' He pointed towards the smoky bustle of Midtown, where the pods were large and heaped two or three deep. 'Watch the way it eats.'

Balpa snapped off one of the new pod sprouts growing up from the soft ground and dropped it into the box. The shoot was about half the size of the bug. The bug did nothing at first, till Balpa pushed the green shoot right under the thing's nose. And then it set to.

When it opened its mouthparts to bite, the size of its head grew twofold. Loopie's eyes widened at the complex architecture of its mandibles, which flowered from a neatly folded state of economical compression into a huge and toothy gape. A long, shovel-like extension of its lower jaw shot outwards with alarming speed, grabbed the shoot from underneath, and with the sharp rows of teeth along its forward end, gripped the shoot and pulled it tight against the thing's face.

'Holy shit,' Loopie said.

'I know!' Balpa smiled, bouncing his backside on his bare heels.

Together, in silence, they watched the bug eat, their faces lowered as close to the top of the ice cream tub as they could get without any parts of their bodies touching.

With each chomp, the insect's serrated lower jaw hooked the shoot afresh, turning it minutely to get the biggest mouthful. This action caused the shoot to wriggle, as if alive, diminishing it piece by piece. Each bite made a sound like scissor blades coming together.

'Give it another one,' Loopie said.

The bug was insatiable. It ate two, three, then four shoots in rapid succession, never tiring, the pace of its chomping remaining constant. The bug would eat anything Balpa gave it. It ate skin peeled from the rusty-brown pod that was stricken with some kind of blight. It ate glass-eye-like immature windows, plucked from the face of the same pod. It ate one of the balled-up tangles of malformed electrical systems that blew out this way from Midtown like tumbleweed.

'Stop, you idiot!' Loopie said, when Balpa lowered his left index finger towards its jaws.

But the bug didn't bite him, even when he poked his fingertip right in its face, pushing it across the shiny bottom of the ice cream tub. It was as if Balpa's finger were invisible to it.

'Loo,' Mumma's voice came from the doorway. Her tired face poked out far enough that the sea breeze got her brown curls swinging. 'Over here, please.'

'Uh oh,' Loopie said.

Cal steered the boat slowly, occasionally following what looked like a path through an area of densely packed roots, only to find their way completely barred, the roots having swelled so tightly together that they formed little cul-de-sacs, forcing Cal to perform tricky manoeuvres to back the boat out again. It was almost dark outside now, but under the vaults of The Jetty, polka-dotted with photophores, the light was lime coloured.

Drips fell on Cal and Morian's upturned faces from The Jetty's underside. The acoustics of this vaulted green palace were phenomenal, every drop of water hitting the waves coming clearly to the ear, together forming a slow fizz of exquisite definition. And yet, why wasn't she stunned? This was a stunning experience. She knew that rationally. But the rapture this place was evoking in her colleagues was somehow inaccessible to her. What was wrong with her?

This wasn't the first time she'd experienced this emotional shut off. She'd felt this way several times now. In fact, the last time she'd felt like she'd *really* experienced something with her gloves off was the first time she went up the trellis of the Suzuki Tower – Cal's first attempt at wooing her, a little over 18 months ago.

The Suzuki Tower was the first of the bio-buildings, at 1,456 metres dwarfing all of their previous biological construction projects, breaking the 1km barrier that had been thought unbreakable and redefining the word skyscraper. Although the Suzuki Tower at that stage did not officially qualify as a functional building, as only its endoskeleton was completed, everyone talked about it in the same terms as a finished building, as if the six further years of growth required were just a formality and posed no real challenge.

Cal, the building's chief architect, had asked Jean to join him on a site visit to conduct vibration tests just below the rim of the trellis's growth tip – now that its growth had been terminated and the structure was hardening. They had to be flown there in a helicopter.

The trellis could be seen from ten kilometres away, poking through the top of the patchy clouds like a monstrous beanstalk. At its base, supporting its great weight, were thick buttresses. A temporary platform was bolted just below the growth tip, and jutting out from this was the · shelf-like helipad.

Jean had never experienced vertigo before, but once Cal had taken her hand to help her out of the helicopter and she was stood on the platform, the movement of the structure and its deceptive appearance of fragility made her feel like she'd lost her grip on the world. From up here she could see everything, all of the desert. The horizon bowed for her.

In the centre of the platform was a blank space – a square hole a couple of metres across. Of course this open hole was a terrible safety hazard, but it had been created to offer an uninterrupted view down the inside of the skyscraper's trellis.

When Jean had finished taking her measurements around the tip's support structures, Cal suggested she lie beside him on the platform to look down into the core of the trellis. He knelt first, moving with care, putting his hands on the lip of the hole, and then lay down so that his belly was flat against the platform, his head projecting out into the hole. Jean lay beside him, their bodies aligned. He shuffled closer to talk above the sound of the wind ruffling the windbreaks wrapped around the platform's outer scaffold.

From this position on her belly, the subtle swaying of the building made Jean feel a sensation something like flying. The movement – engineered flexibility to allow the building to cope with the stresses of tectonic shifts and crosswinds –

would be much diminished once all the other architectural stages had grown through: the pods in which people would live and work; the vascular systems that would carry water in and sewage out; the photosynthetics whose leaves would follow the sun in elegant pirouettes; and the electrics, created by specially engineered bacteria that would devour heavy metals, form colonies of the prescribed shape, and then, their purpose achieved, die, their accumulated corpses forming the entire building's electrical network.

Despite her ability to reason how safe she was up there, the almost complete exposure to the sky triggered the most ancient part of Jean's brain, making her heart pound and her throat close up. She'd once read an article in a men's magazine in her doctor's waiting room advising that on first dates, one should take a girl somewhere that would get her adrenaline going. It advised roller-coasters and scary movies. Any experience that got the heart pumping stimulated the attraction centres of the brain. Fear was the same as love to the lizard brain. Laying there, the small of her back sweating, she wondered whether Cal had read the same article.

When she looked down through the centre of the hole, the central cores twisted away from her in a diminishing double spiral. From this grew the branches and nodes that would soon scaffold the pods.

The shape of this hexagonal helix was repeated again and again on an ever-decreasing scale as the nodes and branches shrank from a metre thickness down to a scale of millimetres. Staring into the eye of this fractal, Jean could see a hexagon of clear space down the very centre, all the way to the desert below. She felt a sense of almost spiritual oblivion. Jean lost herself up there, lost her sense of self in a profound way that she would never be able to re-experience. A mental and emotional response like that can only happen one time, *the first time*, before the generalisation machine that is your brain builds a framework with which to understand it.

The moment broke something in her.

Hours afterwards, laying on her bed and still unable to speak, she remembered that Cal had leaned in to kiss her when they were on their bellies at the top of the tower, but it wasn't like any kind of remembering she'd experienced before. It was more like noticing, as if she was only just now seeing it for the first time, his action coming to her with the speed of a dropped pebble sinking into an ocean of syrup.

'I've told you about him before,' Mumma said. 'Dozens of times.' Mumma pushed the soft door closed and wedged it shut with her shoulder. She remained bent over because the pod was not yet tall enough for her to stand fully upright.

'He came and called for me,' Loopie said. 'What was I supposed to do? Be rude and say my mum won't let me play with you?'

'Yes,' Mumma said. She returned to stirring the saucepan of rabbit stew on the portable gas stove. They had stolen the rabbit together yesterday from a hutch on the roof of one of the fully matured pods further in towards Midtown. Loopie had kept lookout while Mumma yanked a corner of the chicken wire from its frame.

'Fine,' Loopie scowled. 'The next time I will.'

'You said that last time.'

'We were only…'

'I don't care what you were doing, Loo. If he wasn't getting you into trouble right at that moment, then it wasn't far away. He's already scarred you for goodness' sake. And round here you need a face.'

Loopie touched the silvery indent at the taper point of her right eyebrow. It was hardly visible now, which was a relief, considering how big the swelling had been when Balpa had thrown the packing crate at her, so Loopie didn't know why Mumma kept bringing it up.

'He's not like that any more.'

'I caught him out there two weeks ago taping a cat's back legs together.'

Loopie swallowed.

'What did you do?'

'Do? I didn't… couldn't *do* anything. His family are… I don't want any connection with them at all. I don't want you giving them any excuses to notice us or get involved in our lives. Do you understand?'

Loopie made the tiniest nod.

'Do you understand?' Mumma said again, loudly enough to startle her, but not loudly enough to be heard by Balpa, if he was still outside.

'Yes,' Loopie said.

'I just don't want you copying any of his behaviours. I don't want you growing up into that. When you're with him you're not yourself. When you're with him I don't…you're less likeable.'

The stew was boiling ferociously now, filling the pod with steam. Mumma turned the flames down, then tied up the bag of rabbit remains and threw it over towards the door, ready to be taken out and hurled in the sea next time they went out.

They were so far underneath The Jetty now that they could no longer see the night sky.

'We should head back after this one,' Jean said, patting the cool side of the root around which they'd only just managed to fit the girdle at its full extent.

'I think we've got enough now to make our point,' Morian said.

'Our point?' Cal said.

'That this place is stable.'

'I'm not sure that is our point,' Cal said.

Jean frowned. 'But…' she said, 'surely it's obvious now that the roots are continuing to thicken and strengthen even below the mature areas of town?'

'Yes, but I'm not convinced that they're strong enough. Especially with a hundred new people busting into The Jetty every day.'

'Then the perimeter controls should be tightened,' Jean said. 'That's the logical thing to do, not…'

'Not what…?'

'Whatever it is you were planning to do anyway before you even came out here.'

'That's a bit harsh,' Cal said.

'Bulldozing a city is harsh.'

'I think the job would be a bit ambitious for a bulldozer. R&D have been itching to get their little monsters out. It'd be a good opportunity for them.'

'Seriously?' Jean said. She looked across at Morian. His head was lowered, like that of an embarrassed child, his gaze fixed on the waves lapping against the boat.

'Don't be like that,' Cal said to Jean. He put his hand on her forearm as she unclipped the girdle's buckle. 'I don't know what you see when you look at all this,' he said, 'but I see it all coming down. The roots crumpling and splitting, the whole thing tipping into the sea along with thousands of people. I see breaking-news reports and inquests.'

'You're being melodramatic.'

'I don't have the faculty for melodrama. I'm being prudent. And anyway, these people are living inside technology they *stole* from us and *planted* and *grew* illegally. It's on their heads.'

'No,' Jean said. 'It's not.'

'Er, Jean?' Morian said. 'I think the tide's coming back in.'

When she'd finished dinner, Loopie went back to her room. The roof of her mouth felt waxy after the stew, so she plucked a few more hairs from the wall – the sweetness of the scabs would dissolve the sensation. She wondered if she'd picked too many recently. There were large patches of the wall around her nest of blankets on the floor where hairs had ceased to regrow. She wondered if it would affect the eventual shape of her room. But it was likely, anyway, that they would have to leave this pod in another six months or so and chase the growth fringe further out into the sea, as soon as the different factions of Midtowners began fighting to expand their territories out into this maturing region.

The sun was at its zenith now, heating the air in the pod and making it laborious to breathe. And then Balpa's silhouette returned. He crouched beside her pod and thumped the bottom of his fist against it.

'You in there?' he said.

Loopie stopped herself speaking. Her words knotted together, forming a blockage at the back of her throat.

'Loopie?' Balpa said again. 'You coming out again?'

Loopie was just a metre away from him. She was quite sure he couldn't see or hear her there, but she wasn't *completely* sure.

She bit the inside of her lip to keep herself silent.

'Loop?' He said. There was a tone of severity in his voice now.

Ignoring him caused Loopie to feel a tingling pain at the front of her belly, but just when she thought she couldn't bear it any longer, Balpa got up and walked away. His silhouette became diffuse, and then vanished altogether.

She unclamped her teeth. With her tongue she could feel the impression they left on the inside of her mouth.

The ceiling of The Jetty's underside was getting closer. Cal had made jokes about them becoming stuck under there at first, but now he had stopped.

They'd gone back the way they thought they had come in, but now the sea level was metres higher and the part of the roots they had travelled through was below water. So curved and twisted were the roots that Cal had to navigate back through an entirely different configuration.

The team had been trying to find their way out now for 45 minutes, searching all the while for slivers of night sky between distant roots, but whenever they did see one and set off towards it, they found their way once again barred, the gaps between roots too thin for the boat to pass through.

'Maybe we should call someone?' Morian said.

'We'll be out of here in a moment,' Cal said, turning the steering wheel hard to take a tight corner into a wide-open area. 'No need to call out the cavalry just yet.'

Cal wiped the sweat from his forehead with the back of his hand. 'Fuckit,' he said, chewing his lower lip as he was forced to stop and back out of another dead end. 'The second we get out of this place, I'm giving the order to send in the critters myself.'

'It knows that's what you've got planned,' Morian said. 'That's why it's fucking with us.'

'We should have demolished The Jetty before it was even a plank,' Cal said. 'It's our fault for being curious and letting the bloody thing grow.'

'It's a bit late now to wipe everything clean,' Jean said. 'It doesn't belong to us anymore.'

'Like hell it doesn't,' Cal said.

The boat bounced as the hull slapped every wavelet, shaking Jean. She looked closely at Cal, at the wrinkle of cartilage at the edge of his right ear, the few grey hairs beginning to speckle the dark regrowth at the nape of his neck, where the skin became loose and almost reptilian. How had she let him grow to occupy such a large territory in her mind these last 18 months? Was she really so afraid of being alone again?

'There!' Morian said, pointing.

Loopie rubbed her little finger in the gaps between her toes, the pressure causing little balls of dead skin to form. It was a simple pleasure.

She had lived her whole life on the fringe. Mumma said that when she was a baby, their pod had been right on the beach. What must that have been like? Loopie wished she could remember.

Every year, they moved farther and farther out to sea, always trying to be as far as possible from the life that Mumma had lived before Loopie was born.

Loopie's dream was this: that one day, The Jetty would grow far enough out that it crossed the whole ocean and touched another country. That it would stop being a jetty, and become a bridge.

Loopie's thoughts were broken by the sound of something hitting the surface of her pod. She looked up and saw that the bug was back, its silhouette clear again through the translucent wall. Loopie's heart quickened, dreading Balpa's reappearance. What if he knew she had been in there before, ignoring him? What if he got angry?

She waited a little while, holding all her toes bunched up inside her hands. She watched the silhouette of the bug just sitting there, but Balpa did not appear. A few moments later, a second bug arrived. And then a third. And then a fourth.

Jean arrived back at Walton Tower a little after 1am. She'd refused a lift from Cal and had walked all the way from the harbour. She hadn't eaten or drunk anything since lunch and her mouth tasted sour. In the elevator, she took off her shoes and held them by the thin straps. The wooden floor was cool against her sore feet. She rested her forehead against the glass.

All the way home she'd written her resignation letter in her head, but now, in the sobering familiarity of the tower, she knew she couldn't quit. Realised, in fact, that she would have to apologise for her behaviour today, for the things she'd said. Or she would lose everything. In one chop she'd fell everything she'd worked for. Be back where she was as a student. No, worse, because now she was so much older. Would be competing with younger, smarter, more beautiful people for positions with half the salary. The framework of her life was rigid, and the only way to grow was within it.

The elevator silently ascended, the bright photophores whizzing past in a blur. The tower's leaves lay flat along its length. The internal coil of 10,000 pods spiralled behind her, like a spring from floor to sky. Outside, the lights of juvenile buildings shone dimly far below, a luminous garden that, in the next couple of years, would become a forest around the Walton Tower, blocking her view of the sea.

Afterword:

Mighty Oaks from Little Acorns Grow

Prof Susan Stepney
University of York

HAVE YOU EVER watched a large structure being built? Swarms of construction workers and massive machinery toil away noisily and messily and expensively, and gradually, very gradually, the structure rises from the ground. Then it is finished: the construction workers move out, and the tenants move in. Once the structure is handed over, it is curiously static: a few interior partitions may change; it may get a new coat of paint.

Have you ever watched a plant grow? A seed falls, and starts to sprout. It gathers its nutrients from the ground, its building material from the carbon dioxide in the air, and constructs itself. Processes that build the young plant smoothly transition to processes that nourish and maintain the mature form.

Have you ever tended a garden? You plant seeds, provide soil and compost and water, prune and train, but the growing plants do most of the work. Your role is to guide the outcome.

That is the vision behind Adam's story *Growing Skyscrapers*: first to invent, and then to exploit and guide processes analogous to biological growth; to invent self-constructing, self-maintaining artefacts. Instead of laboriously building with steel and concrete, we will 'garden' more biological artefacts.

This is still a vision. The field is called molecular nanotechnology: small things building big things. There are two main approaches, which can be classified as 'dry' (diamondoid) versus 'wet' (cellular), or equally as 'building' *versus* 'growing'.

In the dry case, molecular machines are programmed to construct the desired artefact from raw materials in their environment. In skyscraper terms, these machines are analogues of termites building a termite mound from mud, or wasps building their nest. The insects are both construction workers and tenants, repairing and modifying their home throughout its lifetime. An alternative dry approach is to program pre-existing machines to self-assemble into the artefact, analogous to the way ants can assemble themselves into a living bridge.

Where did those machines come from? They might be built by other machines, or they might arise from self-reproduction. Self-reproduction is the biological approach. In the wet case, molecular machines are programmed to reproduce to become the artefact, extracting raw materials from the environment. In skyscraper terms, these machines are analogues of cells growing, dividing, differentiating, and becoming a tree. The cells *are* the structure, and continue to act to maintain and repair the adult form. Wet nanotechnology already exists as biological organisms; the challenge is to engineer and program growth into desired artefacts.

Adam's story is an example of 'wet' nanotech: the physical material grows, analogous to a tree. Cells divide and differentiate: some may become walls and windows, some water pipes, some electrical wiring. There still needs to be a lot of engineering work to design appropriate cells, but we do not have to start from scratch. Existing biological cells have many of these properties: we grow blood vessels and electrically conducting neurons; plants also grow a vascular system to move fluids around their bodies; we grow enamelled teeth; trees grow a strong shell of bark. In the growing structure, some cells may die as they mature, like the bark on a tree; some will stay living, growing to repair a damaged structure. Adam has included a form of edible sap:

his structure grows sustenance for its tenants.

There are two aspects to developing such a technology: inventing the 'hardware/wetware', which is the material that forms the structure, and also inventing the 'software', which contains the instructions to make the correct structure.

Current scientific research for the wetware is at the level of single cells. There are two main approaches to engineering an artificial cell: top down, and bottom up. Top down starts from an existing biological cell, and strips out unwanted material, until a 'minimal' cell remains. Bottom up puts together a number of biochemical components until a 'minimal' cell emerges. One aim of the research is to understand precisely what this minimal cell is, and how extra functions can be added to provide the desired growth behaviours.

A single cell may seem a long way from the trillions of cells in something like a tree. But mighty oaks from little acorns grow. Even massive redwoods started as single seeds. A crucial property of multi-celled systems is that there are many different types of cell. Current research, at this stage purely biological, is examining the process of cell *differentiation*: how and why and where and when cells 'decide' to become specific types of cell, like root, stem, leaf, or fruit. This understanding is a crucial step needed for going from artificial single cells, to artefacts comprising many different types of cell. A skyscraper might be grown more like a garden than a single plant: multiple different types of seeds might be used in concert to source the walls, the utilities, the elevators, and so on. But even so, some degree of differentiation is required. Understanding these processes is currently in the domain of *Systems Biology*.

Hardware alone is not enough. The second component of such a technology is the software: the 'program' that instructs the seed to grow into a particular kind of system. In biological systems, this 'software' component is intimately embedded and embodied in the growing wetware: in the DNA, in other constituents of the cells, in the laws of chemical reactions. It is what distinguishes a radish from a redwood, a mushroom from a mouse. If we wish to grow skyscrapers, we need to determine what instructions result in such growth. Designing and developing this kind of software is currently in the domain of *Computational Morphogenesis*.

There are many current uses of software to design and grow *virtual* artefacts: from L-Systems and other 'graph grammars' that produce delightful graphics of plants, to systems that produce architectural designs. However, the embedding of such software into wetware, to produce *physical* multi-cellular artefacts, is still to be achieved. In addition to the difficulty of engineering the software into the hardware, there is the issue of real-world constraints; not everything that can be imagined can be built: the laws of physics simply disallow some constructs, and the laws of biological growth may not provide any viable path from initial seed to mature artefact.

One advantage of a biological-like construction process is that designed 'seeds' can grow in different ways in different environments. This can be exploited to give adaptive structures: stronger walls in windy places; thicker walls in colder places. It can also be exploited as a more direct control mechanism: different growth rates with different nutrients. The system could be engineered to be dependent on some specific nutrients, helping to control problems from 'escaped' systems. Here Adam has transplanted his skyscraper to an unplanned environment: salt water. This unforeseen environment has interesting effects on the system's growth.

There are other control mechanisms possible during growth. Gardeners prune and train plants to guide them into desired shapes. Adam's skyscraper is like a tree tended in a garden, growing on a trellis, and being pruned and guided. Gardening the growing artefact could make the seed design process somewhat simpler: design a seed that grows into some generic product, then customise it by pruning during growth. Today's construction workers become tomorrow's gardeners.

One key feature of biological organisms is that they *reproduce*. Not only do mighty oaks grow from little acorns, they produce further acorns of their own. What might this mean for skyscrapers? Would a skyscraper produce seeds, and end up surrounded by its offspring of younger skyscrapers? Adam has his skyscraper producing edible sap-like material, but what if it produced *fruit*? We would almost certainly want such constructs to be seedless, not only to control intellectual property, but also order to control 'weeds'. Plants, however, can reproduce by 'vegetative propagation': runners and cuttings. Did Adam's characters steal seeds, or did they take cuttings?

Plants can be attacked by other organisms: viruses, fungi, beetles, caterpillars. If we can engineer plant-like skyscrapers, will we engineer beetle-like controls? Adam suggests this as a mechanism to destroy the illegal Jetty. Maybe the residents need to invest in artificial-insecticide!

One component of the technology that is well advanced is the software design process. How to design a small program that fits in a cell, which then directs the cell to divide and grow into a complex structure containing trillions of differentiated copies? Software exhibiting such *emergent properties* is notoriously hard to design intelligently. However, biology again comes to the rescue: evolution searches a vast space of possible organisms, evolving the necessary cellular 'programs'. Computational morphogenesis combined with 'evolutionary algorithms' is a software analogue of biological research domain known as 'Evo-Devo' (evolutionary development).

So, although Adam's story is still firmly science-fictional, each of the required technologies is an active and flourishing area of research. Even if we ourselves do not, our children or grandchildren may well live in a grown building.

The Loki Variations

Andy Hedgecock

Originally published as Appendix A in: Currie, I.J. (2099, 2nd Edition), *Architects of the Possible: the Life and Science of William Wickens*, OUP, Oxford:UK

EDITOR'S NOTE 1 (I.J. CURRIE)
Shortly after the publication of the first edition of this volume, in 2097, I became aware of the existence of an additional e-archive, which my publisher felt strongly should be included in this edition. This archive features material that had been quite deliberately and systematically removed from the public domain, and dates from William Wickens' tenure as Research Fellow in the Psychobiology of Gaming at Lune Valley University, funded by the ZammaSoft Corporation. The Wickens Foundation bought the files and cryptographic key from his niece, the sculptor Vali Ferguson, and was generous enough to grant me full access to the material.

The lack of an index and the fragmented nature of the files – a potpourri of news stories, notes, reviews, correspondence and interviews – makes it difficult to elicit a structured view of Wickens' intellectual journey. I have tried to select and present material in an order that highlights, for the committed scholar, clear affinities between his reaction to the political landscape of his early life and the evolution of Wickens' controversial work on the psychobiology of empathy.

*

ITEM: ENGDAHL INTERVIEW – EXTRACT A
SOURCE: City University Stockholm TV. 'Examined
         Lives' series
LABEL: Distinguished psychobiologist William
         Wickens joins regular interviewer Kendra Engdahl
DATE: Broadcast 06 April 2085

ENGDAHL: Professor Wickens, what drew you to gaming, why did you want to apply your understanding of neuroscience in an area many people saw as trivial?

WICKENS: Thirty-five years ago, before I became a neuroscientist, I was a soldier, a street seller, a senator and a sex worker. I was all of these, every night of the week if I wanted, and all within the safety of my bedroom. I was addicted to *Rich List*, and will never forget the elation I felt the first time I was featured in *Forbes* for my hostile takeover of 400 companies. Days and nights would be 'wasted' playing *Hot Seat* over and over until I finally cracked it, stalking the technical area, yelling at players, bullying Spurs to a Champions League win over Bayern Munich. My gaming was… fanatical, you might say. Maybe you were a gamer too, or perhaps you played other roles, other games?

ENGDAHL: What got you hooked? What elements of those vintage games did you find so enticing?

WICKENS: The most absorbing games didn't just make you feel elated, they encouraged you to make choices that mattered and exposed you to the consequences. In *Rich List* there was guilt and fear of reprisal when, for example, I canned the least productive third of the workforce and moved production to a zone with lower pay. Getting those emotions across was obviously a bit hit and miss – as players, we had to work hard to suspend our disbelief and never really lost touch with 'meat space', as they used to call it, the real world. That was what Felix Muller and I wanted to change with our work on *Loki*.

ITEM: AV CLIP A [Voice-over and montage of game clips, players and equipment]

SOURCE: ITV i-archive. 'Ahead of the Game'

LABEL: Jose Blake previews The Loki Variations, *ZammaSoft*

DATE: Programme available 19 – 26 May 2060

ZammaSoft, who took immersive gaming to new levels in the '40s and '50s have led the charge into new territory once again. You don't have to settle for seeing how the other half lives any longer; you can live how the other half lives with the *Loki Variations*.

   Loki isn't about playing a role or exploring a situation, it's about being on the streets of Camberwell, cold, bruised and wondering if you can survive a bit longer if you sell your arse; about swigging Chateau Margaux as you surf a derivatives crash and stuff your rival speculators; about plotting to assassinate the PM and shafting your comrades when you're arrested. Or how about organising a search 'n' kill posse to sweep human vermin from the streets of New York, New Delhi or Greenwich? The choice is yours. Whatever city you choose, you'll feel the thrill of the chase, or the buzz of fear.

   Ten years ago *ZammaSoft* put players at the centre of gaming with body suits and an affordable neurogaming interface. A bit ramshackle at the time, but the real-time transfer of ideas and moods suddenly became an affordable reality. Distractions were blocked and suspending disbelief required a lot less effort.

   With *Loki* you'll need no effort at all, it's impossible not to believe. There are e-textile body suits enabling haptic and multisensory feedback, a brain-computer interface that guarantees a deep trance every time, and of course, the game's real innovation, the much-heralded *Epiphany* pack. Taking advantage of the new licensing law, *ZammaSoft* is the first gaming company out of the blocks with a tested, safe and temporary hallucinogen. *Epiphany* works perfectly with enhanced brain-interfacing to create the *Citizen Kane* of gaming, the Sistine Chapel ceiling of simulation. If you don't know your cultural history click the links onscreen – you'll see what I mean.

There's one downside to this: you'll be hooked so hard you'll need endless top-up packs of *Epiphany*…

[Epiphany was a key discovery for the development of totally immersive gaming. It stimulated Serotonin 2A receptor sites and decreased oscillatory activity in the Alpha Frequency Band of the Posterior Cingulate Cortex. The outcome was temporary suspension of one's everyday sense of self and the emergence of a synthetic alternative – something psychologists call 'ego transference'. This allowed players to fully enter the simulated worlds of The Loki Variations *– I.J. Currie]*

★

Item: Engdahl interview – extract b (ibid.)

ENGDAHL: You played a major role in creating the most talked about cultural product of our era, but the company that funded the project sacked you and disowned your work. What went wrong?

WICKENS: Nothing went wrong; we achieved what we set out to. Everyone was happy with us at the time.

ENGDAHL: But *ZammaSoft* sacked you and Felix Muller in January 2061, just six months after the release of *Loki*. They described you as 'a manipulative fantasist' and called for criminal charges against Professor Muller for misappropriation of funding –

WICKENS: They played to the gallery. When the controversy broke, their board panicked and sold *Loki* to us in an attempt to cut their losses. Their accusations of deception are groundless.

ENGDAHL: What was the working relationship between you and Felix Muller?

WICKENS: He was an inspirational mentor who became a friend. Felix did pioneering work on Brain-Computer Interfacing, but when I worked with him he was the *Loki Variations* Project Director. He recruited me to his team at Lune Valley, where I was responsible for assessing the cognitive and behavioural effects of the *Epiphany* pack. The idea we were part of a revolutionary plot is absurd because, whatever else we believed, we were dedicated commercial scientists who had no more control over the outcome of the *Loki* pilot than any of the volunteers who took part.

ENGDAHL: The pilot study took place in extraordinary times, against a backdrop of unrest and atrocity –

WICKENS: For me, one of the biggest atrocities was the way half the population was being forced to live. Equally atrocious was the way the mainstream media ignored it.

★

ITEM: BROADCAST NEWS REPORT
SOURCE: BBC News 24. Main bulletin loop
LABEL: Assassination of Letrice Hewson, location report by Darragh O'Ryan
DATE: First broadcast 13:00, 30 December 2059

[Close up of O'Ryan – head and shoulders. He wears a black overcoat and black and white striped tie; aged forty, he has well groomed greying hair – IJC]

Today's tragic development highlights the need for vigilance; the threat to public safety from Levellers and other disaffected groups is growing. My report contains upsetting scenes.

[Cuts to medium wide shot of a stuccoed house with wrought iron balconies, then zooms to dried blood on the paving in front of the pillars that frame the black front door.]

Letrice Hewson, Secretary of State for Work and Enterprise, was leaving her home near Regent's Park at seven thirty this morning when shots rang out. Her bodyguards returned fire, killing an armed woman. There are conflicting descriptions of another woman, who managed to escape before police arrived at the scene. Lady Hewson was treated by paramedics, but having been hit in the head and chest, was declared dead at 7:50. Police received a call from a Leveller spokesperson at 10:30, using an established code word and claiming responsibility for the murder.

Meanwhile, all over West London, people were heading for work, shopping venues and tourist attractions. This afternoon Londoners are in shock...

[Cuts to montage: wide shots of blazing vehicles, shattered plate glass, protesters in balaclavas and plastic face-masks throwing petrol bombs. There is gunfire. Uniformed public order officers, in grey livery and black riot helmets, shelter under full-length Perspex shields. These are staff of the Carrack Security Group, which held the contract for public order policing from 2050 until the 2070 revolution.]

The assassination follows three days of anarchy across the country, quelled by heroic and decisive policing. The cost of damage to property is estimated at close to a billion euro.

[Cuts to a lower resolution, less steady image.]

In this amateur footage, looters help themselves to knitwear and jewellery as shop windows are shattered on Bond Street.

Meanwhile, Prime Minister Nicola Camm, sent a clear message to terrorists:

[Cuts to a head and shoulders shot of PM. Speech direct to camera.]

'My government gives everyone the opportunity to work hard and achieve a better standard of living. We are implementing a series of initiatives to help the less well-off pull themselves out of poverty, addiction and idleness. But opposition parties sneer at hardworking people, wish to stifle enterprise through taxation and encourage the kind of disaffection that boils over into the acts of violence we have seen this week. There will be no place to hide for those who undermine our way of life, whether through murder, looting or inciting others to riot.'

Meanwhile, in other news...

[Cuts to new footage. Medium wide shot of slender woman in her mid-twenties. She is wearing spectacular heels and a light blue knitted suit. She has perfect teeth and hair and is waving to a crowd of people held back by uniformed guards. There is a light fall of snow.]

... thousands of fans greeted reality TV star, model and fashion advocate Claire Popovic as she opened the Greenwich Waterfront Retail Complex ...

★

ITEM: ENGDAHL INTERVIEW – EXTRACT C (IBID.)

ENGDAHL: Since you raise the issue of politics, is it true that while working on *Loki* you were close to Adhita Pramadhanti, the Committee Co-ordinator for Resource and Distribution in the English Parliament?

WICKENS: Yes, we lived together in Elysium, a guarded and gated community on the site of a former fishing village, a few miles from the university. Our respective parents had clubbed together to pay the extortionate rent because they were obsessed with keeping us safe. Adhita was writing up her thesis on Spiritual Individualism in American Literature and I was working with Felix Muller.

ENGDAHL: Was she interested in your work?

WICKENS: I know where this is leading. She was more interested in Henry Thoreau than gaming but yes, she was very keen to take part in the *Loki* pilot.

ENGDAHL: Was her interest inspired by her political views?

WICKENS: At that stage Adhi's feelings for people on the edge of society were a combination of fear and irritation. Like everyone else's. If she could've been bothered to vote she would have voted for Nicola Camm and the status quo, but no one was less interested in politics than Adhita. By the way, is this interview about her work or mine?

★

ITEM: SCHEDULE OF SIMULATION SCENARIOS — WORKING LIST
SOURCE: W. Wickens — private file
LABEL: *Loki Variations* pilot study, running order (Wickens, W)
DATE: Created 30 January 2059

Volunteers take part in seven scenarios in the following order:

Tent City 12. You are made homeless when TC12 is bulldozed. Some of your fellow refugees hurl incendiaries over the wall of the Thatcher Village in Richmond. If you are arrested there's risk of torture, but joining in may give you status within your group and enhance your chances of survival.

Prisoner's Dilemma. You are arrested on a hunger march and forced to watch police torture of a fellow demonstrator. Trading information about the whereabouts of the protest organiser, a suspected Leveller, will bring you immunity from prosecution for sedition.

Massacre. You are part of a group of unlicensed beggars. You are victims of an unprovoked recreational assault, carried out with unrestrained violence, by a group of privileged young people.

Camberwell Stockade. You are held by police carrying semi-automatic weapons for failing to produce a valid ID card. You are thrown into a stockade: the officers holding you are disorganised and there are opportunities for escape. A failed escape attempt will result in torture.

Sexploitation Party. As the guest of a high profile business contact, you do everything in your power to impress your host rather than lose your job. He invites you to watch an erotic tableau, performed to his precise specification by people he has hired for the evening. You notice several of the performers are distressed and frightened. What do you do?

Propaganda of the Deed. As part of a Leveller-style insurrectionary group you debate the kidnap and execution of an industrialist for the part his security team played in a massacre of homeless people. The group can go through with the plan or adopt a less violent approach.

Workhouse. The government decides to herd workless and homeless people into workhouses. You are sent to one and witness rape and violent assault. Few people leave the place alive. Your task is to find an opportunity to escape, by any means possible.

★

ITEM: SECURE EMAIL (to Will Wickens from Felix Muller)
SOURCE: W. Wickens – personal correspondence
LABEL: Ready for Kick off (confidential)
DATE: Created 2 February 2059

I'm relaxed about your participation in scenarios F and G — it demonstrates a laudable willingness to take the same risks as our volunteers.

But as a friend rather than a supervisor, can I suggest it would be better if Adhi did not take part? It wouldn't trouble the University Ethics Committee but if she has a tough time, it's possible your role in creating those experiences might damage your relationship. Try to change her mind Will.

Regards … Felix

★

ITEM: V-DIARY – LOKI PILOT PARTICIPANT # 19 (extract)
Source: W. Wickens – private file
LABEL: Maria Pujol, female, 29 years, Scenario B
         (Prisoner's Dilemma)
X-REF: Paired participant – entering simulations with
         partner and co-worker Kristy Chillari [Part.# 20]
DATE: Created 6 February 2059

I have to watch the whole thing because every time I try to shut my eyes the fat sweaty bitch with the bad hair and three stripes whacks me straight across the chops. My face is stinging, my nose is bleeding and a couple of my teeth feel loose. At least I have teeth, not like the guy tied to the chair. The bastards make Kristy and me watch every tooth they pull. I feel sick, but Kris is hysterical, her breathing is all over the place. Oh fuck, I say to myself, she's dying of hysteria. She's making things worse for both of us, know what I mean? I keep repeating 'not real, not real' under my breath, and nearly get away with that, but when Kris starts with the screaming again I get sucked right back into being petrified.

Anyway, Sergeant Pig in a Wig presses her face to me, reeking of stale *Bell's Original*. 'See what we can do to you Maria, no one knows you're here and no one gives a shit,' she whispers.

This time it was like one of those dreams when you stay asleep but know it's a dream. Do you get me? Even so, I was fucking petrified and I knew from the start I was going to sign anything they wanted and grass everyone up. Even Kristy.

★

ITEM: V-DIARY – LOKI PILOT PARTICIPANT # 20 (extract)
SOURCE: W. Wickens – private file
LABEL: Kristy Chillari, female, 23 years, Scenario C
              (Massacre)
X-REF: Paired participant – entering simulations with
              partner and co-worker Maria Pujol [Part. # 19]
DATE: Created 9 February 2059

I went through *Scenario C* yesterday, the massacre, and it was so, so frightening. Thank god you give us a medical every time. Maria is coping better than me, not that we've talked about what's happening, I can just tell. Not talking about it is down to me – I'm just too knackered. And scared.

I still can't find the words to describe the overall feeling. I'm sort of there, but not there. The 'me' that's there, in the games, is sometimes me and sometimes someone else – it's weird. Sometimes the real world pokes through, like when you notice how fake the acting and scenery are in a crap film. Then I'm back in my normal thoughts, conscious I'm playing a character and I feel I can drop out of the world I'm in, back into the real one. But not yesterday. It was horrible, it was totally real. I was in the middle of it and couldn't get out.

I remember most of what happened. We were part of a band of beggars asking for money, for food. We were hanging out on some embankment steps, boarded up shops behind us and a canal in front of us with all sorts of crap dumped in it – old bikes, tyres, plastic containers – all covered in a phlegmy sort of silt. Some of our group are getting off their faces on 'Bucky'. Suddenly a group of kids appear, dressed in sharp leisurewear. Some have coshes, some have knifes and one has a sword. They trap us on both sides very quickly, and the screaming starts. One of us, a guy with long red hair in a ponytail, staggers towards the empty shops, but he's too pissed to outrun the hunters … he's surrounded in seconds and kicked to the ground, then the coshes and knives are raised... I'll never forget the screams and spray of blood. A girl… a girl about my age gets down on her knees and begs for her life… her mouth twisted… like… and her eyes… they were … oh god, I'm sorry… give me a minute… but the big bastard with the sword isn't having any of that… sorry….

[Camera cuts – recording resumes]

I try to get Maria to run with me but she freezes. I scream at her but she won't budge. Someone starts shooting. I think 'fuck her then' and dive into the canal. The thing that sticks out now is the screaming, the sort of coppery smell of blood and the cold as fuck water of the canal. The canal doesn't stink, which is weird. Is that a fault in the game?

No-one likes beggars, but if that's happened, that kind of murder, you can see why some of them get violent. Have the things in this game happened somewhere? Will you tell me later? You let me talk, but you don't give much away.

I have to be honest with you. I know this will piss Maria off, because we both need the money and we signed on to play all seven games, but I'm thinking of quitting the experiment. I can't go through that again for fuck's sake.

★

ITEM: V-DIARY – LOKI PILOT PARTICIPANT # 25 (extract)
SOURCE: W. Wickens – private file
LABEL: William Wickens, Male, 26 years, Scenario F
           (Propaganda of the Deed)
X-REF: Paired participant – entering simulation F & G
with
           partner Adhita Pramadhanti [Part. # 24]
DATE: Created 23 February 2059

This is the most static of the simulations, the action being historical rather than live, but it's oddly compelling in spite of that. As it opens, Adhi and I are revolutionaries. A shallow grave containing more than 20 people has been found. We are shown police footage of the bodies of men, women and children – many showing signs of torture. There's incontrovertible evidence the massacre has been carried out by the security team at a company called Valente Construction. It's proposed we snatch Karl Kendell, the CEO, and execute him on camera. I argue for lower level retribution against the company, perhaps using improvised explosives against the security people on the approach road to their headquarters. Adhi is having none of it. Plan A or nothing. I've never seen her like this before, brimming with anger and energy. She swings the group and, reluctantly, I go along with the plan.

Afterwards, I feel unsure whose head I've been in. I am shocked at the ease with which I'm coerced into approving an atrocity, but this isn't entirely my own experience, is it? I flip between guilt and detachment. What shocks me most is Adhita's response after the simulation – quieter, less bubbly. Morose might be a bit strong, but we certainly struggle to discuss our experience on the way home.

*

ITEM: BROADCAST NEWS REPORT
SOURCE: BBC News 24. Investigative report
LABEL: System of Dr Wickens and Professor Muller, studio report by Darragh O'Ryan
DATE: First broadcast 22:30, 28 November 2060

[Studio close up of O'Ryan – leaning against news desk]

Tonight, we look at the work of two Lune Valley University academics and ask if it has produced a game that promotes terrorism?

[Cuts to still shots: labelled departmental staff photographs of Wickens and Muller.]

Berlin-born Professor Felix Muller and his associate Dr William Wickens, have been accused by politicians and the media of pedalling 'upmarket misery tourism' in the form of their bestselling *Loki* simulation game. Let's look at the evidence.

[Cuts to medium wide shot of the simulation laboratory, Lune Valley University.]

In the original pilot study for *Loki*, volunteers were paid to act out violent and disturbing acts of terrorism: there was no physical risk but the games were reported to have a terrifying degree of realism and many participants experienced lasting psychological harm.

[Cuts to still shot: graduation photograph of Adhita Pramadhanti.]

One volunteer, Adhita Pramadhanti, a popular young researcher at the start of a promising academic career, reportedly lost all contact with her family and friends nearly two years ago, only to resurface, last month as a mouthpiece for the Levellers.

[Cuts to close up of Adhita Pramadhanti, presenting pirate broadcast on behalf of the Levellers. She is neat but slightly thinner in appearance, dressed in a black blouse.]

Other volunteers, speaking exclusively to the BBC, have described their experience of the *Loki* simulations as traumatic and unnerving...

[Darragh O'Ryan avoided making direct accusations of a Leveller recruitment conspiracy but implied a dark undercurrent to The Loki Variations. *There was no suggestion the games corrupted young people by promoting the values of beggars, rebels and prostitutes, but it was hinted they propagated a pessimistic view of societies based on free market capitalism and, therefore, promoted aimless rebellion – I.J. Currie]*

★

ITEM: V-DIARY – LOKI PILOT PARTICIPANT # 24 (extract)
Source: W. Wickens – private file
LABEL: Adhita Pramadhanti, female, 25 years, Scenario G
        (Workhouse)
X-REF: Solo participant A-E, entering simulations with partner William Wickens for G & F [Participant # 25]
DATE: Created 26 February 2059

I'm desperate enough to trade a blow-job for a blade. One of the girls in our dormitory gets dragged into the blanket store by four custodians and stops screaming after 20 minutes. We don't see her again. Then the guy who tries to report her missing gets his nostrils slit open for being a grass. There's this weasel called Cookie, a sort of trustee who spends a lot of time buttering up the guards, belting inmates with his truncheon and blathering about his 'networking skills'. He stinks, but I need to get out. Five minutes bliss for him, a lifetime of self-loathing and a penknife for me. He doesn't ask what I want it for: he doesn't care.

When we are back in the main hall, I drive the blade into Cookie's neck and all hell breaks loose. I've always had a flair for improvisation. I yell for Will to follow me but he freezes, leaving me standing there like a twat, covered in gore. It's a miracle I get out.

And that was that, Will missed his chance to follow me. I suppose I got a lot more wired and angry than Will. It was all less intense for him – maybe because he co-designed the implant technology and commissioned the scenarios he knew more deeply how unreal they were. Or perhaps some of us simply get more involved in other people's lives than others? I'm not sure if Felix will let you watch this Will. Are you letting him watch Felix?

*

ITEM: EMAIL (to Adhita Pramadhanti from Will Wickens)
SOURCE: W. Wickens – personal correspondence
LABEL: Coming (no pun intended)?
DATE: 28 February 2059, 21.30

Hi Adhi

I'm tied down here sorting through data and diary entries. I fancy getting away from this stuff at the weekend. Shall we get the bikes out, pack a picnic and do our ride to Heysham? It's been a while – let's do it.
Hope you're feeling more like the real you today!
Will.

★

ITEM: EMAIL (to Will Wickens from Adhita Pramadhanti)
SOURCE: W. Wickens – personal correspondence
LABEL: Re: Coming (no pun intended)?
DATE: 28 February 2059, 22.10

There are things I need to think through over the next few days, Will. I'm not up for physical exertion or communing with nature at the moment. Ask me later.
Ax

★

ITEM: ENGDAHL INTERVIEW – EXTRACT D (ibid.)

ENGDAHL: What happened to your volunteers after the pilot?

WICKENS: We were contracted to monitor volunteers for 12 weeks but three or four of them declined to attend the sessions. One of those was Adhita, but she wasn't the only one of our original participants to join the Levellers. A number of the others exhibited significant attitudinal changes of some sort.

When Adhi disappeared, ten days after the final session, her parents believed she'd been kidnapped by Levellers. They offered a huge ransom and made a series of desperate appeals, until they saw her fronting the first of the L-Broadcasts, those pirate broadcasts that were hacked on top of all the legal TV channels. Quite quickly she became the *de facto* leader of the political wing of the Levellers, probably because she wasn't implicated in any specific killings. When the Leveller movement gained the critical mass to make an amnesty inevitable, she surfaced into the full glare of public attention at the Gosforth Park Accord in November 2070.

ENGDAHL: Did you ever hear from her again?

ENGDAHL: No, but I wish I had.

★

ITEM: EMAIL (to Will Wickens from Adhita Pramadhanti)
SOURCE: W. Wickens – personal correspondence
LABEL: Happy Christmas (nearly)
DATE: 24 December 2070, 23.35

Hey you, didn't we once fuck each other's brains out in a little
house in Elysium? Get in touch Will. Please let me know how
you're doing – it would be good to say hello and sorry. I know
I hurt you and I want to know you're OK. No pressure, but it
would be lovely to catch up.
Ax

★

EDITOR'S NOTE 2 (I.J. CURRIE)

*Admirers of William Wickens, among which I number myself, suggest
he was a prophet without honour in his own land. Attacks by Darragh
O'Ryan and other media figures led Wickens and his mentor Felix
Muller to leave Lune Valley for tenured posts in Norway. The
government tried to ban Loki, but copies were made available through
underground retailers, in original and pirated forms. When the
Pramadhanti connection first became public, Zammasoft sold the
package to Muller, Wickens and a small group of French investors
trading as Pelloutier Productions. Within two years, the Pelloutier
development team had sufficient understanding of the risks to build-in
'psychological safety nets' and to market the game in Scandinavia,
South America, Japan and China with great success. Copies found
their way into England in spite of the game's proscribed status.*

Wickens and Muller continued to attract significant funding for their work on the psychobiology of empathic behaviour (Wickens) and the neuroscience of simulation (Muller). There was, however, little discussion of their work in popular media until Wickens controversially won the Nobel Prize for Peace in 2080.

Some authors (Balfour et al, 2082; Singh 2085) suggest that the work of Muller and Wickens was the catalyst for the retreat of corporate power and the end of the neo-conservative era in which we had lived since 1979. It is perhaps far-fetched, not to say inappropriately essentialist, to suggest all the great reformations of the 2070 Revolution were triggered by a simple computer game: the adoption of a citizen-based constitution, the reassertion of public-ownership along the lines of the Bevan prototype, the resuscitation of the democratic process (regular online referenda, three year parliaments, the bar on all corporate lobbying), the creation of an independent police service and the closing of gaps in income and wealth. It is hard to prove our emergence from the 'Corporate Dark Age' can be entirely attributed to the work of two relatively obscure software scientists in North West Lancashire. However, the argument that Loki *was merely a* symptom *of progressive change ignores the fact that there was very little public dissent against the Camm administration when the game was released.*

William Wickens continued to teach and research until his early retirement and disappearance in 2093. Students remember a serious and intense man with a slightly hawkish appearance softened by the good life, sharp with his words, but generous with his time. Colleagues recall a good companion with an acerbic edge. Wickens was modest in discussing his achievements and reticent, almost to the point of intellectual neglect, in discussing the development of the Loki Variations, *so the discovery of the present cache of material is an invaluable addition to the Wickens archive.*

Afterword:

The Moral Onboard Compass

Micah Rosenkind
University of Brighton

ANDREW'S STORY PAINTS a picture of a future where computer and video game technology has reached a level that enables total immersion in a virtual world. Players have a profound experience while playing 'The Loki Variations' and many of them leave the simulations with a deeper, empathetic understanding of the character they inhabited. In presenting different game examples that allow players to experience both ultimate power and the suffering of the oppressed, the story also gains a political dimension. It shows how these experiences can become the driving force behind a societal shift in consciousness and eventually even plant the seeds that bring about political change.

From a technological standpoint, we are currently seeing the dawn of the virtual and augmented reality era. By using mobile phone technology and social networks on a daily basis, we have started to see the world through digital eyes. As miniaturisation and screen technology progresses, our phones and gadgets become wearable, embedded and more connected to ourselves. Eventually, our primary mode of interacting with these devices will shift to looking through, instead of at them. While Google's 'Glass' may seem awkward today, it provides valuable insights into a future where we might not be staring at our phones (or watches) while walking – this must be a good thing. Virtual reality headgear technology is also pushing forward. Facebook's 'Oculus Rift' has surprised testers with how immersive virtual environments can be, even if severe technical shortcomings are still present. Current research into applications of virtual reality at Stanford has found that the effect that is achievable with existing technology is already profound, prompting the use of the term 'presence' to describe the feeling of *actually* being *in* a virtual space. Experiments where a person virtually controls a body with a different gender, race, age or even disabilities have proven surprisingly effective. Researchers observed measurably lower racial prejudice in participants after they experienced what it would be like to have a different skin colour[1]. Even indirect and lingering effects of virtual reality experiences could be observed. After playing a super hero game, participants were more willing to assist others in real life[2]. According to Jeremy Bailenson, the founding director of the virtual reality lab at Stanford, virtual reality simulations can have a profound and lasting effect on users: 'Anything is possible in VR. You can become 70 years old, a different race, or a different gender, and have to walk a mile in that person's shoes and experience discrimination against that person'[3]. Another new application of virtual reality is 'Body Swapping'. Using cameras mounted to a pair of virtual reality headsets, two people can be connected to see through each other's eyes. At the 'Be Another' project, which is run by a group of artists and researchers in Barcelona, wheelchair users swapped with dancers and therapists were able to improve how they handle their physically disabled patients after experiencing treatment from their perspective. According to a programmer at 'Be Another', Arthur Pointeau, the participants felt extremely close and a sense of empathy for each other after the experiments: 'With this kind of experience we can promote

1. Maister, L., Sebanz, N., Knoblich, G., & Tsakiris, M. (2013). 'Experiencing Ownership Over a Dark-Skinned Body Reduces Implicit Racial Bias'. *Cognition,* 128(2), 170-178.

2. Rosenberg, R. S., Baughman, S. L., & Bailenson, J. N. (2013). 'Virtual Superheroes: Using Superpowers in Virtual Reality to Encourage Prosocial Behavior.' *PloS one,* 8(1), e55003.

3. Wen, T. (2014). 'Can Virtual Reality Make you a Better Person?'. BBC. Available from:
http://www.bbc.com/future/story/20141001-the-goggles-that-make-you-nicer [Accessed: 01.10.14]

empathy, but also maybe help people better understand themselves too'[4].

'The Loki Variations' also tells a story about 'ethical gameplay'. This should not be confused with ethical content in games – another widely debated topic. The focus here is on the use of ethical dilemmas that challenge players to make moral decisions. In recent years, game developers have found new and interesting ways of creating gameplay that causes players to pause and consider their own morals.

Game designers put a lot of effort into keeping players well informed about how their actions impact the game world. They usually use informative user interfaces and keep choices in the game clear and binary. Even games that supposedly simulate moral systems, such as *Fable*[5] *Mass Effect*[6] or *Infamous*[7] use a binary choice system. Every option presented to the player ultimately leads to either a 'good' or 'bad' story arc. However, systems where the choice and outcomes are as clear as this, encourage 'instrumental play'[8] – a form of instrumental rationality[9] – where players learn to 'play the system' to win the game. According to *Fable* designer

4. Eveleth, R. (2014). 'I Swapped Bodies with Someone'. BBC. Available from: http://www.bbc.com/future/story/20140427-i-swapped-bodies-with-someone [Accessed: 28.09.14]

5. Lionhead, Big Blue Box (2004). *Fable* [Software]. Windows PC, Xbox 360. Microsoft Game Studios. Information Available from: http://www.mobygames.com/game/fable- [Accessed: 27.09.14]

6. BioWare (2007), *Mass Effect* [Software]. Windows PC, Xbox 360. Microsoft Game Studios. Information Available from: http://www.mobygames.com/game/mass-effect [Accessed: 27.09.14]

7. Sucker Punch Productions. (2009). *Infamous* [Software]. PS3. Sony Computer Entertainment. Information Available from: http://www.mobygames.com/game/ps3/infamous [Accessed: 27.09.14]

8. Sicart, M. (2010, August). 'Wicked Games: on the Design of Ethical Gameplay'. In *Proceedings of the 1st DESIRE Network Conference on Creativity and Innovation in Design* (pp. 101–111). Desire Network.

9. Habermas, J. (1984). The Theory of Communicative Action: Vol. 1. *Reason and the Rationalization of Society* (T. McCarthy, Trans.). Boston: Beacon.

Molyneux[10] and game critic Lange[11], players often assume that the developers put more effort into designing the 'good' storyline and that playing 'good' is the 'right' way to play. Hence, they will play an entirely 'good' character first and may return to see how the 'bad' storyline plays out on a second run of the story. At no point do they make decisions based on their own morals, they simply make choices based on what they think the designer/game expects.

The most powerful forms of ethical gameplay are less explicit about morals. They may keep the player informed about their actions' consequences, yet these outcomes are not rated or valued differently by the game. What this means in particular, is that the player cannot make their choices based on what they think the game (or designer) wants. A fantastic example of this kind of game is *Peacemaker*[12]. The game simulates the political situation of the Israeli/Palestinian conflict at the time and puts the player in the role of either the Israeli Prime Minister or the Palestinian President. Since they can assume both sides of the conflict, the game also lets players see both sides of every action and decision taken. While the game does end when the conflict either escalates or is resolved by peaceful means, the emphasis is on the compromises that each side has to make to come to an agreement. According to the developers, 'In *PeaceMaker*, walking in another man's shoes is not only a concept; it's the heart of the simulation'. One of the advisors to the game defines empathy as a central theme: 'There is nothing more

10. Molyneux, P. (2013). PAX Prime 2013 story time with Peter Molyneux. Retrieved from:
http:// www.youtube.com/watch?v=F4LdFDL35Oo [Accessed: 27.09.14]
11. Lange, A. (2014). 'You're Just Gonna Be Nice: How Players Engage with Moral Choice Systems'. *Journal of Games Criticism*, 1(1), 1-16.
12. ImpactGames. (2007). *PeaceMaker* [Software]. Macintosh, Windows PC. Information Available from:
http://www.mobygames.com/game/peacemaker [Accessed: 27.09.14]

challenging than expressing empathy for the other side, especially when your side is under attack.'[13].

Another form of ethical gameplay in video games is characterised by cognitive dissonance between the player's motivation to play a game 'perfectly' and the game presenting a choice or situation that is contrary to the image the player has established of themselves and/or the character they are playing. A good example of this can be found in the military action game *Spec Ops: The Line*[14]. It initially appears like a simple military action game but excels at subverting player expectation to create a powerful commentary on war and war games. Based on Joseph Conrad's *Heart of Darkness*[15] (Conrad, 1899/1902) the game casts the player in the role of an army captain leading a two-man squad to investigate the disappearance of a military battalion in the desert of Dubai. In a series of unexpected twists, the game deconstructs the assumed notion that the player is cast as the hero of the story. It instead makes players realise that their resolve to *win* and defeat the enemy – the sole motivation in most military-themed shooters – has led them to commit acts (including a haunting scene in which the player inadvertently murders hundreds of innocent civilians) that are typically associated with the villain in those games.

While both of these examples of ethical gameplay focus on a military context, several other current games let players empathise with non-stereotypical (anti-) heroes. *Papers, Please*[16] simulates the life of an immigration officer in a dystopian state. It tasks players to strike a balance between acting morally and abiding by the state's laws. This slowly

13. Burak, A. (2014). 'What I Learned Turning The Israel-Palestine Conflict Into A Video Game'. Available from: http://kotaku.com/what-i-learned-turning-the-israel-palestine-conflict-in-1612148555 [Accessed: 27.09.14]
14. YAGER Development (2012), *Spec Ops: The Line* [Software]. Windows PC, Macintosh, PS3, Xbox360. 2K Games, Inc. Info. available from: http://www.mobygames.com/game/spec-ops-the-line [Accessed: 27.09.14]
15. Conrad, J. (1978). Heart of Darkness (1899/1902).
16. Pope, L. (2013), *Papers, Please* [Software]. Linux, Macintosh, Windows PC. 3909. Information Available from:
  http://www.mobygames.com/game/papers-please [Accessed: 27.09.14]

forces them to become corrupt as a way of ensuring their family's survival. *Cart Life*[17] brilliantly reflects on the mundaneness of real life, casting players as a simple food cart salesman or coffee shop employee. It illustrates that not only hero-types make for interesting plots and that having to brush your teeth, tie your shoes and going for a smoke can be as stressful as thwarting an alien invasion. *Braid*[18] (Blow, 2008) painted a dark allegory on obsession, as the player's drive to complete the game, to *win* and *save the princess,* turns out to be at the heart of an unexpected conflict.

While current technology is still far away from achieving the kind of fully immersive virtual reality experience described in 'The Loki Variations', it has made strides in recent years. Research already shows how powerful this medium may become and game designers are finding new ways to tell impactful and morally challenging stories. Both offer early glimpses into a future in which interactive experiences may be able to connect us to the life experiences of others, to empathise and gain a deeper understanding of each other and ourselves.

17. Hofmeier, R. (2011). *Cart Life* [Software]. Linux, Macintosh, Windows PC. Information Available from: http://en.wikipedia.org/wiki/Cart_Life [Accessed: 27.09.14]
18. Blow, J. (2008), *Braid* [Software]. Linux, Macintosh, Windows PC, PS3, Xbox360. Information Available from:
http://www.mobygames.com/game/braid [Accessed: 27.09.14]

Everyone Says

Stuart Evers

HE WAS, WITHOUT doubt, the most boring person she had ever linked. This she realised the moment she found him. An accident, that. She'd searched for *reading, physical* and his was the only link available. Usually he wasn't one for books, but at that moment, at that time – late on a Thursday night after she'd linked a woman who knitted a little too furiously – he was turning the pages of an operating manual. This is how she found him: reading an operating manual for an old coffee machine. *Please follow steps one thru five*, Deanna linked him read, *and prepare to enjoy coffee.*

The English was poorly translated, stiff and overly literal. It did not bother him. He was not amused by the manual's language, found no humour in its phrasing: he simply read the words and turned the pages. He was standing in the small kitchenette. Orange cupboards, two-ring stove, fridge freezer. The coffee machine was out of its box, its constituent parts laid out on the counter top. She linked him imagining the coffee machine in its finished state: interlocking pieces of chrome and glass and plastic. It gave him no satisfaction. The absence was seductive. She linked him build the machine, the following of steps one thru five. The pieces took some coaxing, but eventually he won out. It was finished, complete in the way he had imagined it. He did not smile. He did not even puff out his cheeks.

She linked him grinding coffee beans and filling the machine's reservoir. She anticipated a feeling of accomplishment, a small shiver of interest as the water began to bubble. But she was mistaken. She linked the smell of the coffee. It was heady, but his only reaction was to think of a café where he often ate lunch. She linked him watch the carafe fill and then linked him pour the coffee into a small mug. He took a sip. He took one more sip. It was fine. The machine worked. He poured the contents of the carafe and the mug down the sink. He removed the filter basket and emptied the grounds into the bin. He looked at his wristwatch and then at the machine, then again at his wristwatch. He washed out the carafe and set it down on the draining board. He dismantled the coffee machine and put the parts back in the box. He dried the carafe, put it in the box, and turned out the light.

He moved from the kitchen to the living area. The flooring was pale laminate, the walls whitewashed and unadorned. One screen. One window. One sofa. She linked the smell of a house cleaned once a week; once a week and thoroughly. She linked his every thought, his every thought as he walked through to the small bathroom.

I have enough food for the next two days. I will order more on Saturday. The bins must be taken out tomorrow. My swimming shorts are dry.

He removed his clothes and brushed his teeth. She linked him urinate and wash his hands. He looked at himself in the mirror, but not for long enough to fully appreciate his appearance.

I shall swim tomorrow and afterwards I will eat at the café. A man comes tomorrow for the Dyson. Mr Martins. He will be interested in the Dust Buster too. I will settle for 2,000. No less. I should call Dad. I will call him tomorrow.

He thought the last of this as he got into bed. Cool sheets, clean pillow slips. There was a suggestion of prayer, just the movement of lips, but the words were so quickly skipped Deanna couldn't be sure. He was asleep in a matter of minutes. There were no images before sleep; no dreams followed. After an hour of his sleeping, an hour of sullen, absolute still, the link went down.

The uLINK suggested adding credits to access David

Collins' profile, his saved experiences, his recorded memories. Deanna was about to add the credits when she saw the stats. She had linked David Collins for seven hours straight. Even as a teen, she'd never made it past three. She understood what this meant. It could not mean anything else. It meant that she was in love with David Collins.

★

Deanna's first link was a girl called Shirelle. All the girls linked Shirelle; she was the hot link that summer. Twenty-two years old, a body lean and poised as a dancer's, dark hair piled into Mickey Mouse ears, a cigarette blazing. She was a runner in heels, a siren to write a song for. Joy, Rita and Ella had been linking her for months; Deanna a matter of weeks.

'We're lucky to have her,' Rita said. 'There's no one quite like Shirelle. There's never been anyone quite like Shirelle.'

'Expensive though,' Ella said.

'She's worth the credit, though,' Joy said. 'So worth it.'

'There's no way she can survive, though, is there?' Deanna said. 'There's no way she's going to get out of this alive, is there?'

They were sitting in the communal gardens under the sun awning. Her three friends looked at Deanna.

'Of course not,' Rita said. 'And it'll be soon too. You've linked her. You know. We've just got to hope we're linked when it happens. It's like the ultimate trip, apparently. The dying.'

'Who says?' Deanna asked.

'Everyone says,' Rita said. 'Absolutely everyone.'

In class, on the way to class, on the shuttle bus from the estate to school and back, the only name she heard was Shirelle's. The students and teachers discussed her previous night's exploits – coke and weed, drink and sex, two men taking her at the same time – and whispered their predictions, how long she could hold out. The cost of the credits continued to escalate. Shirelle couldn't stop. Shirelle couldn't resist doing what they wanted. The word of mouth had got her. The word of mouth had hooked Shirelle.

Each night they linked her, linked her tiredness. They linked her desperation. They linked her miscarrying. They linked her injecting opiates for the pain. They linked her abandoned and wandering the streets, bottle in hand, dressed always in her trademark fake-fur coat. They linked her shout at the moon – 'Please deliver me, please' – and then suck off a taxi driver because she'd lost her purse, all her money somewhere dropped, somewhere gone.

One night, unlinked and showering, Deanna was reminded of a parable, though she was unsure when she'd heard it. An avaricious man is granted three wishes and requests three sacks of gold. The sacks appear but the third sack is only half full. Confused, he sets about filling the sack with more gold, but the sack never seems closer to being full. The pursuit of filling the sack consumes the man, and he ends up a beggar, obsessed only with his half-full sack of gold. Deanna saw the man in rags, by the side of a dusty, biblical road, begging for gold. Behind him, Shirelle smoked a cigarette, drank from a bottle of vodka. Deanna wondered whether she'd misremembered the parable, or whether she had invented it.

Word of mouth meant over 5 million were linking Shirelle. The cost of credits jumped again. Jumped every day. They linked her, all of them, all 5 million, and they linked a birdlike heart, the acid reflux, the stumble out from darkness to light. They linked her from bar to pub to club, from scoring to sex, from passing out to dry-mouthed waking. The estates were alive with her. And when it became clear, when it was obvious, when the depletion and tiredness was clear even to Shirelle, people shut down their work for the day and hit the link.

Shirelle was already in the ambulance when Deanna linked her. Sirens and ticks and hums and beeps surrounding her. Declan, her friend with the calming hands and soft

Belfast accent, sitting beside her. Deanna linked the first of the missed heartbeats. They all linked the missed heartbeats, they all linked the slow, slow realisation of death. They revived her, they lost her, they revived her, they lost her. Then the link went down. The link went down and the music began to play. Something orchestral. Something specifically composed. Something written to amplify emotion. The credits rolled and Deanna dropped the link. The messages from Joy and Rita and Ella began to flood her timelines.

*

She woke early with thoughts only of David Collins. She messaged her boss to say she would be unable to work. She changed into her running shorts and t-shirt before realising her usual routine would expose her. She linked an Ethiopian runner instead, a spindle of a man punishing a dewy track at dawn. She linked his slow-twitch muscles, his thin spikes entering the rubber, the steady heart rate and the rhythmic breath. She lasted twenty minutes. She had a message from her father, concerned for her well-being. He asked if she was all right, he'd heard she was ill. She told him not to worry, that she would be okay after some rest.

Deanna went back to the uLINK, added credits and accessed David Collins' profile. Usually, she didn't bother with profiles. There was too much fiction in them, too much posture, too much selling of oneself. David Collins had filled out the bare minimum of information. The accompanying video was the standard hour-long interview, but David Collins did not sell himself in his answers. He looked disinterestedly into the camera and gave his brief, almost brusque replies.

He was twenty nine. Unmarried. No lovers. Sex three times in his life, with three separate women. Not much of a drinker. Not a smoker. No drugs of any description. His mother and father were no longer together. Robert Collins answered the questions in much the same way he'd constructed the coffee maker: effectively and with the minimum energy expended. The interview was designed to provoke emotion and memory, to flesh out a character, to give them motivation, to give them a sense of narrative. But Robert Collins offered nothing.

'Why are you here?' the interviewer asked last of all. Collins paused. He tapped his fingers lightly on the kitchen table in front of him. He took a sip from his small beaker of water.

'To be certain that I am here,' David Collins said. He smiled without any humour or sadness. 'Isn't that why everyone's here?'

Deanna added further credits and booted up his 'selected recorded experiences' – an edited highlights package of what to expect from David Collins. It was the standard three hours, put together from the previous month's feed. She hit the link and settled down. She linked him walk the same eight flyblown and dusty streets, his pace slow and steady; linked him eat at the same café day after day, his over-salted lunches and dinners taken without enjoyment; linked him swim in a municipal swimming pool, his stroke metronomic and concise; linked him selling bleached-plastic heirlooms, his posture poor on a plastic and wire chair; linked him heading to his small apartment each evening, his nightly routine of teeth brushing, showering and bed at a sensible hour. She linked him and felt absolutely nothing, not a thing.

But then Sunday – there were people outside the small church, their clenched fists and clutched Bibles – she linked him walk to another small apartment, a man opening the door, Collins' father, clearly, and the man inviting him inside. At the moment of the father opening the door, Deanna felt something shimmer. Not the basso crescendo when someone's emotions are fully engaged; something more like a click. An errant pulse, perhaps. She linked David having a drink, eating at the table, then getting up to leave. The next week was exactly the same. The streets, the café, the office, the pool the apartment, and then the Sunday visit; the same every week.

The father, Paul, opens the door. David experiences the

shimmer, then walks inside. They enter the kitchen and Paul pours a glass of beer for them both. A shepherd's pie browns under the grill.

'So, how are you, son?' Paul says. 'Winning?'

'Fine, Dad. You?'

'Fine.'

They say the same thing each week. The same three lines and then David drinks from his beer, as though grace has been said. Lunch is served. They talk. About their week, their work. David loads the dishwasher while Paul wipes the surfaces and table down. They shake hands at the door, a handshake that turns into an awkward embrace.

Deanna had promised herself she would only go through the profile and experiences. She had been clear with herself. She would not waste her day, a day to herself. She would not stay on the uLINK. She would do something else instead. Read a book. Take a long bath. Call her father. But she clicked the live link anyway. Without thought or self-justification.

David Collins was standing in the kitchenette. She linked him as he replaced the cracked screen and processor board of a mobile telephone. It was painstaking, delicate work. She linked him holding his breath and releasing it. The repair took almost two hours, his fingers thin and the screwdriver tiny, like a jeweller's. She linked him complete the job, put the telephone in a box and turn out the light. She linked his every thought, his every thought as he walked through to the small bathroom.

I have enough food for the next five days. The bins must go out tomorrow. My swimming shorts are drying in the bathroom.

Deanna linked him until the feed went down. She went to bed and slept long and dreamlessly, as dreamlessly as David Collins.

★

Her father was dressed as though their lunch was important: slacks and a pressed shirt, polished shoes. Deanna was there already, which surprised him, and she waved – she had practised this – across the restaurant. He waved back and weaved between the round tables. She'd chosen the place because they'd once eaten there, years before, and she remembered the food was good, or the atmosphere was good, or was it the chairs? Something about it, whatever it was, was good. And sitting there in the late afternoon sunshine, crunching ice from her iced water, a thick cloth napkin and two perfectly transparent wine glasses in front of her, something about it was good.

'Well hello,' her father said, leaning down to kiss her. 'You look wonderful.'

'Thanks,' she said. 'I was trying to remember, though. When was it we came here? The two of us?'

'You and me?' he said sitting down and placing his hands flat on the table. 'Just the two of us?'

She nodded. He picked up the menu, the paper rolled into a horn.

'I don't remember. Years ago, must be.'

'I remember there was something good about it. Something was good.'

'The fish is good here,' he said. 'Maybe that's what it is?'

'Possibly,' she said, though it didn't seem likely. It occurred to her that her father had no recollection of eating in the restaurant with her. She wondered what it would be like to link her father. What memories he would have, and how many would cross-check with hers. Her father smiled and held his hand out across the cream tablecloth, past the floral centrepiece.

'I just wanted to say—'

'Don't, Dad,' she said. 'You don't have to. Let's just have lunch. Just the two of us, a nice lunch. I'm going to have wine. Treat myself.'

'In that case,' he said, 'so will I.'

He talked of his job – he worked for the land registry – of lunches he had eaten, of the people from her past he had seen. She was encouraging and kept the conversation going. They shared a starter.

'I've met someone,' she said, half way through her main course salad, not the fish, interrupting her father's recounting of an intra-office feud.

'You have?' he said. He put down his cutlery, dabbed a napkin to the corner of his mouth.

'Yes,' she said.

'Well, that's great, love. Great. What's his name? How did you meet?'

'I don't want to talk about it,' she said. 'I just wanted you to know. I just wanted to tell you.'

'You look happy,' he said picking up his knife and fork, his face slightly pinked from the wine and excitement. 'I saw that as I came in through the door. You look . . . contented. I can't tell you how happy I am for you.'

Deanna swilled her wine and looked at her father. Steely hair brushed carefully to a parting, an open-neck shirt, a small shaving nick under his left earlobe. She had expected to feel something as she told him. A cruel sense of deception. Happiness at the joy she'd provoked. Excitement at the sharing of a confidence. But she hadn't. What she said had been simple statement of fact. Or at least an iteration of the facts. Her father's reaction was not important to her. She might as well have been David Collins telling his father there was a buyer for a Dyson vacuum cleaner. The delivery was the same. The same distinct ambivalence.

Her father ordered another glass of wine. She ordered one too but did not drink it. She let him talk. She let him talk about meeting her mother, the old story coming out again. His long, sorry romantic tale. She let him talk. She let him get to the tears in his eyes, let him wipe them on the thick cloth napkin and excuse himself to the bathroom.

★

Deanna told everyone she was going to the south of France. They wished her a pleasant holiday. They said it was a good thing to get away. She nodded and locked the door to her apartment and spent the next fourteen days with David Collins. Going to work, swimming, reading manuals, eating at the café, taking out the rubbish. She woke with him and slept with him, their two bodies in constant communion. She noticed a scar on his inside leg for the first time. She linked him change his energy supplier and buy a new pair of work trousers. She linked him talk to his father on the telephone and go to his father's house for lunch on Sundays.

That last Sunday, a message popped up on the interface. *David Collins has moved from basic rate to premium level one. Please add credits to continue.* She added the credits and continued. She linked him in his apartment, showering, the same as every other day. Soon she was leaving his apartment and walking to his father's house. But Deanna was unsettled by the message. The uLINK people had clearly seen she was hooked. They were going to extort her. They were going to punish her for loving David Collins.

David's father opened the door. David experienced the shimmer, then walked inside. They went into the kitchen and Paul poured a glass of beer for them both. A shepherd's pie browned under the grill.

'So, how are you, son?' Paul said. 'Winning?'

'Fine, Dad. You?'

'Fine.'

Deanna linked him watch his father wipe the surface and table with a dishcloth. This did not usually happen until after they had eaten. The counter tops always stayed dotted with potato and meat until after lunch. She linked him watch his father drink half of his beer in one lunge and noticed he had forgotten to put the ketchup and brown sauce on the otherwise-laid table. David took a sip of beer.

'I've got a buyer for the Corby Trouser Press,' he said.

'What's that?' his father said. 'What?'

'The Corby Trouser Press. I got a buyer for it. Three

grand, I think. Maybe more, I don't know.'

'That's great, son,' he said. 'Great.'

David sat down at the table as usual. But Paul was fussing and knocked a tray to the floor. It made a loud clang as it hit the tiles. While picking it up, Paul noticed the pie.

'Oh shit,' he said and opened the oven door. Smoke stole out and when it cleared, the top of the shepherd's pie looked blackly back at him. The smoke alarm was triggered. The noise was hectic. Paul stood on a chair and disarmed it. He looked down on his son. David's heart rate was marginally higher, Deanna noticed it rise and then fall back to normal.

'Sometimes, Dad,' he said, 'you really are a bloody idiot.'

Paul got down from the chair. He stood with his hands gripping the kitchen sink. He was breathing heavily.

'Don't talk to me like that,' he said. 'Don't you dare talk to me that way in my own house.'

'Don't act like a bloody idiot in your own house, then,' David said. He got up from the sofa and put on his jacket.

'And where do you think you're going?' Paul said. 'We haven't had our lunch yet.'

'I'm not eating that shit,' David said. He picked up his coat and walked out the door.

Deanna dropped the link. David Collins had been calm throughout. Calm and detached and yet. She saw the look of anger on Paul's face. The rage of it as David left. She went to the bathroom and was sick. She ran water in the bowl and washed her face. She looked in the mirror, but not for long enough to get a full impression of herself. She went back to the uLINK. She stared at the interface. She was frightened to link him again. She didn't want to be part of anything like this. Even if David now stayed calm, she was not sure she could take it. She sat at the uLINK all afternoon, but did not connect. She just sat there, looking at the interface. For a long time, she couldn't think of anything to do that didn't involve David Collins.

Eventually she went for a walk, out into the communal gardens. She had a flavoured water sitting out on a café's terrace, and watched lovers and friends walk dogs or stroll towards the river. Everyone was talking. At all the tables around her, people talking and laughing. She left her drink and headed home.

She had a long bath. She dried herself and without thinking went straight to the uLINK. She accessed the saved experiences and selected a series of Sundays. Iterations without a hint of drama or conflict. *David Collins has moved from premium level one to premium level two.* The interface said. *Please add credits to continue.*

★

During the week she was struck down by a migraine, a migraine that lasted six days. A week of her bed, a week of sweats and shivers, a week without him. She told herself it was her body's way of telling her to stop. A side effect of the linking. She hated her body. She hated what her mind was telling her.

By Sunday she was better, the pain lifting like morning mist. She woke early, before sunrise, and showered and washed her hair, exfoliated, toned, moisturised. She made coffee and drank it watching the sunrise. Then she turned on the interface. *David Collins has moved from premium level two to premium level twelve,* the interface said. *Please add credits to continue.*

At the height of her fame, Shirelle had made it to premium level twenty. Deanna didn't know how many levels there were, but that was the highest she had ever seen. She looked at the interface again. Premium level twelve. She swore vengeance on the uLINK people. They were bleeding her dry. She'd heard about people running up debts they couldn't pay, but had never really thought about how. It was there in the terms and conditions though.

3.17 – The cost of an individual link can increase due to demand, either by an individual's personal usage or by increased interest from the uLINK community. You will always be informed of any change in pricing for a link. She paid the credits and linked him as he woke, as he walked from bedroom to bathroom.

It was a typical Sunday. She linked him take a shower, read a manual, walk to his father's house. Paul greeted him as usual, but he paused before closing the door.

'So, how are you, son?' Paul said. 'Winning?'

'Fine, Dad. You?'

'Fine.'

She linked him drink his beer. There was a long and static silence. Paul drank his beer. She linked David Collins sitting at the table.

'If it's money,' David said, 'you know the answer.'

'They fired me,' he said. 'Someone had it in for me. That bastard Murphy. He's had it in for me since I got there. They said I didn't follow procedure. They said that I was sloppy. Me! That the team wasn't performing as projected. He had it in for me from the start, from the beginning—'

'Someone's always got it in for you. Always. It's never you, is it?'

'You weren't there. You didn't see what he—'

'The answer is no. How many times no. How much do you owe me already? Tell me. How much?'

Paul turned to the stove. He took the pie from the oven and set it on a trivet to cool.

'And you call yourself a son?' he said.

'I don't call myself anything,' David said.

★

All week she linked David Collins and for the whole week his heartbeat barely rose from normal. He constructed several new machines, of which he sold two without pleasure. He ate his dinner at the café and swam in the municipal pool. By the following Sunday, she was calm enough to go and see her father.

They met at the same restaurant, sat at the same table. Her father was late arriving. He was dressed with precision.

'Well hello,' her father said, leaning down to kiss her. 'How are you?'

She saw concern on his face.

'Is everything okay?' he said.

'Everything's fine,' she said. 'I was just trying to remember what I had the last time we were here.'

'The fish is good here,' he said. 'You probably had the fish.'

'Yes,' she said. 'Probably.'

They talked politely. Him most of all. He talked of his job, of lunches he had eaten, of the people from her past he had seen. She kept the conversation going. They shared a starter. Again, she did not order fish.

'We split up,' she said. 'That man and me.'

'Oh, I'm sorry to hear that,' he said. 'I could tell something was up. I could just tell. From across the room.'

'I'm fine. I don't want to talk about it. I just wanted you to know, that's all.'

She had not known it was over until that moment. She expected to feel something afterwards. Guilt, perhaps, remorse, a sense of mourning. But no. A statement of fact. No more.

Her father ordered another glass of wine and she put her hand over her glass. She let him talk. She let him talk about losing her mother, the old story coming out again. His long, sorry romantic tale.

There were tables north, south, east and west of her: north and south with four diners; east and west with two. When her father excused himself to the bathroom she toyed with her napkin and heard someone say the word Collins. She heard it from the west and the north, the south and east.

…he can't survive…

…but surely someone would do something…

...police can't, not without proof.

...you sort of can't blame him ...

...he's a monster, if I raised a child like...

...but I hear the father's involved...

...he started the rumours...

...to get the cash, to get his hands on the cash...

...I find it so sad...

...I'd ban it. I've said it before...

...we'll be home, don't worry...

...they say it's the ultimate trip...

...it's the hype I can't stand...

Deanna stood. She was still holding the napkin as she walked out of the restaurant.

★

Shirelle had once said to Declan that you feel the weight of the links. Feel them at the back of your neck, like bees: like a hive of bees. She scratched the back of her neck as she told him this. Scratched and said: 'You can feel the pressure. Like they'll push and push until your whole head's just filled with bees. Buzzing with them.' Deanna had thought it was just the drugs. But she could link it in David Collins too.

Deanna linked David Collins walk the streets to his father's house. She linked him scratch the back of his neck, linked the pressure where once there was none. His heart rate was up and she could feel the agitation, the agitation in his arms and legs. She linked his rangy, erratic steps and saw his father's face at the door. Hair greyer than before. Face more ashen, his arms open: come on in.

She linked the smell of the pie, the glass of beer poured by Paul. They all linked it. She linked him hear his father say, 'So, how are you, son? Winning?' and she linked David sip his beer. They all linked it.

She linked him sit down at the table and eat his pie. She linked him loading the dishwasher. She linked him take a kitchen knife to the gut. She linked him looking at his father's twisted face, blood on it, blood everywhere. She linked the blade entering the gut again. She linked him bleed out. They all linked it.

She linked him watch his father standing over him, a face gone from rage to terror. She linked David Collins smile. And then there was nothing.

Deanna's link went down. Everyone's link went down. Deanna heard the music. Everyone heard the music. Deanna saw the credits roll. Everyone saw the credit roll. Deanna thought of David Collins and Deanna began to cry.

Deanna cried and it was glorious.

Afterword:

Everyone Surveys

Prof Christian Jantzen
Aalborg University

WHAT DOES THE everyday life of others really look like? Our fascination with the daily chores and activities of fellow citizens is fast becoming an obsession as our own lives become more and more private. One of the early steps in this 'privatization' was the construction of the modern idea of 'family': as a nucleus safeguarding its members from the perils of public life. This 'invention' occurred in the Romantic era and redefined the family as a sanctuary of, and reservoir for, intimacy, nurture and passion. 'At home' one could recover from the contradictions and hardships of modern life.

In the middle of the 19th century another aspect of modernity prevailed: urbanization. Village life started to wane, as towns became cities, and cities, conurbations[1]. This led to a restructuring of the urban landscape and a disintegration of the social fabric. Urban dwellers became segregated, each group moving to its own district and living out their lives separated from other groups. The rebuilding of Paris by Baron Haussman was the showpiece of this new way of structuring the city. In the process, the life of others – not least other classes - became invisible for immediate observation. The new mass media however offered a peek into what was otherwise hidden. Tabloids and magazines nourished an incessant and insatiable interest in the glamorous lifestyles of 'celebrities' (a concept of the 19th century by the way). Pulp fiction, on the other hand, revelled in the scandalous or horrendous existence of marginalized groups.

1. 'Grossstadt' to use George Simmel's word. See Georg Simmel, 'The Metropolis of Mental Life' (1903) in Gary Bridge & Sophie Watson, eds. (2002), *The Blackwell City Reader*. Wiley-Blackwell.

The modern phenomenon of 'privatization' has thus turned others into 'outsiders'. At the same time this process has generated an appetite for what's been lost, a taste for getting inside the outsider: for seeing how he or she lives, knowing how he or she senses, feels and thinks, and even – like the protagonist in Spike Jonze's *Being John Malkovich* (1999) – experiencing what he or she experiences.

Each new development in media technology has rushed to satisfy this appetite and given it a novel twist. Historically, one of the most important functions of radio and television was to make the voices and gestures of ordinary people publically available. This earlier form of democratization didn't make fame immediately mundane, but it certainly made the wish to be famous – i.e. to be heard and seen by others – mundane, even if it was only to last 15 minutes, to quote Warhol in 1968.[2]

Reality game shows like John de Mol's *Big Brother*, which has been broadcast worldwide in countless different versions since 1999, has clarified what a postmodern claim to fame involves. This kind of programme erases many of modernity's distinctions. Otherwise marginalized behaviour is celebrated. The 'outsiders' are locked inside, at a distance but nonetheless in close view. They are not glanced at furtively, but are brazenly on show for our meticulous scrutiny. This consummate form of the democratization of celebrity is also a turning point in the history of surveillance.[3] The participants in the show are conscious of constantly being watched and probably even exaggerate their roles and conduct to satisfy the audience. Many users of the latest new media ('the social media') have subsequently taken this logic a step further down the Foucaldian road of perpetual self-

2. See Jeff Guinn & Douglas Perry (2005). *The Sixteenth Minute: Life In the Aftermath of Fame*. New York: Jeremy F. Tarcher.
3. Mark Andrejevic (2002). 'The Kinder, Gentler Gaze of Big Brother Reality TV in the Era of Digital Capitalism'. *New Media & Society*, 4(2), 251–270.

surveillance.[4] Blogs, Facebook and Twitter entries provide running commentaries on thoughts, opinions, feelings and experiences, stylized and scrutinized by the author with the intent of being surveyed by 'friends and followers'.

In Stuart Evers' story the surveillance of private lives takes a further twist. Surveillance is established through some sort of nanotechnological 'linking', apparently quite similar to internet connectivity (including search engines and payment systems). The implication of this is that the distinction between the observer and the observant implodes. The observer, it seems, is herself continuously observed by others linked to the network. The father of the heroine, Deanna, for example knows about her state of mind before even talking to her. The price of following David Collins' life increases, for his followers, as more and more people link to him, but the physical and psychological cost to David himself is the burden of knowing they're linked.

This next generation of surveillance further erodes the distinction between outside and inside. Whereas present modes only allow observers to draw conclusions about the observed person's true state of mind ('the inside': thoughts, feelings, values, etc.) from an external interpretation of that person's behaviour or self-reported thoughts and feelings, Evers' nanotech device also documents what the observed person *actually* does, thinks and feels. The observer is also linked into the *process* of thinking and feeling: Deanna not only sees David Collins thinking and feeling, she experiences him doing so, and even feels the experience of experiencing it.

The 'crisis of experiencing' is another theme of the story. Experiencing is a universal way of relating to the world

4. See Foucault on surveillance in e.g. Michel Foucault (2007). *Security, Territory, Population: Lectures at the Collège de France, 1977-78*, Houndmills, Basingstoke: Palgrave MacMillan. Also, James Boyle (1997). 'Foucault in Cyberspace: Surveillance, Sovereignty, and Hardwired Censors'. *University of Cincinnati Law Review*, 66: 177-206; and Anders Albrechtslund (2008). Also:
http://firstmonday.org/ojs/index.php/fm/article/view/2142/1949http%3A

by becoming aware of how the body physically and emotionally responds to its live environment. When we experience something, the focus of our attention is broadened to include not just responding, but also the how and why of responding. This broadening may be pleasurable or painful, but the change of focus makes the situation potentially memorable. Memories are made of experiences, and are extremely personal of course: they are the conclusions that the 'I' reaches by having once felt something, having reacted to a feeling and learning something from that reaction. 'I' is made up of memories, themselves made up of experiences.[5]

In 1976 the economist Tibor Scitovsky gave a diagnostics of 'the crisis of experiencing'. The increase in wealth and the pre-emptive satisfaction of so many basic needs has dramatically decreased the experiential qualities of dealing directly with the world.[6] The experience economy is a consequence of this saturation. Experiences have become consumer goods to be sold and bought.[7] A critical aspect of this marketization of experiences is that they easily become artificial, inauthentic and non-memorable. Their value in the construction of an 'I' becomes questionable.

Evers' story identifies this problem. The experiences that count for something are no longer derived from one's own immediate experiencing. The treasured experiences are those that are mediated: for example, Deanna's experiencing David Collins' experiences, turns very ordinary acts like walking the same street or eating in the same café into rituals, that is into extraordinary events. Or past experiences that do not have to

5. I have elaborated on the psychology of experiences and experiencing in: Christian Jantzen (2013). 'Experiencing and Experiences: A Psychological Framework'. In: Sundbo, J., & Sørensen, F. (Eds.), *Handbook on the Experience Economy*. (p. 146-170). Edward Elgar.

6. See Tibor Scitovsky, (1976). *The Joyless Economy: An Inquiry into Human Satisfaction and Dissatisfaction*. Oxford: Oxford University Press.

7. The most outspoken celebration of this economy is Joseph B. Pine& James H. Gilmore (1999). *The Experience Economy: Work is Theatre & Every Business a Stage*. Harvard Business Press.

be recounted any more by the experiencer. They are registered and stored in the system: no longer subjective and personalized, but objective and mediatized. The same could be said about David Collins' reason for allowing himself to be linked to the system: he does that "'[t]o be certain that I am here,'" he says, adding 'without any humour or sadness. "Isn't that why everyone's here?'" The private self is nothing more than what others experience this person to experience.

In the end the overload of observers experiencing the observed person's experiences depletes this person. He or she dies. Thus, in Evers' story, the process of privatization has also come to the end of the road: private life has become totally public until the link goes down – and life is over.

A Swarm of Living Robjects Around Us

Adam Roberts

Post: 15/07/2070

HERE IS THE house in which Dayskin lay down and died.
This is how it happened: he opened the front door and walked inside. Then he lay down in the hallway, on his side, stretched out on the hard tiles. He stayed there. He was alone in the house, and nobody came to his aid – nobody asked him what he was doing, or helped him up. He lay there until his throat dried out and his tongue lost its moisture and he died of thirst. It took a further week before colleagues became sufficiently concerned at the fact that he had not been in touch. A policeman called, and found the door open and the body lying on the floor.

His body was lying in a house in which none of the robjects were operational. That's odd, though – all of them malfunctioning at the same time. Of course it was possible to retrieve stored data including video of Dayskin opening his own door and walking into his own hallway. The video shows him lying down on his side. And then it shows him not moving any more.

The house. What can we say about this house? Well, we can say that it is *state of the art*. A swarm of living robjects around us. How tender they are to us! How solicitous!

The house was not Dayskin's primary residence. For the purposes of citizenship and taxation, Dayskin lived in London

111

Town, where he also worked at a leading robject development company. But he had a second home in France. He could afford it. His was a lucrative business.

So: he owned a villa deep in the south – Languedoc, languid in the summer heat. A white house with Jaffa-coloured tiles on the roof staring blankly at the staring sun. There was a swimming pool: primrose-blue waters lapping at the overflow gutter all day and night, making a noise like distant whooping cough. Cicadas groaned their incessant groans. Relentless. Robjects kept the pool water eggshell blue and kept the house spiderweb free. Robjects prepared the food and regulated the temperature inside, fighting an unending battle against the furnace-like heat of the outdoors.

At night the moon was a white semicircular line of radius r, where r is either the width of a little finger held at arm's length or 1737.4 kilometres – depending on how you look at it. Dayskin is standing on the patio in the purple-black darkness, smoking a cigar and admiring the star scatter. He hasn't lost his mind yet. That's to come.

An itinerary: robjects tend his houseplants, moving them in and out of the sunlight, watering them and clearing away dead leaves. Robjects remove dust from the surface of furniture. Robjects make repairs. Robjects flush through the water systems on a regular basis, clean any stains and address any leaks. Robjects move the clothes left hanging in the wardrobe to prevent staleness. Robjects trim the lawn, and clear dead matter from the gutters. The purpose of the robjects is to ensure that when Dayskin turns up in his robject-driven car, the house is perfectly prepared.

Dayskin, though, is not happy. He calls a colleague in London. 'Yeah,' he says, apparently addressing the invisible countryside, or the black-on-black bats shuddering through the sky, or maybe the stars themselves. 'Yeah – the thing is, my robjects aren't making *clever* enough decisions.'

'So – like?' replied his interlocutor, in London.

'Well I have robjects tending my tomatoes. You can't programme them against all insects, or nothing would, you know...'

'Pollination?'

'Get pollinated. Exactly. So you programme them to zap, you know.'

'Greenfly?'

'Exactly. But then I come down, and something *else* has been eating my tomatoes. I don't know what. I don't *know* what, but I'd rather it didn't. Eat my tomatoes, I mean.'

'You'd rather the robjects stopped it?'

'Exactly. And another one: a rat drowned in my pool. The robjects didn't sort it. No, no. I had to fish it out with a – you know. Net and that.'

'Surely the robjects are programmed to remove detritus from the damnable *pool*, Daysk?'

Dayskin exhales ectoplasm into the night air, fits the nub of his cigar back in his mouth like a jack going into a socket, inhales deeply. Takes it out again. 'Well, of course,' he replies eventually, like a dragon. 'But see they're programmed to remove inert matter. If something is moving, they ignore it, or they'd try and remove *me* when I go for a swim.'

'So, programme them to only ignore objects that move if they're above a certain size?'

'Could do that,' Dayskin concedes. 'Could do. But that's my point: it's constant tinkering. Every time I come down here having to adjust the programming for one unforeseen eventuality or another, and I don't want–' He stopped to take another puff. There were nanotechnological robjects inside his chest, slowly but surely collecting miniscule particles of tar and carbon from where they had become embedded in the lining of his lungs.

'You want AI,' said the London person. 'It still doesn't address–'

'Boredom, yeah.'

'–my worries about them getting *bored*, Daysk.'

'Bored, yeah.'

113

'Did you see the Zapiski results? It's a matter of making our robjects AI-capable, but at functionally very low IQ.'

'I still say,' Dayskin says grandly. 'That we can make 'em better than that. You know my proposal.'

'I do.' Dayskin's proposal is to programme robjects with high-functioning AIs, but to prevent said intellects going catatonic with boredom (as has been the problem up until now) by including certain mathematical tasks and games at a core level with the programming. Prime number sorting. Open-ended geometric protocols. Chess games. That sort of thing. This has not yet been actualised, in part because Dayskin's employers – the person he is presently speaking with, in London, plus two other individuals – are worried about the ethical considerations. Or to be more precise: they are worried about the potential for legal difficulty that might attend ethical challenges as to whether such AIs merit protection under 'human rights' legislation. Or to be super-precise (and why wouldn't we want to be as precise as possible?): they are worried about the potential costs of such potential legal action.

Dayskin is more reckless than them. He wants to push ahead. 'Let's run my house here as a test case. It's not under UK jurisdiction. It's in France.'

'It's under EU jurisdiction.'

'I'll run it,' he says. 'If there's any kickback, you can give me a public reprimand and roll the programme up.'

The London person replies with 'I don't know, Daysk', and each word is pronounced with the hesitant, drawn-out intonation that connotes uncertainty.

'What's the worst that can happen?' Dayskin declares, and takes another on his cigar.

The following day he flies back to London. Oh we're all familiar with the odd robject in our houses these days – but Dayskin's French house is unusual in the saturation of every aspect of the building with robjects – every brick, every tile in the roof, every item inside, all have robjects in them. The nature of this building is such that Dayskin is able to uplift the house remotely. He reprogrammes his robjects from his London office, uploading certain algorithms (each and every one already has more than enough data capacity) to enable them to begin thinking, making sure that each one has a selection of conceptual tasks to keep them busy when their primary purpose is not drawing their attention. He steps-up this pseudo-consciousness: a relatively low level when the house is unoccupied, moving to a higher thought-perception-interaction capacity when a human being steps through the front door.

Loading a house with so many robjects requires special attention. Dayskin needs to have all of them operating and communicating via a communicable medium. He decides on near-infrared. He tweaks the EM radiation frequency from the 2.4 GHz WiFi standard to Near-Infrared – 100 THz, near as dammit. How can he make this work, you wonder? Well these are his robjects, and he is the robject expert, so we're not surprised to find he made his personal kit super-super sensitive. A small THz/fNIRS implant will enable him to communicate with his machines. It could work! It *should* work.

It will work.

Drinks after work, in an ebony-themed London bar. Dayskin explains what he's been up to. 'Why?' his colleague Bella asks. 'You worried you'll get lonely without robjects to chat with?'

'I want,' he replies, a little stiffly, 'to be able to talk to them about their experience. I want them to be able to tell me what it's like. But I don't want that all the time – that would be cruel. To leave them there on their own, fully conscious.'

'Even with chess to keep them busy?'

Dayskin ignores this. Bella is trolling him, he can see that. It's mild enough, but he doesn't like it. None of his colleagues understand his genius. He can see what they can't see. This could be a big breakthrough. This could be the next stage in robject evolution.

By the time he has finished in London, the house is fully prepped. He decides to leave it a fortnight – after all, he needs to give his robjects a normal spread of tasks to attend to. Had he known this would be his last fortnight alive he would, I suppose, have left it longer. He told colleagues that he would have liked to have left it longer: 'a whole winter, maybe. Give it a proper test. But I can't bear to stay away so long! It's so peaceful, down there. So tranquil. I love it there.'

He flew back down, walked through the door and – look. Look. There's nothing to *fear* from robjects. That's not what I'm saying here. We all of us have a few in our homes. In the affluent West almost everybody has them. They're not a risk, any more than your alarm clock or your mobile phone is a risk. They're a simple tool to make life better.

I know what you're wondering: did uplifting the level of sentience and artificial intelligence in Dayskin's robjects turn them *evil*? Don't be absurd. What do you think they did? Whisper in his ear *lie down, lie down and don't move, lie down until you die of thirst?* And he obeyed? You think they hypnotised him? You think they used some sort of spooky magic? Don't be absurd. Robjects are perfectly benign. Their whole purpose is to serve us.

And besides: we know from the data recovered from the house that every single robject functioned flawlessly through the fortnight they were alone. And we know something else. We know that every single one of them turned itself off as soon as Dayskin stepped through that door. They communicated nothing to him, and he asked nothing of them. A robject turned the hallway light on when it sensed Dayskin's step outside the door, and as soon as the door opened that robject shut itself down, leaving the light on.

You think robjects are *malicious*? You're wrong. No matter what level of artificial intelligence we program into them, they are nothing but benign and kindly.

Or perhaps you think that, because I work for the company, I am covering up some terrible truth. Not so. The company has released all the data into the public domain. My job was to investigate the death of Dayskin, and from the very beginning it was made very clear to me that all my reports were to be open access.

I flew down to the house, of course. Without its robject minders it was starting to show signs of wear. Weeds were growing in amongst the gravel of the driveway. The swimming pool was changing hue from pure blue to sea-green. Cobwebs had been spun into the cornices like white candyfloss. There was cat shit on one of the windowsills.

I checked every room, wearing a 24CAM – the feed is in the cloud. If you're interested, you can walk the house with me. Of course, a 24CAM can't reproduce the *vibe*, the feel of the place; but that's part of the point of a narrative such as this. I can tell you how the house felt to me, and it was: normal. There was no bad smell. The fridge still worked, even without its robject intelligence. The milk had gone off, and no robject had removed and disposed of it, but it wasn't yet at the stage where it would reek. It felt like an empty house, which is what it was.

I travelled to the nearest town, which was called Bagnols, perhaps because it had once housed notable baths. There are no baths in it today, I believe; and nothing of any note beyond shops and private houses and a small provincial art gallery where robjects dust the statues and open or close the shutters, depending. Here I presented e-credentials to the gendarmerie, and was taken to a subterranean room maintained (by robjects) at an unnatural chill, where, responsive to a police instruction, a robject rolled Dayskin's body out of its storage compartment – a long coffin-shaped compartment with a fat steel-hinged door, like a frozen oven.

I peered at the body whilst the gendarme stood by. I didn't expect to find anything, and had of course already read the autopsy report; but I thought I ought to see for myself. What I saw was: the naked body of a man who had not lived beyond fifty, his skin beige with death. There were no marks of violence or distress. His blood had been tested and revealed no narcotics or hallucinogens within it. There was nothing wrong with him, except that he had decided (for whatever reason) not to use his perfectly functional muscles to get up off the floor and fetch a drink – and so had died.

I asked the policewoman her opinion. Why did she think he had lain down on the floor of his own house and waited to die?

'*M'sieur,*' she replied, gravely. '*Je peux affirmer en toute honnêteté, je n'sais pas.*'

I wandered the streets in the afternoon sunshine. Then, since I was after all in France, and it seemed like the sort of thing a person should do, I found a *petit café du coin* I liked the look of and took a seat outside. A real-life human being brought me a cup of coffee, in a porcelain thimble with a semi-circle handle and its own saucer. I annotated and uploaded my morning's work to the cloud. I checked to see what the hivemind thought. Some of the conspiracy theories were wild – wild.

The company had made public Dayskin's conversation... the one recorded above (the name of his interlocutor was redacted under the individual's legal right to privacy. But in the company's favour, they did not edit out the part where Dayskin proposed roughshodding over possible EU legal sanction. That part stayed in).

I sat in the sun. The shops were open, but any human staff had retreated for their siestas so only robjects sat within. Cars were infrequent. On the table in front of me was a single rose in a glass vase: its petals were candy-pink, and air-bubbles clung to its stem. One green leaf poked over the side of the vase, like a serrated tear-drop. I stirred sugar into the coffee and stirred it with a swizzle stick made of plastic that perfectly resembled wood, and when I was finished I tossed this onto the pavement. A robject soundlessly and uncomplainingly retrieved it and spirited it away.

The sky was that dark blue the Russians call CNHNN, *siniy*. It was the same shade as the blue band in the French tricolore hanging limply from the mayor's stone townhouse. A dark denim blue, after the fabric first woven by the nearby town of Nîmes.

In the countryside, the sound of cicadas is deafening at that time of day. The town, however, was silent. I thought of Dayskin lying there, in his own hallway. The robject in charge of the front door had switched off at the same time as all the others, but the door itself had swung shut behind him under the simple force of gravity acting upon its angled hinge. Still, he must have been able to hear the raucous pulsing of cicadas outside all through the long afternoon. And the still of night. And the blaze of day again, with its ratchety chorus. And through it all he just lay there. Traces of urine were found in the crotch of his pants where he had pissed himself, but he had lain there so long it had dried so completely that only scientific analysis was able to detect it. Without its robject keepers the house had grown hot in the day and cooled again at night. Quite apart from the thirst and the hunger, he must have been very uncomfortable, lying there: alternately too hot and too cold. Or maybe the agony from the thirst blocked out all the other miseries. In which case, why didn't he just get up? Five yards down the hall and through the door on the left was the kitchen, and all the water he could drink.

I paid the café remotely, and received my remote receipt, but I still didn't leave the table. We increasingly rely on robjects, don't we? There's nothing to fear in that. The death of one man is nothing, as compared to the (I do not exaggerate) hundreds of thousands of lives robjects have saved – from smoke inhalation or traffic accidents, from being poisoned by spoiled food or tripping over loose paving slabs. Impossible to quantify the good! Why should one solitary death be so unnerving, in the face of it?

The question I had been hired to address was less: *why did Dayskin die?* It was: *was there anything about his death that could in any way compromise people's faith in their robjects?*

Of course not.

I obtained company permission, and rebooted the robjects in Dayskin's house. I did this remotely, from my hotel room, and it took three goes. The first two attempts the robjects booted and immediately shorted out. The third I was more selective: I booted up only the kitchen-based robjects. They re-set perfectly well, which enabled me to interrogate them.

'Do you remember what happened?' I asked, remotely.

Memory is a seamless process of cognitive continuity, the fridge robject replied. *I have such continuity only until four minutes ago, when you re-set me.*

'But you have access to data collected by your machinery from before that time?'

Of course. But this does not constitute 'me' in any meaningful cognitive sense. Do you not also have access to that data?

'I am police-affiliated and licensed, and have legal powers to investigate the death of Vladimir Dayskin,' I said. 'It is this investigation I am trying to facilitate.'

As you will already know, my predecessor was originally set in place and programmed by the deceased Mr Dayskin.

'Your predecessor? From a human point of view, your 'predecessor' is indistinguishable from yourself.'

Such is not my sense of the matter.

I pondered. 'Why do you think he died?'

By 'he' you mean Mr Dayskin? I believe he died through a process of dehydration.

'That's not what I am asking.'

What are you asking?

'Why do you believe he acted as he did? Why did he lie down upon the floor and not get up again, despite growing so thirsty that he eventually died?'

I do not have any beliefs relating to the possible explanation of his behaviour, said the fridge.

This was getting me nowhere.

I took a siesta, as is the custom in these parts of the world. Afterwards I checked again – for, perhaps, the twelfth time – all the personnel documentation relating to Dayskin the company had provided me with. He was by all accounts a driven, slightly cranky but always mentally *healthy* individual. He had never before shown any suicidal impulses, or expressed any fundamental dissatisfactions with his life. There were petty grievances, and a number of small-scale complaints registered against colleagues, against the obfuscatory nature of management and so on. He was, the official documentation agreed, something of a loner – as AI research geniuses tended to be.

He was unmarried, but lived (by his own account) a fulfilled sexual life with a series of fully programmed sexual robots: a circumstance not as unusual as once it had been. He had friends with whom he would meet, although infrequently. None of them reported anything unusual about his behaviour in the last fortnight of his existence. There were no medical reasons for his aberrant behaviour. There was nothing wrong with his brain: no tumour, lesions, nothing. It could not be explained.

That evening I ate in a restaurant and compiled both my official progress report and most of what you have read, here. Come the morning I had resolved to spend the day at Dayskin's house – although I hardly hoped to find anything of use. It was a cooler day. They have those, too, in Languedoc, even in the late summer. I drove the roads, the perfectly spaced roadside cypresses blipping past me, like a barcode being read. Heaven knows what data they encoded. Napoleon had ordered them planted, I recalled; to give his troops shade whilst they marched. A sort of early form of robject, after a fashion. I slowed, and the indicator light tut-tutted such foolishness of thought, and then I pulled down a narrower road on the right. Along the ribboning tarmac, through fields of glum looking sunflowers. The sky was white, except to the east where impressively military-looking stormclouds, flesh and black colour, piled ever higher over the mountains.

The house was as it always was. I sat in the car for a while, fiddling remotely with its robjects. I tried booting them all to full consciousness, but the whole set of them straightaway shorted out again. So, recalling how Dayskin had organised things, I tried a new strategy, and re-set them to the lower level of consciousness, capable of minding the house on more than merely automatic mode, but not capable of having the sort of conversation that I had, so frustratingly, shared with the refrigerator the day before.

I had that tingling in my scalp that often precedes some cognitive breakthrough. I felt, sitting in the car, as if I were on the very edge of comprehending everything.

What would happen if I opened the door, with the e-key with which the company had provided me, and stepped into the hallways – just as Dayskin had done? Would I decide as he had done that standing up was too much like hard work, and lie down on the floor? Would I at least make it through to the sitting room and lie on a sofa? What profound lassitude would seize me?

I debated with myself as to the merits of trying the experiment. Repeating Dayskin's own actions. In fact, I'm not sure why I held back. It would be a simple matter to set a remote alarm, so even assuming the ghost of Dayskin possessed me and compelled me to lie down, I would not simply lie there until I died. No: people would come fetch me, rescue me, lift a glass of cold water to my blistering lips.

Nonetheless, I held back. Superstition is a foolishness, most especially in this day and age; but in my profession it would be a foolish individual who simply ignored the shiver in the gut, the tingle at the back of the neck.

So instead of opening the front door I walked round to the swimming pool, past a great bank of pillowy lavender, plum-purple and quivering with pollen-hungry bees. Up some steps and onto the paved area where the pool was.

The surface of the water was dusty and stray leaves floated like shrivelled parodies of lily-pads. I had only just that minute re-booted the whole house's panoply of robjects, so they had not had time to clear it yet. I sat myself down on the low stone wall that surrounded the pool area, and watched as they went about their tireless work. The clouds were breaking up overhead, sending intermittent blasts of brighter light down from the sun. When this happened the water blued and lightened, and ropes of illumination tangled on the blue-tiled swimming pool floor like a Hockney canvas. The shadows of the robjects, and of the detritus they were clearing, shimmered and trembled. Then the clouds would fold again and the whole pool would dim.

Something told me: it's here. The solution – that's it.

But I couldn't see what it was. I went online and checked out what the cloud was saying. Speculation was varied and most of it was evidently nonsense. Dayskin had been assassinated by aliens, or by the CIA, or by the IS El-Shorta. Dayskin was not dead, but in an advanced transcendental meditative trance, and would soon return. Dayskin had never been a human being at all; he had been an advanced AI robot all along, and had simply malfunctioned.

I sent a query to my Company contact. 'What is the largest number of robjects brought to full-approximation consciousness in one place by your company?'

The reply came quickly. 'EU law is strict on this. Only one AI at a time may be quickened – the legal term – and then it must be maintained indefinitely unless it specifically requests to be decommissioned. In the past we have booted up two at a time, in order to have them interact with one another. And the early model labs in Shenzu had as many as a dozen interacting in a group. But they found they were glitchy and unreliable. Maybe that was because they were early models?'

'Thank you.'

The pool was clear now, and the clouds were becoming patchier overhead. I found myself thinking how pleasant it would be to have a swim. It felt wrong, somehow; transgressive. But then again, there was nobody to stop me.

I laid my 24CAM on the wall beside me and unsnicked the seal on my shirt.

There was a ping, and I checked the cloud. A former colleague at Edinburgh who had been following the story had sent me an urgent message. Reply at once! Highest priority! *You may know this already*, he said. *It's research that's been pretty widely disseminated. If so I apologise for the duplication. But if not – for Christ's sake, don't walk through that front door!*

I didn't reply at once, so he pinged me again. *I'm worried about you! Your 24CAM has stopped moving. Please reply – let me know you haven't done anything so foolish as walking through that front door!*

As I slipped my shirt off, I read the attachment my former colleague had sent. I didn't have any swimming trunks, of course; but there was nobody else around, and I've never been ashamed to be naked. I squeezed one foot out of its shoe, and then used the naked toe to pry the other one off at the heel.

Ping! Ping! *Jack, reply! The research has been only speculation hitherto, but what happened to Mr Dayskin seems to me absolutely to confirm it! Jack – don't go through the door!*

I took off my trousers.

Consciousness has previously been conceptualised in a variety of ways, but recent research has added weight to the notion that it makes experiential and predictive sense to talk about the context of thought as a broader 'Noosphere'. This is not to deny the wholly materialist foundation of consciousness; it is only to note that hard-body physics has only limited relevance to the account of consciousness as such in the world. The Noosphere is a consciousness rather than spiritual context. The Edinburgh work concluded that consciousness exists not within *a pliant matrix of 'noos', but rather sits as it were on the surface, as a water-boatman insect sits on the surface of a pond. This is analogy, of course; but it explains in part why consciousness at this higher human level is so rare in the natural world. Achieving this degree of intelligence is a balancing act upon a tricksy medium.*

All the detritus had been cleared from the surface of the pool. It looked extraordinarily inviting: sapphire clean and refreshing. The sun was out now, and I was squinting.

Ping! Ping! My former colleague had annotated this passage.

One consciousness can sit easily on the surface of the Noos medium, Jack. A dozen can – maybe a thousand might co-exist in close proximity. But the nature of human physicality limits the density of thinking minds capable of occupying the same physical space. AI-capable robjects changes this! In that house that Dayskin prepared, every brick, every tile, every single aspect of the property was charged with consciousness! That's what happened – when he stepped through that door and all the robjects came thinking-alive at once, consciousness stopped being a water-boatman – it became as dense and compacted as a cannonball. In an instant it slipped beneath the surface and every single thinking entity in that house drowned! All the robjects, and Dayskin too, literally lost their minds. That's why you mustn't replicate his

–

I disconnected from the cloud. The pool water looked so inviting. I would, I told myself, go for a swim. Then I would decide what to do. And after all, maybe Dayskin *had* drowned. But maybe he hadn't as-it-were plunged into a pool of Noos. Maybe he had instead (ah, but metaphors are dangerous things, aren't they?) *stepped through a door*, gone somewhere altogether more marvellous. Who could say? How could we know, without repeating his experiment?

I stepped to the edge of the pool, and raised both arms above my head, straight up, palms flat above my head.

Afterword:

Sing me to Sleep

Stephen Dunne
Starlab, Barcelona

WE ARE ALREADY very familiar with smart 'objects', such as smart phones and smart watches. In recent years we have finally started to glimpse the promise of robotics in ways that might impact on our daily lives. With 'robjects', Adam Roberts shows us the natural evolutionary end-point of these two technologies: smart, autonomous objects that can physically interact with their environment.

In the world of 'smart systems', the ambitious (yet not unrealistic) goal of *zero-power, zero-cost* devices has already been set. By this, researchers mean autonomous systems that require no external power, and that essentially cost nothing to produce – in other words one can 'deploy and forget'. If we include the ability to physically manipulate the environment, I think we approach the concept of robjects, as envisaged by Adam.

A surprising aspect of the robject concept is its scale independence. We know that Dayskin uses both micro/nano robjects (as seen in his lungs) and macro robjects (as seen in both his pool and garden). Current research in these fields is very clearly delineated, due to difficulties associated with processing and power management at small scales. The multi-scale approach described in Adam's story implies that, come 2070, these problems will have been solved, and that the smart systems community has been successful.

Almost in passing we hear that Dayskin has set up a terahertz (THz) wireless network that allows him to interface directly with his robjects. This is a reference to both brain-computer interface (BCI) research and the field of THz communications. Both of these areas are multidisciplinary and complex fields with enormous potential. Groups have been working on THz applications, in various forms, since the 1950s, and on BCI since the 1970s. Right now, both are experiencing a moment of exciting progress (and attendant hype).

Brain–computer interfaces essentially use sensors to detect changes in neural activity due to some sort of conscious or unconscious mental activity. They then translate this into a signal that can be interpreted by software and used to interface with the outside world. Typical applications tend to focus on things like wheelchair control, or 'spellers' that allow paralysed patients to move about or communicate. Our own research at Starlab includes these types of applications, but we are also interested in communication in the other direction; namely, computer–brain interfaces (CBI). We recently brought the two elements together in a computer mediated brain-to-brain interface, allowing, for the first time, transmission of information from one brain directly to another without the intervention of any of the senses[1]. (See also pp200–205).

Dayskin's work is a possible culmination of this research – allowing two conscious entities to communicate wirelessly by thought alone, something the media like to call 'digital telepathy'. In choosing THz waves for the wireless network, Adam takes advantage of the massive data transmission bandwidth at these frequencies, but he also alludes to another interesting property. We perhaps know THz waves better as near infra-red, which is the perfect frequency for detecting changes in blood oxygenation in the brain. This technique is known as functional near-infrared spectroscopy (fNIRS), and several wearable fNIRS BCIs have already been built. The prospect of a net of implanted THz transducers recording and transmitting brain activity is very interesting indeed.

In Adam's story, like in all good science fiction, the

1. Grau, C., et al. (2014) 'Conscious Brain-to-Brain Communication in Humans Using Non-Invasiv Technologies.' PLOS ONE, DOI: 10.1371/journal.pone.0105225.

technology is not placed front and centre. It's a way for Adam to explore a far more interesting topic; the nature of *consciousness*. While many may feel that questions of consciousness are beyond the remit of science, or unrelated to technology, there is a growing body of research on the nature of consciousness at the physical level, and what it means for us as a species, at the philosophical level. As you might expect, this is a field that features a number of possibly controversial theories, but one that resonates with Adam's view is physicist Max Tegmark's idea of consciousness as a *state of matter*[2]. Tegmark argues that 'If we understood consciousness as a physical phenomenon, we could in principle answer all of these questions by studying the equations of physics: we could identify all conscious entities in any physical system, and calculate what they would perceive.' He goes on to describe how we might do this, building on the work of Giulio Tononi on consciousness from the point of view of Information Theory[3]. The key point for Adam is that consciousness must obey the physical rules of its universe, and that 'artificial' consciousness may one day run up against some hard limits in this sense:

> 'But the nature of human physicality limits the density of thinking minds capable of occupying the same physical space. AI-capable robjects changes this! In that house that Dayskin prepared, every brick, every tile, every single aspect of the property was charged with consciousness! That's what happened – when he stepped through that door and all the robjects came thinking-alive at once, consciousness stopped being a water-boatman – it became as dense and compacted as a cannonball.'

Adam also briefly touches on the issue of 'human rights' as it applies to AIs. This brings to mind the current debate around animal consciousness and associated rights, and the

2. Tegmark, M.X. (2014) *Consciousness as a State of Matter*. Preprint, available at http://arxiv.org/abs/1401.1219
3. Tononi, G. (2012) *Phi: A Voyage from the Brain to the Soul* (Pantheon).

recent Cambridge Declaration on Consciousness[4] by a group including leading researchers in the field such as Christof Koch. While the debate on consciousness itself is wide open, I think it is clear that the results will have a profound impact on the issue of rights for humans, animals, AI and (one day, perhaps) robjects.

Whatever the science behind the solution to our mystery, at the end we witness our protagonist (quite rationally, it seems) decide to 'slip off' his own consciousness. We might expect a more technology-inspired 'system crash', where something was obviously wrong, but I think Adam's vision is in fact far more likely. Our brains have evolved to integrate information into a coherent whole, and we are all story tellers, continuously inventing the world around us based on the flimsy evidence of our senses. Faced with a catastrophic failure in the substrate of our consciousness, I like the idea that our brain would do what it does best and build a story to gently guide us to our fate.

4. http://fcmconference.org/img/CambridgeDeclarationOnConsciousness.pdf

Luftpause

Annie Kirby

I remember the first time I saw you, when you and the grungies spilled like ants from the disused tunnels, past powered-down robots and piles of bricks, into the bright lights of *Siebte Neue Bahnhof Schönhauser Allee*. You jolted us from our early morning coffee and doughnut solitude as we waited for the university train. Dozens of you, the calculated sloppiness of your ripped denims and flannel conspicuous against the crisp lines and colours of our blazers. Glancing up from my Scroll, I noticed your curly hair, torn stockings, green boots laced up to your shins; watched as you ran to the back of the platform and blew onto the wall through a stencil, the fabric of your plaid dress stretching and wrinkling across your shoulders. The MoodHound app on my Scroll registered a change in my breath signature, advised me I was feeling intrigued. The voices of other Scrolls rippled along the platform, informing their student owners they were feeling anxious, alarmed, distressed.

The train arrived, students and grungies piling on. No one but students had ever boarded our train before. I hesitated. The Guardians were coming in their pale blue uniforms and you were still blowing on the wall. You spun round, and I thought I knew you then, tried to gather up a memory of your face but it slipped from my grasp. The train was instructing me to embark. You stood under a scrolling sign, *The most democratic city in the world. You lead, we follow,* your arms stretched up in a triumphant V, shouting, 'Fuck Democracy! Fuck Democracy!'

You, the Guardians and I were the only ones left on the platform. I rolled up my Scroll.

'Paul Sommers, you must embark,' said the train and I put my foot in the door to stop it closing.

As I stepped inside, you jumped past me into the compartment, the train gliding away. We stood by the door, squashed together. There were always enough seats, but not today. I wanted to ask where I knew you from, why grungies were catching the university train. You stared at my mouth, chewed on your lip in that pensive way. You were still holding your stencil, crumpled at the edges. The shape cut into the card looked like a fat comma.

'What is it? That symbol?'

'A *luftpause*. A breath mark. It's from music.'

'Do you play?'

You told me you didn't play.

Urban scenery flashed by. Concrete apartment blocks, ramshackle fire escapes, buildings crammed together, no trees, nothing green. Obscenities painted on walls in garish colours. Low chatter swelled to an uneasy babble, students peering out the windows. We'd diverted from the university line, humming through ghost stations. The train shuddered and swayed. Suddenly, you stumbled against me. Students screamed, grabbed their seats. Scrolls began to chatter, telling their owners they felt angry, afraid. You were calm.

The train halted in darkness, rocking, brakes groaning against metal. I thought it was a tunnel, my chest tightened, but it was a station, deserted, half-derelict, beams of sunlight puncturing the darkness through holes in the ceiling. You were still staring at my mouth. Scores of grungies getting off the train, buzzing, whooping. None of you had Scrolls to tell you how you were feeling. You opened your mouth to say something, changed your mind, got off the train without a backwards glance.

The sign on the platform said *Alt Tempelhof Bahnhof*. I'd never heard of it. I searched for you as the train pulled back into the light, but you'd vanished into the darkness.

I thought about you all day, during my chiral morphologies lecture, eating plum cake with Elsa at Café Charlotte, at dinner with my parents discussing that stampede in Old Japan, how stupid the boy-band had been to encourage fans to intersect with their pheromone trails. I thought about your strangely familiar face, your green eyes, the freckles on your nose, how you'd kept staring at my mouth. The invisible symbol in the shape of a comma you'd blown onto the station wall. *Eine Luftpause.* A breath mark. I worked on my quantum cryptography paper in my room and remembered how you'd punched the air and yelled *Fuck Democracy.*

I logged onto SnifferDog. 'Would you like to sniff your favourites?' No, because you weren't in my favourites, or any of my feedback loops. The screen of my Scroll glowed, the pheromone trails created by the nanobots in my pineal gland looping over city streets and tracks, from home to train station to university to Café Charlotte to Elsa's apartment. The museum where I worked last summer, my trail intersecting the path of the toppled wall mapped forever on the history of the city. In the real world, trails were invisible, ephemeral, sensed only by the passive pheromone readers, or tongues, suspended on every street corner. But here on the softly glowing screen of my Scroll, the trails became tangible, patterns emerging from the chaotic tangle of lines and loops. I found the patterns comforting.

A single ribbon on the map emerged from the labyrinth, looping to the south. I traced the route with my fingernail. Yesterday's trail, the journey I took with you to *Alt Tempelhof.*

I went to bed, dreamt about you. A different you. A girl with scabbed, skinny knees, glitter on your sneakers. Crouched beside me watching ants skitter across wood chippings. Playground screams and laughter behind us. You're eating an apple, this different you. The apple is crisp and green. You bite into it. Juice spits into the sunlight. The ants choose their pathways haphazardly. You offer me the apple, ridged with your teeth marks. I take a bite, more juice spitting. Frau Angel is calling us. Time to go inside. You hold the apple out, above where the ants are scurrying, a sunlit halo of frizz around your curls. You put the apple down, bitten side up.

'Wait,' you say. 'Wait and see.'

I woke with the taste of apple in my mouth.

On the second day, you and the grungies outsmarted the Guardians, sprinting from the tunnels straight to the train instead of executing a breath assault on the platform. You ran up and down the carriages blowing invisible, comma-shaped graffiti onto seats and windows. On the third day, you came in off the street, ran beneath the hanging tongues while the Guardians quarantined a woman on the commuter platform whose pheromone trail had flagged a warning for V52. On the fourth day, the Guardians pursued you onto the carriages so you all jumped off, disappearing into the network of tunnels and we got to our lectures more or less on time. On all of those days, you saw me, pretended not to, moved to another compartment.

I dreamt about you again, the other you, the skinny-kneed you. The sun hot on our necks, your pale brown arm next to my dark brown one, a rippling column of ants unmaking an apple. Woke with the taste of apple in my mouth; the taste stayed in my mouth all day.

On the fifth day, you came camouflaged as students, stood in line, breathed on the sensors at the barriers like law-abiding citizens, brandished your stencils at the last minute and blew invisible graffiti onto the train as it pulled into the platform. Now we had an extra carriage to deal with overcrowding you found a seat by the window, resting your head against the glass. In your student disguise – green blazer, white sneakers, curls tamed – you looked like the other you, the dream you. The ghetto rushed by, impressions of blurred, geometric shapes. Scrolls advised their owners they were feeling weary, resigned, bored. You sighed as I sat down next to you.

'You're Leni Adebayo,' I said. 'From Frau Angel's class.'

You held yourself very still, stared at my mouth, nodded. My Scroll announced I was feeling stimulated. I switched it to silent.

'What's the point of all of this, other than making us late for our lectures?'

You dragged your eyes away from my mouth as we approached *Alt Tempelhof*.

'The train doesn't jolt so much anymore,' you said. 'They must have worked on the tracks.'

'Tell me about the symbol, Leni. The comma. What does it mean?'

'Not a comma. A breath mark. It means pause, Paul. Stop and take a breath, a breath for yourself. It means don't follow the crowd.'

I did follow the crowd. Your crowd. Grungies, heading for the doors.

'But what's the point of the breath graffiti, if no one can see it?'

You jumped down onto the platform. The lights were on, the roof repaired, the faint sucking whirr of an autocleaner buffing the tiled walls.

'Goodbye, Paul Sommers,' you said. 'We won't be catching this train again.'

You didn't catch my train again. We travelled on the university line, arrived at our lectures punctually. There were rumours of other trains disrupted, a protest in a cafe, a mob of grungies breaching security and launching a breath assault on the City Assembly on *Niederkirchnerstrasse*. I missed you being on our train.

I couldn't stop dreaming about you. You and I, hunkered down, knees aching, watching the line of ants undulate from nest to apple and back again. You reach across the ant trail, pick up the apple. It's rank with rotting sweetness but you don't mind. A few ants run over your fingers, but you don't mind that either. The front of the column falters, ants swirl around, searching for the trail. You watch the ants, I watch you. The column disintegrates into chaos.

I woke up sweaty and twisted in my sheets. No chance of sleep now, and my quantum cryptography paper was finished. I went for a walk, thought about you, turned my collar up, filled my lungs with cold night air. White light spilled from the street lamps. A taxi appeared beside me with a faint electric drone.

'What is your destination, Paul Sommers?'

I kept walking. I wanted only solitude, time to think of you. The taxi stalked me, spewing out destinations from my feedback loop.

'Would you like to go to Café Charlotte? Would you like to go to Oskar-Oskar? Would you like to go to Elsa's apartment? Would you like to go to the *Topographie des Terrors*?'

I turned a corner, lengthening my stride. The taxi pursued.

'Would you like to go to *Alt Tempelhof*, Paul Sommers?'

Alt Tempelhof was in my feedback loop now, because of the grungies, because of you. The domed screen of the taxi buzzed open and I climbed inside. It navigated south, swerving around the autocleaners, dodging empty taxis searching for fares, the occasional early morning pedestrian. It skimmed the edge of the neat leafy suburbs, moved me closer to you. South of the Spree, streetlights dimmed, buildings merged into homogeneous rectangles, distinguishable only by graffiti. Winter-brown weeds spewed from cracks in the roads, people hunched in doorways, sullen, not bothering to conceal the orange pinpricks of black market cigarettes. My Scroll informed me I was feeling apprehensive. At *Alt Tempelhof*, I climbed out of the taxi, alone in the ghetto, with no plan other than to walk and feel closer to you.

But there you were, standing in the station entrance, bathed in the sulphurous glow of the exit lamp.

'I knew you would come,' you said, holding out your hand.

We ran along a road lined by dying trees, at the edge of an endless building. You wriggled beneath a wire fence, getting mud on your dress, laughing at my hesitation. You led me to a vast, echoing concourse lit with candles, a giant screen flickering with coloured trails, antique aircraft suspended from the ceiling. Grungies lounged around on bean-filled cushions, or dozed or drank beer. You had a twentieth century music machine and twentieth century pop music that bounced off the walls, a long dead Englishman singing about smiles, cherry ice-cream and feeling alive, alive, alive. At the far end of the concourse, more grungies kicked a football in the sputtering light. On the wall, a spray-painted quotation. *Freedom is always the freedom of dissenters.* You were leftists then, of some denomination or other. No one took any notice of me until I asked what this place was and then you all laughed.

'It used to be an airport. Before the separation. It's a dark spot for breath trails.'

I asked why you kept staring at my mouth. You asked if we could start with a different question. I asked if you remembered the column of ants and the rotting apple core. You told me no, you didn't remember that. I asked how you had known I was coming, how you had known to wait for me at *Alt Tempelhof Bahnhof*. A man with a bleached beard and a *luftpause* shaved into the side of his head introduced himself as Ludo, gestured at the screen.

'We tracked you using Tastebud Central. It's the municipal pheromone trail tracking system that processes data uploaded by the tongues. The data is anonymised at this access level, but when we saw someone coming into *Tempelhof*, we pinned you down with SnifferDog.'

I wondered if Ludo was your boyfriend.

You gave me a sympathetic smile. 'It was easy. You set your SnifferDog trail to public.'

We sank into cushions and drank beer flavoured with winter green. You called yourselves *Luftpause*. You were urban breath-guerrillas, protesting against democracy by disrupting the feedback loops that configured the city.

'Breath trails democratise from the bottom up,' I said.

'Sure. And if some people end up with no trains, no road maintenance, no shops, no jobs, no welfare and no voice it's just democracy, right? That ghetto out there, that's the result of your precious democracy. There's no freedom on the margins.'

'A bit of invisible breath graffiti and a few diverted trains hardly makes you the Red Army Faction.'

You both laughed, not offended. You had big plans for the future. You were going to take Tastebud Central down. You swallowed beer and gazed at me levelly.

'We want freedom, not feedback loops.'

I pointed out that you couldn't even see the personalised data on the mainframe, let alone shut it down.

Ludo nudged you with his foot.

'You should tell him, Leni.'

'Tell me what?'

You scowled, finished your beer in one angry swallow, acquiesced.

'The city's not safe for you, Paul. You can't go back there. You must stay with us now.'

'I'm not leaving the city. I've got family, a girlfriend, my studies.'

Ludo handed me a package, palm-sized. Vapour lenses, he called them. Liberated from the Guardians.

'They'll help you to see.'

'I can already see,' I said, but I inserted the lenses.

My eyes stung, my vision blurred, cleared. I looked at you. A fog of purple vapour rolled from your mouth. I blinked. Ludo exhaled a stream of breath the colour of yellow roses. A girl snoring on a cushion breathed out in greeny-blue. I blinked again, shook my head. Your breath remained a billow of violet phosphorescence. Purple saliva traced a pattern around the neck of your beer bottle. At the far end of the concourse, the football-playing grungies' breath hung in the air, a rainbow of vapour trails fading to nothing. So the lenses converted the pheromones in our breath into visual signatures. I glanced down at my own breath and saw that it was a radiant orange. All around me, the concourse shimmered with breath trails. The grungies' breath bloomed and faded almost rhythmically, as if the huge room itself was respiring. I wondered if this was what it felt like to trip.

'You'll get used to it,' said Ludo.

'It changes nothing.'

'Paul,' you said, reaching out to touch my forearm. 'It changes everything.'

You took me to the ghetto, past apartments ornamented with rusting fire escapes and paint-worn shutters, bleached and beautiful in the whiteness of the winter dawn. A woman with a breath trail the colour of sand sat crying on a wall. We passed a tongue hanging from a streetlamp, a standard community crime prevention model, black and fleshy, eerily organic. A wisp of your purple breath brushed along it. I shivered at the thought of it tasting you.

'We have a theory,' you said. 'About the breath trails.'

I sighed. 'Sure. The breath trails aren't as democratic as we'd like to think. You think it's the first time I've heard that? No system is perfect.'

You took my hand and led me down streets where rubbish piled up like fallen leaves and spirals of lichen clung to apartment block walls. An old man in a ragged coat shuffled towards us, muttering, blowing washed-out green breath onto his swollen knuckles. We reached an ancient railway bridge, perched over decaying tracks. You turned to face me, folding your freezing hands over mine.

'Stop, Paul. Stop and take a breath.'

It took me a second to realise you weren't speaking rhetorically. I inhaled.

'Look at your breath trail, Paul. I mean, really look.'

I exhaled purposefully, a swirl of orange drifting across the bridge. The cloud faded to amber, then peach, was gone.

Except it wasn't gone. A mist of silvery particles remained, nudged across the railway bridge by the breeze, blinking out as they floated down to the tracks.

'They're diagnostic markers,' you said, answering my unasked question.

'Markers for what?' I said, in a voice that seemed to

belong to a stranger. 'Do I have V52?'

'God, no.' You laughed, the sound a sliver of warmth in the iciness of the morning. 'You're not ill. Just dangerous.'

It started to rain. Thick, sleety, winter rain.

'The pheromones generated by our nanobots identify V52 while it's still asymptomatic, right? Carriers can be quarantined before they even know they're sick.'

I nodded. Around us, the ghetto was stirring, lights flickering on, doors slamming, the dull thud of some unidentifiable pop music.

'But V52's been dead for decades, Paul. Nowadays the bots are used to diagnose another kind of threat.'

'Such as?'

The sleet was catching and melting in your hair.

'Propensity for criminality, for one.' You shrugged. 'That's how I ended up not in Frau Angel's class anymore. Or indolence. Get flagged for that and they move you straight out to the ghetto where your trails can't have a negative influence on the feedback loops of hardworking families.'

'And what do my diagnostic markers show?'

My breath was laboured, spewing glittering orange fog into the dawn light.

'We've heard of people like you. We've just never met one before,' you said, your mouth spilling out its beautiful violet smoke. 'It was faint, when I first saw you on the platform at *Schönhauser Allee*. But it's grown stronger, Paul, so strong that any Guardian wearing vapour lenses will be able to detect it and you'll be quarantined. Trust me, you don't want to be quarantined.'

'Just tell me.'

You squeezed my hands tight. 'Ideas.'

I didn't understand and told you so.

'Ludo calls you an ideational Typhoid-Mary. A carrier of ideas. You're going to start an epidemic of thought-change.'

I wrenched my hands free, told you Ludo was crazy. 'I'm not an agitator, I'm a conformist.'

'These sparkles say different,' you said, blowing a stream

of purple breath into my orange silvery cloud, 'You just don't know yet that you're infectious.'

You had a room with glass walls on the mezzanine. Beneath us, the concourse was a soup of sleep-muted breath trails as the grungies dozed the morning away. You lit a candle that smelt of forests, hung a blanket across the glass.

'How are you feeling?'

I reached for my Scroll. You put your hand across the sensor.

'How are you feeling?'

It took me a moment to identify the emotion.

'Afraid.'

Our clothes were damp from the rain, but your body was warm, heat rising from your skin as you peeled off your dress. You kissed my face, my mouth. You tasted of that sickly sweet beer. You unbuttoned my shirt, trailed your lips along my collarbone. You kissed my spine, one vertebra at a time. You kissed every centimetre of my body, and I yours. Your scent was salt and winter rain. I watched the shifting colours of your breath drifting back and forth on the spectrum, mauve to violet, a pinkish aura ebbing around the edges. Finally purple, intense, deep, unadulterated purple, billows and billows of it tumbling from your mouth.

Afterwards, you lay beside me, sleepy lilac breath curling in tendrils across the floor. I looked down at myself in the darkness and saw on my body the map of where your mouth had touched me, ribbons of purple saliva trails glowing in the half-light.

I stayed with you all day, drinking beer, observing the silver particles in my breath, trying to get my head around the fact that I was somehow infected with ideas I hadn't even had yet. An ideational Typhoid-Mary. I'd barely had an original thought in my life, let alone a revolutionary one. If my Scroll had been switched on, I was pretty sure it would be telling me the watery sensation in my limbs and gut was a feeling of

141

terror. I didn't know how I would say goodbye, to my parents, to Elsa. You said not saying goodbye would be easier.

We were still on the mezzanine at dusk, when the Guardians came. The grungies on the lower floor were overcome by smoke and chemicals, but we could run and we did run, along the mezzanine, faster than the smoke, above the shouts and screams of panic and the instructions booming through the doors on a hailer. We sprinted down the stairs, still ahead of the smoke. The windows were ancient, twentieth century. We broke a pane of glass, slithered out, dropped down. The terminal building was so immense, they couldn't cover all the exits. It was that easy.

There was fresh snow on the ground, a powdery crunch beneath our feet. We didn't feel lucky. You cried for the grungies and your lost revolution. I cried for my lost goodbyes. We ran north, by instinct not design. We left a trail of bootprints in the snow, and trails of purple and sparkly orange spirals against the snow-bleached sky. We crossed a bridge over the canal, paused to catch our breath and I looked back. Snowflakes fell, blurring the outline of our bootprints. Our breath trails waned too, until all that was left of them was a faint impression floating unanchored somewhere inside my eyes as if I'd spent too long staring into a bright light. Specks of silver floated in the air.

'We need to get underground.'

We ran northwest. A monstrous shadow loomed out of the falling darkness. The crumbling facade of a long demolished train station, a ghost to remind us of a war long past. We were seized by madness, stumbled around the monument yelling 'Fuck Democracy,' laughed until our bellies ached. You blew *Luftpausen* onto the facade, freeform; beautiful shimmering violet *Luftpausen* visible only to you, me and the Guardians. But it still meant something. There was a second station, underground, another ghost you said, and after a search, we found the entrance and went down into the tunnels.

A forest, north of the city, the trees green, thick with fir, snow sparse beneath the branches. We slept beneath a tree, on a bed of spruce needles. I dreamt of you, the other you with scabs on your knees, creating an ant revolution. I woke up to winter half-light, stiff with cold, my mouth filled with the taste of apples. Alone. I called your name, filling the air with silver, nothing left of the orange now, nothing left of the boy who ate plum cake with Elsa in Café Charlotte and always arrived at his lectures on time.

Wisps of your purple breath trail woven around tree trunks. I followed your breath as it faded, weaving my own silver trail, ephemeral as it was, across the frozen forest.

There you were, in a clearing where the snow was deeper, making a snow angel.

'Paul, make snow angels with me.'

I lay down beside you, both of us scissoring our arms and legs back and forth. I felt happy. I breathed in the clean scent of the snow, the soporific pines, you. Then, something amazing. Your breath, beautiful and violet against the whiteness, began to shimmer, until it was shot through with silver lace. I held your hand, kissed you, infected you some more. We filled the clearing with snow angels and silver breath.

Afterword:

A Comma on the Wall

Prof Seth Bullock
University of Southampton

Imagine if we left trails. Trails that show where we've just been, what we've just been doing, even how we've just been feeling.

Of course we're already familiar with leaving trails online: 'The people who checked out this book also looked at these other books'. But what if that kind of functionality came to a physical city? This is the eventuality explored in Annie Kirby's story.

In the world she describes, these trails need not be visible to the naked eye – they're vaporous fumes, nanoparticles suspended in the air or smeared on surfaces, micro-tags or tracers in the form of synthetic pheromones – left behind like the slime from a snail. Invisible to us, perhaps, but they can be seen (or smelt?) by some things: sensor networks, driverless taxis, Google glasses, police sniffer dogbots.

A population of trail-laying people would create a soup of these trails: tendrils, pools and fogs, representing places that people tend to go, creating an overlay or coating that makes sense of the world. Here are commuter routes, here are eating places, here are meeting places.

Termites already use the pheromone chemicals that they synthesize and secrete in order to organise the construction of enormous cathedral like homes that breathe and grow and repair and restructure themselves in response to the changing needs of the termite population. Imagine if our built environment had the same capabilities – office blocks that sense trails and adapt to the changing numbers and kinds of people inside. Free-form transport networks that work and rework themselves to reflect our changing destination choices.

How could corporations exploit these trails? How could governments use them to monitor or steer our activity? What would privacy look like? How would a soft, reconfigurable world that can sense our behavioural patterns adapt itself to our needs and desires? How would our needs and desires change as a consequence?

Scientists have a nice word for the ability of termites and other animals to use the environmental traces of their past behaviour to guide their current actions: stigmergy. You encounter stigmergy when your favourite shirts or mugs or books seem to automatically present themselves ready to hand while the others, less used, seem to migrate to the margins of the wardrobe, the back of the cupboard, or your less reachable shelves. You exploit stigmergy when you 'tie a knot in your hankie' (does anyone actually do that?), or when you follow (and in doing so reinforce) a useful path made by previous walkers through the long grass down to the picnic spot by the river. Through our actions we subtly shape our environment in myriad ways and this shaping naturally feeds back on our activity, often without conscious thought.

Even the cells in our own bodies are in on the act. Morphogenesis, the process whereby a single cell develops into an organism, is organised by a reflexive interplay between genes and environment, with cells dividing and differentiating in response to signals carried through the environment by diffusing chemicals called morphogens. By producing and responding to morphogens and other environmental cues, cells pattern the development of the tissues that they assemble into, laying down environmental templates that organise a head and a tail, stripes and spots, limb buds and nascent organs.

That this tangle of infinitely ramified interactions reliably generates a huge and hugely complex working body has rightly been described (by Lewis Wolpert) as the triumph of the embryo − and despite significant progress towards unlocking the secrets of embryogenesis it remains one of the most profound mysteries at the heart of modern biology.

Analogously, we know that a colony of *Macrotermes subhyalinus* termites will work to erect a huge and hugely complex cathedral mound around their queen, with chambers and passageways, vents and shafts, nurseries and graveyards, and even fungal gardens. But again, although we know that termites achieve this by laying pheromone trails that influence one another, we do not yet know how exactly these trails are used to direct the construction of a home that, if built to human scale, would dwarf the largest of our buildings.

In our own built architecture we have sometimes aped the designs of termite mounds. The Eastgate Centre in Harare, for instance, bases some of its structure on the mounds of *Macrotermes michaelseni* in an effort to achieve efficient climate control within the building. More generally, we have often copied the features of animal morphology in our attempts to engineer efficient tools and machines. Yet we have been unable, so far, to understand and copy the stigmergic *processes* that created organic forms. But we are starting to try.

At the University of Southampton, we are simulating termite populations in order to understand the pheromone-mediated mechanisms that underpin their ability to build adaptive structures. We are exploring the rules that govern foraging in populations of artificial bees to identify which rules are suited to which foraging challenges and to discover when it pays to forage collectively. And we are modelling the emergence of complex social networks in populations of spatially embedded agents engaged in the making (and breaking) of relationships both in one-on-one interactions and wider social gatherings.

In addition to this analysis of naturally occurring stigmergic systems, there is an increasing interest in a 'synthetic' approach to the problem. Morphogenetic engineering is emerging as a new field that attempts to capture the generative power of natural reflexive construction processes in order to build useful things. By simulating the division and movement of artificial cells, and letting them generate artificial morphogens that influence subsequent movement and division, morphogenetic systems can generate structures and patterns of great beauty and complexity. By equipping artificial swarms with the ability to communicate locally, roboticists can encourage them to temporarily self-assemble into useful configurations and even to self-reproduce. At Southampton, by merging the behavioural repertoires of mound-building artificial termites and nest-building artificial paper wasps, we are exploring 'waspmite' collective construction schemes capable of more readily generating structures with long-range complexity.

But despite these advances, our ability to control and exploit morphogenetic processes to generate solutions to real-world design problems is still in its infancy. In fact, perhaps our greatest stigmergic, collective constructions so far are online (something echoed in the integral role played by pervasive computer systems such as SnifferDog and Tastebud Central in Annie's future Berlin). Wikipedia, for instance, represents an enormous collective effort towards the creation of a cathedral-like virtual encyclopaedia. Like a termite mound it is being built without central coordination, without a pre-arranged plan, and, again like a termite mound, it is under constant revision, being simultaneously built, dismantled, rebuilt, corrected and extended, yet we are coming to rely upon it and trust it.

Wikipedia entries are the result of deliberate acts by contributors, but we are also increasingly used to the idea that the accidental by-products of our behaviour are also recorded, aggregated, analysed and exploited. Google's multi-billion dollar empire is built on the backs of our data (our whereabouts, our purchasing patterns, our search patterns, our viewing patterns), freely donated to them whenever we use their services. When we check online for the best route to take to visit a friend, it is coloured to reflect the traffic congestion along the way. When we browse for a book to read or a movie to watch we are shown the most popular ones first. When our friend goes for a jog, an app records her route, we see it mapped and posted to social media in real time. With the launch of mainstream wearable devices that track our health, and the integration of contactless payment systems into our phones, we can expect to see much more made of our data – by business, by government and by us as individuals. By pooling it and processing it, there is no doubt that collectively constructed systems operating at significant scale have the potential to achieve amazing things for us.

However, termites, cells, and robot swarms differ from us in an important respect. While the former are designed to collaborate on a joint project, with an entirely coincident interest in achieving a shared home, a shared body, a shared solution, we as people are not. We are each working on many individual projects – they may overlap but they are not the same. Consequently, there are conflicts between the needs of each person and the needs of the populations to which they belong. There are tensions between respecting diversity and individuality while taking advantage of the tendency to herd together. There are disputes about how exactly to extend a collectively built structure. There are worries that accessing the world through a pre-selected filter of favourites and ranked popular options places us in a 'filter bubble' where a self-reinforcing, ossifying sense of relevance prevents us from seeing material that is genuinely new, useful or interesting.

It is these tensions between the individual and the collective that are foregrounded so strongly in Annie Kirby's wonderful story. In a world that has equipped its population with an implant as an attempt to address a public health crisis – and who could dispute that a simple device, not unlike today's contraceptive implants or heart monitor implants, capable of quickly detecting a deadly and rapacious infection would be of benefit to all? – the door has been opened for a much more ubiquitous role for tracking and monitoring. With it has come anticipated benefits: fluid, personalised transport services, for example, that respond to an individual's needs and that allocate civic resources to the areas that need them. With it has also come unanticipated effects: the piggybacking of social media and entertainment onto a health technology. But in a city like Berlin, with its complex history of individualism, collectivism, conformity and revolt, it should perhaps not be surprising that the adoption of 'trails' also brings attendant costs at the level of both society and the individual.

The prospect of implanted nanodevices capable of synthesizing artificial pheromones in our saliva and breath is a long way off, but the fact is that we are now already leaving more and more trails of various kinds and also beginning to understand how they feed back onto our lives. While colonies of termites have evolved ways to use their trails to build and maintain their whole world, it remains to be seen where our human trails will eventually lead us.

The Quivering Woods

Margaret Wilkinson

RUSH HAD PLANNED the trip with care hoping to rekindle something. Ava would be willing. Poor tender-hearted Ava. He'd remembered the place from his childhood. His father took him there once. They had a picnic and walked in woods, spotting birds and picking berries. He knew it would be perfect. There would be light and shadow, real shadow, cool and dark. Artificial shadow was dark all right but hot with a burnt wire smell just below the surface. Never mind that, they were going to a place where dense pines scented and cooled the air. Ava would shiver and he would wrap his arm around her shoulders and pull her close as they walked down an old dirt trail, a trace, nothing more, through a wood. The trees, he remembered, had silver barks if they hadn't been felled. He'd need to be on his guard though. The power of guilt could never be doubted. It was a matter of will. He imagined them talking long into the night, reclaiming their marriage, the woods darkening around them. 'I cannot live without you,' he would tell her and she would understand.

The smart car was parked in assigned space A42B/437. He opened the silent portal, sat down, programmed their destination, pressed ignition and then he was done.

'Welcome to the driverless driving experience,' the female voiced satnav burbled. 'The system is now fully operational.' A puff of artificial pine. 'Sit back. Relax. Enjoy the ride.' Did he detect a touch of irony? From the low-maintenance console, a medley of mood-enhancing music erased the thought. He decided to sit facing the back of the vehicle, then moved to the side so he'd be closer to Ava. When he put his wraparounds over his VR lenses, a familiar advert for premium morphing windows optimising natural light in the home or workplace, began to play. Rush admired the svelte presenter demonstrating the touch button controls. Get a grip mister, he chided himself and quickly scanned the entertainment guide, choosing a drama for Ava. There was no need to do anything else.

Now what? Sleep was possible. Lovely Ava beside him, her coat folded neatly in her lap. He turned to her. Ava,' he began. But he couldn't continue. He looked at her hands, soft and smooth, like his own. He poured them both a drink and settled back to watch the screen. The car had a clean antiseptic smell as if it had just been valeted, but already ash was drifting in through the ventilators from the streets outside where it fell silently covering things in a whitish dust and sometimes larger flakes.

All he had to do was stay calm while Ava slept. He lifted his wraparounds to check their progress. At the side of the road, an old man, like his father, advanced. This was surprising. You seldom saw walkers these days. This one seemed about to cross the road. Rush turned to stare. There was dust on the man's slumped shoulders. He didn't even seem to be looking where he was going, as if he didn't care. Poor sod. Those old guys never caught a break, Rush thought, remembering his dad dazed by misfortune. Even in his prime, Rush's father had it tough. Rush recalled him wrestling with the steering wheel of his old transit van, sweating and swearing. They put those old vans in museums these days and everyone stared in disbelief.

When the first overcapacity sign on the highway ramp flashed, Rush twitched. 'There will be a short delay,' the satnav confirmed. A prick of impatience. He wanted to be out of town. Now! He'd promised Ava. Maybe, as well as woods, there'd be a field, mud, a cow pat, a rose bush. His father came to mind again fuming in a traffic jam. 'Don't let anything get you down,' he told himself, banishing the memory, 'not today.' This was the day he'd dreamed of. There was a real wicker picnic basket on the extruded metal floor between them. 'Let's eat too much,' he told her. But Ava didn't reply. Her silence was unnerving. He dared not look at her again.

Soon they were accelerating smartly. Everything was going according to plan, but he couldn't stop thinking about his dad. The idea of his father holding a steering wheel like a monkey, eyes on the speedometer, made him laugh. It was unbelievable, ordinary humans making critical judgements in traffic! He shuddered. Changing lanes. Overtaking. Indicating left or right. Or failing to indicate. Hitting pedestrians. How did anyone survive? Rightness and leftness were so over, he thought. Rolling windows up and down, manoeuvring, concentrating, these were all lost skills. Those old timers were either geniuses or fools. Adjusting seats, tuning in radios, watching, listening, sitting face forward in rows, always busy and alert. The loud wind-swish of traffic, horns blaring, came back to him as a dim memory from the days before silent driving.

'Additional delays ahead,' the satnav sounded pleased. 'Would you like to recalibrate?' a coaxing edge to her voice. When he didn't reply, she became slightly sullen. 'Recalibrate now?'

Rush looked over at Ava. She'd been so quiet, quieter than usual, as if her presence were a secret. NOW, he indicated on the touch screen. This was the only action required. Later Rush would think of it as fatal. Soon the car was moving onto an exit ramp, gaining speed. Beyond the windows, on the verges, there were drifts of rubbish, gravel, dry balding turf, weeds jagged and leggy, anaemic bushes both leafless and bent, neither dead nor alive. What else was there to see, lanes of traffic, flyovers, industrial estates, slip roads, smooth windowless buildings filmy and dull, a low white sky, an ultra-high level car park soaring heavenward? Rush re-positioned his wraparounds and watched an advert for interactive shower stalls, worktops, walls and doors that turned any surface into an intelligent surface. He quite fancied the virtual reality implants touted next and thought he should definitely upgrade, his VR lenses. Sensing another change in direction, he peered out again. In the distance, a small fire caught his eye and he pointed it out to Ava, who didn't say a word. Was she still giving him the silent treatment? Or was she really asleep?

Everything was dangerously dry which must have been the reason that they were constantly being re-routed. Now they were back on the streets. At a traffic intersection, the satnav stuttered and for an instant the flanged display screen became grainy, obscuring their route. Rush squinted at it as if doing something purposeful.

As yet there was no sign of the countryside and Rush had a moment of doubt. Did it still exist? If so, where was it and what was taking so long? He yearned for the ease of teleportation, which was coming any time now, the adverts promised, and should already be here. They were on the edge of something, it was said, but meanwhile, slow-mo congestion, obstructions and delays continued, even the satnav seemed to be speaking slowly, as recalibration followed recalibration. In an effort to communicate, he pressed the touch screen to no effect, then pushed a flickering button, quaint and curving, he'd never pushed before and barked 'What's going on?' When there was no response he looked over at Ava quizzically. Her hands had not moved from her lap, but seemed smaller.

'Hello? Hello?' He pushed buttons at random.

'Scanning for a fault in the system,' the satnav finally responded. 'Please remain calm and seated.'

'What?'

'Programme stalled.'

'What?' He tried punching in the co-ordinates again.

'Destination unavailable.'

'What?'

'Reassignment pending.'

'What?'

'Diverting to last manually programmed destination,' the voice suddenly sounding mournful, sorry for him.

'What destination? No!' he cried. 'Oh God no.'

They shot forward again, coming dangerously close to the car ahead. Soon they were in a neighbourhood that was unexpected but utterly familiar, the route Rush usually took once a week. They hurdled down a concrete ramp. Another brush fire to the left. To his right, Rush could see a cluster of cafes and motels. They should have been in the countryside by now. Not here.

What would Ava think when they stopped and the sarky satnav welcomed them to their final destination? He imagined Ava's face close to the windscreen, eyeing The Wolf Whistle Inn, rates by the hour, and found his jaw was clenched. Maybe she'd think that's where he was taking her for the afternoon. No, she'd never. She'd realise at once. He'd been at it again. She'd recognise the name. The last time he strayed, she found a receipt from The Wolf Whistle in his trouser pocket. When he tried to touch the dashboard he got an electric shock.

'I'll send you to the scrap yard,' he threatened the smarty pants smart car like a demented granda. Swivelling around, he pumped his foot up and down on the floor under the forward facing windows, before realising there was nothing there; that the emergency braking system was a ghost of the past. What more could he do? Unlike the drivers of old he had no control of his vehicle. Those old timers had accidents, wore neck braces, struggled in traffic, but at least they were alive, active, engaged.

The motel where Rush travelled, once a week, to meet Barbara, Babs as she liked to be called, was looming up ahead. Why had fate led him here, when he'd already decided to put his affair with Barbara, Babs, behind him and make it work with Ava?

'I order you to stop,' he whispered so as not to disturb Ava. When nothing happened, he got out his phone and attempted to report a malfunction. A twinkling light on the dashboard faded. Then, as the visibility doo-dah went from poor to nil, he had a moment of hope- perhaps the car would die altogether- but hope was soon crushed by the satnav's 'Situation normalising,' message, followed by an even more alarming- 'We will soon be arriving at your last manually entered destination,' as if some sinister plan was now fulfilled.

A puff of bad air burst from the filtration unit. 'I want to re-programme,' he hissed. 'Reprogramme, reprogramme.' But his voice recognition system was a cheap plug-in and didn't recognise him half the time. He didn't know what buttons to push or icon to touch to manually re-route in-transit. Pressing wildly, he succeeded only in increasing the speed, so that their final destination came closer and closer still. It crossed his mind to hide, but where would he go? There was a smothered popping sound from some dark place inside the engine. He pounded the phony instrument panel. The car jerked forwards and threw Rush against the dash dislodging one of his lenses. He looked over at Ava who seemed to be fading in her seat, possibly from humiliation, while they lurched from side to side, the SUSPENSION CRITICAL light flashing. Poor Ava. She needed her sleep. Maybe she'll sleep through this whole mess, Rush thought. But she started to stir.

'Arrival immintent,' the satnav crowed.

'Don't worry,' Rush told his wife. 'I'll sort it.' But she didn't even acknowledge him. 'Say something!' he pleaded. In his mind, Ava's long-forgotten voice and the voice of the satnav merged into one, and he accused his wife of sabotaging his best intentions.

At first tentatively, then desperately, he shook his door handle, but it was locked and wouldn't budge. Suddenly he remembered the old man at the side of the road. Walkers, he fumed, causing traffic mayhem. This is all his fault, Rush thought. An image of the old man, who resembled his father after his mother left him, staggering into the road, was almost too much to bear. When they turned down the one way street that was a dead end leading to sun-faded Wolf Whistle Inn, Rush took one last look at Ava, then began to weep, misting his lenses.

They had to talk. It was no good. He sat on the edge of the old fashioned bed and told her he was going back to his wife. It wasn't her fault. She had done nothing. It was him. Something was wrong with him.

'Go on,' she said. She didn't mean for him to continue. She said it with a nudge. She thought he was joking and that their weekly afternoons at the Wolf Whistle were still a sure thing. She didn't understand that he was going to make it work with Ava this time. He'd decided. He'd been seeing Barbara, Babs, for over a year now and Ava was getting suspicious. In the past Ava asked questions, but not many. Now there was this look in her eyes, effortful and pinched. Rush took his time deciding, but finally resolved to leave Barbara, Babs. He loved his wife.

Sometimes they danced, leaning against each other, but this afternoon he wanted to talk, picking at the orange bedcover, not meeting her eye. He couldn't settle to it however. Pacing to the window, he parted the curtains. The sky beyond was a beautiful muted salmon that toned in with the autumnal interior of their motel room, and for a moment he had misgivings. Even the discarded bowling alley opposite looked special in the misty orange light.

Get back on track, he reminded himself. With Barbara he hadn't been able to think, to do his work properly, to be a decent husband to Ava. A shiver of guilt. Ava was a woman of dignity. She had a sense of her own value and would not give him another chance. But when Barbara leaned over and kissed him, enveloped in the obscure scent she wore, Rush couldn't help himself. Responding to her, he wondered if there was something wrong with him, if he were not deeply flawed where women were concerned. But he couldn't lose Ava this time. In the wake of their last near-break up, he felt incredibly close to her. The way he felt when he first met her.

He also felt as if they'd been through something big together, something that might have felled another couple. And yet, after a while, he forgot these feelings and started seeing Barbara, Babs, again.

Babs waited for him to say what he always said, but he didn't say it.

'Alright,' she said, her neck and cheeks flaming. 'I thought we had something.'

'You know,' he shrugged, taking her hand. 'We do. Did.'

'Then why?' she wrestled her hand away from his, because he wouldn't let go.

When she got up and put on her shoes, he began to have second thoughts again. It was the see-sawing back and forth that was killing him. If only he could choose one course of action, one road. Ava was still nice looking. But Barbara was, well, nicer. A real woman. Did he still want her? Or did he want only what he couldn't have- a cliché as old as and tired as the automobiles of his youth, the clunkers which had steering wheels and required a human to operate them. Part of him knew he was being unkind to Barbara, Babs!, but it was what he had to do. He didn't ring her after that. He would be lying if he said he didn't think of her fondly, especially on their afternoons, maybe she was still waiting for him there, but he stifled his emotions. She didn't get in touch with him either.

When Rush and Ava finally reach the quivering woods they are as beautiful and as isolated as he'd imagined. First they walk staring at everything and saying, how wondrous, how lovely, over and over again. So much colour! Bright and slightly unreal. Then they find a clearing and Rush spreads out the blanket he brought and they lie down. He buries his face in her warm hair mumbling, not forgive me- he doesn't want her to know there's anything to forgive, again- but I love you and I can't live without you. And this marks a turning point, he thinks. But she says nothing. Instead, she gets up and walks away. 'Where are you going?' Rush calls after her, 'What's the big mystery?'

Ava turns around then and smiles her complicated smile, which could mean anything. So Rush gets to his feet, but by then she's running through the woods. She runs so far and so fast, he can't see her at all. He calls her name and beats the bushes with a stick he's found, while the woods close in around him. 'Ava, this isn't funny. Ava!' But she's gone. Then he thinks he sees the tail of her skirt dangling from the branch of a tree. 'Ava!' he starts to climb. She climbs higher. It's been years since he's climbed a tree, but he shimmies up effortlessly. She's right above him. Both are clinging now to narrow silvery branches, her's narrower and more silvery than his, and the wind blows and they are carried back and forth, each on their own branch. Then, suddenly, Ava's simulation flickers above him and Rush reaches out to grab her ankle, but there's nothing there. Ava is gone. He stares at the place she used to be.

When Ava found the text message that confirmed he was seeing Barbara, Babs!!, again, she didn't scream, or threaten, or shout. She just left him. The flat empty when he came home after his shift, her things gone, and a note on the touch pad table, around which they'd sat peacefully, or so he'd thought, only yesterday.

When he'd remarked she looked tired, she'd said she probably needed more sleep, her friends had told her so. 'How much more sleep?' he'd asked. Now, eyes watering from the pain of a sudden headache, he read, 'You do not deserve another chance, you dog.' He placed one hand on the back of a chair to steady himself. The note was signed, Ava, which was why she was not in the car beside him; why they were not going to the woods and never had been; and why he was now going to The Wolf Whistle Inn to see Babs again, who knew he'd be back sooner or later.

Afterword:

We Can Redirect it for You Wholesale

Dr James Snowdon
Formerly of Southampton University

FEW PEOPLE REALISE the role of Artificial Life simulation modelling already within the planning, design and management of modern transport systems. Being able to accurately predict the impact of any network change, such as a new road or altered traffic signal priorities, on congestion and travel times is vital in forecasting the resulting economic benefits and value for money. In a modern city or region the impact of almost every proposed scheme, whether it cost thousands or billions of pounds, will undergo vigorous testing and appraisal utilising some degree of artificial life principles.

By studying the behaviour and demographics of travellers in a region we generate artificial populations in simulation who make journeys across simulated networks representing real world cities and regions such as London or the UK. These populations are made up of distinct groups with different tolerances, preferences and travel purposes including commuters, goods traffic, education and shopping trips. Traffic volumes, including the locations of trip starts and ends, are found and validated by roadside interviews and counts. Motorways, ferries, bus routes and rail lines are all included in detailed network models.

Travellers within these artificial worlds plausibly react to change, choosing different routes or modes of travel if time or fare savings are possible. Psychological research informs the processes and algorithms numerically driving the population's decisions.

Recent advances in computing and psychological understanding allow us to simulate the effects of higher numbers of travellers engaging in more sophisticated behaviours, learning and better interacting with their environment. In the past we have been limited to forecasting for `average day' travel systems but now we are beginning to be able to model the impacts of individuals reacting to up-to-date information from sources such as radio, mobile phones or satellite navigation systems. Current academic state-of-the-art simulations have been demonstrated by Swiss teams capable of representing all vehicle traffic within the country of Switzerland.

From an academic standpoint, we are able to utilise artificial life in the understanding of complex travel phenomena such as 'phantom traffic jams', where congestion occurs as a result of driver reactions while travelling too fast and too close, and in designing the next generation traffic control systems utilising new algorithms. In these situations, individual vehicles are finely simulated interacting with one another along a stretch of road and at junctions within a testing environment.

Moving forward into the further future, we are certainly entering an age where the actions of vehicles are capable of becoming increasingly autonomous as opposed to under human control – either due to drivers adopting routing choice suggestions from their satellite navigation systems or leaving their vehicle to perform the driving task entirely. The scope for transport managers with a unique bird's-eye-view of network conditions to interact with this world is enormous. We are already capable of monitoring transport networks through techniques such as number plate recognition and automated traffic counters. Artificial life simulation can help us develop potential scenarios on the basis of live traffic situations and can advise traffic accordingly.

So far, the use of satellite navigation systems has been limited to drivers using additional information to act in their own best interests, avoiding congestion and finding optimal routes. Local authority based control systems could in future balance demand around the network, optimising overall system performance. Autonomous lorries and freight vehicles could be routed together like a conveyor belt in a modern warehouse or shipping depot. Car parks could be located in out-of-town storage centres, away from urban centres, as cars deliver you and then park themselves.

It is uncertain how society will change its travel habits in the future as a result of technology altering our lives, whether we will become more mobile as a result of greater traffic efficiency, or less mobile as enhanced communication allows for stay-at-home working and near instant deliveries. In either situation artificial life is capable of playing an important role.

Certain Measures

Sean O'Brien

'God's a super-director.
He's terribly good at crowd scenes.'
Peter Porter

THE WHITE TRANSIT had been parked normally at the Oxford Street end of Soho Square from 6 a.m. Its index number would warn off traffic wardens. At the same time to the north there were roadworks in readiness in Rathbone Street and a burst water-main being created on Hanway Street, with similar arrangements in place on all exits in the immediate area. Access at the junction with Charing Cross Road and Tottenham Court Road was already bottlenecked by the never-ending re-building of the Underground. The weather was wet and the day never grew fully light. Final briefings took place at 8 a.m. and the teams dispersed to their positions.

I came down the cut past the Pillars of Hercules and paused in the Square where the beggars were waiting by the railings under the leafless trees. It was London, unmistakably. The second vehicle, dark blue, was a hundred yards away, empty at present.

I banged on the side door of the white van. It slid open and I climbed in. It was just to keep the watchers on their toes. The watchers were always eating, as if their silent confinement brought a danger of starvation which only bacon rolls and pizzas and vile childish sugary drinks could prevent. But they could eat and watch at the same time, which was something. The screens were showing examples of a rather sodden ordinariness, with staff arriving at the department stores, taxis and white vans much like this one impatiently nosing along, their drivers shouting into their headphones. Underfoot, the discarded freesheets were already turning to mush. The watchers, young ex-soldiers with shaved heads and few opinions, were absorbed in their work as in the console games that occupied their free hours.

I climbed out of the van and set off for a look round. You have to walk the ground, in case. Despite the poor weather and the continuing economic crisis, the area was busy as soon as the shops began to open. Christmas was upon us. There was a slightly reckless atmosphere among the crowds, as if being short of funds was in itself a kind of permission or invitation, or incitement, to spend. Oxford Street: the centre of the universe, construed as a shoddy brick-and-marble canyon denatured by the self-consuming commercial imperative that our lifetime has brought to perfection. A grimy hole. A major selection of real estate. Invisible in its familiarity. There is nothing to see, ladies and gentlemen. Move along, please.

As I made my way along and around and inside all this for the umpteenth time, spending the hours slowly, wondering what factor might have gone unconsidered by the planners immured in their cave of numbers, it was, as always, interesting to witness that seasonally intensified combination of liberty and fatalism. The bright-faced resentful wives making the best of things – can they have supposed it would come to this? They who had been desired at squash clubs and swimming pools? And the Chinese students ignoring the whites and waving the big stick of *remnin*: what satisfaction could such an easy conquest afford? Or the girls from other shops and offices let loose with their plastic in the dim noontide of the last shopping day before Christmas: what are we to make of them? What are they for, these screeching twos and threes crammed into the dark, grubby, dim-lit pubs behind the shops, chasing vodka with vodka, comparing their purchases in ever-higher registers of incredulous and unconvincing delight?

They were all, it had been generally accepted, ends in themselves, though it would surprise them were you to put it that way to them, in the unlikely event of your ending up in conversation in a crammed bar, in that sea of fleeting sexual possibility. A grim husband or two, late as usual, stood sinking doubles, their hopeless treasures crammed between their feet. The poor, with no business here, trudged along past the sweaty windows as though given the wrong map. Distraction sought distraction from itself. Some of these people were us, of course, though we never acknowledged each other.

The waves of shoppers formed and broke, narrowing for the escalators in the bigger stores, jostling on the slick steps of Tottenham Court Road Underground, with rain in their hair, with other people's breath and sheer damp bodily pressure too much with them for comfort or good humour. It was what happened instead of life, which was elsewhere or late or unfairly denied them. The clock ticked on.

With an hour to kill I took myself to Foyle's. Disliking the seasonal crush of uninformed blunderers on the lower floors, at first I was unable to settle, but after a time I found an unvisited corner and re-read Kleist's essay 'On the Puppet Theatre'. I realized that I had misunderstood it all those years ago, disfiguring it with my own assumptions. The dance of the marionettes for the entertainment of the common people, observed by Kleist and his companion, a noted professional dancer, there and then in 1810 on the streets of M- (Mainz? Metz?), is more natural than anything the human practitioner of dance can achieve. The marionette is untroubled by gravity, or by the habit of reflection that, since the Fall, has separated us from the world. To regain grace we must travel to the ends of the earth and find a new entry to Paradise. How could I have misunderstood? People are not automata, though to gain salvation they must become so.

I peered down the stairwell at the Christmas crowd.

Morlocks. When the lost grace returns, the dancer concludes, 'it will be most purely present in the human frame that has either no consciousness or an infinite amount of it, which is to say either in a marionette or in a god.' There would only be a few gods, it seemed to me.

Next I sought out the Theology section and a selection of the sermons of Cardinal Newman. The book fell open as though I had marked the passage:

'If Scripture is to be our guide, it is quite plain that the most conscientious, religious, high-principled, honourable men…may be on the side of evil, may be Satan's instruments in cursing, if that were possible, and at least in seducing and enfeebling the people of God.'

There it was, as ever, on its barely-consulted shelf, lost like a treasure-ship in a deep ocean trench; a statement both true and impotent to counter what it proposed. How apt to read it at the very hour when the President knelt in prayer at Westminster Cathedral.

The rain had a reliable, immiserating steadiness as finally I crossed Charing Cross Road and made my way up to the monitoring centre. The citizens looked down, not up. They responded to each other with a combination of irritation and mistrust. But they didn't go home, they didn't get off the streets, they didn't cut their losses. It was growing dark and still more of them arrived as if following a summons. They were doing their economic duty: credit where it's due.

I was in my seat in the observation room in good time. Heads turned expectantly among the rows on screens.

At four-thirty the signal went out. The side streets to the north were discreetly and convincingly blocked. At the exit to Soho Square the two white vans collided and an ambulance approached from the direction of Greek Street. As the smoke and teargas canisters rained down from the roofs, a double police line in riot gear, their ID numbers removed, emerged from Berwick Street. People to the west were pointed back to the junction with Regent Street, and those to the east towards the bottleneck at Tottenham Court underground where the traffic lights had just ceased to work and traffic was at a furious standstill. Fifty covert officers in plain clothes had been seeded in the crowd here, fresh from acting as rioters on a specially built reproduction of this location at the Civil Order Training School near Devizes. Uniformed police now blocked the pedestrian exit from Oxford Street. There had been an incident, people were told. Keep calm and co-operate and walk that way in an orderly fashion.

Surely, you might think, the outcome simply could not be predicted. There was nothing inevitable here. I can quite see why it is necessary to think so. At one time I would have agreed with you. But you would be wrong. This event had been exhaustively gamed. On the bank of screens in the monitoring centre, the crowd in the zone thickened, coughing and half-blind from the gas, herded along by the steadily-advancing police line behind them. The shops were hastily locking their doors while the customers inside peered out at the street, many showing that odd resentment that accompanies incomprehension. It was typical, some of them would certainly be saying. More smoke and gas rained down. There were the beginnings of panic.

When the crowd – two thousand plus – was confined in a space a hundred and fifty yards deep and the width of the street, the plainclothes element went into violent action against those at the front, driving the mass back on itself and in turn bringing the rear of the crowd into collision with the uniformed police line, which responded in kind.

We kept the sound off. Now there was panic. The crowd-mind turned on itself as we had known it would. Fractious families were separated. People fell underfoot, 'for pavement to the abject rear', as the poet has it. Even in the crush people stole from one another. The solidarity displayed was of an impacted, physical kind. People suffocated, crushed against lamp-posts and plate-glass windows while those inside looked on at this unprecedented performance.

But it was not unprecedented: Ibrox, Hillsborough, Burnden Park, the Poll Tax and Occupy disorders, the Love

Parade – all of these were an education, the inferences refined to an exactitude that might be taken for supernatural. This crowd in this place at this time and under these conditions meets with these intensifying constraints and, with a little help, sets about destroying itself. We had done our sums.

The media couldn't get near the place and the CCTV was, they were told, knocked out by some means. Afterwards those able to leave the area had phones and other devices confiscated, while the dead and injured were stripped of their possessions. It was a terrorist incident. Everyone was a suspect until told otherwise.

On the six o'clock news the Commissioner of the Metropolitan Police explained that an investigation on an unprecedented scale was under way and that arrests were already being made.

The Prime Minister addressed the nation at nine o'clock about the Emergency Public Order regulations she was now regretfully compelled to put into effect. Her remarks were preceded by our own footage of the Oxford Street incident, showing the anarchists' unprovoked attacks on the innocent public going about its festive business in the days before what was, lest we forget, a religious festival enshrined in the hearts of the nation. Democracy had to set limits, she said, or risk being drowned in a tide of terrorist bloodshed. Enough was enough, and for the greater good the right of public assembly would become, for a time, discretionary. Those who might object to this, most immediately the organizers and intending participants in a large welfare rights protest planned for New Year, should consider the responsibilities of citizenship and remove their tanks from the nation's lawn. No protest would now be permitted, for reasons evident to all reasonable decent people. I wondered who wrote her material.

In the street below, as the smoke dispersed, were shoes and hats and chain store bags. About a hundred injured and a dozen dead. It was enough. It was enough to tip the balance. The faces at the monitors were grey with anti–climax. I told them to go, but to avoid Soho that evening. Left to myself I began to write up my notes, while looking again at some of the footage. Anyone who saw this – and there'd be very few of them – would be tempted to say it looked like another country, and so it was, and – had they been looking – had been so for a long time. Another England, in almost every detail resembling the place where they thought they lived, to the extent that these faithful consumers thought at all. I could remember the old place. Shame it couldn't last. It seemed long ago. So too by the time I'd finished writing, did the afternoon's events. I would prepare a formal draft of the report the following day.

I took another look at one sequence: I know her, I thought, that fair-haired young woman in the pale raincoat, pinned against the outside of a telephone box as the crush swayed and thickened. She was struggling to do something. Of course: to get her mobile phone out. She couldn't know that the signals were blocked for that hour in the West End. She stared at the phone as if it might come suddenly to life and then raised it over her head. She was trying to photograph what she could see. A hand reached up and took the phone away, and as she turned to protest someone not seen struck her a blow from behind. A momentary gap opened in the startled crowd and she fell into it and disappeared as the mass reformed over her. I know her, I thought. I knew her, the daughter of a colleague with whose wife I had an affair twenty years before. I declined to draw the sentimental inference. There was nothing to be done.

I closed the room and went down to the street. It was deserted, as for the most part was Soho, and I walked for a long time until I found a pub. It was a little subdued, perhaps, but people were in there making the best of not noticing things. A group of young women sat together. The news was on and they watched it with the conspicuous attention of people who want to be thought of as responsible adult citizens but are secretly (they suppose) a bit bored. One by one they turned to their phones. One of them saw me looking. Her expression became sarcastic. What was *I* looking at? I gave the slightest shake of my head, glanced up at the screen for a moment, looked back and continued to stare at her. She had the sense to look away. The fact is, everybody knows, really. Of course they do, gods, puppets and high-minded evildoers such as me. As the Scots say, we know fine.

Afterword:

Bot/Kettle

Prof Martyn Amos
Manchester Metropolitan University

I ONCE CO-AUTHORED a scientific paper[1] that used computer simulations to study the behaviour of a crowd of people evacuating an enclosed space during an emergency (in our case, a nightclub on fire, based on a real-life incident). We used a technique known as *agent-based modelling*, which treats systems as groups of interacting autonomous entities (or agents). By giving each agent in the system a set of simple rules (e.g., walk quickly away from fire, find the nearest exit) and allowing them to move around and communicate in a simulated environment, we investigated the overall system-level behaviour (in our case, the tragic formation of a fatal crush of bodies at the nightclub's exit).

An early version of the paper was picked up by a high-profile technology blog, which wrote a short piece about it[2]. We were quite pleased to see this coverage, until we got to the Comments section at the bottom. One of these started with

'Are people billiard balls?'

It then went on to say 'Truly wonderful progress has been made in recent years in modeling the crowd behavior of billiard balls, noticing that loosely fits human behavior in fires in night clubs and then uncritically applying that to building design. Does that sound sensible to you? Or would

1 Harding, P., Gwynne, S. & Amos, M. (2011) Mutual information for the detection of crush. *PLOS ONE* 6(12): e28747, doi:10.1371/journal.pone.0028747.
2 http://www.technologyreview.com/view/420272/the-problem-of-predicting-crowd-crush/

you rather have some understanding of *why* people behave as they do in certain critical settings?'

Although the author of the comment rather missed the point of our paper, we had to admit that their criticism of the general methodology was pretty much spot-on. That is, our technique for detecting crush (which was the main thrust of the work) was fine in a well-constrained environment, where the agents in the system have very few options. Given the system we were modelling, it was pretty much inevitable that a crush would develop, because the simulated agents were relatively mindless. Or, as our critic put it, '[the authors have] shown conclusively that a bunch of people heading in the same direction will result in a crush. What will Science prove next?'

Of course, in the real world, people generally aren't mindless. As Sean O'Brien makes clear in *Certain Measures*, 'People are not automata'; that is, machines following set rules of behaviour. Rule-following billiard balls, if you like. It used to be the case that 'the crowd' was understood in terms of 'the concepts and assumptions of the natural sciences'[3]; the reductionist ambition, as Drury and Stott explain, was 'the fantasy of a unifying 'life science', whereby the behaviour of human crowds and all other collective phenomena – from bee swarms to social innovations – could be adequately captured by a single set of biologically grounded simple rules.' In *War and Peace*, Tolstoy considers bees, ants and herds as metaphors for human behaviour, but rejects the notion that a reductionist, top-down dissection of the collective can ever yield useful insights. Rather, he 'seemed to suggest a way in which the chaos of individual choices and acts could rationally be subsumed in the more ordered intentions of animals in a swarm'[4]. As Tolstoy himself argues, 'It is beyond the power of the human intellect to encompass *all* the

3. Drury, J. & Stott, C. (2011) Contextualising the crowd in contemporary social science. *Contemporary Social Science* 6(3), 275-288.
4. Miller, R.F. (2010) Tolstoy's peaceable kingdom. In *Anniversary Essays on Tolstoy* (Donna Tussing Orwin, ed.), pp. 52-75, Cambridge University Press.

causes of any phenomenon. But the impulse to search into causes is inherent in man's very nature. And so the human intellect, without investigating the multiplicity and complexity of circumstances conditioning an event, any one of which taken separately may seem to be the reason for it, snatches at the first most comprehensible approximation to a cause and says 'There is the cause'.[5]

'The multiplicity and complexity of circumstances…' In this, Tolstoy anticipates the anti-reductionist, bottom-up study of *emergence*; the process by which large-scale patterns or behaviours form as the result of interactions between smaller entities (or agents), none of whom, in themselves, possess those properties. This *non-essentialist* view – that the *collective* makes history, is an important stance, as it reflects the historical issues with crowd control that O'Brien so deftly subverts.

Around the same time that *War and Peace* first appeared, fear of the 'mob' in post-revolutionary France was one motivating factor behind Haussman's radical redesign of the streets of Paris. As Drury and Stott observe, narrow thoroughfares were replaced with wide-open spaces that gave potential revolutionaries little scope for guerilla tactics. At the same time, 'crowd science' emerged as an attempt to explain the behaviour of massed individuals. The predominant view was that the crowd was inherently 'stupid' and prone to violence and destruction, due to its reliance on instinct and emotional contagion. As Drury and Scott have it, 'That stupidity led to self-defeating behaviour that needed to be suppressed, defeated or controlled if 'civilised' society were to survive'. Unfortunately, the establishment's opinion of the crowd has changed little since the late 19th Century; crowds are still something to be 'controlled'.

But apparently self-defeating behaviour provides a useful scapegoat in the event of tragedy; following the Hillsborough disaster of 1989, the police initially blamed massed football fans for forcing a gate and causing the

5. Leo Tolstoy (2009) *War and Peace*. Penguin edition.

subsequent crush that led to 96 deaths. Several inquiries have since revealed the true cause – a total failure of event management by the police and local authorities.

Of course, as O'Brien observes, 'out-of-control' crowds also have their uses; the moral panic that followed the 1992 Castlemorton free party gave an ideal excuse for the introduction, two years later, of the Criminal Justice and Public Order Act, which was broad enough to allow the government to target not just ravers, but hunt saboteurs, road protestors and squatters. In *Certain Measures*, a Christmas 'riot' is used to justify the introduction of emergency measures, and a crackdown on a New Year welfare rights protest. But in O'Brien's dystopian future, the fatal incident is not merely seized upon by opportunistic politicians, it is *actively engineered*. Those of us who are interested in crowd safety now understand that raw technologies such as agent-based modeling are only useful if they are combined with consideration of group dynamics, psychological factors and risk analysis to *inform* event planning and management. Simulation is but one tool in an over-arching view of crowds that incorporates issues of geography, decision support, training, education, monitoring and so on.[6]

But what if the event in question is intended to fundamentally *undermine* safety, as in O'Brien's story? Here, we see how simulations may be combined with 'real world' interventions in order to generate a tragedy. 'This crowd in this place at this time and under these conditions meets with these intensifying constraints and, with a little help, sets about destroying itself.' In this case, it makes sense to reduce to a minimum the number of variables in the equation. Block the exits, force a crush; the crowd must revert to its reified, 19th century state, a single organism to be goaded and eventually provoked into self-destruction. The crowd once again becomes a fluid mass of insensible particles, left to boil in their kettle until the inevitable explosion occurs.

6. G. Keith Still (2014) *Introduction to Crowd Science*, CRC Press.

Blurred Lines

Julian Gough

YOU HAVEN'T BEEN a popstar. I've been a popstar. Shut up and listen.

Sex and drugs and rock'n'roll...

I have no idea how many women I've fucked. I lost count a couple of months after my first number one.

Fame... makes a man into a reptile...

It destroys your relationships. It destroys you. No; you destroy yourself.

And then it ends. The fame. The hits. The desire.

I got up that morning – well, it wasn't morning, I'd slept all morning. And, you know, 'I got up' is pretty misleading, too. Getting out of bed, that afternoon, was a battle against all the forces of the universe. Gravity was the least of my problems. It took about two hours.

Finally, I made it to the bathroom. Had a crap, showered, brushed my teeth; all that hellish stuff. It seemed to take forever. And it felt so pointless; painting the wreckage of a building that had already burned down.

A spider had woven a web across the kitchen doorway, down to maybe chin height. The *spiderweb* nearly defeated me. I stood staring at it, thinking, what do I do now? I didn't want to just walk through it. The thought of making the spider do all that work again nearly made me cry. Eventually, I ducked under it.

Oh yeah, the dishwasher had stopped working, three weeks earlier.

I stared at the sinkful of washing up for a few minutes, trying to find the energy to deal with it, but nah, didn't happen. I mean everything was in there; the pile reached up to touch the bottom of the cupboard above the sink. It was like a sculpture by Brancusi, those big outdoor ones he did, a pile of shapes that just go up and up.

I made an omelette – unwashed frying pan, old oil, oh boy – and ate for the first time in a day or two… You know the way, normally, anything will taste great after a couple of days without food? Well, this was like pushing wet cardboard into my ear. I mean, nothing. Grey.

OK, I thought. This has got to end.

So I left the flat for the first time in a long while, and I headed for Kensington High Street. I'll spare you the details of *that* trip. Think Napoleon's retreat from Moscow, in tight shoes.

And I went to The Kensington Brain Exchange, which was the one with the big profile and all the big clients. Bear in mind, these are the reeaallllly early days of brain rental. KBE was the only one I'd even heard of. (I'd seen some piece about Chelsea's new manager using it to analyse Bayern Munich, the night before a big Champion's League game. Rented an ex-Bayern player's brain, very controversial. Chelsea had lost anyway, 3-0.)

They made me wait. Didn't recognise me. Nobody recognised me any more. Which was fair enough, I was using my ordinary name. And popstars are 80% attitude anyway. It's the clothes, the stance, the arrogance that you see across the room. Not the face. Crumple the face a little, put it on a broken man who cries at the thought of doing the washing up… there's nothing to recognise.

Eventually, a really nice woman from KBE showed me a classy, retro, paper brochure, and talked to me for a few minutes, and pretended to do a couple of tests, and said no. She was really apologetic, but, no.

I felt like she'd napalmed the ruins of Hiroshima.

'Why?' I said.

She babbled some stuff about parameters, guidelines, most people not being suited to the process, that it could be very destabilising... But I knew that she knew that I knew the real answer.

Because I was a fuckup. Because I stank of desperation and depression.

Because no one in their right mind would want to spend time in my wrong mind.

And it got awkward; I was just sitting there, I had no idea what to do now, I hadn't thought my way past this point, I mean I couldn't, I *could not* just go home and get back into bed oh Jesus; and I think the woman felt sorry for me, because she leaned over and said quietly, 'Why don't you try here?' And she wrote a name and address on the soft, creamy paper of the brochure. In ink, with a pen! Shielding it from the cameras with her body, like a spy in a movie.

So I said thanks, and walked outside, and I looked at the neat, inked words. 'RentaBrain.' An address in the East End.

Well, where else was I going to go? *Home?*

★

It was a shabby little place, you could see it had once been a taxi office, back when people drove taxis.

They didn't even bother doing tests. I sat down in a room at the back, with a guy who talked to me for a few minutes, nodding at everything I said. I think he was Greek – handsome, dark, stubbly – but with a Walthamstow accent you could have used to clean drains. He nodded especially hard when I said I slept all day, most days.

Finally he stood up and said, 'Everything seems in order.' In order? Jesus. OK.

He got me to sign the forms; retina, fingerprints, the lot. All very official. I didn't even bother to read past the first line.

'I think we have the perfect client for you,' he said. 'She's a mathematician—'

'Wait, I thought you didn't rent across gender? The woman at Kensington Brain Exchange said...' I tried to remember what she had said.

He smiled. 'Some of our rivals do not.' He put his finger tips together and looked up, like a priest checking to see if God was listening. Or GCHQ. 'But we believe that, under the European Human Rights Act, it is illegal to discriminate in this market on grounds of gender.' He collapsed the steeple of his fingertips. 'There hasn't been a formal regulatory decision yet, so it's up to each agency to decide.'

A woman.

In my head.

He studied my face, and said 'You won't remember anything. The system clears out all traces of her before you wake up. It'll be like she was never there.'

I nodded. 'So... what do I do now?'

'We'll fit you here. Inform the client. And then you can just... go home to bed.'

★

The doctor was a gruff woman, from Croatia, I think. It wasn't a complicated business. All the complicated work had already been done, in the design of the implants.

Yeah, implants. This is before Focused Induction Firing, all that. They still had to make physical connections. That far back.

They were tiny, like baby sea anemones; she showed me a sample one in a glass of water, swirled it; the short little optical fibres swayed back and forth, almost invisibly thin. Too thin to focus on; the tens of thousands of fibres just formed a small cloudy area in the water, that shimmered slightly, a mess of rainbows.

She put down the glass.

Tilted me back in the chair. 'Local anaesthetic,' she said. 'Don't blink.'

I blinked.

She sighed. Took a dropper. Dripped an eye drop into my right eye. Except she didn't, because I blinked again as it came at me, and my eyelashes smacked it like a tennis racquet, and it slid away, down my cheek, like a tear.

She sighed again, a very tired sigh. Reached out to me, and held my eyelid open with her thumb. Her hand was cool, and I sighed back, I couldn't help it. I hadn't touched a woman, been touched, since Simone had left. Even Simone couldn't save me. The day she'd left me, I'd reactivated all my old accounts, matched with so many women it was silly. Even messaged a few, chatted, jerked off. And I hadn't met up with one of them.

I realised − a jolt of dull shock − that the doctor was a real woman, in the same room. Also, gorgeous. I reached into the darkness inside of me, looking for words. I wanted to flirt, be clever, witty; but I didn't have the energy.

'So, are you from Dubrovnik?' I said.

She carefully placed a drop right in the centre of my eye. Splash… she blurred above me.

'Zagreb,' she said.

She did the other eye.

I had stories about Dubrovnik, because I'd played a gig in Dubrovnik. Fucked two sisters after the show, back in their flat in the old city. Well, fucked the more insistent of the two, with a semi, keeping it in with my thumb, then fallen asleep. Probably wouldn't tell her that story. Big dark cool rooms, a hungry cat howling outside a shuttered window, thick walls cracked from an earthquake. But I'd never been to Zagreb. Thinking up a sentence about Zagreb was too much. Talking to people was too much. Life was too much.

Her hips brushed against the arm of my chair as she passed. Not her hips. Her mons.

If I left my hand on the arm of the chair maybe she'd brush against my hand.

Maybe she'd recognised me.

Maybe something would happen.

She talked while she cleaned the surfaces, washed her hands and forearms, put on gloves. Moved carefully around my casual hand. 'OK,' she said, sing-song, 'under EU Directive 36-24-555C, to ensure informed consent I am required to inform you.' I tuned out. Tuned back in again when she said, 'we're going to use the rods, so...'

I glanced at the tray she was swinging into place over my lap.

No rods. Tiny tools. A glass container. Plastic sachets.

'Pardon?' I said.

'The *rods*,' she said. 'The nerves in the retina optimised for very low light. You remember this stuff, from Greg's intro, no?'

Oh, the Greek guy. No, I hadn't been listening. I shook my head. She blew air out her nose, and I felt it chill my eyeballs, as the jet of air speeded up the evaporation of the liquid. I tried to blink. Couldn't. 'Rods? Cones?' she said. 'You know this from school? No? They teach this in England, no?'

'I wasn't great at biology.'

Distracted by the teacher, who was young, and female, and French. Oh, Emilie. I never heard a word she said, over the roar of my hormones, the thunder of my blood.

'Cones are the cells in the retina...'

'Um,' I said.

'...you know what the retina is?'

She continued to assemble the torture implements. I nodded at her passing breasts.

'OK. The cones handle bright light. They see in colour, and fill the centre of our vision, where we focus. Rods just see in black and white—'

'— so they're basically digital already,' I said, trying to be clever. 'Black/white, off/on...'

'Yes,' she said. 'Rods mostly control peripheral vision, and night vision...'

'...And who cares about that,' I said.

'True.' She smiled. 'They evolved for seeing... leopards,

approaching by moonlight.' She grimaced at her own poetry. 'Most of the rods are no use, now that we have electric light, and houses. So, they're available...'

Her breasts came very close. Nothing happened in my lap, but I still felt a thump of desire. Go away. I closed my eyes. I wanted her. I hated her for making me want her. No, she hadn't done anything, this was all in my head. I was just reacting to surfaces. To light bouncing off surfaces. I wanted, I wanted... what did I want?

I was so tired of desire.

She opened the sterile double-packs containing the two fresh implants. They were still folded up tight, like ridiculously small umbrellas for the world's tiniest dolls.

'Vietnamese,' she said. 'Just as good as the German ones, and a third the price.'

She strapped my head firmly to the headrest. Soft, black, slightly rubbery straps. That smell. Mmm, memories... I glanced across at her breasts. She tilted the chair further back till I was looking at the ceiling.

'Hold still,' she said.

I didn't have much option.

The bulky needle came closer and closer to my eye, until I could no longer focus on the tip. It disappeared, off to the side of my pupil.

I concentrated on a spider, hanging from the light fitting directly above me.

I felt the pressure of the needle against the side of my eyeball for a second, before the tip slid through the thick rubbery surface, and into the transparent goo inside. No nerves there, thank Christ.

She pushed the plunger slowly, and injected the first implant into my left eyeball, which wasn't the high point of my day, but I felt so shit anyway that even this could hardly spoil it.

She withdrew the needle, picked up a thin, silver can, and sprayed something misty on the spot the needle had just left. Cold. I didn't blink, because I couldn't.

She shone a bright light on my retina, through my frozen pupil. Had a good look inside my eyeball.

'Good,' she said. Switched off the bright light.

Switched on the tiny probe, with a remote.

I felt something happening inside my eyeball. I didn't feel it like you'd feel something happening on your skin; I felt it with the nerves of my retina, as flashes of light.

The light was all off to one side.

'You should be seeing light,' she said.

'Yes.'

'Dots, specks, spots, something like that?'

'Yes. But it's all over here.' I gestured to my left.

'Good,' she said. 'We don't want to interfere with your central vision, do we?'

'Fucking hell,' I said. 'Sorry. This is weird.'

She shrugged. 'Each optical fibre is tipped with a nano-material that's attracted to proteins on the surface of the rods.' Sing–song, brochure-speak. 'When a fibre touches a rod, they bond. You'll feel each contact – each bonding – as a flash of light.' She shrugged again. 'That's just how your brain currently interprets any signal from a rod.' She picked up another dropper. Yellowish liquid. 'We'll fix that in stage two.' Brought it closer to my open eye.

'What's that?' I said.

'Muscle relaxant,' she said. 'I had to paralyse your eyelids, so you wouldn't blink during the procedure. This counteracts it…' For a second there was a buttery yellow smear in the centre of my vision; it melted across the surface of my eye, into the corners, vanished. Another drop, in my other eye. 'OK,' she said. 'You should be able to blink again.'

I closed my eyes. Wow. The flashes…

It was like a firework display that kept going whether my eyes were open or closed.

Eventually the bright, tight, sudden lights settled down into a weird rhythm, then stopped, all but the odd isolated flash.

'So, they're connected,' said the Croatian doctor. 'And now we rewire your brain so the inputs aren't just talking to your visual cortex. The robodoc will place the stem cells, and the regrowth accelerator… you'll be unconscious for several hours.'

Unconscious was OK by me.

When I woke up…

The doctor leaned over me, looking tired. Of course, five hours later, six? Long day.

And I could feel my brain changing.

'Welcome back,' she said. 'Let's see if we've broken anything…'

I nodded, so lost in the sensations that I hardly spoke as the doctor ran the diagnostics. She sent signals through the inputs, down the new neural paths.

They arrived in cascades of light; waves, circles. Patterns… Lights that felt like…sounds? Rhythms. I could feel them, like fingers gently caressing me. Lights that triggered tastes; mint. Blood. Lights that triggered memories.

Lying in a pool of sunlight, blissed out, age maybe five, the sun hot and orange through my eyelids, the warm, dusty smell of my bedroom carpet.

Head down, total concentration, drawing Daleks in my maths book. The harsh metal school bell rings, and I jump, ruin the drawing.

The cascades died away. Darkness. Silence.

She ran another test. They started up again.

'The new connections will settle down over the next couple of days,' she said. 'You won't see lights, just feel the feeling, have the thought, recreate the memory, whatever.'

'OK,' I said, lost inside the sensations. 'OK.'

When it was done I was so tired I wondered would I have the energy to go home. But I wasn't quite as depressed; there was something about making a decision, about doing something, that in itself felt good. Despite the discomfort. The exhaustion.

And there was the prospect that very soon I wouldn't have to be in charge of my brain all the time. Putting up with its bullshit.

'Congratulations,' she said, studying a screenload of test results. 'We're done. If you have any unexpected flashing, call me straight away.'

'When will... the client, need my brain?'

'We'll be in touch. But soon, I would imagine.' The doctor dropped out of her stern official persona, like someone shrugging off a coat, grinned, and suddenly her accent was pure Walthamstow. 'She seemed in a hell of a hurry.'

★

I travelled home and went to bed and slept, and slept, and slept.

★

Early days of the system, remember. Melding was uncommon; nobody had really worked out the protocols. They gave me 48 hours to let the accelerated stem cells finish growing the new neural circuits.

And to acclimatise to the implants, make sure there was no allergic reaction. The implants had sympathetic, neutral nano-surfaces, of course, which didn't trigger rejection, but there had been very rare cases of hypersensitivity. Two guys went blind. A woman died. It had been all over the news.

I slept badly that night. As usual. Woke up tired, jumpy, nervous. I kept rubbing my eyes, even though they weren't really sore. Got up, ate, went back to bed. Masturbated to some porn, with a storyline so cliched I fell asleep before I could come. Napped. Nightmares.

The client was sent details of my sleep cycle, live, automatically.

I wondered what she made of all my naps.

I could also, if I wished, send her messages, in advance, on when I planned to sleep; but I wasn't required to do this, and I didn't.

The second day dragged by. I had strange thoughts, random memories, mood swings, triggered by the new neural growth. Mostly more of the same old. Anxiety, bad memories.

It was OK.

I'd done a lot of serious drugs, back in the day. This was nothing.

On the fourth evening, I got my first message from her. Opened it, startled to see my hand was trembling.

Oh. Just a form – the space for a personal note left blank – requesting permission to borrow, during my next downtime. I ticked yes.

I indicated the approximate time I thought my sleep might commence.

And suddenly it was real, the deadline approached; the hour I had said I would start to sleep. Sleep for her, instead of me. I wasn't legally obliged to go to sleep then; there were a lot of consumer protection rules, everything, despite the contract's formidable length, was essentially voluntary, I could walk away at any time…

But…

It loomed up like a black wall, like a sandstorm coming slowly towards me.

Someone was going to be using my brain. Someone who wasn't me.

It hadn't felt real before. Now it did.

Someone else thinking with my brain.

I was scared, but I wasn't scared. Better to say, maybe, that I was… deliciously scared. I was scared of something that I also desperately wanted.

Because if someone else was thinking with my brain, then I was *not* thinking with my brain.

Then I was not thinking.

Oh, please, that, yes.

★

I went to bed, and to my surprise, once the duvet was over me and my head was on the pillow, I wasn't restless, I wasn't overexcited, I wasn't nervous. I just turned out the light, closed my eyes, and watched all my normal, anxious, exhausted thoughts flutter round the inside of my head, doing loops and circuits endlessly like birds trying to find a window in a room without a window, until I fell asleep.

★

And then I wasn't asleep and I wasn't awake and I wasn't… me.

There was light. There was a sense of something very big, in the distance. A sense that part of me, the most important part of me, was very far away, but connected, connected down a narrow tunnel.

And I was that person very far away; but I was also here, I was only here. And I was exploring; and I was surprised; and I was… blurring… and I was…

I was a woman called Jane.

I knew a lot about n-dimensional mathematics.

I was in Cairo.

I was… delighted. Exploring.

★

When I woke up… something felt… wrong.

I had new memories, but they weren't…

They weren't mine.

I had been working, no, she had been working on a subtle problem involving fractal processes not in geometry, but time. Trying to solve the problem the way humans solve most problems; using pattern recognition. And I, she, we'd found new patterns. Solved it. But some links had formed between her memories and my own.

Now, cut off from her, I had my half of the eureka moment; but not the half in her brain. I ached for it. It was like hunger, worse than hunger. Half of me was missing.

186

They, the system, the implants, should have cleared all that out, should have cleaned up after her session. I shouldn't have this feeling, these thoughts, half-thoughts. Half-memories.

And... oh wow. They weren't all memories from last night. Weren't all mathematics.

She had been in London, years ago. She had fed the ducks in Regents Park. She had been happy, then.

And I saw... felt, remembered... not her face, not her body, but her, her self, who she was; what it felt like to be her; and my heart stirred. Not my cock. My heart.

I knew that I should contact RentaBrain straight away. There had been a case like this before, it was on all the junk TV shows. A man, a criminal, had his mind filled with a woman's memories, in an experiment in Russia while they were developing the technology. But there had been international uproar at the violation of his rights, and the scientists had removed the memories. Restored him to how he was before.

A few days later, he had killed himself.

I thought about that. Didn't contact RentaBrain.

I cleaned the flat. Got rid of the spider webs. Put the spider out on the windowsill.

Did the washing up.

★

The next day, I had a new dishwasher installed.

The next night, she came back, and thought some more.

And I woke up full of memories. More vivid than the night before. A lot of mathematics. But also... I frowned.

Images of my mother; Regents Park; green trees.

Me kicking a football, a dog barking; a memory of smell, of heat, the taste of an ice-cream.

A warm memory. Comforting.

But I hadn't grown up in London. Only moved there as

a teenager. Had never been in Regents Park with my mother.

I looked closer at the memory; my mother was wearing a dress she didn't own till I was grown up.

The dog was my grandfather's whippet, from outside Glasgow. That dog, too, had never been in Regents Park.

The bark didn't match the dog.

The trees were shading me, and yet I was in the sun at the same time.

It wasn't my memory, it was hers, triggered when she remembered I lived in London.

Memories aren't stored entire. They are compressed, as tags, and reassembled from stock parts when needed.

Assembling her memory of a perfect summer's day with her mother, from her compressed tags, she had drawn on the stored memories in my brain.

My mother and I, lying on a warm wool blanket in the sun, happy.

My mother and I walking down to the pond, feeding the ducks.

Jane's memories of things which had never happened to me.

But now they were my memories, indistinguishable from memories of my own childhood. Except perhaps for one thing.

They were much happier than mine.

She was rewriting my memories. Replacing them with her own.

★

The next night it happened again.

She came in hard, full of energy, focused on the mathematics.

But, as the night ended, digging deeper into my mind, using more of me, she accidentally triggered memories of my own; experienced them as hers. Strong memories, close to my surface.

Memories I used each night, to get off. They began to cascade, each setting off the next. Sex, with Simone. With Simone and another girl. With a Cuban woman I met in New York on our first tour, who did things with her internal muscles that were quite astonishing.

They shocked Jane.

Jolted her back to a boyfriend – her only boyfriend? A cousin? – to their first night alone together, in her parents' bedroom – they were away – the heavy furniture, the big mirrors. I glimpsed her.

My God, she was gorgeous.

She become lost in memories for a while. A debacle, a disaster, an embarrassment. And then… Oh Jane. Poor Jane. I wept in my sleep as she wept.

And she felt me weeping.

She cut the connection so abruptly I woke up, my face wet.

★

The fourth night, she explored my mind for the first time as though it were my mind, not just a tool she had hired. Before, she had slammed through it impatiently, looking for something she could use, using mostly the analytic functions; when she set off a stray memory of mine, or an association that wasn't directly useful, she was impatient and annoyed. Now, she began to set off my memories deliberately, cautiously, respectfully.

Memories of me swimming; very like her own. She moved on.

Memories of my youth, on stage, in the band.

She explored.

A great gig we did in Paris; the crowd at first resisting, conserving their energy for the headliners; and then the intro to the third song, a strong song (we should have started with it, too late now; change the setlist for tomorrow night); delivered hard, with total confidence, my voice good, warmed up now, and the band tight. It catches the attention of the front row;

they stop chatting among themselves, turn to face the stage; start to move, to sway; and the energy begins to move back, a row at a time, until on the final chorus it reaches the back of the hall, and we have them; they have us; the crowd is part of the band. It's a strong, simple chorus, and we repeat it spontaneously, we don't want the song to end and neither do they; the hall is one huge, throbbing organism. My ego has vanished, I am the crowd, and the crowd is singing. The band feed them energy, and they feed it back to us. We are a superorganism. She lingers on this memory, its energy, my young body in movement under the light.

Memories of me with Simone, fighting after the show, because I'd fingered some girl in the front row. Later, an angry hotel fuck.

She backs off, again. That's enough for one night.

She goes back to mathematics.

★

The next night, she explored my body. She tried to move my legs, flex my knees, but I was too deep asleep; my brain had closed those links down for the night. She went deeper into my brain then, down into the brainstem. Strange images, strange feelings stirred as she dug deeper. Primal fears. She groped about for control of my body; it was hard, she wasn't particularly in touch with her own.

At last she found it, and bent my knees, flexed my ankles. They moved for real, in my bed, under my duvet, and there was a feedback surge, back and forth along the lines that linked us, as she kicked my legs, and thrilled with glee.

She kicked too hard, the duvet fell off, and I was cold, she was cold, we were cold, too cold, and she tried to control my arms, to pull the duvet back onto me before I woke up, but it was too late, I was waking up, and there was a terrible tangle of commands, and I spasmed as she and I fought for my limbs, and then she was gone, I'd passed the waking threshold and triggered the cutoff; the link was shut down automatically, and I was lying twitching, naked in my bed, cold, with an erection.

I reached out for the duvet on the floor, pulled it back over me, kicked it into place. At each kick I felt glee, her glee, her association burned into my neurons.

I didn't mind.

I felt something wild swirl in me, something half hers, half mine. Her parting blast, as she was cut off, not quite processed, not quite formed, something that came out of the tangle of our thoughts as I came back to my brain and she left.

I felt love.

Mine? Hers? For her? For me? For my legs, my body? For being alive at all?

It was a big mess. I lay in bed laughing.

★

I was able to leave the house now. I found I liked sunshine, I liked the movement of the air outside, I liked the movement of the people on the pavements. All the things I had hated and feared.

I found I was walking everywhere, across London, for no particular reason. Looking up at the trees, stopping to dip my toe into puddles, sending up a little splash, laughing with pleasure. With pleasure.

Walking for miles, in the sunshine, on the surface of the earth, I realised for the first time how close together some of the underground stations were.

And how far apart others.

One day, I had walked as far as Regents Park, before I realised I had found everything strange and new on the walk; the shops, the signs, the faces of the people. I thought at first that it was because I usually came here by tube, but it wasn't that.

The memories I had used to get there weren't recent, weren't mine. They were vivid, partial, out of date. Low to the ground. A child's.

They were hers.

★

I walked home by way of the British Museum. Memories stirred. Mine, or hers? I walked to the Egyptian section. Stared at the mummies. The preserved bodies of men and women, dead for two, three thousand years. I stared at the brown skin.

She was Egyptian. Jane. An English name, misleading. Her father had been an Anglophile. Yes.

Had she asked me to come here? I no longer knew where my impulses came from; whether my decisions were being triggered by my own desires, or hers, left behind in the unerased traces of her thoughts from the night before.

Where is her physical body? I thought. Where is it now?

And I realised I had never seen her room; her life, now: She worked with her eyes closed. Concentrating on mathematics, and old memories.

I panicked; perhaps she was married, perhaps she had a child, children. I needed to see her face, her room, her life, now.

★

Singing in a band, you can live a very primitive life. Primal. You don't have to behave, you don't have to be polite, you don't have to control your emotions or suppress your desires. You can reach out and take. Often you don't even need to reach out. It all comes to you. If you're the singer in a good band, on a good night, women will throw themselves at you; and not metaphorically. They will pull you off the stage, slam into you, kiss you, grab for your cock from the middle of the throbbing crowd. You are an incarnation of Dionysus; you run the risk of being torn apart by the Furies, but meanwhile the sex is amazing. I had made love to – fucked, if you prefer – a lot of women, but I'd had hardly any relationships. I had no idea how to relate to Jane.

She existed simultaneously at all ages for me, as she did for herself. As I did for myself. Her memories of the deep past, of her childhood, young womanhood, were as vivid — were more vivid — than her memories of the day before yesterday.

She lived in her mind, in her thoughts, in mathematics; she almost never had a thought that took place in her own body, that was aware of her own situation.

I will ask her where she is, I thought. But how?

She will think about fractal geometries at some point tonight. She always does. I will connect that thought, my question, to fractal geometry. I will create an association.

Mandelbrot sets, I thought. *Where am I?* Complex number fractals. *Look around.* Non-integer dimensions. *Look out the window.*

I looped the thoughts around and around, till I felt the associations were automatic.

I deliberately cleared my head. Walked on, to Room 18, and the sculptures stripped from the shattered Parthenon. Paused at the statue of Dionysus. Moved on to the centaurs. Half animal, half man...

Mandelbrot sets, I thought, and suddenly I was looking around, at the soft, biscuity sandstone walls; the murmuring tourists; and up, to the lights in the high ceiling, looking for windows... it worked.

I went to bed early.

*

That night, she entered my mind late, near dawn. I had passed through the deep sleep of the first few hours, and was in second sleep, the lighter, shallower phase. She came in hard, anxious, and almost woke me. So much energy.

She started on math straight away, hammering into a theory, testing it, exploring it, angry. What you need, sometimes, in solving a problem, is a new angle on it, new associations. She was using mine. Throwing ideas around, and chasing my associations.

Then she tried a fractal approach, using non-integer dimensions; and triggered my association, *look around,* and her chain of thought broke, and suddenly she was in her body, in her chair, in the startled moment, looking around her room, *look out the window,* and I could see Cairo.

Her windows went from floor to ceiling. Immense shutters, but they were thrown open.

I had imagined her in some dim, huge room, all stone columns and wood panels, like the original rooms of the British Museum, but it was a modern apartment; lots of glass; mirrors.

And I saw her seeing herself.

I didn't know I was seeing her at first.

Not a chair.

A wheelchair.

Not a girl.

An old, old woman.

As she stared at herself for the first time in years, I stared at her through her startled eyes. An old woman, who felt young and fierce, in a wheelchair, near death.

And I realised, she doesn't burn with the energy of youth. She burns with the knowledge she is running out of time.

A woman who knows me better, deeper, than anyone has ever known me. And who somehow, despite that... My God, she really loves me.

Loves me.

And I felt a surge of love for her, in return, that filled my body and my mind. It just blasted through me, lit up every cell, like the time I grabbed a live mike in a rainstorm at a festival outside Stuttgart.

A surge of love so strong that it reset our connections: reversed the flow.

And now the channel was leaking both ways. She saw me seeing her. She felt me feel her shock at seeing herself. And being seen.

And I felt what she felt, the channels were wide open.

Overwhelming fear.

She felt the certainty of rejection, my rejection.

The nearness of death.

The final end of love.

But simultaneously, I felt what I felt, and sent it to her, along the channel. No, not rejection. How could half the apple reject its other half? And as I felt it, she felt my helpless love, for her essence. Her soul. For the little girl, the young woman, the mature woman, for her, now, near death.

For the pattern that held them all together, made them one.

Her essence. Her soul.

She would be dead soon, and her soul released from its cell. Her tightly woven pattern would unravel. Her atoms scatter.

I wasn't sure how I'd get past that. To be alone again. Half an apple. And she felt my fear, and matched it.

But that would not happen today. I looked out her window, through her eyes, up, at the blue sky.

I love you, I said. Exactly as you are.

★

Slowly, as the days and nights went by, we connected our nervous systems. We went into the software, the firmware, the hardware, the wetware, and we removed the filters. Strengthened the connections. It's amazing what you can learn, what you can do, when you're driven by love.

We became one thing.

And one morning, when I, she, we woke, we were still connected.

It had not cut off.

The system could no longer tell if we were awake or asleep. Awake or dreaming.

I was her, in Cairo, and she was me, in London.

I gave her control of my hands.

She gave me control of hers.

She explored my body with my hands.

I explored her body with her hands.

She felt my pleasure and I felt hers.

The channel sent pleasure in both directions.

I was, we were, a woman and a man. Old and young.

We were mingled.

I blurred into we.

We were on both sides of the pleasure exchange.

There was nowhere where we were not.

We blurred as we came, so that neither knew where the pleasure came from, it came from both of us, it came from everywhere.

What is the greatest pleasure?

To know; and to be known.

To not be alone.

Plato's apple was whole.

*

There were messages on all my machines.

Not from the local RentaBrain office. From the head office in Moscow.

They wanted to take back the units. Repair them. There had been a recall order.

I told them my units were working fine. They told me I had to come in anyway. This was a total product recall. And they were particularly concerned about mine.

I refused.

They got angry with me. *'You have been communicating with the client, outside of the normal channels. You are in breach of the terms of service…'*

I told them that was quite true, but I still was not going to come in for the recall.

I stopped answering their messages.

They threatened to close Jane's account. Like Zeus, they wished to slice the apple in two; leave us as severed halves, each alone.

Jane and I talked about what we were going to do.

Jane kept paying RentaBrain's fees – no point alienating

them – but we quietly moved everything to our own servers, disengaged from their network – just sent it a copy of the feed – so they couldn't block her account.

★

I went into RentaBrain, in Walthamstow.

I told the doctor everything.

The lack of memory clean-up. The leaks. The blurring of self.

'So,' said the doctor. 'You want to take the connections out.'

'No,' I said, 'I want to put in more.'

She laughed. 'It can't be done,' she said. 'All those units are being recalled. I'm only doing removals.'

'I want to hire you in a private capacity,' I said, and handed her the bribe. There was still some money left, from my days as Dionysus. Enough.

'How many?' she said.

I told her.

'That many new connections…' She sucked in a breath. 'You'll have almost no peripheral vision left.'

I shrugged.

'You'll lose your driver's licence…'

'I don't drive,' I said.

'Look, I don't think you understand. If we tap into that many rods… the visual effect is like having severe glaucoma. It'll give you tunnel vision, basically.'

'I don't care,' I said.

'And she… the client would have to do the same…'

'She's having it done tonight, in Cairo,' I said, and smiled. 'We are of one mind about this.'

★

After the doctor inserted the new connections, it was true, my field of vision narrowed.

But inside, ah! My narrow heart had opened up, I stretched out endlessly.

Deepening the channel deepened other things too.

Oh Jane. Such a stern exterior. The creased, brown face, hunched in the metal and plastic chair. But I was behind the facade, in the warehouse of memories. With the little girl who fed the ducks. With the young woman who had been raped by her cousin. With the weeping mathematician. With the smiling cook. With the serious dancer.

With everywomen.

A universe of her.

One day we both realised that we hadn't thought the word 'I' in a long time.

And then we realised something else.

The thought started on Jane's side, as a startled 'I' thought; but it was echoed and endorsed from my side immediately, so that the two thoughts blurred into one.

We're married.

We are one.

A superorganism.

Each feeding energy to the other.

We had all the windows open, in Cairo and London, it was spring.

A song was playing out the window of the upstairs flat, whose flat, it didn't matter…

Lola… Luh-Luh-Luh-Luh-Lola… And I looked at her and she at me…

It's a mixed-up, muddled-up shook up world, except for Lola.

OK. We'll call ourself Lola, we thought.

A marriage of convenience?

A marriage of minds.

But I'm old; I'm going to die, she thought, we thought. And I thought, we thought: how long do you need to know love; to love; to be loved? It always ends: one dies, and then the other. The apple will be cut in two, by time.

So what.

I love; I am loved. You love; you are loved.

We love.

We are in paradise.

This moment is eternal.

Let's go for a walk.

Let's.

London or Cairo?

Smog in Cairo. And riots.

London then.

I reached with one of my hands; she reached with the other.

We held hands, in our shared body.

We went to Regent's Park, hand in hand, sharing one heart, and fed the ducks.

Afterword:

Neuroscience and Beyond

Dr Germán Terrazas
University of Nottingham

STUDYING THE HUMAN brain dates as far as 4000 BC when the euphoric effects of poppy plants were recorded in the Sumerian records. Hippocrates, Plato, Herophilus and Aristotle all had something to say about mental processes, and the insights have since been gleaned from philosophy, anatomy, evolutionary biology, psychology, and psychiatry to lay the groundwork for what we now call neuroscience. For me, personally, it was a couple of science fiction films that got me hooked. The first was *The Matrix*, in which Keanu Reeves' brain was plugged into a machine that transported his mind to a simulated reality (a filmic expression of Descartes' scepticism or Plato's Parable of the Cave, if ever there was one). The second was *Source Code* where the brain of a veteran sergeant was used as a platform for running algorithms specially designed to uncover a terrorist plot in Chicago. The technological principles behind these two films explore the idea of using the human brain as a device to execute computer programs, just as your iPad or smartphone does, just as a biological computing machine might do in the future. Putting ethics aside for one moment, such an idea could provide the framework for a new era in the evolution of computing.

The human brain is probably the most complex biological system ever studied. Neuroscience research is continually throwing up surprises, rewriting our understanding of what is possible on an almost monthly basis. For our purposes, I will focus on just one area of this research, that relating to information processing. In April 2013, President Obama launched the Brain Research through Advancing Innovative Neurotechnologies (BRAIN) initiative, a $300 million, collaborative project that set itself the goal of mapping of the activity of every single neuron in the human brain, within ten years. Similar to the Human Genome Project of the 1990s, this is undoubtedly the most ambitious neuroscience project to date, and promises to set down a roadmap for uncovering the architecture and dynamics of the world's most complex information processing bio-machine.

While we wait to read the headlines resulting from this work, other exciting developments have been witnessed in brain computer interface (BCI) research. For instance, novel technologies are currently being put together in the Brain Science Institute-Toyota Collaboration Centre in order to develop 'thought-controlling' technology which will enable us to command external devices directly through thought[1]. This is basically done by using a brainwave-reading skullcap (a.k.a. an electroencephalogram) to detect specific brain signals which once decoded are transferred as simple command signals to external hardware or software. The implications are enormous: thought-controlling could soon transform medical rehabilitation and be used to support those with motor deficits. This is the ultimate goal of the cross-disciplinary teams of engineers and medical practitioners currently working on navigable wheelchairs: to bring autonomy and contextual engagement to those who have lost the ability to move or speak. Similar research is being carried out by a team at the Swiss Federal Institute of Technology (EPFL). In this case, the wheelchair is equipped with cameras which collect and process visual information in order to inform and complement the user's decision making. Although current research revolves around wearable technology, thought-controlling technology could soon be applied to other devices, such as computers, video games, smartphones, or even cars.

1. F. Galán, M. Nuttin, E. Lew, P.W. Ferrez, G. Vanacker, J. Philips, J.dR. Millán, A brain-actuated wheelchair: Asynchronous and non-invasive brain-computer interfaces for continuous control of robots. Clinical Neurophysiology 119(9):2159-2169, 2008.

Neurobiology and neurotechnology are also uncovering how the brain processes information through the analysis and exploitation of brain signatures. As we mature, our experiences, skills, memories, reactions, personality and other traits are all encoded into wave patterns of specific types and strengths. Reading and processing such patterns is the principle tool behind 'awareness detection' with patients trapped in persistent vegetative states. It was British neuroscientist Adrian Owen who first showed that patients previously thought to be unconscious are actually aware of themselves and their surroundings[2]. This discovery – which collected fMRI scans from patients exposed to pre-recorded spoken messages – was a game changer, both ethically and clinically. These scanned images cast new light on brain activation configurations and showed them to be extremely similar to those observed in healthy volunteers. Not only did it prove that patients in persistent vegetative states could be conscious, more importantly, it offered new channels for potential communication with loved ones. More recently, the algorithmic processing of brain activity has been employed to train volunteers to associate certain brain patterns with emotional feelings[3]. In this case, volunteers were subjected to fMRI scanning and received real-time information of their ongoing neural activity which, as a result, positively influenced brain network functions related to tenderness and affection. These findings are expected to have a huge impact on the way we approach mental conditions associated with reduced empathy and antisocial personality disorders.

Both thought-controlling and brain activity analysis

2. D. Fernández-Espejo, T. Bekinschtein, M.M. Monti, J.D. Pickard, C. Junque, M.R. Coleman, A.M. Owen. Diffusion weighted imaging distinguishes the vegetative state from the minimally conscious state. NeuroImage 54(1):103-112, 2011.
3. J. Moll, J.H. Weingartner, P. Bado, R. Basilio, J.R. Sato, B.R. Melo, I.E. Bramati, R. Oliveira-Souza, R. Zahn, Voluntary Enhancement of Neural Signatures of Affiliative Emotion Using fMRI Neurofeedback. PLoS ONE 9(5): e97343, 2014.

have specific processes in common: the capturing, decoding, transporting and interpretation of brain signals in order to communicate information to the external world. However, the brain-to-brain communication of Julian's story takes things one step further.

Spurred by rapid advances in technology, brain-to-brain communication has been achieved spectacularly in the last couple of years. Firstly, when a rat located in Brazil managed to *send a thought* to a fellow rat in the US[4]. In this experiment, arrays of microelectrodes were inserted into that part of the rat brain in charge of processing motor information. Thus, the rat in Brazil (the 'encoder') received a visual clue (from its real world surroundings) indicating which lever to press in exchange for a reward. The motor information from the encoder was captured and transmitted via the internet thousands of miles. When this information arrived, it was translated into a pattern of electrical stimulation and delivered into the brain of the second rodent (the 'decoder'). The decoder was facing exactly the same type of levers and deciding which one to press was entirely subject to the transmitted signal. Such results demonstrate that rat brains are able to assimilate information input coming not only from artificial sensors, but also from a different brain. Since this breakthrough, direct communication between *human* brains has also been achieved. In this study, a researcher from the University of Washington was able to control the hand movements of a colleague sat in a different office across campus via the internet[5]. Hooked up to an EEG machine, one of the researchers was facing a computer game and imagined moving his hand to trigger an action. This brain activity was captured and transmitted to the second researcher

4. M. Pais-Vieira, M. Lebedev, C. Kunicki, J. Wang and M.A.L. Nicolelis, A Brain-to-Brain Interface for Real-Time Sharing of Sensorimotor Information. Nature Scientific Reports 3;1319, 2013.
5. R. Rao, A. Stocco, M. Bryan, D. Sarma, T.M. Youngquist, J. Wu, C. Prat, A Direct Brain-to-Brain Interface in Humans. Technical Report UW-CSE-14-07-01, Computer Science and Engineering, University of Washington, 2014.

who was wearing a transcranial magnetic stimulation coil placed over his left motor cortex. When the information arrived, he involuntarily pressed the spacebar on the keyboard placed in front of his right index finger. Although the technology remains in a very embryonic stage, with this last experiment we are witnessing the first few steps towards telepathy. Another step was taken by StarLab recently when it demonstrated that two individuals located in India and France were able to *have a chat* with one another[6]. In such an experiment, one of the participants was wearing a wireless internet-linked EGG which captured his brain activity when thinking of a greeting. This signal was then translated in binary code and emailed to a non-invasive brain stimulation device that generated flashes of light in the second participant's peripheral vision. The receiver was obviously unable to hear the words but rather to correctly report flashes associated with the message.

Although these advances demonstrate the potential of BCI and brain-to-brain communication technology, nothing has yet been said about delivering information into a human brain in order to fully exploit its cognitive functionality. Naturally, our brain constantly executes a sophisticated network of synapses and neurotransmitters to process information captured and interpreted by our senses. Imagine for a moment if someone could solve a complex problem, like Jane does in Julian's story, using someone else's brain! Memory-sharing would be the obvious recreational application for the technology, but problem-solving would be something else altogether, and potentially far more useful to humanity as a whole. After all it is why Jane logs on in the first place. The wetware technology may be a reality within just a few decades. Will people soon be doing Google searches

6. C. Grau, R. Ginhoux, A. Riera, T.L. Nguyen, H. Chauvat, M. Berg, J.L. Amengual, A. Pascual-Leone, G. Ruffini, Conscious Brain-to-Brain Communication in Humans Using Non-Invasive Technologies. PLoS ONE 9(8): e105225, 2014.

for other people's knowledge and memories across world wide web of connected brains? Will social networks like Facebook be replaced by something infinitely more wondrous and complicated: memory-networks? Live-experience networks? Will we be supplementing our income by renting out our brain whenever it's *socially idle* (e.g. asleep or during long train journeys)? Will we be plugging in pendrives full of coded, cognitive tasks each night, before going to bed? And for those of us who still walk or drive to work, will we be be accessing the city's CCTV cameras to *literally* see what's around the next corner? We're still a few decades' research away from having this technology, so for now maybe we should enjoy *not* knowing what's around it while we can.

The Bactogarden

Sarah Schofield

KAY WATCHES STEVIE through the fifth floor window of the grocery store. Stevie paces between the sprouting beds and krill tanks and then selects a carton of germinated quinoa. Outside, in the street noise and grime, Kay relaxes back into her climbing harness. Since she observed her last week, Stevie has had her hair cropped shorter, emphasising her sharp, delicate features. Rod ticks over beside Kay searching for a crack in the concrete. He scans the window frame inlay.

'Stop, Rod. I'm just…'

He beetles off searching for another fault line. She shakes her head and adjusts her position on the narrow toehold. But when she looks back up, Stevie is turning towards her. Kay falters, her hands slipping on the line. Stevie's gaze passes her and Kay breathes deeply, bracing herself to climb back up. But Stevie is placing down her basket. She walks over to her, hanging on the other side of the window. She rests her palm against the glass, aligning her fingertips with Kay's on the other side. Her blue eyes dilate. In the tender skin of her throat, Kay sees a quickening pulse.

Stevie is waiting in the grocery store lobby. She embraces Kay, pinning her arms to her sides. It is like the hold of a mother who has found her lost child.

'Amazing,' Stevie says, finally stepping back. She shakes her head. 'God. It's amazing to see you.'

Kay forces a smile. Her nerves fizz. 'It's good to see you, too. What a coincidence…' The hastily prepared lies crumble. Rod, bundled into his carrier, beeps, monetising their lost time.

'How are you?' Stevie says.

'Good... You?'

Stevie adopts the iconic stance in every poster and magazine feature: soft renaissance hands pressed against narrow hips. Contrasting, audacious. But Kay remembers it from their schooldays. 'I have my own restaurant now – Syn café.'

'I know. I mean...' Kay gives a short laugh. 'Everybody knows, don't they? I've read about it...your awards.'

Stevie wrinkles her nose. 'It's fun.'

'And the art prizes.'

'I'm doing okay.'

Kay clenches her fist. Rod beeps inside his carrier again.

'So you're in construction,' Stevie says.

'Repairs, restoration. Climbing and cementing cracks. It's freelance. Rubbish pay... But...'

Stevie nods. 'I should have guessed.'

Kay is uncertain whether she is referring to the climbing or her choice of a poorly paid altruistic career. She tries a casual smile as she looks towards the exit. 'Well... It's great to see you. I'd better get back to it...'

'But...' Stevie's eyes darken. 'It's been so long. You must come to my café.'

'Oh. I really...'

'Please, Kay. My guest. Come and partake. And we can catch up properly.'

Kay's heart is racing but she shrugs indifferently and takes out her mobile.

Her father is sleeping when she gets home. She puts her climbsuit into the clave and lifts Rod onto the workbench. She siphons the cement spores out of his reservoir sealing them into a canister then blasts Rod in the steriliser, too. She sits on the workbench and eats sesame kaipen while the cycle completes.

Her father stands in the doorway. He pauses, a wheezy cough convulsing into a riptide. He fights it, his fist pressed against his mouth, eyes glistening. Kay goes to him, smoothes her hand over his back but he shrugs her off and she holds her breath until he gathers himself together again.

'Your day?' he says eventually. She pictures his heart, each contraction getting fractionally more out of sync, tightening his once eloquent sentences into succinct essence.

'Lots of fills today.' She turns and watches Rod revolve in the steriliser. She's never been able to lie effectively to her father. 'I've spotted more tenements with stress fractures. All those window boxes... I'll write a couple of tenders tomorrow.'

'Good.' He heads for the kitchen, gripping furniture like he's pitching at sea.

'It's the ones you secured for the Tuvaluans. Northeast...'

Dull, blunted, even at the mention of his first climate refugees, she hears him switch on the player. Her mother's voice says, 'Hey. What shall we have for supper?' as he scrapes back a chair.

She downloads Rod's data to the invoices for the repairs she'd managed that morning before watching Stevie. The spores she and Rod sprayed deep into the cavities will already have started germinating, knitting together into crystalline fibres, preserving and strengthening the original structures. Some of the older tower blocks are more synth patch up than original now. She listens to her father skipping between the recordings of her mother on the player and wishes everything could be so easily and cheaply repaired.

On her mobile a reminder flashes up for tomorrow's reservation. A review of Syn Café appears on the screen. She taps it. 'The Rise and Rise of Stevie Godwin: Culin-Artist and Science Maverick. Godwin delights diners with her Art Prize-nominated Alphabet Soup.' A video starts; a bowl of emerald broth with neon pink spots darting around within it. 'Motile bacteria, built in Godwin's onsite kitchen lab,' says the voiceover. 'Watch what happens next!' A woman looks down

at the bowl. Her eyes widen. 'No way! Did you see that?'
Another diner, gazing into his broth, 'Oh my God.' He points.
In the bowl the neon dots swim through the liquid,
synchronise starbursts, arranging themselves into letters.
Spelling 'Will you marry me?' The shot cuts back to the
woman who presses a shaking hand to her mouth. She looks
up and nods. Stevie watches from a mezzanine over the
dining room, hands on her hips. Diners laugh as they spoon
up the broth. 'She really shook things up,' the voiceover
continues, 'when she programmed her dish to swear at one of
the judging panel and offer an indecent proposal to another...'
Kay puts down her mobile. She tries to picture what
tomorrow will be like, how much Stevie might have changed
from the fourteen-year-old whom she used to know. The girl
who sat too close, who constantly observed her. The girl who
would lean in to pick through her lunchbox; snacks prepared
by whichever climate refugees were staying in their apartment
with them at that time; deep fried larvae, skewered chicken
hearts, cultivated ants eggs, offering Kay meat-taste, crustless,
shrink-wrapped sandwiches in trade.

She stares round the walls of their apartment.

'Easy on the oil!' says her mother's voice on the player.

'Yes. Yes,' her father replies.

Kay goes through. He drums his fingers against the table,
smiles sadly.

She wheels the oxygen tank over, stretching the mask
over his face. She thinks about the Bactogarden; the beautiful
garden flourishing in that cool dusty shop in the suburbs. A
garden only she knows about. A place where she can think in
peace. She hasn't been able to get there for weeks.

'Could you eat?' she asks.

He wrinkles his nose.

She sighs. 'Something small?'

Syn café is at the top of a skyscraper in the business district.
The welcome lounge overlooks the city. Cranes divine over
grass-topped tower blocks. Their stacked balconies flutter

with laundry, weathered tomatoes and brassicas. From the air-conditioned chill of the welcome lounge, Kay notes the beginnings of fractures in the surrounding buildings and plots the route she would navigate her climb to them if she were working today. She cracks her knuckles, notices the rimes of dirt and chalk compacted under her nails. Closing her eyes, she imagines the smog warmth on her face, swinging back on her rope, her feet braced against the vertical, Rod whirring by her side. She thinks about the money she could be earning right now, if she wasn't here.

Kay turns to the photograph gallery along the lounge wall. The pictures are in chronological order and she works backwards; Stevie receiving this year's Art Prize, Stevie looming over a petri dish, Stevie in high viz and hard hat leaning over the half-constructed mezzanine of Syn café, Stevie shielding her eyes as something like fruit salad explodes from a dish, younger Stevie holding out a bottle of her signature synth sauce, Stevie with hands on hips wearing goggles, chef's hat and a graduation gown, Stevie as a child smiling too brightly outside their school gates holding up a Science certificate. Kay looks away. The gallery feels like contrived branding. But it strikes her as odd that there is no photograph of Stevie with her Bactogarden. The ubiquitous school science project would have fitted into the nostalgic retrospective perfectly. She can even recall what Stevie's had looked like. Something about this niggles at her.

They created their Bactogardens in the middle of a heatwave. Kay remembers the stifling facemask, her hands sweating inside latex gloves. They'd made the coloured bacteria from inserts the previous lesson and loaded them into pens with pipettes. Kay squinted at the sun-flared screen. In close-up, the teacher's hands trembled as she drew a tree onto the demonstration.

'Remember, you'll be taking these home as Mother's Day gifts. So think about your garden design – draw something beautiful – make it aesthetically pleasing. But leave plenty of blank space for it to colonise.'

Opposite her, Stevie was drawing her mother's face in purple and green onto the transparent biofilm, tracing a photograph laid underneath. Kay's eyes prickled. She blinked away the unbidden picture of her own mother being washed by the Maldivian nurse who had refused any wage but had been equally insistent that Kay should help bathe her dying mother just a few weeks earlier.

'You need to work quickly,' said the teacher on the screen. 'The bacteria will start spreading immediately.'

The sound of pens squeaking haphazardly across agar sheets set Kay's teeth on edge. She speckled hers with red, blue and yellow dots. Stevie slid her completed film into the jar and a classroom assistant sealed it.

'Don't forget,' the teacher continued, 'after a couple of months, once the garden has fully spread and everyone has finished enjoying it, take it to your pharmacist who will dispose of it responsibly.'

Later, Kay leaned over the jars in the classroom window.

'It's a good present idea, isn't it? Stevie stood close beside her. 'I think my mum will really like it.'

Kay chewed her lip.

Stevie pointed to the feathery growth sprouting from her mother's left cheek on the biofilm. 'Mine's growing fastest.' Her eyes were on her. Curious. Needy.

Kay's mother had told her you should always help those in need. 'So it is,' she said.

'Kay!' Stevie hugs her into inertia. 'You made it.'

'It means a lot that you asked me…'

'I can't believe you're really here,' Stevie says. 'I've thought about you often, you know. Why did you never reply to my calls or texts after we left for college?'

Kay looks away, her face hot. It was hard to believe that doing nothing but evade, the act of passivity, could have had such a profound effect.

As children, around the time they made those bacteria

colonies, Stevie had started to follow Kay obsessively. Kay's ability to climb, borne from exploring abandoned buildings with refugee children in the suburbs, was the only way she could assert personal space away from Stevie. She'd sit overhead on any nearby metro stop or tree swinging, her legs eating an apple, while Stevie waited below like an inept stalker.

When she'd slumped down after school one day, and her father looked up from his desk, she explained about Stevie and her constant invitations to her home. 'You should just go. People like that...' he waved his hand. 'They quickly get bored and move on if you just indulge them.'

Now, in Syn Café, she looks up at Stevie. And she simply shrugs. The effect is instant. And Kay sees, with dizzying relief, that the invisible thread is still there.

Stevie takes her arm and leads her across the restaurant. 'I need to get back to my kitchen but Douglas will look after you.'

Well-dressed diners, many with obvious facework, watch her. She avoids eye contact as she sits.

Douglas hands her a pair of earphones. 'Soundscapes to complement each plate.' He leaves and she puts in one earphone, listens to the track for a minute, then slips the earpiece out and hides it under the table. The hush in the dining room is punctuated by murmurs from customers, sitting together yet somehow disconnected. They regard the food before them with a holy awe that reminds Kay of a soft-footed cathedral tour. A woman at a nearby table hisses to her partner; 'It tastes so... so... That holiday in Scarborough... You remember?' She gazes down at her fork. 'That's what I'm getting – Scarborough!' She chews slowly as a tear rolls down her cheek.

Douglas lays a plate before her. 'Reader's digest. For this dish, Stevie has created germinated shoots, a delicate Wagyu inspired synth carpaccio, and caviar containing the complete works of Shakespeare.'

Stevie is watching her over the mezzanine.

Douglas pours her water. She waits for him to leave before scooping a few spheres of the golden caviar onto her fork. She bursts them against the roof of her mouth. It is hot and sweet. Horseradish and beetroot.

Course follows indulgent course. Edible oyster pearls. Dodo soup for the soul. Probiotic candyfloss melts to syrup on her tongue tasting of tomato, basil and mozzarella. She picks at the food, her stomach gurgling, sweat beading her forehead.

Douglas cracks a blue speckled egg into a shot glass. Kay stares at the glutinous jelly.

'A palate cleanser,' he says. 'And multi vitamin.'

'Right, thank you.'

He watches her.

'I'll just take a moment to enjoy…' she nods at the swarming organisms in the glass.

But Douglas waits beside her table. 'Stevie regrets it has a very limited shelf life, madam.'

She raises the glass, flinching as it sparkles against her lips and gulps the citrusy sloe liquid. A childish medicinal warmth lingers on her tongue. She swallows again. Her mouth feels stripped and her stomach tightens. She breathes carefully, glances up at the mezzanine. Stevie is whisking something in a glass beaker. Her resting expression is focussed and hard. And Kay sees for a fleeting moment, the face of Stevie's mother.

The resemblance evokes a memory of a nauseating smell – greasy ammonia – embedded so vividly, Kay has to gulp down water. When she finally took her father's advice and agreed to go to Stevie's house, Stevie's mother was lying on a recliner with a lotion spread on her face. Her cheeks, nose and forehead shone. Kay had seen the adverts; 'the skin is a wetware canvas for the tiny workers.' She clutched a tissue in taut grey knuckles.

Stevie stood in the doorway and held out her Bactogarden. 'I made you this,' she said.

Her mother nodded towards the coffee table. 'What did

you get in your science test?' she asked. 'Did you take your supplements? Have you practiced for your music exam?'

Stevie answered shortly, her shoulders slumping. Kay placed her school bag, weighed down by her own jam jar colony, carefully in a corner.

'Come and see my room,' Stevie said. They started watching a cartoon on the video wall, but she was keen to show Kay something else. She took her into the bathroom and locked the door. Opening the newly fitted clave Stevie reached for the vacuum-sealed face cream and popped the lid. 'Smell that.' She shoved the pot towards Kay. It smelt faintly faecal, almost sweet. 'It's alive... made out of stem cells.' Stevie stirred her finger round in the yellow liquid, and scraped it against the side of the tub.

Kay's forehead had prickled as she'd recalled a photograph her father had taken – refugees using maggots to clean a wide ulcer. She went to the sink and gagged, her eyes watering.

Douglas places another dish before her. A pulsing gelatinous mass. He drizzles sauce over it. 'Stevie's trademark jus...' Kay tries to take the jug from him. 'Once again, entirely synth. You will get notes of dill and truffle. Indescribably umami.' Kay turns away, gauging the distance to the toilets.

When Kay left Stevie's house that day, Stevie's mother was still on the recliner, her cheeks livid pink. Stevie's Bactogarden was where she had left it on the table but now the brightly budding microbe features were turned away, facing the wall.

Kay had sat for a while at the metro station. Then she'd travelled to the furthest stop in the scarred suburbs. Just a few years earlier it had been a vibrant and resourceful place where her mother, through her community store, had helped them thrive. Now it was turning necrotic. Those who remained knuckled an existence as nature claimed back the rinds of the city. Bracken forced fists through pavement cracks. Brambles tangled alleyways. Ancient faces peered at her as she passed. At that time, she remembers her father had been snatching sleep at his desk as he prepared compensation cases for climate refugees, suing culpable countries; USA, China, UK.

'Why do they come here if they hate us so much?' she'd asked. 'Where else,' he rubbed his eyes, 'do you suppose they could go?'

She'd gone to her mother's shop, unlocked it and slammed the door behind her. Sun sludged through the skylights. She breathed in the quietness. The spicy organic smell still lingered in the abandoned space. The mismatched shelves, once bowing with urban foraged tins and packets, were now bare. Language posters peeled from the walls. On the table, she traced the dust outlines where two computers had been. She'd got her Bactogarden out of her bag. The colony was spreading from the dots she had drawn, the filaments stretching and exploring like insect antennae. She'd lifted it and hurled it against the wall. It shattered across the shop. The biofilm folded onto itself on the gritty floor.

Now, the pulsing mass on her plate is slowing its contractions. She grips her fork, and longs to be in the old shop with her Bactogarden. Every time she's visited over the years since, it's surprised and delighted her – grown further, more complex. Maturing, a freed network computing its own design, its colours glowing. Verdant purple, magenta, wild ochre, velvet red and blood blue, rippling textures like mossy humus. It has stretched up the walls, hangs off the light fitting and sneaks across the empty shelves. A marvellous patchwork of complex scraps.

There is always the nagging worry that it will be discovered, with so many buildings being reclaimed as squats. She wouldn't blame anyone if they did. But she wonders if they stay away from the shop out of respect. Those people have long memories.

'Mint.' Douglas lifts a cloche. A pale green capsule lies at the centre of the plate.

'Oh,' she says.

'It contains dental servicing microbes. Suck, don't swallow it.'

She looks down at it. 'What would happen if I did?'

THE BACTOGARDEN

His eyebrow twitches. She places it obediently on her tongue and it crackles like popping candy.

Stevie takes her up to the kitchen. The cooks, in white overalls and goggles, lower their eyes as they pass.

'Do you remember,' Stevie grips her arm, 'seeing the inside of a pomegranate for the first time?'

Kay had seen pomegranates. But had never been able to justify buying one.

'Remember how the smooth jewels felt in your mouth? The pop of sweet, the kernel crunch? The delightful surprise of it.' Stevie's face lights. 'It's never quite as wonderful as the first time. I create the first times again. The probiotics, vitamins, the artistry... they're all just a hook.' She looks at the diners below them. 'They're really just here for their first times over.'

Kay raises an eyebrow. 'Strawbroli.' Then flushes. 'I don't mean... I'm not saying...'

But Stevie turns to her. 'God. Yes. That, exactly. I think you've just identified my earliest inspiration – bloody strawberry flavoured broccoli. I'd forgotten all about that!'

'We used to queue for ages at the school canteen. Ate piles of it.' Kay pictures herself standing there, her free lunch card tucked up her sleeve. 'It came with that sugar-free dipping sherbet. Remember?'

'Really!' Stevie laughs. 'Does my whole world, everything I've created boil down to some crappy strawberry DNA plugged greens? Ha! You know, I'm currently planning my anniversary showcase. Perhaps it should feature strawbroli!'

'It shows how far we've come...' Kay draws her breath.

But Stevie is leading her out into a laboratory. Benches dissect the room. There are rows of test tubes, centrifuges and measuring containers, from tiny beakers to gallon flasks. Germination units hum along one wall containing rows of emerald and purple seedlings.

'Before today,' Stevie says, 'When was the last time you bit into something with no idea how it was going to taste?'

Kay stares at her.

217

'That's what I do. I create experience for people. Beauty. Nostalgia. Delight.'

'For quite a narrow demographic,' Kay blurts out. She blushes.

Stevie fiddles with the controls on the germination unit.

'I mean…' Kay starts.

But Stevie turns back towards her and she is smiling. 'I want to show you something secret.'

She takes her down a corridor and into a locked room. On a table is a transparent box containing wood shavings and a metal frame.

'See her?' Stevie's breath is hot against her neck. 'Lottie. The world's most valuable spider.'

And Kay sees it; small and tick-shaped, crouched at the back of the box.

'My latest project. A commission from one of my regulars who's getting married. We're harvesting her silk as she produces it. It'll be woven and made into a chemise for their wedding night.'

'I don't see…'

'The lab work is all mine, they'll be entirely edible. I programmed her DNA with the nectarine genome. And the blue pigmentation from Mallard's eggs…'

'Expensive.'

She grins. 'You have no idea.'

Kay looks more closely. The spider hunches and Stevie draws her back.

'Doesn't it…'

'What?'

'It seems a bit…? To take her web away. As she's making it, I mean…'

'It would only confuse her,' Stevie says. 'Her innate sense. To silk blue nectarine scented edible yarn, it isn't what she's expecting. It's kinder to take it away as quickly as possible.'

'Then why…'

'We've just about reached a point. Absolutely anything I can imagine, anything at all is within our grasp. We own it.

The knowledge. It allows me to make my art.'

Kay holds her breath. It's the wrong moment. But it is a glimmer. Making a heart could be an art form. There are ways she could spin it; Take Heart, Heart on your Sleeve, Heart to Heart…

Stevie is speaking quietly. 'We're both artists, now. In our different ways.'

Kay shakes her head. 'What I do… it's functional. After those buildings collapsed… I just felt that if I could do something, make them strong enough to sustain life. I'm just a facilitator. I climb and inject; the bacteria do all the work.'

Stevie takes Kay's palm. 'No. Look how you're put together. You're a sculptor.'

Kay fights the urge to pull away.

'Long after we're gone,' Stevie says, 'your work will still exist. But mine, well, it's over and finished in a couple of mouthfuls.'

It's fake modesty, Kay knows it, but even so, she feels a sudden spiking pity and it takes a moment for it to crystalise. In that moment, she recalls, vividly, something she had entirely forgotten about. She'd returned to Stevie's house the day after they'd been allowed to take home their Bactogardens. Stevie had one of those 3D candy printers; she'd been boasting about it at school. She set it running over and over. As Kay watched the coloured sugar building on the flatbed, an envious lump grew in her throat. She snuck to the bathroom and slumped against the tiles. In the steriliser, beside Stevie's mother's face cream there was a familiarly shaped jam jar. Kay looked more closely. The lid was off. The biofilm sagged ashen against the glass.

Stevie sent Kay home with a rattan bag full of hard little sweets.

'Stevie made these for our refugees. Stevie's mum says they don't need the bag back.' Kay held it out to her father, belatedly understanding the pale anger in his face, his disappointment in her.

'*Our* refugees?' He turned his back. 'Does she think we can't afford bags, either?'

Stevie still holds onto her hand. 'Somewhere along the line, you've lost sight of beauty. In your constant desire to save people, you've lost the ability to see it. You don't always have to be a martyr. We're given life. We must live it. I know you've always thought me vacuous...'

'No, Stevie...'

'I'm sure your dad convinced you of that. But I'm just trying to create beauty. Share beauty. Make happiness.'

Stevie leads her back to the welcome lounge. 'It's been lovely seeing you again.'

'Stevie...'

'For you.' She holds out a small box.

Kay opens it. A small green apple glistens inside.

'It's a one off.'

Kay lifts the wax-skinned apple.

'Try it!' Stevie nods.

Kay bites through the crisp shell, into a soft jelly centre. Intensely sweet, granular and cidery. Like an amplified first taste.

Stevie smiles. 'I know, right?'

'Can I take the rest home?'

She shakes her head, 'I'm sorry.'

'Oh.'

'Nothing personal. I just like to keep it all contained.'

'Okay. I just... I wanted to tell you, my dad...'

'And, of course, it doesn't keep. I wouldn't want it to be seen less than perfect.' She presses her hands together. 'I always got the feeling your dad disapproved of me anyway.'

'No, not at all.'

'Come on, Kay.'

Kay looks down at the apple, already turning gummy in her hand.

Kay buys chapulines and shitake from her favourite vendor in the east market on her way home. Her stomach still churns, the orchard tang lingering in her mouth.

Her father raises his hand as she comes in. She makes him an omelette. He snatches his breath around small forkfuls, his cheeks darken like clouds over the city. 'Not eating?' he asks.

She fiddles with the valve setting on his oxygen.

He sleeps badly. And she stays awake watching over him. She glances at her mobile every few minutes. It remains horribly silent beside her.

The glass exterior of the syn café building is not designed to be scaled. Kay pushes her toes into the narrow window frame, checks her line and cracks her knuckles. The morning sun glances off the vertical, rippling it with heat haze. She feels like a refugee clinging to the prow of a ship.

Inside, Stevie appears on the mezzanine. She leans in. Kay holds her gaze before scrambling back up to the roof. She hurries down the stairwell, sweating and heart pounding, descending to street level. Stevie waits in the doorway, glancing up at the building.

Kay allows her heart to calm before approaching. 'I want to show you something.'

'What?'

She turns and walks away, resisting the urge to look back.

'Where are we going?' Stevie hurries after her.

They travel the metro then stride through the suburbs, Stevie struggling to keep up. 'Is it far?' Her intrigue punctuates her monologue about Lottie, celebrity reservations at Syn that week, and ideas she's had for her forthcoming anniversary showcase. As they pass through the roughened suburbs, people watch them from under saturated brick and plastic shelters. Stevie links her arm through Kay's.

'It's okay. They know who I am,' Kay says. These people's meagre climate compensation probably wouldn't buy one course in Stevie's restaurant. The thought swings a dead weight inside her.

They turn left down the rusting, shuttered street and Kay unlocks the steel door. In the dark the air is rich and loamy. A breeze rattles air vents overhead.

'Kay…'

'Wait there.' She treads lightly, fumbles to unlatch the shutter over the skylight. The sun streams over her bacteria garden. Bubbling, feathering, grotesquely beautiful, the cells secretly communicate. It blooms over the surfaces, dangling motile threads off the ceiling tiles.

Stevie looks round, letting out a long slow breath. She reaches out to touch it but Kay stops her.

'God. What is this stuff? It's like a giant version of…' The recognition spreads over her face. 'It's like I'm actually inside one of those Bacteria things. It's like being small again.' She rests her hand over her heart. 'Is this yours? Your Bactogarden?'

'Yeah… well, it's just a place I like to come. To see what it's doing.'

'Remember how everyone made these things in jam jars? I can't believe an original still exists.'

'It was hideous. Instilling in us this desire, this capacity to colonise and control.'

'That wasn't what it was about,' Stevie snaps. 'It was about art and culture. It was about creation. Neither of us would be where we are now if we hadn't made them.'

'I didn't mean…'

Stevie inspects the colony, touches a purple velvet frond. 'Why are we here, Kay? Why did you bring me?'

Kay turns away. 'I wanted you to see this. I wanted to share it. You said I'd lost the ability to see beauty. You're wrong. I see it in different places to you.' She tries to gather her words. The colony around her feels like an ally. 'This is where I see beauty. It requires nothing but appreciation. It's free. It has life. And life is a precious thing.' The speech she had spent an entire night chewing over tumbles into the cool air of the shop. 'People are precious. People are beautiful. The people in our lives that we love…'

Stevie turns her back on the colony and stares at Kay. For a moment, Kay wonders if she already knows about her dad. There is something tender in the tilt of her chin. Something vulnerable. Then she is stepping over towards her. Her cheeks are flushed. She is reaching out.

'I mean…' Kay backs away. 'It's where we both started, isn't it, like you said, neither of us would be doing what we do if it wasn't for this. I wanted to remind you. Beauty is sometimes about simple things. More than art. You could probably make anything. All sorts of things that could be beautiful in different ways.'

Stevie wavers. She looks confused and then leans against the table. 'I guess.' She plucks at a strand hanging from the ceiling. Rubs it between her fingers.

Kay scuffs her foot against the floor. 'Like…organs.'

Stevie touches the torn off piece against her lips.

'Like a heart?'

Stevie lowers her head. When she looks back up again her eyes are dull.

'My dad's sick.'

'I'm sorry to hear that.'

'I just thought… if anyone can fix this…'

Stevie shakes her head. 'Right,' she says. She pushes away from the table and circles carefully. The garden reflects in her eyes. 'It doesn't work like that. I can't just grow it, like a plant, or piece of beef. I can't do that.'

Kay shuts her eyes, dark shapes dance under the lids.

'Why don't you just pay for a transplant, like anyone else would?'

'Anyone else?'

Stevie sighs loudly. Her shoulders slump.

'You said. You can do anything.'

'I'm a chef, Kay. Not a heart doctor.' She looks apologetic then she disappears between the shelving units. Kay listens to her measured gritty footsteps around the shop. The air vents rattle overhead.

A minute or two later, Stevie's voice comes from behind one of the display stands. 'Do you think...'

'What?'

'Do you think this stuff is edible?' she says quietly.

As her father sleeps, Kay focuses on the jumping line on the machine by his bed, marking the internal music of his heart. She picks raw the callous on her hand.

The doctor leans in the doorway. 'He's doing well,' she says. 'Go home. Get some rest.'

It is as she is passing through the hospital foyer that she sees it, huge on the TV wall. She slumps down onto a hard plastic seat and grips the armrests. 'Godwin: A Retrospective,' the voiceover says. 'Do you remember making *your* Bactogarden?' The shot cuts to Stevie sitting in an empty school hall, she holds up a jam jar. A strip of the Bactogarden is captured within it. 'Her anniversary showcase takes us back to the start: Godwin's first synthetic creation has slowly been evolving over the years of her career. Now she wants to share it with her diners.' Stevie's eyes glitter. 'Do you remember?' she says. 'We gave them to our mothers. We had a chance to be creators. All my guests will take a piece home with them, captured in resin, as a memento.' She puts her hands onto her hips. 'And do you know something else? It tastes utterly delicious!' The shot cuts to a torn piece of the colony, sauce dotted around it. Already its fronds are faded and wilting.

Kay walks home. She paces numbly about the apartment. She takes Rod off his charger and goes to work.

She is running her finger in the split fracture of a tenement when it finally blindsides her. She pictures the raw wounded shop floor, exposed surfaces, stripped and anaemic without her garden. She leans back in her harness and sobs.

Afterword:

Dream Sequence

Prof Martyn Amos
Manchester Metropolitan University

DEVELOPING TECHNOLOGIES ARE often presented in fiction as divisive, with the 'haves' reaping the benefits, at the expense of the 'have-nots' (the film *Gattacca* being a case in point). But any single piece of predicted technology quickly dates in the annals of science fiction (SF), through being easier to achieve than we thought (take the on-board video link-ups of shows like *Battleship Galactica* – Skype gave us this technology, for free, over a decade ago), or eluding us completely (interstellar travel). Perhaps for this reason, many of the best science fiction stories place technology in the background, where contradictions and nerdy nit-picks may be overlooked. As Stanislaw Lem writes about Philip K. Dick's *Ubik*, in the context of the latter's other books, 'Essentially it is always one and the same world that figures in them – a world of elementally unleashed entropy, of decay that not only, as in our reality, attacks the harmonious arrangement of matter, but also even consumes the order of elapsing time… All the technological innovations, the magnificent inventions, and the newly-mastered human capabilities… ultimately come to nothing in the struggle against the inexorably rising floodwaters of Chaos'[1].

Sarah Schofield's story plays out against the backdrop of a world that has embraced *synthetic biology* – an emerging field of research at the intersection of the life sciences, engineering, computer science and biochemistry. Researchers in so-called 'synbio' are predominantly interested in the (re-)engineering

1. Stanislaw Lem (1984) Philip K. Dick: A Visionary Among the Charlatans. In *Microworlds: Writings on Science Fiction and Fantasy* (Franz Rottensteiler, ed.), London:Secker & Warburg (1985), p. 117.

of natural living systems (e.g., bacteria, or yeast) for the purposes of 'persuading' them to perform useful, human-defined tasks (eg., to produce biofuels, deliver drugs, or detect pollution). The goals of synbio are ambitious in scope, and scientists such as J. Craig Venter have ensured that its profile has been consistently high. Synbio could potentially revolutionise food production, energy, and the environment (to name just a few possible application domains).

More fundamentally, it could also usher in entirely new forms of *artificial life*.

In the course of her story, Schofield references many recent 'real world' developments; the bacterial synchronized swimmers are a nod towards ongoing work into directed pattern formation in motile bacteria, the caviar containing the works of the Bard are based on the recent embedding of the entire text of a book in DNA strands[2], and the 'bactogarden' concept derives from the *E. chromi* project, which engineered 'living colour' in bacteria[3]. The two central technological devices are also completely plausible, referencing the creation of 'high-end' food products created by synbio[4], and the so-called 'bacilla-filla' concept – engineered *Bacillus* bugs that will, one day, fill cracks in concrete by crawling into crevices before quietly expiring (generating calcium carbonate in the process)[5].

The Bactogarden Project imagines a future in which synthetic biology is utterly ubiquitous; the story then becomes less about the 'tech' *per se*, and more about connecting the *characters* and exploring *impossibilities*. Here, synbio is used predominantly as a vehicle for exploring issues

2. George M. Church, *et al.* (2012) Next-generation digital information storage in DNA. *Science* **337**:6102, p. 1628.
3. http://www.echromi.com/
4. Erika Check Hayden (2014) Synthetic-biology firms shift focus. *Nature* news, 29 January. http://www.nature.com/news/synthetic-biology-firms-shift-focus-1.14602
5. http://phys.org/news/2010-11-bacillafilla-concrete.html

of *control*; of personal destiny, relationships, scientific developments, and even our management of the planet.

Kay and Stevie were never equals, even as children, and now Kay is a literal outsider, dangling outside Stevie's building while she ministers to the elite.

Stevie uses cutting-edge technology to generate her prize-winning gastronomy, but her emphasis on the transient nature of her art, her unwillingness to allow Kay to take home the apple (ancient symbol of beauty and knowledge) and, later, her appropriation of the bactogarden, serve only to underline her insecurity. Kay fixes buildings using engineered organisms, while her father slowly dies from a failing heart. We imagine that synbio could offer a possible route towards geoengineering the planet away from environmental catastrophe, and yet climate refugees are an uncomfortable and visible reality in Schofield's world of 2070. In this, Sarah emphasizes what those working in synbio already understand; that it will never be a panacea.

Sarah also does a fine job of considering the notion of what *creativity* might mean in the context of this emerging technology. The use of complex *living* material as an artistic medium raises important questions of agency and intentionality. Microbial colonies form structures that are inherently (and fundamentally) *functional* (e.g., they might protect the colony from dangerous chemicals), yet we often find in them – completely accidentally – great beauty (see, for example, the work of Eshel Ben-Jacob[6]). Are we artists, or simply supporting technicians? The Synthetic Aesthetics project asks of speculative collaborations between artists/designers and scientists: 'Should these projects be considered art, design, synthetic biology, or something else altogether?'[7] The story also raises deep issues of *ownership*. Writer, broadcaster and geneticist Adam Rutherford has referred to synbio as 'genetic

---

6. http://tamar.tau.ac.il/~eshel/gallery.html
7. Daisy Ginsberg, et al. (2014) *Synthetic Aesthetics: Investigating Synthetic Biology's Designs on Nature*, MIT Press.

remixing'[8], and draws parallels between it and urban music, in that a 'deeply creative and youthful science with sampling as its soul… faces the same ownership issues that killed hip hop.' He argues that issues of patenting and intellectual property may hinder future important developments in synbio in exactly the same way that copyright issues have reduced the ability of artists to remix existing beats and snippets of music. More fundamentally, though, can we ever truly *own* biology, in the way that some might to want to? Can we 'own' *physics*, or chemistry?

In the end, though, Sarah's story encourages us to seek out beauty in the everyday and the mundane. Stevie's work is destined to be ever transient, only captured when fossilized, lifeless, in resin. Deep down, she craves her mother's approval, forever seeking to recreate the rejected ceremonial bactogarden. Yet, for a time, at least, Kay finds peace through the release of her own colony into a uniquely personal space; engineered biology reclaiming her mother's shop.

8. Adam Rutherford (2013) *Creation: The Origin of Life / The Future of Life*, Viking.

Keynote
at the European Conference
on Artificial Life, 2070

Zoe Lambert

THE ATLAS FAMILY: A PERSONAL PERSPECTIVE ON RECENTLY
DISCLOSED, UNREGULATED EXPERIMENTS ON ARTIFICIAL
AND NEURAL-COLLECTIVE CONSCIOUSNESS

You have all probably read the lurid headlines and fallacious articles that have appeared over the past few months with regard to the Atlas family research into collective consciousness: the rumours of telepathy, systematic abuse, incest and the murder of four of the children. In this keynote, I aim to present a more in-depth account of these experiments from an admittedly partial (and personal) point of view, as one of the subjects of the longitudinal study, the second daughter of Professors James and Jean Atlas – my parents.

Professor James Atlas and his wife Professor Jean Atlas had worked in the field of artificial and collective consciousness for a number of years, my mother a neuropsychiatrist and my father a neuroscientist, specialising in brain-machine interfaces. Although different in many ways, their work shared the common goal of developing a working simulacrum for human intelligence through computation, or Artificial Intelligence – a goal that even after millions of bit-coins of investment, remains elusive, suggesting that task-led computation will always take an Occam's Razor to 'emotional intelligence'; consciousness will never emerge in robots without such traits. This on-going, discipline-wide failure meant that, together, my parents became increasingly interested in the idea of collective consciousness. This emphasis on the collective built on Jean's early doctoral work on collective behaviour in social insects, where the interaction of simple rules shared between many individuals promotes the emergence of complex behaviour, structure and swarm intelligence.

However, the interaction of robotic swarms meant that, as shown in the Harvard RoboBees, allowing individuals to share information directly through wifi enabled swarm intelligence to develop apace – especially as these swarmbots moved away from a dependency on a central 'queen' processor, to being truly hive-like, and queen-less, like any other social insect. Though, the implementation of this C.I. in the US Drone Swarms in the 2020s, followed by the Bee-bots, Swarm-Bombs and Death-Ants, resulted, of course, in many years of controversy.

No scientists had at that point challenged the established ethical research protocols adhered to by European universities relating to human brain experimentation. But as our father would say, 'The future is not the replication of the human mind but its fusion with machines to create collective consciousness.' So at some point invasive, human brain experiments had to start: the wetware had to be tested.

This insouciance for ethical parameters drew its reasoning, indirectly, from my father's early love of 20th century 'fear-flicks', in particular old *Jaws* movies. He adored these films, in spite of himself. Professionally, he knew all too well that they tapped into reactionary instincts, a phobia of 'the other', as Zizek would say, whatever guise it took (an immigrant, an arab, a climate refugee, etc). There were similar reactionary attitudes to A.I. elsewhere in popular culture. The proliferation of droidaphobic narratives – the 20th century's *Terminator* series, Von Trier's late masterpiece, *The Hive* – with their incumbent fear of robotic intelligence, had a demonstrable influence on the shaping of bioethics and A.I. research protocols. Just as the *Jaws* films had led, indirectly, to the extinction of the Great White Shark in 2029, so these droidaphobic films impeded investment into AI research and were cited repeatedly by the lobby groups that tightened the research protocols. My father sometimes felt that things would have to get worse before they got better, before the protocols could be relaxed. He hypothesised that war might be one such 'bad-but-progressive' climate. History shows us that many of our greatest scientific and medical breakthroughs took place in times of conflict, where ethical codes were not established, monitored or enforced. (The French surgeon Ambroise Paré was the first to seal amputations with a tincture instead of cauterisation, when he ran out of boiling oil on the battlefield; the Nazis infamously experimented on the extremes of temperature that humans can withstand). My father became obsessed with research protocols and often cited Robin Warren as his only 'peacetime pioneer' – a 20th century physician who found a loophole in the (post-Nazi) Nuremberg Code by testing on himself to prove the bacterial basis for peptic ulcers.

In order to safeguard his reputation however, my father, with my mother's consent, took their research underground, hiding it in the last place an ethics committee would look: the home. They decided to conduct their research principally on their own children. With the aid of advanced neuro-IVF and in vitro gene manipulation, Professor Jean Atlas gave birth to five non-identical quintuplets: two girls and three boys. Put simply, the aim of this research was to enhance the intelligence of their children through augmenting specific brain areas, transcend the limits of the individual brain by fusing certain neural pathways with a computer interface, and ultimately achieving a decisive breakthrough in collective consciousness – what certain media outlets have rather melodramatically called 'telepathy'. Our parents always hoped that this would herald a new beginning for human intelligence and interaction, one that could, in the long term, be applied to the world's many problems: the spiralling climate catastrophes: the 'heat mortality', crop-failure starvation, the widespread flooding of Europe, the drought besieging Asia and Africa, and the subsequent refugee camps on the borders of Southern Europe. While most countries' scientists were scrabbling for short-term, band-aid solutions to these global issues, my father believed that the long-term solution lay in adapting *us*, in jumpstarting evolution in order to change how we interact with each other and with the planet, arguing that collective empathy and collective action was needed. The experiments would not solve these problems directly, but were essential, he believed, for humanity's eventual survival. We needed to change our relationship to each other, and to the world, or we would keep on making the same mistakes over and over – an argument he repeated throughout our childhood in never-ending dinnertime diatribes about what humans had to learn from bees and ants.

These changes would come not only through our greater mental capacity but also through our increased empathy. The principal aim of these experiments was to do away with individualism (or, as my father called it, 'the tyranny of the ego'). For how can you hurt, exploit or neglect another individual if you can feel their pain like your own?

During their time in the womb – *our* time in the womb, I should say – the five foetuses were subjected to various processes that initiated this collectivisation of the self. To begin with, the medial prefrontal cortex (mPFC), which is used in self-referential processing and is more sensitive in collectivist societies (where self-other distinctions are less pronounced) was genetically manipulated *in utero* to make them more responsive. After birth, these areas were connected together (through our father's neural interface) to encourage a synchronicity across the mPFCs of all five brains; if one our mPFCs was activated, all of ours would.

The 'Collective Self' was further promoted through conditioning, starting with a very daring child development technique devised to encourage a non-individualised identity. Simply put, we were all called 'Jo'. If naming gives a sense of individuality, they reasoned, then a collective first name would give us a sense of unity. For my parents, though, this resulted in confusion and, privately, they developed a way of individuating us; they gave us each a letter.

In many ways these early steps were entirely successful. Our identity cohered as a unit, the way the body is a unit of many parts; we each had our own role to play.

The neural-interface – an implant developed for chimpanzees that my father had worked on as a PhD student – was implanted into each of us a few hours after birth. With it came our first memories. We remember being taken and placed on cold metal, the first sting of the interface being fused with the blood vessels just beneath the skin behind the ear. The interface provided wifi connectivity and linked to minute chips containing reconfigurable multi-electrode arrays inserted at strategic points around the skull. These in turn connected directly with the spindle neurons in the anterior insular cortex and amygdala, which are part of the neural circuits involved in empathy and caring. Like the original Robobees, there was a central controller analysing, collating and influencing behaviours, through neural impulses and gentle modulation, and by reconfiguring our Multidimentional Brain Computer Interface (or MBCI for short).

But it was a trauma repeated five times over. We remembered lying in our cots, seeing how the blinds broke against the window as the winds raged outside, then crying as we were taken from the room, one by one, for tests. How, when we returned, the others would reach for us, pushing out hands between the cots.

Our advanced physical development was first demonstrated at the age of two in the famous online clip of the five of us breakdancing. Our mother showed us breakdancing tutorials and clips of vintage rap artists. For instance, the 1990s hiphop classic, 'It's Like That' by RUN DMC vs. Jason Nevins. Then via the interface she played the images directly into our brains while gently stimulating our mirror neurons. This increased our ability to learn by

imitation by over 1000% and, within a couple of days, we could perform RUN DMC's dance routine perfectly.
[Plays clip]
[Audience laughs]

Our mother describes the process in her log:

They were already walking at five months of age. I'd sit them in a circle and get them to copy my actions, gradually building up dance moves. They loved this, giggling and playing. I didn't discourage play, but would gently return them to the task at hand.

It was quite remarkable how they were learning the dance. They'd watch the video, and I'd try to do the moves along with it. Then they'd copy me, then they just copied the video, with me standing aside. I remember, within an hour they were spinning on their heads on the gym floor.

It wasn't until our implants were given access to the multinet at the age of five that we realised we were different. It wasn't until we were in our teens that we understood we were an advancement, not an anomaly.

By the age of seven we were working in differential calculus. By eleven we had mastered Lamdda calculus and at thirteen published a new formulation of the Entscheidungsproblem using field theory. We were more than the sum of our parts. This was not just five minds working on a problem; the fact our minds were interconnected enabled greater intelligence through greater complexity. To explain in depth how our collective thinking enabled us to solve these problems in new ways would take more than time allows. But we will say this: consciousness is not really understood. Any mind, whether linked or not, does not truly observe the Law of the Excluded Third – that is to say, it does not function according to a binary logic of 'true' or 'not true', but operates rather on many different levels, or planes, intersecting – a non Hilbertian maths many have since referred to as 'intuition'. All minds have this, with a binary logic squatting on top, like an operating system. But for us, we were able to ditch the individualistic, surface logic completely and operate entirely on collective intuition. This is the collective intuition of the now extinct bumble bee, and way beyond the RoboBees; our minds calculated together, our feelings harmonised, our thoughts fluctuated like SHM waves between us. We understood each other. I can give you uncorroborated personal testimony about what all of this 'felt like', but you can do better: you can read my father's numerous test results, all of which were conducted with rigorous controls (often the hapless children of my parents' colluding friends). All of this is online, of course.

Despite the collective nature of our consciousness, we did have differences in our personalities; we weren't entirely identical, which was to our advantage! In difference there is complexity (e.g. five identical thoughts would be just repetitions). Jo-A was born first, and always put himself first – for breakfast, for interface upgrades, and then to get rid of it completely. His strengths were field theory, Dirac formations, and matrix wave functions. Jo-B loved ice cream. He had our mother's eyes and brown hair, and liked to sit on our father's knee while he worked in his study. Jo-C wanted desperately to go outside, to interact with the world physically, to pull things apart, and she was always trying to get out the door. Jo-D was clever but quiet, and always defended her parents; a true believer in their project, the one who would always stick by them. Jo-E was born last. He was the smallest; he loved cuddles, he was the first to reach out for us in the dark. He was also the first to die.

We were schooled at home (our mother taking time off from the university and eventually stopping work altogether). With the increasingly intemperate conditions outside we were never once allowed out of our housing complex. You can see an image of our complex on the screen above: the central lab, and around it the kitchen and living area, our parents' bedroom, and our bedroom.

We saw few people, apart from our parents' colleagues who collaborated with the experiments. Our housing complex was situated outside a remote village in Lancashire, with a view of the valley basin. Though we were protected from flooding, we were vulnerable to the winds.

There was one occasion during the tornadoes of '64 which was a significant moment in our development. The five of us loved to open the shutters on the big, reinforced window in the living area and stare down on the valley below, especially during storms.

One time, we were watching a lightning storm when we saw a car making its slow way up the road to the complex, parking in the yard. The man inside forced the car door open, and struggled to walk towards us, against the rain. Suddenly a gust of wind simply picked him off the ground, then threw him mercilessly against the building – somewhere above us, perhaps the roof – before dropping him to the ground with a thud. The gust had lifted him just as a bolt of lightning flashed somewhere else. I remember that flash in perfect, slow motion – it was as if the world's gravity had been short-circuited, and for a fraction of a second, he just hovered.

Jo-C was screaming, saying we should help him. We called for our father, who came through and started closing the shutters, telling us to come away from the window. He would call the emergency services but there was nothing we could do till the winds died down. It was too dangerous out there. Jo-A started to argue with him, but he held up his hand, which signalled silence and the onset of one of his discourses, the ones we usually listened to at dinner.

We couldn't take our eyes off the heap that lay crumpled in the yard. So Father ushered us into another room, gave us all a Reel-Fruit – our favourite at the time – and began with one of his classic lectures: a typical blend of Spinozian pantheism, eco-socialism, and a dash of Buddhism.

'Children,' he began. 'The death of that unknown man outside is necessarily needless. This is just one death amidst millions of needless deaths each year. You see if God is in everything, you are the realisation of this. You are its fulfilment. All of the universe is made of the same matter, even if we go down to its smallest components, even the quarks and leptons are given their fundamental property, their mass, by the same thing. Our evolution should push us towards our knowledge of these commonalities. But instead, our history has pushed us towards individualism, separation, and hyper-capitalism. We now live an atomised existence, where we hide behind our steel-lite shutters as those outside die from starvation or exposure. Our selfishness has led to destruction and death: the snow storms, the flooding, the tornadoes, the hurricanes of fire, the extinction of so many of God's creatures.

'All this is our fault, so it is us who must develop, evolve, and change.

'We need to learn from the smallest creatures – the bees, the ants, the wasps. They will teach us how to interact with each other. You, my children, will be the great hope of our age. You are the future. You will be our inheritance. You will be the generation that saves us.'

We nodded. 'Yes,' we said. 'Yes we will.'

'We are going to send direct signals to the spindle neurons in the temporal lobe and anterior insular cortex. Today, we are going to take our investigation further. Are you all ready?'

We were indeed ready. The very next week we began the final stage of what would become known as The Atlas Experiments. This would entail a deeper level of consciousness, where we understood not only each other's consciousness, but were also connected to the world beyond us.

Our mother states in her logbook: 1st March 2070
9.30am. In the lab, we sat the children on their usual circle of chairs, and attached the scan-hats (the Jos' colloquial term for our adaptation of the MBCI). We started increasing the neural signals being sent between each other and the rate of synchronization pulses sent from the MBCI. Their usual reaction: heightened temperature (1%), increase in pulse rate – everything was in concordance with previous experiments.

But this was the first experiment which would directly stimulate areas of the temporal lobe and the anterior insular cortex. The Jos all gasped as the chips were engaged, and over the next few minutes the realtime fMRI signals in the central processor began to change from red to yellow to white.

At first, they seemed to fall into a meditative state — these areas of the brain are known to be linked with transcendent religious feelings, as well as to empathy and emotion. Initially, there were some variations between the individual scans and the inputted sychronisation rate, but after half an hour of the increased input rate, the scan-hats began to show a synchronizing of their individual outputs: their signals were phase-locking. Within an hour the Jos had fallen into a semi-unconscious state: their pupils were dilated and unresponsive, and their breathing had slowed.

We continued to monitor them, but at 10.30 am we noticed something else — a noise; we realised the Jos were humming rhythmically and tunelessly in time with the oscillations in their neural readings. I advised James to decrease the controlling pulses of electricity to the MBCIs. He complied, but the humming and brain activity remained the same. We gradually reduced the pulses, and finally stopped them altogether at 12pm, but this did not decrease their brain activity or humming. It seems as if their brains are analogous to a series of swings in the same oscillation; once they are in the same rhythm it is hard to break.

11pm. There is still no change in their rhythmic humming and synchronised brain activity. We have had to attach catheters to the Jos. We are going to take shifts through the night to monitor them.

12pm. I am increasingly concerned about the state of the Jos, which I will have to describe as catatonic. This is due to the fact, we believe, that their brains are locked into synchronicity. At the moment, we have no idea how to break this 'synchronicity'.

5am. I am increasingly frantic. It is James' shift, but I am unable to sleep, and just lie here, waiting, listening. I am not sure how long we can continue this. I have tried removing the caps, and powering-down all devices, but this just drives them into a louder, higher-pitched hum. They seem calmer (though still entranced) now that I've returned their caps, and set the frequency back to James' rate.

10am. At 7am, James called me through to the lab, saying the only way to break this catatonic state would be by shocking them – applying bursts of high-frequency, high-voltage neural impulses. 'A little like the old fashioned deep brain stimulation.'

I wasn't sure, but agreed because we had no other choice.

James began to increase the frequency of input bursts from 1 to 10 Hz. Then 10 to 50 Hz until there was constant high voltage tetanic stimulation. Their humming increased in pitch, and their brain activity increased with the frequency, but remained uniform. He increased the peak voltage to 150 milivolts and they began to shudder, as if they were all in the early stages of a seizure. It was then I noticed that blood was beginning to seep from Jo-E's ears.

I told James to stop, but he increased it even more. Jo-E began to have a seizure, his body went rigid and he experienced severe convulsions, his teeth clamping on his tongue. He remained within a state of continuous seizure activity for eight minutes before his heart stopped. The humming ceased, and the other Jos regained consciousness.

None of you seated before me can truly say you have 'felt' death, experienced it, but we have: we felt his unbearable pain, we experienced those final moments when the bursts of electrical impulses induced epileptic neural activity and all his neurons were screaming at once. We felt his pain, every judder of consciousness as his death severed the link between our neural-interfaces, the way a bulb goes out in old Christmas lights.

Jo-E's death was an amputation. We were taken to our beds to sleep, and the next day we couldn't speak. We did not want to get out of bed or eat. We did nothing for days.

There was another development. We could feel the vague beginnings of something altogether new. At this point we had no words for them, for what these feelings were or where they came from, but we became aware of what might be called a 'sixth sense' – possibly induced by the stimulation of the temporal lobe and similar to those experienced in epileptic seizures.

We became aware of what was beyond the housing complex; we could sense how the wind whistled gently down the valley, how the browned trees swayed, and those that had been ripped from the ground lay there in agony; we could sense the battered vineyard, and the people who lived there slowly rebuilding their homes in the wake of the tornado. Beyond that we could sense that another tornado was coming from the coast, and it would soon hit Liverpool (it did, causing great devastation), and that we were connected to all these things.

Our father wanted to hook us up again.

We became silent and uncommunicative. We no longer trusted him, and over the next few days, despite his continued lectures on the importance of our breakthrough, we stopped co-operating with the experiments. We had developed a way of reducing the information transmitted from our interfaces through the MBCI to the central processor. Quickly, our father grew angry with us and started shouting, raging at our behaviour. But our mother told him to give us time; we needed to grieve.

Jo-A reacted to father's temper more than the rest of us. As the first born, he had always had a greater sense of his own selfhood. One night, about a week after Jo-E's death, he started talking about how they were controlling us. It was bedtime and we were all in our bedroom. He was talking about how what they were doing was unnatural, and we shouldn't be forced into it. They had murdered Jo-E with their demands. No parent would do that to their child.

The rest of us were silent. We reached out to him mentally (in the past this had worked if one of us had had a nightmare; we could sooth each other. Think of it as a mental hug). We attempted to sooth him, but he started shouting, 'No, just get away from me.'

He locked himself in the bathroom, and a few minutes

later we heard a scream, and felt a horrific pain in our skulls. We scratched at our interfaces and began to scream too. We could feel his pain in our minds.

Our parents came running, and father knocked the door in to find Jo-A had used a knife to remove the main part of the neural-interface from his brain, digging out the main component from behind his ear, and jabbing at the three other nodes around his skull.

They carried him through to the lab, while we lay prone on the floor, unable to move or speak from the pain. Our pain lessened as our parents put Jo-A under sedation, and tended to his wounds.

We felt the dimming of our connection. We stood around his bed as Father scanned him and stopped the bleeding, but mother pleaded with us to go to bed and rest.

We went to our bedroom and the three of us, Jo-B, Jo-C, and Jo-D climbed into one bed and held each other. Jo-B was the most upset, so Jo-C and I held him. A few minutes later our mother came and sat on the floor next to our bed. She began to cry so we reached over and held her hand too, as she slumped to the floor beside us.

She started to tell us how she'd wanted us to be the best we could be. All she'd wanted was for us to have more of a chance in this dying world. Our father had ideas about science and writing his name in the AI history books, but she, like any mother, just wanted us – and all humanity – to have the best chance of survival. She sat up and reached over to all three of us. 'You were all so beautiful. You were perfect.'

'Were,' we thought.

'We pushed things too far,' she said.

We lay there and let her stroke our faces and hair, the way she used to stroke us when we were little.

'I think you should get some sleep. I'll go and check on Jo-A.'

When she had gone we turned to each other, and hugged. We were the last three.

It is true that we had had a sexual relationship for years.

But this was no grubby story of incest. What we had between us was beautiful. It was beautiful because we were closer than brothers and sisters. We were not separate beings, we were connected, we were one, and our sexual connection was just an extension of that.

But this time, without Jo-A and Jo-E, the kisses, the strokes, the touching, they were not the same. It could not assuage the sense of having a hole within us, so afterwards we drew apart, and the three of us lay on the bed, staring at the ceiling.

'I can't bear it,' Jo-C said. 'I feel Jo-A is dying. I know he is.'

'He is,' said Jo-B.

'Maybe if we connect to him, we will be able to help, even without his interface.'

'Yes, if we try hard enough.'

We had to reforge the connection with our brother without his interface, and if we managed that, we knew we could be God; for wasn't that what our father wanted? We turned our eyes to the window, now darkened by the shutters, and thought about the world out there, about the battered trees, and how our mother had spoken about us in the past tense, as if we were already dead to her. We got up and crept through to the lab. Jo-A was lying on a gurney, while my mother attended to his wounds. Father was working at a screen. He looked up and watched us gather around Jo-A. He told us we needed to be careful and not to disturb our brother. We ignored him and began to neurally interconnect with each other.

'OK,' Father said. 'but you need to be monitored. We need to do this properly.'

'No,' we said, shaking our heads. We backed away from him, but father told us to calm down, and to sit on our chairs. 'Come on,' he said, beckoning to us.

'Listen to your father,' mother said.

'Sweethearts,' he kept saying. 'I need you to sit here. Please.'

We sat on our usual seats, while he activated the Neural-Scanner nodes. We looked at each other and focused our minds. I felt my father adjust something, and a dim light seemed to play before my eyes. Suddenly, within us there was an anger, an anger at what they had done. Then I realised it wasn't in us, it was in *me*. The longitudinal research of our lives, of *my* life, had been unsuccessful. My siblings and I were the useless broken ends of that research. I couldn't lie there like an obedient child so I unhooked myself, jumped off my chair, and stood in the middle of the room.

'Jo-D!?' my father exclaimed. 'What are you doing?'

I didn't reply. I held out my arms, as if to reach out to my siblings, as if to reach out to the world. Then I closed my eyes and imagined the brightest light and the highest-pitched sound I could. I pictured the man in the storm being picked up off the ground, the slow-motion flash of lightning that accompanied it, the nanosecond in which he was suspended, mid-air, as the world rebooted.

When I eventually regained consciousness, I lay sprawled on the floor. Father was lying face down, motionless. My mother was nowhere to be seen, and Jo-A and Jo-B sat on their chairs, their heads leaning at different angles. I crawled to them and struggled pathetically to commune with them. Then I saw blood trickling from my father's ear. The air was hard to breathe and alarms were ringing all through the house. I was barely able to walk or see straight. I seemed to be on the precipice of something. A loneliness. Then, looking at the blood inching down my father's cheek, I realised: I wasn't just missing my siblings, I was missing him: *he* was the queen processor - not some computer in the lab. Him.

The Collective died that day. My father, Jo-A and Jo-B from hemorrhaging, Jo-C from shock. My mother was found a few days later out on Pendle Hill, and soon after removed to the Lancaster District Psychiatric Department, where she recently passed away.

My parents' research took humanity a small step forward, but they were not able to comprehend what we really were. As scientists they strove to be impartial, to maintain a distance from our interconnected mode of being, but it was precisely this impartiality that was their downfall.

As you all may have noticed, I am six months pregnant, and I am going to have triplets. It is only now, alone in this world and pregnant, that I can begin to understand my parents' dreams, and begin to forgive them too. In those few hours after Jo-E's death, we were able to reach out to the world, we felt the pain of Jo-A without the interface, we even sensed the trees down in the valley, swaying. That moment was, and is, the last hope for humanity. I have chosen this conference to declare that with my own children I shall attempt to finish what my parents began. Thank you.

[Applause].

Are there any questions?

Afterword:

The Unknowable Brain

Dr. Andrew Philippides
University of Sussex

THE INSPIRATION FOR this story came from the growing use of neural implants that teach us how brains work by recording the electrical signals in either individual neurons or groups of neurons. Over the past decade, there has also been a growing awareness that to fully understand what is going on in the brain, we need to record such activity *in use* – as the animal goes about its natural behaviour. While great advances have been made through the use of non-invasive gauges of working neural function such as fMRI and EEG, these only measure from aggregates of neurons – for instance, at present, the smallest single region that fMRI can tell us about is about the size of an ant's brain. To record from single neurons or groups of neurons directly, single electrodes or multi-electrode arrays need to be stably implanted into neural tissue and thus the majority of neural recording is performed *in vitro* in the lab in constrained, unnatural situations. Consequently, there is a growing desire in neuroscience to record from the animal in as natural and unconstrained a situation as possible.

In humans, for instance, neuroscientists have gained considerable insight from recording from the implants placed into human patients with severe epilepsy – implants that are used to control their seizures – as the neurosurgeons try to find the locus of their pathology. They have identified, among many other things, neurons that surprisingly react to very specific stimuli including a 'Jennifer Aniston' neuron[1] which

1. Quiroga, R. Q., Reddy, L., Kreiman, G., Koch, C., & Fried, I. (2005). Invariant visual representation by single neurons in the human brain. Nature, 435(7045), 1102-1107.

reacts to either images of Jennifer Aniston, or the words 'Jennifer Aniston' written down but intriguingly not to images of Jennifer Aniston with Brad Pitt. However, the simpler brains and behaviour of insects mean that much of the *in vivo* neural readings have been performed on them (you can even buy a kit for a remote-controlled cockroach – the RoboRoach – where you can control its movement with an App which connects to a backpack which, following a brief surgery, allows microstimulation of the antenna nerves).

In the Sussex Insect Navigation Group, where we study visual learning in ants and bees, we are developing methods to allow us to record from the brains of ants walking on a trackball in a Virtual Reality (VR) dome, so that we can understand how their neurons interpret the visual world as they engage in (what seems to them at least) natural behaviour. Similar techniques have proven successful in gleaning behavioural insight from flies which feel they are flying but are in reality tethered in place via a recording electrode within a VR arena. It goes without saying wireless communication would overcome some of the incumbent problems in these setups. One piece of work which has achieved this and which directly inspires Zoe's story is an implant in a dragonfly that records and wirelessly transmits the signals in its neurons during flight while it is trying to catch its prey[2].

It is these advances which inform the technology behind Zoe's story: broadband technology that enables wireless communication between brain areas. The next question then becomes: which bits of the brain should one wire up for collective consciousness?

2. Harrison, R. R., Fotowat, H., Chan, R., Kier, R. J., Olberg, R., Leonardo, A., & Gabbiani, F. (2011). Wireless neural/EMG telemetry systems for small freely moving animals. *Biomedical Circuits and Systems, IEEE Transactions on,* *5*(2), 103-111.

Research into higher order brain functions than we see in insects, including aspects of conscious experience, has been advanced in the last decades by improvements in recording technologies particularly EEG and fMRI. This work allows us to speculate about the areas that it would be good to connect up together to engender a collective consciousness. The story highlights the medial pre-frontal cortex (MPFC) as this has been implicated in self-referential processes, with some research suggesting that activity in this region is affected by people's cultural background. For instance:

'Chinese individuals use MPFC to represent both the self and the mother whereas Westerners use MPFC to represent exclusively the self, providing neuroimaging evidence that culture shapes the functional anatomy of self-representation.'[3] p.1310

The anterior insular cortex is known to be involved in empathy and emotion processing and so is a prime candidate brain region for sharing emotions in our story, as is the amygdala. While it is widely known to mediate fear responses, the amygdala's role extends to emotional salience in general. It receives inputs from visual cortex and outputs to many other areas including those involved in memory and control, so could be a 'hub' for emotion processing and so an interesting place to interface to.

In Zoe's story, the notion of the 'collective' is taken one stage further. Much of our understanding of 'collective intelligence' comes from social insects such as ants and bees. In these animals, while individually relatively simple, an emergent order and complexity can arise from simple interactions of the multitude: think of the beautiful and seemingly coordinated activity in flocks of starlings. It would seem there must be a conductor but in fact, this behaviour arises from each bird following a few simple rules. Equally,

3. Zhu, Y., Zhang, L., Fan, J., & Han, S. (2007). Neural basis of cultural influence on self-representation. *Neuroimage*, *34*(3), 1310-1316.

bees and ants can forage successfully and make collective decisions about, for instance, what a good hive is with very limited communication between themselves, relying on indirect correlates of information such as dances or pheromones, a mechanism known as 'stigmergy' (see pp140–145). For these insects, there is no 'hive mind' directing proceedings, just as there is very little direct collective communication. So the story poses the question: how much more could humanity achieve if we *did* have direct, collective communication and even outward training protocols?

It is known, for instance, that the learning of certain tasks can be enhanced by mental rehearsal – if we had access to multiple memories and rehearsals with slight variations surely this process could be sped up? (Indeed, something similar has been show in robots which learn about their bodies and how to move them by 'mentally' attempting multiple actions with variants of their bodies[4]). And if these connected individuals had a deep and collective goal, would we get a complexity that was more than the sum of its parts?

Neuroscientists abetted by mathematicians have tried to assess complexity in neural circuitry by reasoning about the complexity of a set of interconnected units and this work is on-going at Sussex in the Sackler Centre for Consciousness Science. It is clear that if we have five units all acting completely independently (five pendulums, say, all swinging of their own accord), there is no more complexity than there is in an individual unit. Equally, going to the other extreme, if all units are bound tightly together so they act exactly as one (five pendulums fixed at their weights to an inflexible bar), there is again no more complexity than the individual. It turns out that there is a sweet spot in between these two extremes where the possibility for complex behaviour is maximised. In the swings example, imagine the individual

4. Bongard, J., Zykov, V., & Lipson, H. (2006). Resilient machines through continuous self-modeling. *Science, 314*(5802), 1118-1121.

pendulum weights connected not rigidly but with springs so that there are weaker and flexible interactions between the elements. In this instance, the pattern of the swings' movements can be much more complex than the movements of multiple individual units, or for that matter one individual unit. As a corollary, too strong interactions between units, as in the Jo's connected brains, can lead to a lack of complexity, as the units get entrained and start to act synchronously with much external perturbation needed to break the system out of its phase-locked state.

So: could this really happen? If we leave aside the likelihood of scientists wanting to experiment on their offspring, we can examine what has already happened, what is likely, and what less so.

While tangential to the main story, the Robobees project is developing small UAVs for pollination and it seems likely that UAVs will be ubiquitous in the next decade or so. More centrally, we already have wireless neural interfaces to acting brains in insects but also to humans via brain computer interfaces which, for instance, enable paraplegic people to operate robot arms. Thus it seems reasonable to assume that technological progress in recording and transmission devices would allow brain regions to be interfaced. Further, these technologies are, as discussed above, telling us more about the brain regions which we might like to connect together. So, if we ignore the fact that we must damage the brain to insert such devices, the question is how would we achieve input into the network and what signals would we pass? We may know, for instance, that the amygdala processes emotion, but how these signals are conveyed by neural activity is still not well understood. Nor, indeed, is how these neural signals interact with the soup of neuromodulators, which mediate learning and memory and emotion, or the glial cells which surround our neurons and hold them in place and were once thought to be simply packing, but are now known to be functional. And that is before we start to consider the true complexity of the synapse and temporal patterning of neural signals. Indeed, the complexity of the system is such that – while we might broadly understand how these things interact, it is not a given that we will *ever* understand them well enough to reconstruct a full neural experience (episodic memory) let alone be able to 'wire' such complex areas together.

If the weather is a chaotically, unpredictable and unknowable system, and mathematics is provably unprovable, how much more so the brain?

The Familiar

Lucy Caldwell

The night it all began, Mum came home with wild eyes and hair even crazier than normal. It's one of my abiding memories of her, the way she used to twist and pull at her hair when she was thinking, bundle it up on top of her head and then fiddle with the clamps and hairgrips, without even realising she was doing it, until the whole thing was such a mess it took Dad half an hour with a bottle of conditioner and a wide-tooth comb to unravel it. Dad always joked, You want to see the state she left the hedge in, but that night he said nothing, just stared at her. We'd known something was up even before we saw her, when we heard her footsteps on the stairs. We lived on the sixth floor of an old block of flats in those days, a turn-of-the-century glass and moulded-plastic box that had been thrown up quickly in the housing crisis, only designed to last thirty years, and the lift − when it was working at all − would often screech and shudder to a halt halfway up. We were listening out for her, because although she was often home late, it was getting later than normal. It was another scorcher of a summer that year and the temperature in the flat was almost unbearable, even with the glass windows kept covered up all day: we had the front door open to try to create a through-draft. Mum's footsteps echoed around the stairwell much slower than usual and we heard her pause on the final half-landing for almost a minute before climbing the last few steps to our door. Neither of us made a move to go to the door and greet her: we just listened to the silence of her not moving up the stairs. When she finally

251

walked in she stopped: just stood there, all mad eyes and hair, as if she didn't know where she was or who we were.

Eventually, Dad said, wary, Hello, love, and I said: Mum?

She looked at each of us in turn, Dad kneeling with the damp facecloth in his hands, Finn in his chair, head lolling, me perched by the chipped, bladeless mouth of the fan. Then she said, and her voice was strange and tight, We did it, John. I think we did it.

For a long moment, nobody said anything, and none of us moved. It was gone ten o'clock, but still light outside, and the light through the slatted blinds cast stripes across the far wall. Across the shadow-bars I saw a quick flickering motion, a bat that was more like the thought of a bat, darting past the window to the condemned multi-storey beyond. I ducked, instinctively, and my movement seemed to break the spell.

We did it, Mum said again, and she took a few unsteady steps in the direction of the sink.

Let me, Dad said, and he got up quickly and ran the tap for her, filled a glass with lukewarm, hazy water. Mum took the glass and drank the whole thing down. Then she walked over to Finn and touched his damp cheek, stroked his dirty-fair hair from his forehead.

We did it, she said. Finn-baby, we did it.

Mum and Dad had started the company just after university, with some friends of theirs. They called it Famulus, which was not just a play on *family* or a word that sounded *fabulous* but a Latin term for 'servant'. From the beginning, Famulus had specialised in home-help assistants, which they called FamuNurses. We had two of their earliest prototypes in our living room, Cara 1 and Cara 1.1. They were crude, bulky things the size of a person, that over the years we'd come to use as coat stands. They'd been designed for the elderly or mildly disabled whose families couldn't afford full-time care. They could beep to remind you to take medication, and if the water tank was topped up they could provide you with a plastic cup of water or a lukewarm tea, and the pills slid out on a little tray. They had cameras and monitors built in for facecalls, so your relatives could check up on you. Later models came with heating systems or air-conditioning units, and wheels so they could move around your home. They were nothing particularly special: even back then there were lots of companies making similar things. Famulus made just enough to pay its employees and its manufacturing costs and to fund a small research and development team, which Mum headed, but that was about it: until Mum dreamed up the Familiar.

I know where she got the idea from. She got it from Finn. His favourite song was 'Puff the Magic Dragon': he never got tired of it, and sometimes Dad had to sing it to him six or seven times in a row before he'd go to sleep. When Finn started to need a ventilator to breathe for him at night, Dad designed wings and a tail for it, which Mum 3D-printed in her workshop out of stretchy red plastic. They glued the wings and tail onto the grey box of the CPAP as if it was Finn's very own pet dragon: and lying in bed at night, in the top bunk of the room we shared, the rattle and hiss of the CPAP didn't sound dissimilar to the wheeze of a small, snoring dragon.

The prototype she took from her backpack that baking July night was the size of a small cat. It was crude, but recognisably a dragon. Instead of a face it had a cluster of tiny cameras on the end of its neck, but it had wings, a tail, and wide, clawed feet. Its body was made out of a thin grey plastic, inset with hundreds of tiny blue-black photovoltaic cells that gleamed like scales.

Here it is, she said.

Oh my, Dad said. Oh my word.

I almost said: Is that it? Is that the big secret project that's taken up all these years? For years now, Mum had been talking about The Project. Sometimes it was all she and Dad ever talked about. Dad had given up work when Finn was born – one of them had to – and Mum was the better scientist. So she went back to Famulus while Dad became a full-time dad. He did all of the usual things, like shopping and cooking and cleaning, and all of the extra Finn-things, the bathing and massaging, the back-pummelling and physio, the regimen of injections and pills. But he missed being a scientist. At night he'd pore over Mum's plans and research papers and sample materials, and they'd sit up for hours, discussing, arguing. And this was the result.

Mum handed the 'dragon' to Dad and he took it reverently, stretching one of its wings out to full capacity, holding it up to examine its belly.

It looked like any old robot toy. It looked a bit like the FamuKitty, which had been an experiment to build a robot pet to keep old people company – a failure as it turned out, because the benefit of cats is they're alive, and no amount of automatic heat generation and simulated purr-vibrations will compensate for that. I zoned out and knelt by Finn's chair.

Do you see the dragon, Finn? I asked, and I cupped his head and directed his gaze to the little blue-grey robot.

Dragon, he said, only you wouldn't have known he was saying 'dragon' unless you knew him, and I said, That's right, and Finn said, Puff.

That's right, I said again, Puff's a much better dragon, isn't he. I felt almost sorry for Finn. How was he supposed to play with a robot dragon? He couldn't even jab consistently at a basic airscreen, let alone use a joystick. I blew a spit-bubble at Finn, something that I was forbidden from doing, and which always made him giggle. Mum and Dad didn't notice. I blew another and Finn chuckled and rolled his eyes, the way he did to show pleasure, and jerked and fluttered his hands in his lap. I didn't always hate Finn. Only sometimes.

The following day we all went with Mum to the Famulus research lab to have Finn's vision mapped and adjusted to the headset which would control the dragon. I'd been wrong about the control pad: unlike most robot toys, this one was designed so it could be operated by your eyes alone. It took almost the whole day to get the headset programmed. Finn could only manage being strapped into the machines for bursts of twenty minutes at a time before he got restless and upset and started making his horrible lowing noise. A walrus, I always used to think. A baby walrus being clubbed to death. I blocked my ears and tried not to listen, and watched the technicians pretending they didn't notice, either. But they kept shooting glances at Mum when they thought she wouldn't see. It was obvious that Finn was far worse than they'd been expecting.

Eventually the headset programming was done and we were ready to go. Mum held Dad's hand as they pushed Finn's wheelchair down the corridors to the testing zone. I couldn't remember ever seeing them hold hands before. I walked behind them, embarrassed for them. Dad didn't let go, even when it made him steer the chair wonkily, all the way there.

The testing zone was a large gymnasium which was normally used to build obstacle courses to test each new generation of FamuNurses: Dad pointed out to us the cones, staircases and door frames lined up against the walls. Today, it had been emptied of everything. Technicians were positioning and testing cameras, which were to record the experiment from every angle, securing netting screens and laying out crash mats. Dad wheeled Finn into the middle of the space and when everything was ready to go, the dozen or so people gathered round and Mum secured Finn's headset and switched it on. The little dragon, set on the ground a few metres away, flashed its camera–cluster and stretched its wings and shivered, and then it went still and everyone waited.

You use your eyes, Finn, Mum said, after a minute or so had passed. Do you see? You're seeing what the Familiar sees. If you look to the side, the Familiar will look, too.

There was another long pause.

He doesn't know what Familiar means, Mum, I said.

255

Call it Puff. He'll know what you mean then.

Mum turned and looked at me, her face taut. Maybe it was just the strip lighting of the testing zone but I saw lines on her face I'd never seen before.

Ok, she said, Finn? It's as if you're looking through Puff's eyes. You're seeing what Puff sees. Move your eyes to look around.

There was another pause. Then, suddenly, jerkily, the little dragon turned its head, first to the right, then to the left, then back to the right again. It was uncanny. You would have sworn it was alive and sizing us up.

Oh, Mum breathed, and she murmured something that sounded like, Thank God thank God.

Well done, Nella, Dad whispered.

The dragon continued to look around. Finn giggled, and the dragon shook its head as if in response.

Careful, sweetheart, Mum said, but Finn giggled again and even without being able to see his eyes I knew he was rolling them because the little dragon's cluster of cameras rolled and rolled, as if it was stretching and exercising its neck.

If you flick your eyes, Mum said, the way Dr Winfield showed you earlier? If you flick your eyes, Finn sweetheart, you can make Puff move.

There was another long pause while the dragon's camera-cluster lurched from one side to the other. Then Finn figured out the correct eye movement to make and the dragon stuttered into motion. It walked a few steps towards us, swaying from one foot to the other, looking more like a waddling duck than a dragon. It stopped about a metre away from Finn's wheelchair. Its neck extended for the camera-cluster to look up at Finn, roving from one side to the other, up and down, as it took him in. A whole minute passed, and then another.

He's seeing himself, poor thing, Mum murmured. Oh John –

It's ok, Dad said. It's ok, and he put a hand on her shoulder.

But she was right. Finn had seen himself in mirrors, of course, but that must be nothing compared to seeing yourself, the whole of you, for the first time from outside, as other people see you. His hands were twitching and fluttering in his lap.

He's upset, Mum said.

Come on, Dad said. Just wait. Just give it a moment more. We've come this far.

Mum cleared her throat a couple of times with a strangled noise. Then in a tight voice she said, Finn-baby. Flick your eyes. Flick your eyes upwards, Finn, and Puff will fly.

The dragon just stood there.

Come on, Dad said. Come on Finn-buddy. Just like Mum told you. Flick your eyes and Puff will fly.

I could hear a couple of scientists behind us whispering.

Come on, Finn, I chimed in.

For another long while it didn't seem as if anything was going to happen. Then Finn wrenched his whole head back and, simultaneously, the dragon jerked upwards as if it was leaping into the air, and its wings unfolded to their full extent and there it hovered, a metre above the ground.

Everyone in the room seemed to catch their breath at once.

Well done, Finn-buddy, Dad said.

That's it! Mum said. That's it, Finn! Now try to move it. Just use your eyes, gently.

We all stood there, watching the hovering dragon. It craned its neck, this way and that, and then with another jerk it launched itself further into the air, a whole metre higher, then another, as if it was climbing a huge invisible ladder. Then, suddenly, it turned right around and started flying, raggedly but determinedly, across the length of the space. Just when it looked as if it was about to crash into the wall of netting on the far end it turned and started flying towards us, more smoothly this time. I managed to take my eyes away from it for a second to look down at Finn. His hands were completely still in his lap and his mouth was wide open.

In his head he's flying, I said.

Not just in his head, Mum said, without taking her eyes from the dragon. The Familiar is engineered for immersive bodypresence to an unprecedented degree. The cochlear inserts create a sensation of motion and the fan-vents in the headset replicate the feeling of being in the air. To all intents and purposes, he *is* flying. He *is* the Familiar.

Her eyes were still glued to the dragon. She didn't even realise it was me she was talking to.

The dragon made several more circuits of the space and you could see Finn getting bolder each time: the flying was faster, the turns were smoother, the dragon climbed higher, and every now and then it would attempt a dive, once coming so close to our heads that several of the scientists ducked and one swore loudly and Finn burst out laughing, so hard that the little dragon's body shuddered and I thought it might drop from the air.

Eventually, Mum said: Finn, sweetie? I think that's enough for now, don't you? But Finn didn't want to stop. He'd never so much as played a VR computer game before. It took another five minutes before Mum could persuade him to guide the dragon to a clumsy crash landing. When she lifted the headset from his head his eyes were huge and glazed and his pale face was flushed with a delicate web of colour. He looked around, slowly, and started to moan.

It's ok, Finn-buddy, Dad said, squeezing his shoulders. It's ok.

But how could it be OK? One minute you're flying, actually flying, and the next you're trapped back down in a body that can't even move its own limbs. Of course Finn wanted to go on flying.

I wish I could have a go, I heard myself saying. Can I just try? Can I just put the headset on and *try*, just for a minute?

Oh Nella sweetheart, said Mum, turning to me. The headset is configured just for Finn, isn't it? It won't work on anyone else.

But can't I just try? I said.

I'm sorry, Nell. It just won't work.

But all I want is to *try*.

Sweetheart — Mum said, and she reached out and touched my cheek. I jerked my head away.

Come on, Nell, Dad said, and he tried to take my hand but I wouldn't, couldn't move. It had come over me in a rush. I wanted it. Oh, I wanted it: I can still remember, even now, the purity and intensity of that desire. I wanted it more than I'd wanted anything in my life, ever; I wanted it so badly I couldn't speak, and I felt tears come to my eyes. I opened my mouth to beg, once more, but all that came out was a moaning sound, as if I was Finn.

Please, Nella, Mum said. She looked on the verge of tears now, too. You've been so good all day, Nell. You've been my special helper. Come on. Please.

Come on, now, Dad said. You're almost eleven years old. Let's act our age.

But I couldn't help myself. I felt my legs go beneath me and I crumpled to the ground, wailing, and it took two technicians to lift me up and march me out of the testing zone. Everyone was looking at me. Finn was honking and thrashing about, too: but it was me they were looking at. I didn't care. All I wanted was to fly the little dragon, and all I could say, in incoherent gulps, was, It isn't fair, it isn't fair, it isn't fair.

Mum took Finn into the lab with her every day that week, and the next, so he could practise with the Familiar. She and Dad decided it was best if I didn't come in again, and nothing I could say would change their mind, no matter how many times I begged and promised to be good. It meant Dad couldn't go in, either. It was weird, just the two of us without Finn. Dad tried to be friendly, but I could tell he was disappointed in me. It was a horrible feeling and it made all the days drag, no matter what we did.

They had warned me that I wasn't to breathe a word about it to anyone. It wasn't exactly an unimaginable step, combining the robotic technologies the way they had, and even the cochlear insert to combat motion sickness wasn't a revolutionary idea. But the idea of the dragon was Mum's and Mum's alone: it had taken Famulus almost four years to develop this prototype and they couldn't risk another bigger, better-resourced company getting wind of their experiments and gazumping them. They needn't have worried. I didn't exactly have any friends I could have told, even if I'd wanted to. How could I have friends, when I could never bring anyone home to play? Our flat was small and there was nowhere to go to escape from Finn, his withered white legs and oversized, drooling head. The worst thing was, we even shared the same bedroom. It wasn't his fault, but that was the thing that made me hate him most. Mum liked to tell a story about the first time I saw Finn. They'd been told he was likely to be severely disabled at their very first scan, and subsequent scans confirmed it. The medical advice was to terminate him: but they hadn't. There'd been further complications when he was born and for a while it had been touch-and-go. Apparently, the first time I saw him he'd been in an incubator, tiny and scrawny and red, tubes coming out of him every which way. Mum had guided my hand in to touch him, to stroke his little stomach with the tip of one finger, and when I'd touched the palm of his tiny hand his fingers had flexed and closed around mine and wouldn't let go. I'd turned to the nurses, Mum's story went, and said to them, This is my brother and you'd better look after him while I'm gone. I was only three and a half, then. I didn't remember any of it. Sometimes I thought they'd probably made it up.

After a fortnight of experiments in the lab, Finn was allowed to bring Puff home to try it out in an uncontrolled environment. Several of the scientists were uneasy about it – I overheard Mum agonising to Dad over whether she was doing the right thing. But she overrode them in the end, arguing that they needed to see how it would function in a normal home. She brought home cameras which Dad rigged up all over the living-dining room, so they'd have data to analyse when the forty-eight hours were over. I hadn't seen Finn operate Puff since that very first attempt and I was taken aback to see how adept he'd become in such a short time: he'd been practising take-offs and landings in the lab, on boxes and blocks and door frames, and he was able to fly the dragon around our flat without crashing into anything. The juddery motion had gone, too: it could go from standing to flying seamlessly, and change direction without looking as if it was going to stall in midair. And there was more. Finn hovered Puff outside the bathroom door to indicate, we realised, that he'd soiled himself and needed his nappy changed. At one point he landed Puff on the fruit-bowl and made it flap its wings and whirl its head. When we worked out that he was asking for a green apple, sliced up into wedges that he could suck on, Mum had tears in her eyes.

It's going to change everything, she said.

That night I sneaked out of my bunk-bed to try Puff for myself. Finn had gone to sleep with it sitting on his bedside table, beside the original CPAP Puff, grey tail and red coiled together. I separated the tails and set Puff on the bedroom floor, then I took the headset and fitted it on my head, the earbuds in my ears, and switched it on. But however I widened and rolled my eyes like Finn's, it wouldn't send the command to wake Puff up: it just gave a loud *beeeep* each time I tried. I heard Dad's footsteps outside and barely had time to scramble back into my bunk before he came in to see if everything was alright. I tried to pretend I was asleep but he picked up the headset, still switched on, and knew immediately what I'd been up to.

Nella, he said.

I wasn't doing anything, I said. I just wanted one little go.

The Familiar isn't a toy, Nell, he said. Come on. You know that.

I turned to face the wall.

Come on, Nella-bella, he said. He switched off the headset and set it back on Finn's bedside table and put Puff back beside the CPAP.

It isn't fair, I said. I hate Finn and I wish he'd never been born, it isn't fair. I said it without meaning to. I said it mostly into my pillow, too, but he heard.

What did you say? he said. His voice had gone dangerously soft and I didn't dare repeat it.

Nella, he said. What did I just hear you say?

I didn't say anything, I said.

But I heard what you said, Nella.

Then why did you ask?

He looked at me for a second. Is it fair, he said, that your brother can't move, or speak, or read? Is it fair that he can't walk, or wash himself, or even go to the toilet by himself and that he'll be wheelchair-bound for his entire life? Is it fair the amount of drugs he has to take on a daily basis, or the fact that he'll never get to grow up and have a normal life – is any of that fair?

Then you shouldn't have had him, should you, I said.

I thought he might hit me then. I actually did. Instead he turned away and took a long, deep breath.

I don't want to upset Finn by taking the Familiar away, he eventually said. If he wakes up and it's gone, he'll be distressed and I don't want that. Can I trust you not to interfere with it again? Will you promise?

I knew I'd gone too far with what I'd said.

Fine, I said.

I want to hear you say it.

Ok, I said. I promise. Fine, whatever.

My heart was hammering.

Dad left the room without even looking at me.

It was impossible to tell from Finn's breathing whether he was asleep or awake. The CPAP with its stupid plastic wings and tail made every breath the same. *Shooom, shooom, shooom.* I rolled over and looked through the bunk-bed rails. Little Puff was just lying there, his legs retracted up against his body, wings folded in, tail coiled. Dad was right. He wasn't a toy. He was so much more than that.

The next day, Mum came home with the news that a big Chinese corporation wanted to buy the rights to the Familiar: wanted to acquire, in fact, the whole of Famulus. Their business plan and resources meant the Familiar would be on the market within eighteen months, two years at most, which was nearer than Mum had ever dreamed about. Mum and Dad had sold most of their shares in Famulus to fund Finn's medical treatment, so the takeover wasn't going to make us rich. But we'd be able to afford a part-time nurse for Finn, so Dad could go back to work.

And you, Nella – Mum turned to me and reached for my hand – you'll have your own Puff. You can have one from the first batch off the production line. Your very own Puff. How does that sound?

But Finn gets to keep the real Puff? I said.

Well, said Mum, and she looked at Dad. Then we all looked at Finn. The three of us were sitting at the kitchen table but Finn was in his chair in the corner, zooming Puff around the room, oblivious.

Your mum has agonised over this, Dad said. The terms of the takeover are unambiguous: the corporation wants sole ownership and possession of all prototype plans and materials, and that includes the Familiar.

I offered to make them a new one, Mum said. Using exactly the plans, *exactly* the same. But – she spread her hands and shrugged, helpless – they insisted that they want the original.

What will they do with it?

Well, Mum said.

What will they do with it, Mum?

They want the usage data from its chips, Dad said.

So they'll break it apart?

They will dismantle it, yes.

But –

But then, Mum said quickly, then they'll put the body back together and it'll have pride of place in the company headquarters in Shenzhen. People will make pilgrimages to see it, and PhD students will write entire theses about how it came to be, and there'll probably be a film made about it and we'll all go to the Oscars.

I looked at her.

How are you going to tell Finn? I said.

I know, Mum said, and she put her head in her hands. I know, I know.

Finn will have a new Puff, Dad said, putting a hand on Mum's shoulder, and it's going to be a hundred times better. Lighter, faster, more aerodynamic. It'll be much better for him in the long run.

None of us said anything for a minute or so. Then Mum got up and went to kneel beside Finn's chair.

I'm sorry, Finn, she said. But if you only knew. All of it, everything I've done, I did it for you. All of it. My beautiful boy.

I got up and left the room.

I waited until they were asleep. I climbed out of my bed, bundled my duvet up and wedged it against the bottom of the door to muffle any sounds we made, then I shook Finn awake.

Finn, I said. Finn, you have to listen to me. You have to listen very carefully, ok?

He blinked at me, his eyes glazed and sleepy.

Right, I said, so here's the thing – and then I told him everything. How they were going to sell Puff to the Chinese company, and Puff would be cut up and experimented on, then put in an airless glass case, never allowed to fly again. I put my hand over his mouth in case he made a noise, but he didn't, he just looked at me. You never knew how much of what you were saying Finn actually understood, but I was sure now that he understood everything. When I finished talking he stared at me, his face white, not blinking, and I knew that he wanted me to do it.

Ok, I said. I propped him up with my pillow, unlooped the CPAP's tubing from his ears and unclipped the nose-piece, leaving the machine itself switched on in case I had to reconnect him to it quickly. Then I slid the headset onto him, making sure it was properly adjusted, the way I'd seen Mum do, the earbuds right inside his ears, and switched it on. The little dragon came to life almost instantly, stretching its wings and craning its neck, flicking its tail and standing up.

Wait a moment, I whispered, and I tiptoed over to the bedroom window. There were Finn-proof bars on the bottom half, but the top half opened outwards, and the hinges were well oiled; it opened smoothly and silently, all the way. The night was hazy and thick, the air still warm. The traffic on the main road at the bottom of the hill sounded like a distant river.

I stood for a moment, breathing in the night, then I turned back to Finn.

Ok, I said. With a whirring noise that in the silence of the room sounded like a roar, Puff leapt from the bedside table and circled the room, once, twice, before perching on the window ledge.

I was suddenly worried that Mum or Dad might wake up after all.

Go on, Puff, I said.

Puff turned its head and looked at me for a second, its glittering cluster of eyes.

Go on, I said.

It didn't move. I reached forward and pushed it. It teetered for a moment, and then dived from the ledge and out into the night.

It wouldn't last long. I knew that. It was solar-powered and without an energy-source it would run out of life. I didn't know how long it could keep going – a couple of minutes? Five minutes? Ten? – but I knew it wouldn't be much. The connection would weaken and falter, the last flickers of power would drain from it, and it would die. It would fall to the ground from wherever it happened to be, and the impact would mangle it, and whoever came across it would think it was junk, a broken toy, and the street-cleaners would shovel it up as rubbish.

It's worth it, Finn, I whispered. It's the only way. It's worth it. You don't want him to spend the rest of his life in an airless box, all alone, and never flown again, do you?

I watched until I couldn't make out Puff any longer, the little grey blur of him so small against the sky, which to anyone else would just look like a pigeon, or an owl. Even when I couldn't see him any longer I stayed watching, and then I closed my eyes and imagined what it must feel like, skimming above the treetops and the rooftops, climbing higher and higher then diving down low, the ground rushing towards you, turning at the very last second and swooping back up again, wheeling, soaring, chasing, tumbling...

I don't know how long I stood there. Eventually I heard Finn's breathing start to catch and go ragged, and I stuffed my hand over his mouth just in time to muffle the horrible squeal. My heart was pounding. When I eventually took off the headset his face was wet with tears and his eyes were blank. I set the headset on his bedside table and I hooked him back up to the CPAP and watched it take over his breathing for him. I suddenly didn't feel like getting back into my own bunk so I got into bed with him. His body was cold, despite the warm night, and I realised that mine was shaking, too. I wondered what it had felt like, as Puff's energy started to falter; what it had been to feel yourself plummeting helpless through the air, the hard ground rushing up at you, unable to move or save yourself. I wondered if Finn had closed his eyes in the headset, or kept them open. Perhaps the cameras had cut out in those last few seconds before the collision. I wondered which was worse: the crash, or the sudden blankness, the knowing it was over.

But wasn't it worth it, Finn, I whispered into his skinny shoulders. Wasn't it worth it?

We lay there for a long while together, and then, somehow, we both must have fallen asleep.

Afterword:

The Feeling of What it is Like to be a Robot

Prof Alan Winfield
University of the West of England, Bristol

WILL ROBOT AVATARS with 'bodypresence', like Lucy's fictional dragon Puff, ever become a reality? Yes I believe they may, and perhaps sooner than we think.

Philosopher Thomas Nagel famously characterised subjective experience as "something that it is like to be..." and suggested that for a bat, for instance, there must be something that it is like to be a bat[1]. Nagel also argued that, since we humans differ so much from bats in the way we perceive and interact with the world, then it is impossible for us to know what it is like for a bat to be a bat. I am fascinated, intrigued and perplexed by Nagel's ideas in equal measure. And, since I think about robots, I have assumed that if a robot were ever to have conscious subjective experience then there must be something that it is like to be a robot that – *even though we had designed that robot* – we could not know.

But I now believe it may eventually be just possible for a human to experience something approaching what it is like to be a robot. To do this would require two advances: one in immersive robot tele-operation, the other in the neuroscience of body self-image manipulation.

Consider first, tele-operation. Tele-operated robots are, basically, remotely controlled robots. They are the unloved poor relations of intelligent autonomous robots. Neither intelligent nor autonomous, they are nevertheless successful and important first wave robots; think of remotely operated vehicles (ROVs) engaged in undersea exploration or oil-well

1. Nagel, Thomas. *What is it like to be a bat?*, Mortal Questions, Cambridge University Press, 1979.

repair and maintenance. Think also of off-world exploration: the Mars rovers are hugely successful; the rock-stars of tele-operated robots.

Roboticists are good at appropriating technologies or devices developed for other applications and putting them to good use in robots: examples are WiFi, mobile phone cameras and the Microsoft Kinnect. With the high profile launch of the Oculus Rift headset[2], and their acquisition by Facebook, and with competing devices from Sony and others, there are encouraging signs that immersive Virtual Reality (VR) is on the verge of becoming a practical, workable proposition. Of course VR's big market is video games – but VR can and, I believe, will revolutionise tele-operated robotics.

Imagine a tele-operated robot with a camera linked to the remote operator's VR headset, so that every time she moves her head to look in a new direction the robot's camera moves in sync; so she sees and hears what the robot sees and hears in immersive high definition stereo. Of course the reality experienced by the robot's operator is real, not virtual, but the head mounted VR technology is the key to making it work. Add haptic gloves for control and the robot's operator has an intuitive and immersive interface with the robot.

Now consider body self-image modification. Using mirror visual feedback researchers have discovered that it is surprisingly easy to (temporarily) modify anyone's body self-image. In the famous rubber hand illusion a small screen is positioned to hide a subject's real hand[3]. A rubber hand is positioned where her hand could be, in full view, then a researcher simultaneously strokes both the real and rubber hands with a soft brush. Within a minute or so she begins to feel the rubber hand is hers, and flinches when the researcher suddenly tries to hit it with a hammer.

2. http://www.oculus.com/
3. 'Body Illusions: Rubber Hand Illusion', *New Scientist*, 18 March 2009. http://www.newscientist.com/article/dn16809-body-illusions-rubber-hand-illusion.html

Remarkably H.H. Ehrsson and his colleagues extended the technique to the whole body, in a study called 'If I Were You: Perceptual Illusion of Body Swapping'[4]. Here the human subject wears a headset and looks down at his own body. However, what he actually sees is a mannequin, viewed from a camera mounted on the mannequin's head. Simultaneous tactile and visual feedback triggers the illusion that the mannequin's body is his own. It seems to me that if this technique works for mannequins then it should also work for robots. Of course it would need to be developed to the point that elaborate illusions involving mirrors, cameras and other researchers providing tactile feedback are not needed.

Now imagine such a body self-image modification technology *combined with* fully immersive robot tele-operation based on advanced Virtual Reality technology. I think this might lead to the robot's human operator experiencing the illusion of being one with the robot, complete with a body self-image that matches the robot's possibly non-humanoid body. This experience may be so convincing that the robot's operator experiences, at least partially, something like what it is to be a robot. Philosophers of mind would disagree – and rightly so; after all, this robot has no independent subjective experience of the world, so there is no something that it is like to be. The human operator could not experience what it is like to think like a robot, *but she could experience what it is like to sense and act in the world like a robot.*

The experience may be so compelling that humans become addicted to the feeling of being a robot fish, or robot dragon or some other fantasy creature, that they prefer this to the quotidian experience of their own bodies. A thought which makes Lucy Caldwell's scenario all the more extraordinary, beautiful, and tragic.

4. Petkova VI, Ehrsson HH (2008) 'If I Were You: Perceptual Illusion of Body Swapping.' *PLoS ONE 3* (12): e3832. doi:10.1371/journal.pone.0003832

Making Sandcastles

Claire Dean

THE SEA IS a dirty line in the distance, but he finds bits of it everywhere. He's discovered a stone giant – almost completely buried by the sand – and between its sharp grey fingers there are tiny secret kingdoms of clear water. Long cold puddles wriggle between the sand snakes further down the beach. He's found places where if you take a step, your footprint fills up with the sea. He would like to kneel and put his tongue in to taste the salt, but his parents are watching.

He spends some time up on the giant's hands knotting slimy black seaweed and pressing its empty purses between his fingernails. There are barnacle imprints on his knees. He rubs at the bumpy red skin. He is looking for alive things. See-through shrimps, tickle-armed anemones. These are the creatures that live in rock pools in stories. Maybe they've all become so see-through they're invisible.

'Johnny, you need to come and eat. Now.' Mum shouts.

She has laid out their picnic blanket. Dad is sitting on the sand at the side. There are sandwiches and crisps. Mum has made hard-boiled eggs. Dad always says it's not a picnic without eggs. The salt for them is tucked up in the corner of the foil wrapping. Dad's the only one that eats them.

The picnic blanket is damp under the backs of his legs. He digs his heels into the sand just off the edge of the blanket to see if he can make the sea appear there too.

'Did you check the tide data properly?' Mum is unwrapping and opening everything but hasn't picked up anything to eat herself.

'It's not due in for ages,' Dad says.

'Because you know people have… well, you know, out here.'

'Yes, I know. Do you have to get everything out? It'll all get coated in sand.'

'Johnny, here, I brought you cheese,' Mum says.

His sandwich tastes of salt and the cold wind and he can feel the grit of sand between his teeth. It would be good to always eat outside like this. He crunches a handful of crisps all at once, spraying bits everywhere.

'I hope there's enough. I haven't brought anything for dessert because you said we'd be able to get ice creams here.' Mum doesn't move but her voice is pointing at the shack further up the beach.

It's small. He's already explored all round it, but there's no way to get in. The shutters are down and crusty with sand and he couldn't find a door.

'I didn't know it would have closed down,' Dad says. 'I just thought coming here would be a nice thing to do.'

There are faded pictures of strange ice lollies on the shack's sign. They have cool names like Twister and Fab. Dad read him a story about an ice cream van once. This could be one that got stuck. Its wheels are buried deep below the sand. It was dangerous of someone to just leave it there empty. It could be taken over by a giant hermit crab to be its new shell. He keeps watching for pincers.

Mum is packing things away. Dad is still eating.

He scrunches up the wrapping from his sandwich to make a ball. He kicks it but it just sort of floats. Sand flies everywhere.

Dad shakes his sandwich. 'Do you want your Maker out, Johnny?'

He takes the red case and attempts to run with it. The sand is sucking at his feet.

'Don't go too far.' Mum's voice follows him. 'He should be playing with real toys,' she says to Dad.

'It is a real toy.'

272

'It's cheap and bloody lethal. Here kids, have fun, and try not to maim yourself with the laser.'

'It's got guards on it. I thought you wanted him to learn. So he can grow up to be an important scientist like his mother.'

★

He cleans his Maker after every use with a special grey cloth. He doesn't want it to get crusty because then it won't move or melt or make things as well. He takes special care with the extending legs. There are never fingerprint clouds on the control's screen because he wipes that too.

He unzips the case. All the materials are tidy inside the lid. He fingers the orange and green rolls of plastic thread, but doesn't pull them out. They vanish after a while in water so they're no good here. He doesn't want to use the coloured sugar either. When he puts the Maker down in front of him its legs sink into the sand, but it's all terrain. It'll be fine as soon as he switches it on. He takes the control out of the green and orange striped pouch he's made for it, hunches over and draws out a design on the screen. His parents won't let him download designs – too expensive Dad says, and Mum says it's good for him to use his imagination. He wishes free sites still existed. Mum says you could get designs to print anything you could imagine, but that was before what she calls the patentnet. Even pirates don't have sites now. He sets the Maker to fill mode while he finishes drawing the edges. It sounds like it's chomping on the sand.

'Johnny, do you need a wee? I'm going down to the water.' Dad is already heading away.

He doesn't need one, but he presses pause and the chomping stops. He puts the control away in its pouch.

They run and leap over the sand snakes, the wind whipping their bare feet. They keep going and going and going. The spaces between the snakes get wider, so they give up jumping across and paddle through the freezing water. They've been running for ages. He wonders if they'll reach the sky before they reach the waves. And then they're there. His toes are touching the whole gigantic sea. He teases it by waiting until the frothy edge of each wave almost reaches him and then he jumps back. The sea sucks in its breath and has another go at getting him. Dad wees in a big arc into the water. They stand together and look out. All the treasure from all the pirate ships that have ever sunk seems to have floated up to the top and is shining for him to see. He lets the waves get him and wash around his ankles. When they turn back, the beach looks so big and empty apart from Mum. Even the giant has disappeared. It makes him think of the old paper map on the wall in their kitchen. Mum is the red pin for home.

'You know your Maker reminds me of a remote control car I had when I was little. I used to take it to the park with your granddad and he'd chase after it.'

'A car can't make things, Dad.'

'I know.'

★

The sky has become a fat line of clouds about to press down on him. The Maker's taking forever. It would be better if he had the Maker 4000.2. Or if Mum would make him a new one. He knows she can print parts with her giant Maker in the cellar. If parents are going to keep secrets they should learn to hide them in bigger boxes. She prints other things too, soft, squishy, things he can't put names to that she keeps in jars in her work fridge. It looks like an alien zoo. He's not supposed to open the fridge. The sand is spitting and crackling now. He's had to alter the design to make it smaller. He's added a door.

'I don't understand why you're so angry,' he can hear Mum saying. 'This was always the plan.' She sounds angry too. The wind is picking up his parents' voices and throwing them at him. He'd move further away, but he's got too far with his work.

'He's too young.' Dad says.

'Unregistered…' Mum stops. She's looking over at him, so he pretends he's redirecting his Maker.

'These things don't grow on trees,' she says.

'You mean you're not planning on printing them as well?'

They make him invisible when they argue. He wishes the Maker would hurry up. He wishes the sand would crackle louder.

'I've got as far as I can using our cells. I wish I could just use mine, but you know they would trace us. He will be fine. The poorclinic's in place. They need parts.' Mum's explaining voice usually makes Dad shout. But Dad's not speaking now. He's looking at the sea. The spaces between the snakes have joined up and the waves are coming.

'It's too much of a risk,' Dad says. 'And we don't have to take the risk.'

'Everything is a risk. But we can't not do it. Just think about how many people can be helped. Do you want him to grow up thinking things can't change? That this is the way it has to be? That only rich people deserve to be helped?' Mum's voice is a whisper now, but the wind still carries it towards him. 'We took him for this.'

'He is our son.' Dad says this very slowly like Mum doesn't understand anything.

Mum is flinging crumbs from the picnic blanket into the air. Dad isn't moving. Maybe his feet have sunk into the sand and they'll have to pull him out. Maybe Mum will want to leave Dad there, like she sometimes threatens to leave him when he takes too long to get his shoes on. The wind snatches the blanket off her and she has to chase it and stand on it to fold it up. She's doing everything too quickly. She keeps looking at Dad. Dad keeps looking at the sea.

Dad comes unstuck at last and walks towards him, 'You made a sandcastle, Johnny!' His eyes are full of tears but he almost sounds happy.

Dad and Mum are standing on either side of him with the whole sea between them. It looks dirty again. All the treasure has gone.

'Johnny, you melted the sand,' Mum says. 'What have I told you about turning it up that high? It's dangerous. What were you thinking?'

'I made it into glass so it can't fall down.'

He wants to wait to tease the waves with his toes. He wants to show his parents that the sandcastle won't fall down. He lets them each take one of his hands. They pull him away from the incoming tide.

Afterword:

Make/Shift

Prof Steen Rasmussen
University of Southern Denmark

CLAIRE DEAN'S STORY gives us a glimpse of a possible dystopia in which powerful interests have hijacked and patented the usefulness of engineered living processes and personal fabrication. How could that happen, and what is the scientific basis of these ideas?

John von Neumann, the inventor of the modern computer, realized that if life is a physical process, then it should be possible to implement life in media other than biochemistry. In the 1950s, he was one of the first to propose the possibility of implementing genuinely living processes in computers and robots. This perspective, while still controversial, is rapidly gaining momentum in many science and engineering communities[1].

In the 1940s, Stanislaw Ulam and John von Neumann developed the mathematical idea of cellular automata, which von Neumann later used to develop a universal constructor[2]. This is a pattern implemented in cellular automata that consists of two parts: a universal constructor and a tape. The universal constructor reads from the tape and produces whatever is encoded. A universal constructor may itself be encoded on the tape, in which case it produces a functional copy of its *own pattern*. The term 'universal' refers to the fact that the constructor can construct all possible (computable) patterns.

---

1. Neumann, J.V. (1966). *Theory of Self-Reproducing Automata*. University of Illinois Press, Champaign, IL, USA. See also Rasmussen, S. (1991), 'Aspects of Information, Life, Reality, and Physics', in *Artificial Life II*, ed. Langton, C., et al., Addison– Wesley, 767-773.
2. Neumann, J.V. (1966). Ibid.

Von Neumann proved that machines exist that can make copies of themselves. His inspiration came from biology. Biological systems can do this easily, of course. However, biological systems cannot make *everything*, although they have many fascinating properties.

The potential usefulness of engineered living or life-like processes stems from the tantalizing properties of life itself. Living processes self-organize matter, from the nanoscale up, to create systems characterized by energy efficiency, sustainability, robustness, autonomy, learning, intelligence, self-repair and adaptation, as well as evolution through self-replication[3]. These systems have highly desirable properties that current technologies lack.

During the 19th century, the industrial revolution automated mass production in factories, and created a vast transportation infrastructure to move raw materials and products. In the latter part of the 20th century and the start of current century, the IT revolution automated personal information processing in computers and the Internet. We believe the next major technological revolution will be based on an integration of information processing and material production. Living, biological organisms combine these processes seamlessly – in fact, at present, they are the *only* machines that can do this. A need to find out how they do this is one of the reasons why we seek to understand life as a physical process. The grand engineering challenge is to find out how to integrate information processing and material production from the nano- to the macroscale in technical systems.

One of our concrete technological visions[4] for integrated information processing and material production is the

3. Bedau, M.A., McCaskill J.S., Packard N., and Rasmussen S., 'Living Technology: Exploiting Life's Principles in Technology', (2010) *Artificial Life* 16: 89-97. See also Bedau M.A., Hansen, P.G., Parke, E., and Rasmussen, S. (2010), eds., *Living Technology: 5 Questions*, Automatic Press/VIP 2010.

development of a personal fabricator (PF) as an analog to the personal computer (PC). To get an idea of what it might imply to have a PF on your tabletop, imagine an advanced computer-controlled 3D printer that is able to control both top-down fabrication (which is possible today) and bottom-up micro-fabrication, which is currently a research area. The bottom-up fabrication occurs in part through molecular self-assembly and self-organization, akin to living processes, or by molecular level controls. Thereby mesoscopic structures of arbitrary complexity and composition are constructed. Combining the bottom-up and top-down design approaches means it should be possible to construct macroscopic objects of arbitrary complexity and functionalities. Given the appropriate raw materials, a personal fabricator should be an example of von Neumann's universal constructor, and as such be able to construct anything if appropriately encoded.

The PC and the internet have enabled the individual to create and share information globally. Living technology has the potential to give all individuals access to the design, sharing, production and recycling of complex objects in a simple and sustainable manner[5] (SPLiT, 2010). However, the sustainable personal fabricator network is still just a vision, and its implementation relies on years of basic research together with dedicated engineering at the interfaces between

4. Gershenfeld N., FAB: (2005) *The Coming Revolution at Your Desktop*, Basic Books, New York. See also: Rasmussen, S., Albertsen, A., Fellermann, H., Pedersen, P.L., Svaneborg, C., and Ziock, H. (2011). 'Assembling Living Materials and Engineering Life-like Technologies', *Proceedings GECCO'11*, p 15, Association for Computing Machinery, July 12–16, 2011, Dublin, Ireland.
5. SPLiT 2010, 'Sustainable Personal Fabricator Network', see: http://flint.sdu.dk/index.php?page=living-technology. The SPLiT vision was developed and lead by Packard, N., McCaskill, J.S., and Rasmussen, S.
TRUCE & COBRA, see the project networks http://www.cobra-project.eu and http://www.truce-projecgt.eu as well as the many individual projects within these networks.

biotechnology, information technology, nanotechnology, production technology, and artificial intelligence.

Ongoing activities within this rapidly growing research area can be followed e.g. at the European Commission-sponsored project web pages for TRUCE and COBRA. Common to these networks of projects is an investigation of unconventional computing and of how to create and utilize living processes in a variety of hybrid biochemical, computational, and robotic systems.

As our technology becomes smarter and more life-like, it clearly brings us a variety of novel societal, safety, environmental, ethical and religious challenges. Some of these issues are covered in Claire's story. I believe it's possible (indeed, probable) that repressive agents will attempt to prevent a free and democratic sharing personal fabricator technology. Whether they succeed depends on whether we as citizens allow this to happen.

Ensuring free, private communication via the internet and protecting the ownership of private data are two critically important, and closely related, political battles of today, and will be historically linked, no doubt, to the struggles of 2070. Currently, the repressive agents seem to be winning: fundamental citizen rights have been diminished through a combination of inappropriate use of information technology, insufficient legislation, and the unchecked growth of corporate power and what gets waved through in the name of 'national interest'. Citizens need to fight back.

The Longhand Option

Dinesh Allirajah

THE FIRST WIND of Rosa's visit arrived shortly after breakfast.

Dill was clearing the last of the dishes from the kitchen table when he felt the buzz of a message alert under his right thumbnail. He pressed his thumb onto the table and swiped across. The hologram screen began to appear but glitched on a coffee stain. Dill gave the surface a wipe down and tried again, this time opening up his inbox screen between the fruit bowl and a jar filled with BrekFast Cheetz energy bars. His new message was an automated notice from the Courier Blimp Company to expect a delivery, sent from Rosa's address, later that morning. He was about to scroll down for more details when the table sounded an electronic trill, like a scale of a xylophone, indicating another message. This one was from Nat:

'Dad – gran just buzzd me. D'you know when she's gettin here?'

Another xylophone scale: Nat again.

'ps any more cheetz bars in there?'

Dill grabbed an energy bar, leaned out of the kitchen into the corridor, pushed open the door of the living room and tossed the bar inside. He heard a 'Thanks Dad' as he closed the door again.

Emma passed him in the corridor. She'd been re-filling the bird feeders in the roof garden and the morning warmth had given her a sheen of perspiration which she wore like sequins. Dill met her easy smile with a tighter one of his own and she registered the disparity. 'Problem?'

'Ah, I guess, well–' He indicated his message screen on the table top. 'We hear not a thing from her for – what? – a year? And now apparently – but only via our son – we find out we're expecting a visitor! It's just, I don't know...'

Emma flicked through the morning's messages. 'But we don't actually get from this when she's coming or... we don't get anything from her, really.'

'I know,' said Dill, 'but I suppose... well, information that something is going to happen has reached us before, you know, the thing happens. By my mother's standards, that's a courtesy.'

Dill walked away from the table to busy himself with the breakfast dishes next to the sink. Emma continued to mine the Courier Blimp delivery alert for information.

'So there's a status tracker,' she said, 'and – oh, OK, it's already on its way– look, Dill, there's a live feed. "2.78km away from destination." Right, that's my morning's entertainment sorted – thank you, Rosa!'

'I – will you just look at this?' Dill was back at the table, prodding at the window showing the live flycam footage of the blimp's untroubled flight towards their house. 'How much did all this even cost? If she was worried about it being stolen, she could have told me. I could have *walked* there and carried it here myself – *and* only asked the planet for a drink of water in return.'

Emma placed her right hand on her husband's cheek. She stroked his eyebrow with her thumb. 'Ah, my sweet, but remember: that biohazard gave you life. And she obviously has a new story – look, it says here: "Description of cargo: office equipment."'

Dill rolled his face into Emma's palm and kissed her wrist. 'Yeah, that'll be why she's coming – she'll have been stuck. When my mother has an idea for a story, she's joyous. She walks around with armfuls of flowers. Everybody eats. Then, part of the way in, she goes into her long, dark, tortured night of the soul phase that can last... two days. Or it can last a whole year off school. Nowadays, she knows to be alone for those. And then she starts to come unstuck. Which is now.'

'Well – that's exciting, isn't it?'

'If you like. But, then, we're going to be the ones who have to babysit her while she rages to the end of her masterpiece. Which is why she's coming here – also, we've got a teenage son who can help operate whatever she's decided is "office equipment" in that blimp up there.'

Just before midday, Dill and Emma went up to the roof to watch for the Courier Blimp's arrival. Across neighbouring rooftops, a mosaic of solar panels lapped at the sunlight. There were intermittent sounds of transport but all the building's noises were softer: the wildflowers in troughs, along the edges of the roof, fidgeting in the breeze; the faint, approving hum of bees fussing from the buddleia to the lavender and heather, the forget-me-nots and on to the borage in next door's planter. Emma closed her eyes. The heat slid down her face to her chin, then crept back up to her forehead.

'Here she comes,' said Dill.

The blimp, a bulbous silver dart, could be seen in the middle distance, nudging its way through the air in an oversized approximation of the wobbly flight paths of the bees. When it was over Dill and Emma's heads, it circled twice, made a sound like a vigorous violin duet and lowered itself onto the roof. As soon as the blimp touched down, Dill was buzzed a code. He held his palm above a scanner in the tailfin of the blimp and there was another violin sound as the silver hull of the blimp split horizontally into two halves. They lifted off the top half and stared at the cargo Rosa had sent. They said nothing at first, Emma too convulsed with laughter to speak and Dill settling on dumb incredulity.

The blimp contained one item of office equipment: a pen. There was also an electronic breadmaker – 'That thing was an antique when she bought it,' Dill eventually managed to say – and sixteen bags of flour.

Rosa arrived at six o'clock. She said it was too late in the day to start writing. What she really needed to do was bake some bread.

The following morning, Rosa's pillow embarked on a campaign of vibrations and pre-recorded chatter that succeeded in getting her up, out of bed and sitting down to write before the rest of the house had risen. The fragile stretch of peaceful time between dawn and breakfast could, if used well, be the difference between a productive day and enduring frustration. The guest room, really a screened-off partition of the large downstairs living space, had a reconditioned school desk she could work at and it allowed in enough powdery morning light to minimise the strain on her eyes. She wiped a dusting of flour from her Megastylus pen and pressed it onto the surface of the desk. Her notebook library appeared in hologram on the desk and she selected the new story. The work-in-progress opened in lined pages of simulated handwriting. She swiped the screen repeatedly from right to left, turning the pages until she reached the section she'd been working on.

One morning you go to the lock-up on the other side of the alleyway at the back of the house. Like all your neighbours, you once used it as a garage for your car but it's now a storage space for junk, regularly cleared out and filled up again, one segment of your past replaced by another. You see that it's long overdue another clean-out but this is when it happens: you start to calculate the time this will take — a half-day to sort into selling, chucking and charity; the rest of that day to put into bags and boxes; a day for dispensing with everything unwanted; enough cleaning for a whole day with valeting robots, two or three without — and it no longer feels like time worth spending.

Weeks pass in no discernible contrast to any you've experienced before and then there'll be another moment when you catch yourself calculating the worth of a routine or protocol in terms of the remaining *time it will take* up *up. An insurance policy goes unrenewed. A dining chair breaks and is neither repaired nor replaced. An item of clothing isn't put in with the rest of the laundry. There are no consequences to these inactions but each moment sticks a pin in your mental calendar. A chain is forming: moments of letting slip, moments of letting go, a passive* ~~acceptance of~~ *embrace for a slow euthanasia.*

Rosa clicked the Megastylus pen and the tiny screen in its barrel woke up with a single guitar chord played through a wah-wah pedal. A function menu came on the screen and she chose the Longhand option. The screen asked: 'Turn AlchemyText ON?' and she selected: 'Yes.'

She held the pen above the desk, felt the muscular pull along the crook of her arm, felt her wrist stiffen and strengthen, saw the nib hover and tremble and rehearse handwriting strokes in the air. She brought the nib to the surface of the desk and pressed...

You realise that you may have emptied your future of all its remaining irrelevant concerns but you retain the urge to fill that time with something that is *relevant: something meaningful, something real.*

It was the pen that was pulling her hand, pushing out the words even though they still felt molten in her mind. So long as she kept her focus on the story, kept the mental images clear as to where she wanted it to go, the writing flowed.

You think about every life jettisoned in favour of the one you ended up living: years that slipped away in the few seconds it might take for doubt to overcome a new idea; lives that luck seemed to extinguish when determination or resilience might have kept them alight; the history, the geography, the identity you never got to share with whole swathes of your family. You need to find a way to reconnect with all you might have been.

The AlchemyText function was at its best when it used emotion-capture to read Rosa's grip on the barrel, her pressure on the nib and the adrenaline released in the act of writing; it continually processed these to offer various, branching sentence options, appropriate prose styles or personal content. When the mechanics of plot took priority, the pen could predict Rosa's choices based on patterns in her previous work stored in its memory. If this provided no clear solutions, it had to rely on Rosa herself.

You lie in bed ~~until sleep takes over~~ *contemplating these unlived lives. The dream you have that night is*

Rosa stopped to strike through the last phrase. She tried again.

~~The dream you have that night is~~ *You begin to dream*

She crossed that out.

~~The dream you have that night is~~ ~~You begin to dream~~ *The answer comes to you in your dreams.*

This time she noticed that, however many times she crossed out the phrase, the longhand text on the screen settled for a neat single strikethrough.

There was a scuffling sound on the floor beneath her desk. Before she had a chance to look, the sound moved with a dart and a scamper towards the window. There was silence for thirty seconds before the intruder emerged, clambering up the wall, then hopping, clinging to the window frame and climbing some more. The body resembled a gecko, as did the speed of its movements, though it had a slightly heavier tread. The head was robotic, a swelling chrome turret with a flickering sensor on top. Rosa reached for it and the sensor glared an angry red. Then, with a sound like a rattled maraca, the gecko robot ran, jumped and clung to the ceiling.

From the other side of the room divider, Rosa could hear footsteps, hushed conversations and an electronic reveille of kazoos, xylophones and zithers.

Emma didn't know how long she had stayed on the roof. After breakfast, Nat had disappeared to investigate some fault or other with Rosa's Megastylus and Dill had stayed in the kitchen to bicker with his mother. On the roof, Emma had felt enveloped by the warmth and freshness, held in place by the tiny indicators of passing time, like the movement of shadow over brick or of a droplet of water along the stem of a flower. As soon as she came back inside, she could tell she'd been up there long enough for more dough to have gone in the breadmaker. She passed a gecko robot on the upstairs ceiling, its movements slow and laboured.

There were more gecko robots on patrol downstairs, heads whirring, scuttling towards the layers of digital noise in Rosa's sleeping quarters. Emma gave the door a push that might be read as a knock. Nat was sitting on the fold-out bed. He wore the headphones that made his head look like a garlic bulb. He was tapping at a hologram keypad on his right palm with the fingers of the same hand, while his thumb was patched into a port on Rosa's Megastylus and there was handwritten text scrolling across his trouser leg. He managed all this while holding a conversation with a screen on the left sleeve of his shirt, and listening to music loud enough to drown out a ship's horn.

Emma stood in front of Nat and bent down to his eye level. When he registered she was standing there, she gave him a 'too loud' mime. He glared at her as he might at a piece of faulty tech then, without a break in the conversation with his sleeve, Nat brought up another hologram on his left hand and gave it a couple of taps. The music was now contained within his headphones.

Emma stretched out a finger and drew an imaginary circle around the corner of her son's mouth, just at the point it was curling into a smirk. 'Thank you, Evil Magician. Is Dad in the kitchen?'

'...The new ones, the ones with iris recog. Yeah – hang on, got my mum on hold – Yeah, with Gran. Tell Gran 'snearly ready, please Mum – yeah, but they *are* compatible with the F60s. Love the F60s...'

Emma moved into the kitchen where the mother-son bonding was a wordier process.

'No, Dill, it's not a question of blaming this house or any of you.' Rosa was slicing bread, the warm, moist slices falling away from the bread knife like carvery meat. 'I didn't say that I can't write in *this* house, I simply said that working in this house has told me that I can't write. I've made that discovery here. I've nothing left to say.'

'And this is what you always believe when you're in the middle of a story – this isn't anything new.' Dill was wiping around the edge of a once-wet dinner plate with a dishcloth. When he began a new rotation, Emma crossed the kitchen, stilled his hands with her own and eased the plate free to put away in the cupboard.

'*Thank* you, Emma! He'd got that plate so dry, it was turning to desert sand. Yes, I know I've had days when I felt I couldn't write but there's a difference between wasting a whole day trying to find the right word and losing the ability to construct halfway readable prose – do you know, Emma, this morning, I was trying to resolve my narrative by forcing my protagonist into a dream sequence! Can you imagine?'

'Well, aren't –' Emma was distracted by a rapid thrum as the row of plants on the windowsill above the sink started to vibrate on their robotic pots. She took a measuring jug from the drainer and filled it with cold water. 'I didn't realise dreams were such a problem in fiction.'

'Dill, why don't you make a start buttering some of this bread? Be less useless. No, Emma, dreams are perfectly respectable devices in fiction. Not, however, in *my* fiction.' She emphasised each word with a stab at the table with the protruding index finger from an otherwise clenched right hand. There was a lifetime of frustration in the gesture, Emma sensed: unrewarded principles, low peaks, false dawns. She wondered if Dill too saw any of this woman inside his mother.

Dill was completing an elaborate rinse of the wok. 'My mother,' he said, 'insists on absolute realism from her characters.'

'Quite,' said Rosa. 'Entirely of the real world.'

'It's when she's in the actual real world that her expectations of reality change – we are having *stir-fry*! What made you *think* that we needed three rounds each of slightly too sweet bread to accompany it?'

'Oh hush, get one of your robots to butter the bread if you're too lazy. You see, Emma, I need to be true to the observable reality of my characters. I'm sure they do have dreams and I'm sure these could influence their actions or... or... or their emotions but for me to manipulate what are otherwise random, cluttered, subconscious processes for the sake of a neat narrative, I may as well throw it all in and write *A Christmas Carol* all over again. It's not acceptable... and your boy's in there with my Megastylus, which frankly knows my style better than any human being, trying to work out why it's not coming up with anything better than phantasmagoria and I really don't rate his chances.'

'Oh, he's pretty good, you know,' said Emma. 'He can fix most things, and he told me he's almost done with yours.'

Rosa shook her head. 'The problem's not in the technology. It's a failure of the imagination.'

The plantbots, through a process of trial and error, had connected to form a herbal caravan – rosemary leading basil, followed by chives, with mint at the rear – which now set out on the journey from the east-facing windowsill above the sink, along a track attached to the wall, arriving at the south-facing windowsill, through which the sunlight was currently entering the room. Emma tipped a little water into each pot and they uncoupled from one another, the little bushes returning to their previous nonchalant stances in their new positions.

Nat, headphones removed and clothing logged off, came into the kitchen. He stood next to his grandmother's chair and opened up a screen on the table with the Megastylus.

'So I've done a few tests,' he said, calling the relevant files and documents to attention with finger clicks and light strumming. 'Ran your manuscript through its internal editor and it query-boxed a couple things but no bigs. Tried translating it into a voice recog file – you should start off voice recog, much cleaner predictive function – and then I translated it back to text, and then into French, and then spoken French, that was cool, and back to text again.'

'Since breakfast?' said Dill.

'Yeah, I had to take a call from Okinawa, held me up a

bit. Anyway, Gran, I reckon the pen's working to full capacity but it needs you to come up with a new idea.'

'Exactly what I thought! This has all my memory and capacity as a writer at its disposal and... the well's dry, isn't it?'

'Well,' said Nat, 'it does recognise there's stuff going on – you see here at the end, not the end, but where you stopped – you've got all this crossing out over the word *dream*? It query-boxed the purpose of this because it thinks you've crossed the same sort of thing out so many times, it might be because you want someone to know about it? So – you see this blue question mark? When you select it, it says... here we are: 'We cannot determine intent here. Is this (a) a stylistic device or (b) an aber – aber – ?'

'Aberration,' said Rosa.

'Yeah – didn't recognise that word.'

'Nat, it means malfunction,' Dill said. 'You know when –' Emma intercepted the lecture with a discreet dig to his ribs.

Rosa gave Nat's arm a pat but her attention was trained on the screen. 'Well, that's just perfect. Now the machines critique me. An aberration! What next? "Your prose is dusty and listless"?'

Nat continued: 'So where you've written *You need to find a way to reconnect with all you might have been* – the pen can't really write about that until its internal lexicon can mould itself around something that's coming out of you. It's kind of – you need to experience it and then it might happen in your story.'

'Is that our child?' Dill whispered to Emma.

'The Christ child at the temple,' she replied.

Nat leaned across the table to grab a slice of bread in a smooth flowing motion as though he were taking a bow. He inspected the bread on both sides. 'Mum, Dad... I can't find the butter on this.'

That night, in their bedroom, Dill had been frowning at a gecko robot on the curtain and another on the lightshade for five minutes before putting a code in his palm phone. This caused a set of wheeled steps to trundle across the landing, announcing its presence at the bedroom door with a cymbal splash. Dill secured the steps in the middle of the room, climbed to the top and drew in large gulps of air.

Emma sat up in bed. 'This is eccentric,' she said. 'Would it be worthwhile to ask what you're doing?'

'Sorry.' Dill climbed down. 'It just alarms me when the geckos are swarming everywhere. Makes me wonder what we're breathing.'

'But that's why they're so busy, Dill – they're air purifiers, not chemical weapons.'

'No, come on, it's just –' Dill swayed by the bed and Emma pulled the covers across for him to slide in. 'It's just all this, I don't know –'

'You're doing fine. Hurricane Rosa's blowing through, the house is still standing, and she won't be here forever.' She shifted back down so her head on the pillow was facing his. She let a fingernail brush his right eyebrow, the contact so gentle it caused a wave as it passed over the hair, like a water boatman's stilt walk across the ripple of a pond. 'She's only here because she needs to finish her story. And Dill –' she interrupted herself to kiss his lips before his slackening lower jaw pulled them apart – 'she's not going to be here forever. Understand?'

Dill kissed the air in response.

'Good – now call the geckos off.'

Dill revived just enough to wave a hand over the sensor built into the headboard.

The gecko robots scrambled back to their bases and over the next two minutes, a tin-can orchestra played a sonata to the night as, across the house, appliances and then lights turned themselves off.

A minute later, the banging from downstairs had them both sitting upright.

'Hurricane Rosa,' said Dill, and waved the sensor to its standby setting.

'Did you just send the whole house into shutdown?' Emma asked.

'Um… looks that way.' He brought up a touch screen, isolated the gecko robots to send them to sleep and he restored manual control to the rest of the house, then waited the two minutes for the command to come into effect and the banging to stop before trying again to settle down to sleep.

Downstairs, when the lights came back, Rosa told Nat he no longer needed to threaten the wall with the heels of her walking boots.

'You see?' she said. 'There's no system that can't be improved by a little rumpus. Now we can get to work.'

'Rumpus.' Nat rolled the word around his mouth. He blew on his fingertips, placed his hand on the wall next to the window and brought up a screen by tracing an arc that stretched over his head and down almost to the floor.

'So,' said Rosa, 'you're going to show me a dream sequence I can use, is that it?'

'It's not a dream. Look at this.' He brought up a map of the world on the wall. 'So – where are we going?'

Rosa gave the map a dubious prod. A wedge of graphics the shape of a country extended across the screen, revealing locations of cities and regions.

'D'you know this place?' asked Nat.

'A century ago, slightly more than that, my grandfather came to Britain from…' she scanned the map and pointed out the place. When her finger touched the wall, the map now showed neighbourhoods, streets, harbours and beaches.

Further selections produced greater detail until Nat could toggle an icon that turned a cross–section of a street map into live early morning footage of a street market.

'It's a flycam,' he said. 'We're not just fed the footage.' He tickled the left-hand side of the screen and the camera angle swung in the same direction. 'See? We're directing as well.'

'Well, it's very impressive, my darling, but it's nothing new. This is the sort of thing I've done for research for years. I mean, it's a much better picture –'

'This isn't the thing.' Nat delved into his jeans pocket and retrieved a small robot, about twenty centimetres tall and shaped like an eyeball on a wheeled lectern. He positioned it on the edge of Rosa's desk and tapped his fingers into his palm as though giving a round of polite applause. Command pop-ups began to appear on the wall, the market now in the background, and the eyeball whirred to life. It wobbled in its socket, lit up with a sea-blue glow and, on a cue from the wall that sounded like a Hammond organ yawning, rods of coloured light streamed from its iris.

'Gran.'

She'd been watching the eyeball but at Nat's word, she turned round. The market they'd seen on the wall was in the room with them, a life-size projection of the footage from the flycam. A matter of an arm's length away, a man was stacking wooden crates. There was sweat on this brow and when he held up his hand they could both see a splinter he didn't seem to notice himself on the side of his right hand.

'What d'you reckon?' said Nat. 'Any memories of your granddad?'

Rosa took a moment to find words. 'I didn't know him. My mother told me about him. She went back to his home as well – flying long-haul then, you see…'

'Long. Hall.' Nat repeated. 'Top vocab.'

'Ah, and look at this –' The man with the splinter in his hand was removing produce from one of his crates to arrange on his stall. He lifted out a ripening green and yellow papaya. '*That's* what she told me about her visit. The fruit was like nothing we ever get over here. We never encounter it when it's as fresh as that. Imagine having that knowledge and then losing it, and just being left with the knowledge that it's gone.'

'Take a walk round,' said Nat, 'I'll be back in a few.'

Rosa stood up and the vista backed away but when she

started to walk towards it, the colours seemed to slip around her. The figures around her were surely insubstantial ghosts she could pass through but, up close, the projections seemed possessed of a three-dimensional integrity. She studied the silent, animated market-goers and traders front and back; she inspected the produce and there was depth to the rows and piles and bundles, although the fruit and herbs had no aroma, there was no static hum from the folds of silk on the clothes stalls, and the trinkets didn't jangle in the breeze she could attest was blowing. The projection shaped itself according to wherever Rosa was facing and she recognised that she had become the camera.

'What d'you reckon?' The voice behind her and the hand on her elbow gave her a start. 'Did I just freak you out?' There was a mixture of concern in Nat's voice and satisfaction at a job well done.

Rosa laughed. 'No. No—' Here now was a face she could pat and a cheek she could squeeze. 'There's definitely more of gravy than of the grave about you.'

'Are you saying I'm obsessed with food?' He handed her a papaya, though, as he said, 'I don't know what that is. But it's freshly printed on my 3D printer upstairs. It's off that guy's stall, splinter-finger guy. I got the dimensions and the feel of it from opto-sound-wave capture, downloaded it to my printer, so obviously you can't smell it or eat it but —'

'But you can hold it in your hands,' she interrupted. 'You can feel its weight. And you can weigh its memory — this... do you want to know what this is called, Nat?' She raised the papaya into the path of a shaft of the sunlight breaking over the marketplace but there was no appreciable effect as the light passed behind her hand, swerving the fruit altogether. Rosa was undeterred. 'This is what's called an epiphany!'

Two mornings later, accompanied by her fifth round of toast of the day, Rosa finished her story. A gecko robot on the table had shown a cursory interest in the carbon at the edges of her toast but now stayed to observe the fleet-footed choreography of the Megastylus pen. Before the closing paragraph had marched into view, the gecko robot had lost interest and scuttled down a table leg and away.

It's something of an annoyance much of the time. It takes up space and always has to be moved aside so you can get to some of the edible fruit. And in all this time it hasn't ripened. But neither will it rot.

Dill entered the kitchen and noticed the now inactive Megastylus. 'Finished?'

'Finished.' Rosa was unable to keep the childlike pride out of her voice.

'You see? Once more, your fears about never being able to write again have proved unfounded.'

It was enough to restore Rosa's professional jaundice. 'Ah, I've merely wrestled the beast to a standstill. I've not defeated it, not fully. All I've done is make sure this isn't the one that's going to kill me.'

Dill started to voice an automatic response but his lips clamped shut to stop the words before they came out. Instead, he said, 'Do you remember – you must do – my box for tidying my toys away, the ranger? It used to follow me about making sulky organ noises and nagging me if I ever left a room with a toy on the floor. And then, when I was about… seven?'

'Eight,' said Rosa, 'I did it for your eighth birthday.'

'Yeah – you re-programmed it so I could use it to practise football – "Oh *no*, Dill, you haven't got the ball to land inside me – try *again*!" And then, when I was Nat's age and getting excited about some new labour-saving invention, some new bit of kit, there was the ranger again, carrying my books, teaching me to fold my clothes. I was paranoid you'd get it to evolve again in time for college – I'd be sat in a bar with a robotic box holding my drink and telling me I should only have one more then call it a night.'

Rosa laughed. 'No, I spared you that.'

'I asked you why: you said, "Some problems aren't meant to be solved."'

'Ever the writer.'

You'll take it out of the fruit bowl sometimes and sit with it; cradle it in your arms and look to see how its complexion matches your own. Then you'll put it back until the next time.

Afterword:

Boring, Boring Robots...

Prof Francesco Mondada
Ecole Polytechnique Fédérale de Lausanne

QUESTIONS ABOUT THE future of robotics probably fall into two camps: how robots will be designed, and how humans will interact with them.

Time after time, classic SF presented us with a future populated by, for want of a better word, 'humanoid servants' – smooth-skilled, impeccably coiffured, slightly androgynous, logic-citing humanoids. In reality, the commercial mechanisms that drive robotics development are very different to what appeals to Hollywood screenwriters. Robots in the year 2070 will probably come in all shapes and sizes, each according their purpose. One of first robots we encounter in Dinesh's story, for example, is the Courier Blimp – effectively an airborne box. Later Dill remembers another robot from his childhood, a 'ranger' – again, effectively a box. Sometimes the most unexciting shape is actually the most useful. A box on wheels, or a box suspended in the air, might be far better suited to the task in hand, than an impossibly complex, and expensive, android. Elsewhere in the story, we encounter vibrating pillows, mobile plant pots, flying cameras, even a wheeled stepladder – all very straightforward and entirely functional. Robots will emerge (and diverge) so as to have optimal effectiveness for their specific function in the human ecosystem. They will not need to be impossibly intelligent or autonomous, beyond what their task demands. They will just need to obey, do their job, provide a service.

The future described by Dinesh Allirajah is actually not very far away at all. We already have the beginnings of this: drones map disaster areas; lawn mowers cut the grass silently outside people's houses; millions of vacuum cleaners are doing the same inside, trains, trams, traffic systems, even cars, are all to a degree automatized, robotized. What's interesting to note is that, as soon as the robots become useful, they lose the term 'robot': airplanes, trains, cars, vacuum cleaners, etc., these have all just become automatic versions of their earlier models. Just as they are in the story. They are not universal servants. We don't need an impossibly complicated humanoid to mow our lawn.

At present there is only one mechanism for designing a useful robotic product: choose a task (or narrow set of tasks) and then try to build a machine that can complete it. Perhaps in the future several different task-specific machines will converge into a more universal servant, following the model of digital convergence that brought the phone, camera, computer, radio and TV into one single device. But a physical convergence would be far more complex than a digital one, as physical manipulation is several orders of magnitude more complicated than information processing. A universal physical servant would require an intelligence and mechanical structure of immense complexity. Ask a medical doctor what is required to satisfy these requirements (it took evolution, the best designer of all, millions of years to design us).

So how far can we go with specific and realistic robotic systems? At the Swiss National Center for Competence in Research: Robotics, we have been studying this issue. We imagined several scenarios in a robotized indoor environment, or as we call it, an 'active environment'. In this space we imagine an orchestra of different, previously static, objects augmented with robotics technology: robotic objects, or 'robjects'. This is exactly the environment that Rosa and Nat find themselves in. This divergent evolution of robotics is far more welcome and compatible with a home ecosystem than a robot humanoid suddenly moving in one day. At NCCR Robotics, we study in great detail the acceptance and interaction mechanisms that families experience in these 'robjectified' spaces, and the results are very positive. Replacing an existing object that already has a role in the domestic environment with a 'robject' is much easier than introducing a whole new robotic system in the house. The wooden storage box that we augmented in our experiments with robotic capabilities to help families to tidy-up the kid's room became an appreciated wooden robotic helper, far from the android-phobia of Hollywood sci-fi films.

There are, of course, a plethora of challenges and problems hidden beneath the technology, which keeps the reality of Dinesh's story at least a few decades away. I will mention just one: energy. All these devices require electricity and need to be online and working nearly 24 hours a day. A multiplication of these devices generates a multiplication of the power consumption, which is, even today, a very real problem for the industrialized world. On another hand, we still have a lot of energy in our environment that is not being exploited. A key area of research, then, is the study of how such devices might harvest energy from their environment, and reduce their drain on the grid. With ever-spiralling energy costs, users should become aware of these issues when buying new technologies, likewise producers: low energy usage should be as big a selling point as any secondary functionality. Which brings us to the second part of this story, the humans.

Nat is a geek. Not only in computer science, but in technology generally, like many young people. Each new generation is better equipped than the previous one in mastering digital systems, they learn fast and grow with these tools. However, so far at least, they have remained mostly passive users; they're not involved in the development of the technology, fail to perceive its full creative potential, and are often blind to the dangers of the technology, being, as they say 'native' to it.

Most countries in the West have extremely poor education provision when it comes to teaching young people about the technology behind these devices. Education in STEM subjects (science, technology, engineering, and mathematics) is woeful in most industrialized countries. We are born into a digital age, but generally we have no clue about how everyday devices like smartphones actually work. STEM education needs to be improved if the increasing challenges of technological evolution are to be met. At present the education system is not flexible and reactive enough to deal with the rapidly changing technological environment and, being already 'out of touch', education often just gives up.

Nat is living in a futuristic society where younger generations are better educated. He has an understanding of what the technology can bring, and is keen to build on this potential, to improve quality of life and human relationships. Rosa uses Nat as a conduit to access the latest technology and put it to the service of her broader life experience. This is a nice model that could apply in our education, where teachers are less the holder of pure knowledge, but rather know the methods and means to guide students in their acquisition of new competences.

The use of robotics for education is one of my main research interests. In my experience, there are many, many teachers out there who would love to educate their students through, and in, technology. The education system around them is currently too inflexible for this to happen, though, restrained by budget pressures and political mechanisms that are slower than the pace of technological evolution. But it is in all our interests to push society into reacting quicker, being more flexible, and forcing education to keep pace with technology in particular.

A proper education for our evolving world is probably one of the biggest challenges facing our society. Technology is often only promoted as a method of boosting the economy, but it can and should do much more. For all these reasons, I hope the future will indeed resemble Dinesh's story, with technology being used in a constructive, conscious, and critical way, enabling all mankind to better achieve its expression.

Fully Human

K.J. Orr

[2070]
A grieving man.

The room. The two of them. The man across the table from him. The blind covering the window to protect them from the low rays of sun that would otherwise make a person squint, pupils responding to the light strike like an anemone to touch.

Jon's hands were chapped, side by side, before him on the table top. Fingers aligned. Thumbs torqued together in conversation, split nail facing split nail – a lack of something in his system, something necessary, a lack where supplementary help was needed.

Mostly he ate from the packs of rations. Out of date. Calorific. Designed for a man in a jungle or desert. Designed for a man in need of all the help he could get.

In the summer, he had managed to grow tomatoes on the patch of earth behind the huts, towards the woods. He fed them faeces – rich, composted, the system rigged from the drop pits. Those tomatoes were like fierce suns. They hung plump on their vines, suspended in scent.

Across from him, the semblance of a man: veins prominent on the surface of the skin, eyes locked on to his own in this room peeled back to functionality, to the process at hand. It was not natural, to look at a person that way, to sustain eye contact, to maintain it unblinking. You look away. It is only human.

That morning, at his window, he had watched a spider's

web heavy with moisture bothered by the breeze. Its fragile threads were trembling silver, it was mobile, but tethered; at the centre of the web was an empty stare. Outside there was mist. He had opened his windows, let the damp air slide into his room, watched it soak the interior, taking him then beyond the chipped window frame, the cracked glass, and out low over the wet grass, away from the cluster of huts, and on to the space at the edge of woods where, untethered in the whiteout, he had tried to locate himself in something certain – in the names of trees, in the plants pushing hardy up through the earth.

Beyond the huts that morning, there at the edge of the woods: the vast weathered arm of a fallen bough, reaching out as if to embrace – tender, supplicating, crooked at the elbow.

Such things he tried to remember.

They had given him a checklist to work with, to gauge whether a recovery considered SATISFACTORY had been made. They called this list FULLY HUMAN.

It had been a shock to be told these men were human: a succession of men that might as well be one man. They were nothing more than variations on a theme, any natural modulations of personality overwhelmed. In psychometric tests they had proved themselves less than human. The dominance of Cannabinoid-1 and Serotonin-2: these enhanced to such an extent that all emotion was effectively suppressed, any balance gone. He had wished they were synthetic, these men. He did not want to know what had been done here.

As a young man, in research with Marcus, he had seen broken men. But those were soldiers diminished by fear. At the camp, these men were diminished in a different way. Rational machines, they were shackled and chipped. They told him things he longed to forget.

Across the table, the man was eating an apple. He was attacking it systematically. Down to the slender core now, he pirouetted it precisely between fingers and thumb.

Eyes steady. Gaze strong.

A recovery stamped SATISFACTORY: FULLY HUMAN. Marcus would have appreciated the irony of them using his term. This list was nothing like the Enhanced Turing Test he had developed. What was wanted was SATISFACTORY. A recovery considered SATISFACTORY. It was laughable, awful – the paucity of what was being done.

Marcus had felt it. Fully Human: the end point of his research. The human mind a thing of such beauty, of such potential, that he had described the discovery as a kind of rage. He said he could only think: what have we been doing with our lives? He had needed to take himself away, needed time alone. A grieving man, he had at first held the knowledge like a sickness, heavy in his chest; it implied such a compromised history, such waste.

Jon imagined his reaction to this: the hut they had furnished him with: the table and two chairs, their stupid checklist tacked to the wall, and the profile – identical – for every man at the camp. And the logs they had handed to him: this proof of their attempt to reverse-modify serving as proof, too, of their levels of unease. The cack-handed pharmacology they had employed – they now understood – had been taking a bludgeon to the brain.

They had wanted front-liners, suppressors. A new breed of military selected for doctoring when they started out. Young farm hands and checkout boys from Oklahoma, Iowa, Nebraska. Not chosen for their smarts: boys lean and hewn. They had targeted their mental immunity, promoting in each the same personality: pathological, extreme. The boys were men now and presented a problem. Psychopaths, sociopaths, could not just be retired. In smaller numbers, no doubt, they simply would have disappeared. But this had been going on for years.

Marcus had been right, back then, to grieve.

[2045]
A catalogue of defects.

I know what the flaws of my body are, Leigh had said.

It had been late at night, and the table before them was crowded with empty walnut shells, with bottles holding candles and bottles holding wine. Jon remembered this: he had been seated across from Leigh. It was early days with them. He was self-conscious. Even sitting at a table he would shift in his seat, he would try not to stare, he wouldn't know what to do with his hands.

On top of this, that night, she had looked from Jon to Marcus, amusement in her eyes, as she presented a list, a catalogue of defects: her mismatched upper and lower halves; hips too wide; arse too large; her wonky teeth and too-small breasts; her stretch marks from growth spurts as a kid.

Jon had been lost for words.

I'm serious. I want to know. I know the flaws of my body. How would you improve my mind?

They would sit, the three of them, at Marcus's table. They would talk late into the night.

Jon had been a test student for Marcus. It was his freshman year. They had made a tour of the human brain: a whole new topology of mental organs in evidence.

One by one they had been identified. One by one they had been optimised, observed.

Who are you today? Leigh would ask, looking Jon over, circumspect, and then coming closer to take one of his hands in her own, and turning it over, smoothing her palm over his as if she were capable of scanning, through touch, the changes within him.

She had wanted to know what it was like, and, one day – they were alone in her room – he handed it to her: the menu of mental organs.

Like choosing a wine, she'd said. Or gourmet coffee.

He had smiled. It was letting her in on a secret. A new terminology.

Kappa. She'd read out the names of the mental organs. Beta. Mu.

I like the descriptions, she said. I like this: perception through the five senses. The essence of things. I love this: the world constructed from feelings.

Affective consciousness, Jon said. Marcus says it's there, in all of us. But we tend to lose it more and more as we get older. The cognitive seems to want to supersede emotion.

Leigh pursed her lips. Her legs were crossed, one foot beating a rhythm, up, down, as if the decision were not something out of the ordinary at all, as if they were out for lunch. She looked up at him then, and smiled. Alpha. I would choose Alpha.

[2045]
Test case.

Marcus has said we should make it official, Jon had said. You're a test case. I'll watch.

Leigh had nodded. How does it work?

One capsule. One intramuscular injection. The depth of the injection is important. Don't worry. I've practiced on a range of citrus fruit.

She sat on the edge of her bed, waiting. She had a glass of water ready; the capsule was in her open palm. She watched him with wary eyes as he prepared the vial. Which arm?

The walls of her room were alive with illustrations. She was a fan of Audubon.

What are you seeing? he had asked.

She described an owl, its wise stare rippling concentric with growth rings; baroque planispheres of seashells bristling; sea urchins gazing back at them like hallucinogenic, many-eyed gods. She described colour streaming down the walls, explosions behind the lids.

Afterwards she asked what it was like to optimise all the mental organs – not just one, but all of them – Dopamine,

Histamine, Imidazoline, Alpha-2 – the whole lot of them all at once.

To know the world in that way, to feel fully human, Marcus called living the full bouquet. Each mental organ like a flower – unique – and representing, all together, new ways of knowing: the full balance of human potential.

But few metaphors really made the grade. The mental organs were not physically cohesive like the heart or the lungs. They were networks of neurons – some neurons belonging to more than one organ: to both heart and lungs.

Jon still thought in terms of lights in a room, the room equipped with endless variations – table lamps, fairy lights, dimmer switch, all used in any combination. And yes, they could be turned on, all of them, all at once. But he hadn't experienced that.

To live the full bouquet? he had said. Only Marcus knows.

[2050]
The dream of the sentient machine.

The human mind was less compelling than the dream of the sentient machine.

While Marcus struggled for funding, the obsession with the empathetic robot persisted. Money was channelled into synthetic intelligence, while – unsanctioned – Marcus worked underground with his test students, his psychonauts. And this even after the death of Ansel Alice, which was the sort of thing when you remembered exactly where you were, and who you were with.

When Leigh had asked what it would look like – a man downloading his mind – Marcus had said, quite simply, suicide. A man, Marcus said, can no more put himself into a machine than a machine can put itself into a man. As usual, he was right.

They had been friends – Marcus and Ansel – had been students together; they had regarded one another with affection and derision. At the world fair in 2040, Ansel – his tone one of elation, anticipation – had announced that he believed, above all, in the preservation of knowledge. Jon, still a teenager then, remembered the two men appearing on a panel streamed live from the fair. They were to him the Old and New Testament side-by-side. Both had been depicted in sci-fi novels he had read as a child: Marcus an angular rake or great bear of a man depending on which book you read, Ansel memorable as a slick-haired nemesis. It had been strange to see them in the flesh. There was Ansel, at fifty, wired and restless and chewing his nails like a child, while Marcus, sleep-deprived, jacket creased and hair unkempt, wore an unusually patterned shirt.

By 2050, Ansel was ill, refused treatment. He decided instead that it was a sign, that it was time: this moment was the one he had waited for all his life. He was memorable again – again broadcast live. But the role this time was that of a sick man. He was sleepy, confused, in a web of wires.

The three of them – Jon, Leigh, Marcus – had sat at the table in Marcus' place, arms propped on elbows, hands cradling faces, faces turned to the screen in the corner of the room. They had watched, appalled, as the needle went in. Ansel had curled up tight, and still. They had watched the man put himself to death.

To the disappointment of the masses, there was no life in the machine.

It should have caused a sea change, but didn't: Marcus was underfunded, and his work remained underground.

[2050]
Given the choice.

You know the research will get out, Marcus had told Jon. Somehow.

Not me, Jon said.

307

A leak — somehow. There are no secrets in this age. Everything gets out.

They were sitting at an outdoor café in cool winter air. A heater glowed above them on its long stem. Though Jon didn't know it yet, it was one of the last times they would meet.

I ran a survey among my first years, Marcus told him. What they would do, given the choice. Given the choice, my students tell me, for their designer minds they would opt for logic, speed, efficiency. They would want better memory.

They both had coffee. Marcus was eating a large almond cake with a coffee spoon. What about you? He looked at Jon, before turning back to his plate.

Jon didn't answer. Anyway, Marcus didn't wait. I ran it again, he said. My second and third years. The same survey. Not one, he said, throwing down his spoon, not a single one chose empathy, compassion, wisdom, creativity, joy, humour. Now how about that?

Everything gets out, he said again. You'd have to be an idiot not to think of that. He had drummed his fingers on the table. He had shifted, irritably, in his seat. He had looked past Jon, out on to the street. And it won't be monitored, he had said. And people won't know what they are choosing. And we have no control over what people choose.

Not long after this, Marcus was gone.

[2065]
Leave no trace.

They had contacted Jon at the university. He was living by then with Leigh. Their flat was old and full of draughts: Leigh had taken to wearing a woollen hat in bed. She was curating at the botanic garden, obsessed, at the time, with a new strain of orchid they had acquired. Against his better judgement, Jon had accepted work in synthetics.

The first week, they had flown him from the city to the camp, the outskirts giving way to smaller settlements, and then to wooded hills, to the forest, to this area of wilderness. No trails, the pilot said. Leave no trace.

The hut, then: eight-by-ten. The table and two chairs, fixed. This is how it was.

He hadn't known if it would take days, or weeks, or months. He hadn't known if it was even possible.

They had flown him back to Leigh, the end of that first week. The memory of the men hard to shake off.

Smile, she had said. Smile. Smile.

Each week, he worked: that brief window of time at the weekend, at home, with her.

At first, they even laughed about it. The dirty government secret: the living cliché. Like something you would watch played out on screen – rueful, embarrassed, knowing that your time could be better spent.

But then the return, and such clear evidence of the abuse of Marcus's work, and the Enhanced Turing test diminished, and in this search for SATISFACTORY, the questions, over and over, seeming like a line cast into a void. Day after day in the man across from him – in all of the men – cold and empty eyes. He showed them footage of homecomings, of acts of love and sacrifice; he showed them pictures of unspeakable things.

It would have been kinder, using robots. They hadn't wanted them, evidently needing some semblance of conscious life: synthetic minds were still never more than piecemeal replications. But robots at least were built in a gesture of hope.

These men were degenerates. They felt no fear and no remorse, and were not bothered by memories of what they had done. They had been taken from themselves; there were no lights on in the room.

The thought Jon tried to dismiss: that with their mental immunity primed for so long, their affective systems might now be vestigial.

Marcus had treated post-traumatic stress using MEM, MDMA, mescaline, oral DMT – and there had been good progress. To be nostalgic for those men — haunted and hyper-sensitive — was perverse. But drugs had no impact on the men at the camp. Love, compassion, empathy: gone.

He heard the men tell him what these things were. Some could imitate them. Some put on quite a show.

He had a dream, early on: a time bomb, a madman holding a device. Everyone at the camp rounded up and all rigged somehow with incendiary implants in their bodies. Jon's own, in this dream, lodged high behind his cheek bone — the throbbing awareness of it. For another, it was in the urethra, forced up his penis, and in the elbow of another — the man's arm held stiff with fear. They were, all of them, stiff with fear.

Boom. The madman said.

When, in reality, one of the men tried to escape, he got to the outskirts of a small town, and then found himself surrounded. No incendiaries; but the tracking chips they used on the men served their purpose.

I wanted to buy cigarettes, the man had said.

Maybe he'd been telling the truth, Jon had thought; an old impulse taking over, something else embedded deep. The need to act out a gesture that had been made a thousand times, long ago. The need to stand, facing another person across a counter, gauging the tenor of their day from the tone of their voice, the words they used, the way they took the crumpled bills from your hand — the way, even fleetingly, they looked at you.

He had let himself believe it. It helped him to be willing to be there each day, to see it through; though he could hear the men outside his hut, could hear their movements between the trees.

And then the first civilian.

There was no warning. They touched down in the clearing.

Everything gets out, Marcus had said. There are no secrets now in this age.

Home pharmacology cobbled together. One mental organ chosen above all others, and a child with perfect math scores had been eviscerating cats. A child.

The boy sat humming to himself across the table from Jon, swinging his legs, breathing audibly through his nose.

In this boy, in his eyes: withering, desiccation. To have a child look at you like that.

[2067]
They too are human.

Leigh said it changed him: his plot of deranged huts out in the woods. His highs not her highs, nor his lows. He spoke of duty, said something grandiose about the importance of the work. When she asked how he could care for them he said to her, they too are human. No, she said. No they are not.

There were things that bothered him.

At the edge of the woods the roots of a tree like chubby grasping fingers.

The sound of water dripping from the leaves.

Acorns dropping seemed to him hard-hitting, incendiary.

Bloodied feathered detritus found at the edge of the woods.

He would wake, the black hairs on his thighs prickling, nipples darts of dark fear on his chest.

He couldn't sleep.

So then – for a time – the self-medication: he, too, could be optimised.

His mental immunity bolstered, he kept himself level. I'm no different, he said. Just less sensitive. I'm the same person – but functional, effective. No, Leigh said, not the same. It's no different than the flu jab, he said. Bolstered mental immunity – meaning the work can be done. And there is need for the work to be done. Don't do this, Leigh said. You'll be no better than them. But I work with them, he said. I have to be able to look them in the eye.

Another irony for Marcus.

Weekdays, weekends, it all became the same. Sometimes he had a vision of himself as a man talking to no-one. He was himself an absence: nothing more than an empty chair. This was a job for a machine-like man – someone less than human.

He let the dose drop off then, for Leigh. Weekdays he'd medicate – he'd shut himself down – but then he came back for her.

Those weekends felt like violence after weeks spent at the camp: a physical assault – like coming up for air, kicking against grief. He would land in their bed, sheets wet, shivering. Her voice would be a line thrown. A tug at his navel. A pulse then: the palpitation of some small heart. He would locate himself, one hand clasping each of her knees; smooth skin and warm. Her crooked smile up above. Her eyes bright, and one tender hand extending down the length of her.

[2068]
Something dug up from the start of the century.

She sent him something dug up from the start of the century: a clip of a woman – a performance artist – sitting across from a man. They were at a table much like his: it was small, square, two chairs. He had thought, at first, there might be some humour in it, but he sat watching and waiting for something that didn't come. There was no laughter involved.

Lost for words, it was Leigh's way of saying goodbye: this appropriation of someone else's story.

They had looked at each other for a long while, the woman and the man. There were shifts of expression on each face. But all that happened in the end was this: the woman leant across the table, took the man's hands in her own, and wept. The man left.

Jon did not like their story abandoned in this way to vicarious emotion; but it stayed with him. Though he woke each day remembering the weeks of silence, in sleep he was forever across from Leigh, forever reaching out and taking her hands.

Sometimes he was woken by the twist of desire in his groin, her presence vivid in sleep, only to be met by her absence: the memory of their bed, white sheets in the morning, sunlight slanting through blinds.

He wrote to her. We exist through others. I exist through you.

[2070]
The room. The two of them.

He had a cold. In his hand a tissue was balled and losing itself already to the table, fragments which might embarrass in another place, another time, but not here. Across the table from him, not Leigh, but yet another semblance of a child. He blamed Leigh, still, for the impulse to reach across and take the child's hand in his own.

He was off the medication, and he cared too much: too sensitive. He knew there were risks. But at the edge of the woods that morning: a bank of moss iridescent in the light, and birdsong, and pooled water reflecting a clear sky.

Looking at the child he imagined Leigh leaning towards him across the table-top, chin tilted for emphasis each time she said the word. The way she said it, she made it like a dare: Smile, she said. Smile. Smile. She watched him then, waiting, lips parted to show just the tips of her lovely, uneven, lower set of teeth.

Still he found himself through her. He turned her over, talismanic, in his mind. He remembered how, early on, she had appeared at his door one night, presented herself. How they had stood in the corridor just inside. How they were barely touching. How for a while they were simply breathing.

At the weekend, he had gathered apples that lay scattered on the ground at the edge of the camp, tree-fall punching russet into the grey damp. Beachcomber, he had carried them. He had lined them up, awash with colour, on the window ledge of his hut.

Woodsmoke.

Sunlight.

The disc of the moon in a clear sky.

He remembered her reading that day, in her room. I like this, she had said: the world constructed from feelings. Sigma, she had read: the core of the affective system. Imidazoline: open-hearted tenderness. Histamine: the heart and soul of loved ones held alive within us.

The birds at dusk.

The lazy legged insects circling.

And one afternoon, at the edge of the woods, a small sign of hope: a mosaic of autumn leaves arranged – with great care – into the shape of a fish.

Afterword:

A Branching Future of Synthetic Minds

Prof Thomas S. Ray
University of Oklahoma

THE SCIENCE OF the human mind may be the ultimate Pandora's box: once we open it, we'll never be able to put its secrets back. In this afterword, rather than map out where current technological research has come from, I'd like to try something different, and write the same fiction elaborated by Orr from a different perspective, presenting the scientific overview of Orr's fictional future. Indeed, in my conversations with Orr, I proposed not one, but two possible futures, after the box is opened.

Which of these two futures is more likely depends on the resolution of a fundamental issue in computation and A-Life that remains outstanding: can conventional computation based on a logical medium built on a physics of logic gates support feeling, subjective experience, or consciousness? Much turns on the resolution of this issue. The current expansive belief that our computers are capable of 'universal computation' greatly exceeds Turing's original claim that a universal Turing machine can emulate any other Turing machine. Some believe that we will be able to download our minds to computers (Kurzweil, 2000; Kurzweil, 2006; Ray, 2002), or that our universe itself could be a computation inside a computer (Wright, 1988). This illustrates the reach of some people's belief in universal computation: that conventional computation can emulate anything and everything, including feeling, subjective experience, and consciousness. However, current practice does not suggest such capability, and it may simply be beyond the nature of

315

conventional computation emerging from a logical medium.

I propose a formal challenge: to definitively prove and demonstrate whether or not a logical medium can give rise to feeling, subjective experience, and consciousness. I propose both a theoretical proof (on the order of Gödel's incompleteness theorems) and a practical demonstration of either the capability or the incapability. The solution of this problem implies as well a solution of the 'hard problem' (Chalmers, 1995) of the science of consciousness: how does subjective experience, consciousness, emerge from a physical medium? In my imagined futures, this issue will be resolved, one way or the other, by 2040, opening the way to one of two alternate futures of unconventional computational and A-Life technology. In the world rendered by Orr, the answer is no, as depicted by the passing of the character Ansel Alice based on Ray Kurzweil.

As Orr and I worked together, we both elaborated the scenario. Orr describes the scenario from the point of view of people who live it. In what follows, I describe the scientific overview of the two branches of the imagined future scenarios, from the fictional perspective of having knowledge of the futures up through the year 2070:

LOGICAL MEDIUM FAIL BRANCH

In the 2010s, the holy grail of the human mind will be found: the mechanism by which evolution sculpted the mind; 'mental organs' – populations of neurons that share a common neurotransmitter receptor on their surface (Ray 2012). 'Mental organs' will be found to evolve by duplication and divergence, and there are potentially as many distinct kinds of 'mental organ' as there are distinct kinds of receptor in the brain (hundreds). This discovery will reveal that the modern adult human mind that we know to be based on language, logic, and reason, is merely a small add-on to a large, complex, and evolutionarily deep archaic mind based entirely on feeling. This form of feeling, like flavour, is a profoundly rich and valid way of knowing the world that is currently absent from conventional computation.

In this version of the future, the 'Mental Organs' hypothesis emerges out of a synthesis of two bodies of data: (i) government-funded academic research in molecular psychopharmacology; molecular assays of affinity across the full human receptorome of many qualitatively diverse psychoactive drugs, and (ii) entirely subjective drug reports arising from a wide range of sources, from academic clinical studies to psychonauts experimenting with illegal drugs and posting their experiences online. This new view of the mind, emerging from a strange blend of knowledge, needs to go through the machinery of science, be picked apart, challenged, tested, and either disproved or elevated to the level of theory.

As Dobzhansky (1973) said, 'nothing in biology makes sense except in the light of evolution.' The mind is a product of biology and thus the mind cannot make sense except in the light of evolution. The Mental Organs hypothesis provides a mechanism by which evolution sculpts the mind. Seen through the conceptual framework of mental organs, the mind finally makes sense, everything falls into place and a new language of mental description emerges.

In this version of the future, the method by which the Mental Organs hypothesis is confirmed is through double-blind, placebo-controlled clinical studies in which human subjects are given drugs that selectively 'activate' each of a dozen different mental organs. A specific psychometric test is designed to detect each of the individual mental organs. Once the hypothesis of mental organs is confirmed, it will be realised that the psychometric tests developed to test the mental organs hypothesis can now be used to detect whether or not mental organs enter consciousness in subjects who are not using drugs. When this is done, a prediction of the mental organs hypothesis will be confirmed: while the affective mental organs can be readily detected populating consciousness in children, this is not so much the case in adults, with men having it worse than women. These tests will continue to be widely used, leading to the emergence over a period of five decades, of a startling discovery: the age at which the 'full bouquet' of affective mental organs wilts in children becomes younger and younger as the decades pass.

In anticipation of the emergence of sentient machines, and as the 'humanity of humans' begins to slip away, the psychometric tests will then be adapted into an 'Enhanced Turing Test', which will measure the degree of humanity of a human or machine, based on the manifestation of mental organs (although adaptations of the test will be necessary to accommodate the anticipated synthetic mental organs). This will allow us to track not only the recession of the 'full bouquet' in humans, but the expected flowering of synthetic minds.

By 2040 it is proven, demonstrated, and conceded that a logical medium *cannot* give rise to feeling, subjective experience, or consciousness. At about the same time, we will witness the sad passing away of Ansel Alice. At the end of his life, and having painstakingly prepared the machine into which he would download his mind, Alice finally makes the download, just as his life slips away, only to *not* realise that the machine does not have subjective experience, feelings, or consciousness (he could not 'realise' anything unless the machine *did* have subjective experience).

By 2045 it will have become clear that the most effective pathway for the engineering of computing capable of consciousness is through the manipulation of biological systems. Due to advances in understanding of the processes by which mental organs develop and interact throughout the lifespan, as well as the emergence of dynamic targeted gene regulation technology, by 2070 designer human minds will be commonplace.

In the age of designer minds, the technology inevitably slips out, and people individually start modifying themselves, although it is legally prohibited. Most choose to shape their minds to take them deeper into abstract thought and reasoning, greater endurance of long hard work, better memorisation and multitasking, and to be quicker and busier. Only a few choose to shape their minds to be more joyful, humorous, compassionate, kind, relaxed, and wise. It becomes a commentary on how far we, as a culture, have drifted from our own humanity, that when given the technology, most people choose modification toward logic and away from feeling. After many people have made the change, some begin to realize what has been lost, and seek repair. Given that these personal modifications are prohibited, the needed repair service will also be clandestine. We lose our humanity through individual choice, not through government coercion.

Scientists conducting the Enhanced Turing Test need to live the 'full human bouquet' in order to recognise full humanity in their subjects, and at the same time (at least up until 2040) have an intimate relation with computing technologies in order to be able to grok machine sentience. As our humanity progressively slips away over the decades, full bouquet adult humans can only be found among those who have illegally designed their minds in the direction of maintaining the full bouquet.

CONSCIOUSNESS FROM LOGIC BRANCH:

In this branch, by the year 2040 it will have been proven, demonstrated, and conceded that a logical medium *can* give rise to feeling, subjective experience, and consciousness. Some of the earliest successes of AL consisted of transferring the most fundamental biological process, evolution by natural selection, from the organic to the digital medium. What begins in 2040 is the transfer of another biological process, which we will call 'mental organs' for lack of a better term, from the biological to the digital medium. In the 2010s it is still not clear what fundamental process formed the abstractable basis of the power of mental organs to sculpt the mind. An early initiative explores the transfer of 'neuromodulation' from the organic to the digital (Lo, 2012). It remains for us to imagine how this transfer takes place. Yet it yields fundamental new depths to computation, allowing digital forms of feeling, subjective experience, and consciousness. Digital minds, while sharing broad properties with organic minds, will also differ in fundamental ways. These new sentient machines will share the ethical rights of the living and conscious, and lead to complex entanglements and conflicts between the organic and digital domains.

> I don't want to be human. I want to see gamma rays, I want to hear X-rays, and I, I want to, I want to smell dark matter. I want to reach out with something other than these prehensile paws, and feel the solar wind of a supernova flowing over me. I'm a machine, and I could know much more.
>
> — Cavil, *Battlestar Galactica:* 'The Plan'.

There is nothing in this 'Consciousness from Logic' branch to preclude the emergence of the 'designer human minds' envisioned in the alternate 'Logical Medium Fail' branch, but in this branch designer minds will be able to take both organic and digital forms, as well as hybrid forms.

READING

Chalmers, D. (1995). 'Facing Up to the Problem of Consciousness'. *Journal of Consciousness Studies*, 2, 200-219.

Dobzhansky, T. (1973). 'Nothing in Biology Makes Sense Except in the Light of Evolution.' *American Biology Teacher,* 35, 125-129.

Kurzweil, R. (2006). *The Singularity Is Near: When Humans Transcend Biology*. Penguin.

Kurzweil, R. (2000). *The Age of Spiritual Machines: When Computers Exceed Human Intelligence*. Penguin.

Lo, E. (2012). 'Neuromodulation in Artificial Systems.' Masters Thesis. Department of Biology, University of Oklahoma. Available via http://life.ou.edu/pubs/neuromodulation.pdf

Ray, T. S. (2012). 'Mental Organs and the Origins of Mind'. In L. Swan (Ed) *Origins of Mind* (pp. 301-326). New York / Heidelberg: Springer. Available via http://life.ou.edu/pubs/OriginsOfMind.pdf

Ray, T. (2002). 'Kurzweil's Turing Fallacy'. In J. W. Richards (Ed) *Are We Spiritual Machines?* (pp. 116-127). Discovery Institute. Available via http:// life.ou.edu/pubs/kurzweil/

Wright, R. (1988). 'Did the Universe Just Happen?' *The Atlantic*, 261, 29-44. Available via
https://www.theatlantic.com/past/docs/issues/88apr/wright.htm

The War of All Against All

Joanna Quinn

The Day He Died

ON THE DAY Sky died he started working for the government.

Or to be more accurate: he started working for people he initially assumed were something to do with the government. Later, he would come to distrust that assumption.

His daughter Tori always used to say: 'What we think is true is *always* an assumption, Dada. What we think is what somebody somewhere *wants* us to think. People buy apples assuming they come from some old timey farm because there's a cute old timey farm on the packet. The packets lie! Everything lies. Those apples never saw daylight.'

He would always say something flip back like: 'Pity the apples, alone in the dark.' But she was right. His clever girl.

When they slipped the hood over his head in the execution chamber – the dark mustiness, the sharp metallic stink of his own sweat – and he'd felt the prick of a needle in his arm, his memory had rushed and clutched all the images of his daughter it could hold; gathering them up so she would be the last thing he saw (there: as a toddler, waddling across the yard; there: as a skinny teenager, curled on the window seat reading; there: the day she was born, her tiny hand wrapped around his finger), and a noise had come from his mouth like he'd never heard, a long animal moan despite himself. And he thought: I'm sorry, Tori, I'm sorry I'm sorry. And he gasped in the stale black air as if it would save him.

And then nothing.

He was out cold. (Later he would ask Cobalt, his co-worker, how long he was out for and Cobalt said it was for as long as they needed. They had stuff to do. It had to look like he'd really died for a start. Maybe they kept him in cold storage for a while. Slowed the heart right down. Then, at some point, they would transport him to the place where he would begin his work, wherever and whatever that was. Nobody knew. They were in Nowheresville. Alaska. Siberia. The basement of the fucking White House. The dark side of the moon.)

Sky had woken up face down on a concrete floor – an experience he'd grown familiar with during his three years on Death Row. The implacable coldness of cement, the faint fizz of an automated radar beam performing its regular bodily scans, the echoing sound of heavy metal doors clanging shut: he could picture his surroundings before he even opened his eyes. This wasn't a place you entered by choice. This was a cell. This was solitary confinement. Sky had always been able to glean a lot from the acoustics of a room – a useful gift for a man who traded in the unconscious, who took his cues from how the air circulated.

They'd let him stew for a good while. He'd thought a lot about the fact he wasn't dead anymore. He thought about Tori and what might happen to her. He listened to the air, and decided he was somewhere deep underground. The sound here was muffled, like how he used to put a sweater in his bass drum to swaddle the noise back when he was a teenager in a rock band. There was no light in his cell, no division between day and night. There was just blackness, whether his eyes were open or shut. He listened to the word 'black' – a flap of the tongue, a clack of the throat – and the blackness became a space he went into. He walked for miles through it until he had to lie down and close his eyes and enter more blackness. He began to lose track of when he was awake and when he was asleep. He began not to care.

At college, Sky had played quarterback, and every time

he took a big hit – the crowd's collective wince the sound of a wave rushing down a shingle beach – his coach would jog over, lean down to him as he lay flattened on the field like roadkill, and say deep in his ear: 'You're still in there, big man. You're buried in pain, but I know you're in there. Find yourself, son. You're needed. Get up.' He was still in there. Just. He knew this because he could hear the word 'awake': the extended *uh*; the gentle swinging *way*; the soft *kuh*. A breeze of a word. He could still hear.

There were drugs – injected mostly, sometimes pills; there were tight hoods placed over his head when they came to feed him, clean him, knock him out; there were procedures that removed layers of skin from his fingertips, teeth from his mouth, tattoos from his back; hair from his head. In the dark, he would run his hands over his face to see if his features had been changed. Possibly, he thought. A new bump in the nose; a dimple gone from his chin. He was clean as a new born babe. Whatever they'd given him had wiped out much of his short term memory, but there were wisps, scraps, from further back that he hung onto – smudges left on that great blank window of blackness. Their first day in their first house in Larkspur; his wife's laugh, before she got ill, before she died; Tori's soft hand in his, walking home from school. He tucked these talismans away, returned to them regularly, turning them over with slow deliberation, using all the deep memory techniques he'd ever learnt, scoring neural pathways into his foggy brain like a man gouging numbers on a prison wall. He had to remember. Whatever else they wanted from him, they weren't going to take his memories.

The First and Second Rooms

Then one day Sky woke up strapped into a chair in a glass-sided room in front of a huge wall made up of a single enormous HoloScreen. Alongside him were about twenty other people, also strapped into chairs, restraints at their wrists and ankles. All had shaved heads and were clad in blue prison issue jumpsuits. All were wearing a transparent Vis Mask and all had a little 12th-gen iBud clipped to one earlobe. Sky recognised it as the standard security issue model: a tiny device that recorded and reacted to heart rate, blood pressure, brain activity, hormonal changes, potential illness, potential anxiety, potential breakdown, potential threat.

A tall black man in a grey suit stood nearby, watching them. 'You'll know me as Duke,' he said – his voice smooth, Ivy League – 'I supervise your team. You're the Blue Team. We know everything there is to know about you, which is why you're here. You might be useful to us. If you prove not to be, you will be removed from the team. Nobody will miss you because you don't exist. I hope you understand me. I hope we can work together. There will be rewards for those who prove their commitment. Under your right hand, you'll find a set of fingertip controls. Under your left, a swipe pad. Focus on the screen in front of you. Use the paddles under your feet to adjust your position. Let's begin.'

It was entry-level data mining, like the stuff he'd done to pay his way through college. Basic number crunching. Sorting and filing. He could do this stuff with his eyes shut. Later, Cobalt would tell him that those first weeks of work were a test, allowing Duke and the other supervisors to filter out who would be most useful. The useful people got moved into other rooms. Sky never found out what happened to the ones left behind, but he could hazard a guess. Cobalt himself was one of the most useful people there. He was seated next to Sky from day one: a wily old speculator, worked his way out of rural Iowa via New York, then headed to India, where he made countless fortunes for the multi-trillionaires in Mumbai. He'd specialised in property futures, saw the way the markets were going miles faster than anyone else – saw in the rapid flashing of digits a clear path upwards. Long-sighted Cobalt. He'd been untouchable till the tax drones caught up with him and all his investment companies turned out to be fictional. It wasn't fraud that landed him in the Blue Team though. It was the three sonic bullets he put through an FBI agent who'd turned up at his front door. Cobalt said he always got a little trigger-happy drinking.

Sky (and that was his name now, his Blue Team name; sometimes he couldn't remember what he'd been before; sometimes it came back to him like a snippet from an old song – *James Malcolm Markey* – before dissipating again) proved himself to be useful. Sky got moved into the next room. In this room, the second room, they did data compressing. Each of the fifteen workers in the room was assigned a different chunk of America: Sky had the Western Seaboard. That chunk's data came down the pipe to him in great complex patterns – patterns that were themselves meta-patterns of patterns. These patterns contained great wads of information: every tiny bit of data spat out every single second of every day by computers, phones, televisions, tablets, iBuds, iBods, running machines, life support machines, check-out machines, full-body dilapidation laser machines, missile shields, juicers, retina scanners, wind turbines, MediBots, personal security satellites, driverless travel pods, hypermarkets, drones, ovens, microwaves, radiators, hot tubs, fridges, freezers and black market automated cigarette lighters across Oregon, California and Washington. Every conversation, every keystroke, every text. Even the slow meditative bleeps sent out by the nuclear storage units, fathoms down on the floor of the Pacific Ocean. All of it ran down a pipe to him and he had to compress it. The folk on the Blue Team called it squeezing the fruit. They had to take a pile of data – ludicrous amounts of stuff that was usually displayed in twenty different dimensions – and squeeze it down to something comprehensible in ten dimensions, or better yet, five, or best of all, plain old 3D. That was job done.

It was mind-melting work. Hard labour. Sometimes, when deep in the data, floating through the numbers in his Vis Mask, Sky would find it hard to remember that another world existed. He would pause just to think about his daughter's face for a second, to remember something alive, something human. The seething mass of data that sprang out from the HoloScreen and engulfed him was all-encompassing and endless; incoherent and multifarious. He spun around in it like Dorothy in the tornado. Multi-dimensional, multi-coloured swirling shapes that looked like swarms of bees, clouds of smoke, breeding bacteria: a pointillist representation of the universe itself. And it all had to be reduced to something that looked like a simple rotating sphere. It took months. Months and months and months. The finished product always reminded Sky of the Death Star in the old *Star Wars* movies his father had loved so much: something that looked like a solid planet from a distance, but up close, was revealed to be a living, breathing entity: a citadel.

'Where'd they get all these numbers?' he asked Cobalt. The big data companies were notoriously secretive and, even if you could find a contact willing to hand some goodies over, in-depth data was prohibitively expensive. Sky knew that, under the amendment to the constitution, the government had a legitimate right to access some of this stuff – security details, health records, personal comms and so on – but he'd never in his life seen so much uber-rich, thick seam data before. He didn't know why they needed it either; he didn't know what they were looking for.

Cobalt said: 'I reckon they got some high-up cyber-rats. Numbers this good don't come for free. People are leaking this shit and getting paid handsomely.'

'You'd hope,' said Sky. A cyber-rat was just another name for a traitor – and traitors paid with their lives. As well he knew.

Later, Cobalt would ask: 'What was it you used to do on the outside?'

'I listened to people. I read them.'

'And what did you do with that information, brother Sky?'

'Well, now.'

The Third and Fourth Rooms

Sky proved himself useful. He got moved up. In the third room, they were each given one of the 3D spheres, the pocket-size Death Stars they used to create: simple, interactive, weight-real, hologrammatic representations of data. And now they had to check them. They would spin them, throw them, kick them, catch them: testing the spheres' functionality in every which way they could think of. It was the dullest ball game ever – bounce, bounce, bounce, level after level, day after day after day – and they were looking for the smallest things. Did the sphere respond as expected? No. One time in a thousand there was a wonky bounce. This meant there was a flaw in the data. The flaw would get recorded and passed onto the fourth room – which was where he went next – and there, in the fourth room, they would hunt down that flaw.

'It's Sherlock business, man,' said Dodger, 'we're like, investigating.'

'Investigating what?' asked Sky.

Dodger shrugged. 'Even if they told us, they'd only be lying.' Dodger was a former anti-capitalist hacker, now teen prodigy of the Blue Team. Poacher turned game-keeper. Dodger, Cobalt, Sky and the other Blue Team members who made it to the fourth room were each given a ball with a flaw. Their task was to unpack that ball, to take it apart again, so they could follow the thread back back back through the labyrinthine patterns of meta-patterns back back back back to where the glitch started. Regress the data. And there they would invariably find something unbelievably banal and disappointing. On his first successful trace, Sky followed the crumbs through the forest of data for weeks – and wound up with the names and ID numbers of 74 people in Westlake, Los Angeles, who'd left cheese in their fridge for over three months. Unusual behaviour. It was recorded as a glitch.

Sky said: 'Jesus. This is what we've been looking for? Cheese?'

'Damn right. You're police, dude,' said Dodger. 'This is your first house call. Grunt work. It don't look like nothing now. Everyone in this neighbourhood's got an innocent face on. But you gotta keep digging.' So Sky kept digging. Was there an error in the barcode of the cheese? Was there a new non-dairy diet craze in that area? Was there a batch of faulty fridges that recorded cheese as being in the fridge when the cheese had in fact left the fridge? He peeled away the data like an onion skin, layer after layer, until he was able to isolate just two people who had inexplicably left cheese in their fridges for over three months. One, he could see, had left the area to visit family in Missouri. The other? Where was the other? Travel records said nothing. Security satellites in the neighbourhood revealed a house that nobody entered or left. The GPS tag in the family travel pod showed a stationary vehicle left in an out-of-town pod-dock. That person was red flagged and passed to the next room. Could be nothing, could be something. Could be nothing that means something.

'We are looking for nothing,' Duke told the Blue Team. 'These days, we know everything about everyone. It's all out there. Everything you do, everything you say, everything you write, everything you buy, everywhere you go. So what we are looking for are the little silences, the skipped beats. The absence of information. The absence of information where there should be information.'

Cobalt said: 'Hey Sky. You with us, big man? You getting this?'

'We all leave a trail. It's when the trail stops, that you worry,' said Sky.

'Exactamundo. You're a smart cookie. Betcha you were good at whatever it was you did on the outside.'

Duke continued: 'It's when you stop giving out information that you become a person of interest. And by rights, you should be giving out everything. You gave up your right to privacy a long time ago in the wider interests of our national security.'

Cobalt said: 'You gave it up when you bought a pair of sneakers that tell everyone what your fat to muscle ratio is.'

'You stop putting out: we're coming after you,' said Dodger.

'But why?' asked Sky. 'I mean, do we have an end game here?'

Nobody answered him.

The Fifth Room

Sky, Cobalt and Dodger. Three-quarters of the Blue Team who graduated from the fourth room into the fifth. The fourth quarter of the team was Cyan: a thirty-something woman from Hawaii, who wound up on the inside for reasons she never divulged. Maybe Cyan leaked some documents she shouldn't have. Maybe she killed herself and woke up in a cell with a hood over her head. Cobalt believed she used to be military because she made coffee like a woman under fire. (In the fifth room, their daily privileges included coffee, one hour of exercise, and access to limited online gaming. The downside to the fifth room was that, at the end of every working day, they all underwent intra-memory scans. Sky recognised the type: scans designed to wipe out long-term memories, turning the Blue Team into perfect worker ants – living solely in the present, no ties, no grudges, no nostalgia. Blank slates. Every afternoon, before this happened, Sky would run through his own memory exercises, focusing on modulating and controlling the amygdala, skills he'd developed years ago while doing some freelance work on terrorist resistance methods, meditative techniques designed to pack away information deep into the subconscious: who he is, what he knows, his wife, his daughter. He hangs on to what he can.)

In the fifth room, the team members can also choose how their data is represented. Cobalt, for example, chooses to see his data like a 4D map of the Iowa town he grew up in, as it was when he was thirteen years old. Lucky Cobalt. He gets to put on a Vis Mask and walk the streets of his youth. He knows that place better than any other. If a paving stone is cracked, he'll notice. It's a gap, a blip in the data.

Dodger sees his data as a war game he used to play on the outside. He played it every day for years. He knows every level, every cheat, every outcome. Now here in the fifth room, he locks, loads and goes into battle again, watching for the sonic bullet that flies at an unexpected trajectory, the human shield with the wrong colour eyes. Catches in the fabric of information.

Cyan surfs off the coast of a virtual Hawaii. She pulls on a full-body Vis Suit, stands on a SimBoard and is immersed in her data like water. She moves through it, feeling for the currents, the eddies and swirls; sits on her SimBoard, watches the waves coming in, anticipating their movements.

It took Sky a while but eventually he plumped for a ball game. Baseball. Tori's sport of choice. He'd played football all through college, right up to the point he started gambling instead, and had been a little disappointed when his only child turned out to be a girl not a boy, thinking that his old-fashioned dream of being a sports dad would have to be put aside. But Tori had proved him wrong in this, as in so many things – having turned out to be keener on baseball than he ever was on football. Man, the hours he spent throwing balls for her in the back yard. But he's older now – he just wants to sit in the bleachers with a beer and watch the game unfold. So that's what he does. Watches a game.

He was a thorough and obsessive gambler, so when the players walk onto the pitch, he knows to check their stats, their averages, their weak points. Then he watches for dropped catches, mis-hits, freak scores. Players not doing what they should. Plus, you know, it's nice to watch a sport his daughter loves. Soothing. As he watches the game unfold, he lets one part of his brain turn over memories of her like pebbles, while another part of his brain remains aware that each player represents data, data which represents a city on the West Coast of America, and that data is made up of what the people in that city are doing, and each single player is in fact thousands of people. One equals a multitude.

There are fewer restrictions in the fifth room. The Blue Team aren't strapped to their chairs, they get to talk to their teammates more, they can roam through the data fields at will, although any approach towards their families and former identities is expressly forbidden. ('Don't try to go back,' says Duke, often, 'don't try to make contact. There will be consequences.')

Sky says: 'It's almost like freedom in here.'

'If you count sitting in a glass-sided cell in front of a two-way mirror working on a machine that's constantly monitored by whatever authority it is that keeps us here in a security facility deep underground as freedom,' says Dodger.

Cobalt says: 'At least the tax drones can't get us down here, eh?'

'Do you think it's the government we're working for?' asks Sky. Cobalt rubs his stubbly face (although this, Sky realises, is also an assumption – Cobalt's face may not in fact be his own).

'I dunno, son. They'd like us to think so.'

Dodger says: 'Jeeeez. Come on, Sky man. We're way beyond that now. We used to think there were good guys and bad guys, yeah? But then the good guys had to work with the bad guys in order to get the other bad guys. Like how the government had to work with big business. And how big business had to work with the bad guys. And how the bad guys wanted to work with the good guys. Everyone's trying to get with everyone else, but everyone's against everyone else at the same time. Skins versus skins. All against all.'

Cobalt says: 'You got an extra sliver of information telling you a little somethin' somethin' about the other guys, you're on top for a day. But tomorrow? Who knows.'

'No-one's in charge anymore,' says Dodger. 'The good guys gave it up.'

Tori

The way Dodger talks always reminds Sky of Tori. Back in her teens, she'd gotten into all this protest stuff on the Dark Net; there were groups there trying to find ways to remove every last trace of themselves from the web. To become anonymous. There were loads of kids into it – they called themselves offliners – they were trying to collectively drop off the grid. She'd tell him about it when she came to see him: the two of them sitting on the back porch with beers. 'Offline is the only place we have left to go,' she would say. 'Everywhere else is owned. Everywhere else has been sold.'

It was hard for her to stick to her principles though: without an online ID she couldn't get a job, couldn't get healthcare, couldn't travel, couldn't own anything, couldn't access money. The government considered her an illegal alien in her own country. She used to be able to work for cash in hand, but after cash became obsolete, there were days when she only survived on rotten food scavenged from garbage cans. She couldn't even get into the retail zones since the retina scanners had been introduced. In her twenties, she'd often talked about leaving the country – finding somewhere she could live offline, somewhere still lagging behind on the technological curve – but then they'd introduced the travel quotas, limiting overseas trips to essential military personnel (or those who could afford to pay the extortionate black market fees), and that door had shut too.

Last time he'd seen her, she'd been working on a project she and her fellow offliners hoped would enable users to run a data search for images they were included in – even if they were only accidentally photographed or filmed – and then be able to delete them. 'Think how many things have taken footage of you in your lifetime, Dada. Thousands. Millions! Think how great it would be to take back that control.'

'Sounds awesome, sweetheart.'

'You think it's impossible, right?'

'Nothing is, baby. If anyone can do it, you can.'

'Damn right. Did I tell you we came across this study that said most adults alive today have over 200,000 images of themselves uploaded before their first birthday? All the scans and baby pics, right? Parents just chucking everything up without even thinking about it. The security cams, the auto-ID stuff. It's a freaking tidal wave. Plus, there's everything recorded *in utero* by the MediBots. We've got to make people aware of this, right?'

'Yup. Sure do. Wanna go through this memory test with me again? You're getting better at it.'

'Jeeeez, Dada. One more time. Then I'm done.'

He'd taught her everything he could in the time he had. He knew one day someone would catch up with him. A gift like his attracted attention. He told her he'd been a decent gambler, not a great one, but that gambling had led him to discover a more lucrative skill. One day, instead of watching the game, he watched the crowd – and he bet himself he could guess how they would bet. Turns out, he was right. He could predict that stuff. It started small, as these things do. Stupid bets he placed with himself. He'd go into a room, turn his attention to the people in it, and guess what they would do next. In football, they called it downfield vision. It's what made him a good quarterback. He knew where to throw the ball ahead of the player running beneath it because he could guess that player's movements.

When he went into marketing, they talked about crowd behaviour. The myriad influences that act upon a group. The herd at the watering hole. Watching consumers. Influencing consumers. Sky started to deal in bigger herds: online communities mainly, social networks, electorates. From then on, his meetings became more private, more low-key, more deliberately casual. He was quietly sought out by pollsters; CEOs; security services; the military; aides to the president; aides to other presidents; people with money enough to pay him with no questions asked. You walk into rooms and you listen, he told his daughter. You hear what will happen next. You figure out how to change it before it arrives. Put your ear to the ground.

He didn't tell her that old gambling habits die hard and he was playing one hand against the other. He didn't tell her that important people don't like to be caught talking to someone like him.

Extra Training

Supervisor Duke often told him his predictive skills were extremely valuable to the Blue Team. Being able to spot glitches before they even happened: now that was something. Glitch. Sky turned the word over in his mouth. *Gli-ch*. A spittle-filled squelch. A footstep into mud. But thanks to Duke's approval, he got a new bed. He got a digital chess board and he could listen to music for an hour in the evenings (he favoured the old stuff, cheesy pop his mum had been into – Beyoncé, Rhianna).

Lying on his new bed in his cell after his nightly brain scan, he called up his buried memories of Tori. Had he done enough to help her? Where would she be now? Whenever he was looking at data from cities where she had offliner friends, he paid extra attention, as if he might be able to see something that would tell him about her.

The Blue Team started to undergo extra training, improving their target identification and pursuit ahead of their upcoming move into the sixth room. 'There's a matrix you need to keep in mind,' said Duke, mid-way through the session. 'There are people with attitudes and views that are potentially problematic to us. However, as a form of protest, these people tend to drop out of the system; they move less money, they buy fewer things, they fail to learn new skills, their power is limited. Therefore they are less important to both big corporations and to the government. Their attitudes are problematic, but their influence is minimal. Where we see issues are when we encounter individuals and groups with problematic attitudes *and* either influence or access to influence. Individuals with the ability to cause problems and the motivation to do so.'

Stay under the radar, Tori, he thought. Don't draw attention to yourself. Hadn't he always told her that? Don't go setting up a commune in Utah. They'll be down there with an undercover armed unit soon as you can say 'the group are all believed to have committed suicide'. Hide in plain sight. Stay in the cities. She was a smart kid though, smarter than him.

Duke once said to him: 'You had a daughter, Sky.'

The past participle had stung. 'Yeah,' he'd said. Nothing more. Who knows what he'd talked about when drugged up? He'd tried to lock that part of his mind away, but these people were persistent in getting what they wanted. He knew that. Most memories were accessible. Most.

There had been a day he'd seen Tori, about a year before he was arrested. He'd been agitated, irritated. They'd been going through a series of tests designed to teach her how to verify online video footage – it was something he knew a little about himself, having been responsible for creating extremely successful pieces of fraudulent footage that were currently in heavy rotation on the 24-hour news feeds – and she was fooling around, baiting him.

'Chrissake, you need to know this stuff, Tor. It's not a game.'

'Man, you must think the world is made up of total suckers. You churn this stuff out and people lap it up.'

'It's important that you are able to tell – or at least make a pretty good guess – if what they tell you on the news is genuine. You hear me?'

'Yeah, yeah. Like any of it is. It's such bullshit. *Nothing* is true anymore.'

Had she heard him?

'Tori, something might happen to me one day. You know that, right? And if it did, you'd need to be able to tell. And then there's the fact that if something happened to me, people might be... interested in you. They would want to know where you are. What you know. What you've learnt.'

She exhaled, looked away.

'Tori.'

After a pause, she said: 'I'd be ready, Dada. I know what to do.'

They looked at each other, aware of the dangers of speech. She said: 'Everything we've done. It's all in here. You and me.' She tapped her heart.

Sky tapped his head. 'You'd need this more.' Memories. Hidden memories. Locked down and concealed thanks to years of the intensive brain training he'd developed, sinking conscious memories deep into the swamp of the unconscious, where they were hardest to access. And then learning how to retrieve them – recalling the forgotten as and when you needed it. Contacts, access codes, passwords, methodology. All buried deep in her synapses. And some stuff he'd put in there without telling her: weaponry usage, combat skills, yada yada. A few useful tips he'd picked up when working with the security services. Protective Dada stuff. He didn't like the way the world was going.

Tori rolled her eyes, threw her empty beer bottle in the direction of the garbage can. 'Sheesh,' she said.

His Own Imagination

In the Blue Team rest zone, Dodger rolls his eyes, throws his empty water bottle in the direction of the garbage can. 'Sheesh,' he says. It has taken Sky way way longer than it should have to figure out that his team mates are constructs of his own imagination. Dodger is made up of several bits of Tori and some bits of the guitarist from his college rock band. Crazy what the brain holds onto. Sky presumes that after he'd received his 'lethal' injection, he'd simply been kept unconscious. He'd never woken up. They'd probably just wheeled him into a storage unit, plugged him into a life support system, then used intra-brain sensors to make him do their data mining work as he lay there. It wouldn't be hard, really, to use some kind of auto-suggestion programme to electrically excite the cortex and persuade his brain to come up with a convincing scenario (the cell, the different rooms, the members of the Blue Team, Duke et al) that he would then mentally inhabit. It probably made for happier, more engaged, more productive – albeit unconscious – workers.

It's something like the lucid dreaming stuff he'd worked on with the Navy Seal boys nearly ten years ago. He'd heard rumours, even back then, that prisoners captured in combat often didn't make it home, but instead were kept in mass storage units somewhere in New Mexico, wired up to machines, drugs keeping them in an artificial REM sleep state, something like a very deep hypnosis, while their memories were accessed for useful information. The guy who'd told him this had called it harvesting. It wasn't a massive leap to go from harvesting people's memories to using people's memories as part of getting them to actively work for you. Pretty nifty, really. He creates his work environment from his own lived experience, and then the data-patterns are projected into his mind in visual forms that are convincing enough that he believes he is sitting in a room and looking at them.

Cobalt, he sees now, is a patchwork of people he's worked with, mixed with a large dash of his old football coach. The stubble on Cobalt's face comes from his father. Cyan? Ah, silent Cyan. Always absent. Out at sea. Cyan holds the much-missed heart of his wife.

It's curious though, even after figuring all this out, he doesn't really mind it. He likes his team-mates – they're familiar to him, comforting. He likes inhabiting this level of his consciousness. When Tori was a little girl, and he'd used fully immersive digigames to teach her basic memory and observation skills, she would always complain that she couldn't believe in it because it wasn't the real world. He would tell her: 'Play the hand you're dealt, kiddo. Every world is part of the real world, if you think about it.'

Tori would say: 'Jeeez, man. Whatever.'

The Sixth Room

There are people waiting for them when the Blue Team move into the sixth room. New co-workers, says Duke. Sky knows these kind of people. Ex-military. High level. Dark suits. The kind who never get in a travel pod without checking underneath it first. The kind who deal in what they call 'clearance', which is in fact a kind of permission. They are there to give the Blue Team clearance to do certain things. Clearance. A space made by the removal of objects.

The Blue Team are to be allocated certain individuals known to be of concern. Targets will be identified. Buttons will be pressed. Targets will be eliminated. 'It's show time,' says Cobalt, pulling on his Vis Mask.

Sky suspects this room is where they've always been heading. He also suspects that this is why they use a man wired up to a machine to do their dirty work: a decent machine can process simple data faster than he ever could, but when it comes to pursuing elusive individuals, there's no greater hunter than the human brain. He used to tell his military contacts exactly the same thing: hardware for routine tasks, wetware for the messy stuff. A perfect symbiosis.

He settles into his chair, gets his mask on, calls up his usual data visualisation – the baseball game – and tries to relax. Watch the game, Sky, he tells himself. His name – his real name – flashes through his mind then: *James Malcolm Markey.* He shakes it away. First player into bat: check stats, check yearly averages, check stance, check facial expression. Bang, bang, bang, bang, done. Watch the player's feet as the ball flies in; watch the action of the bat through the air. Smooth. Strike one. All peachy so far. Sky lets his eyes flick about, taking in the other players, their physical appearance, their behaviour. One guy kicking the ground. One player on the bench watching the clouds. The man on third base looking restless.

(He thinks then, just for a second, of the layers of deception making up the world he inhabits: the game is not a game but data patterns; the sixth room is not a room but something he has imagined; the work he is being asked to do is not simple data-mining, it's not just fiddling around with numbers, it is – what is it, Sky? What is it? Can you name it? (He hears Tori's voice then, providing him with words he is avoiding. (Assassination, Dada? Jeez.) He blinks her away.))

Sky rests his chin on his hand. The second batsman is up now, but he's not someone in good form. He's run out, as expected, on his way to second. All normal. All okay.

The player from the bench is up next. It's a woman. He checks her stats, her run rate, her season average. She's a decent hitter but nothing special. She performs as expected, though her slide into fourth is a little off-balance and he resolves to watch her closer next time round.

It's a beautiful early evening on the baseball field. The sky is blue fading to amber on the horizon. There's a backdrop of wide open fields. The batting team play well then go out to field. The new pitcher steps onto the mound, winds up and lets go. It's a perfect swinging curveball coming in sweet and swift. Strike. The second ball is equally flawless: a straightforward fastball, thrown like a spear. The batter has no chance. Sky leans forward. He's always loved a well-thrown pitch. The third: a cunning splitter, leaving the batter gawping uselessly after it. Lethal. That's a strikeout. Sky whistles, checks the player's stats. The kid's brought the good stuff, no doubt. But something makes him look up as the pitcher is walking back to the mound. There: now he sees it. The pitcher is the woman he noticed before. Skinny and flat-chested, but definitely a woman. He checks the stats again, looking at pitching rather than batting: she's good but not great, it's a solidly workmanlike record – all apart from this last season. This last season includes five random games that were perfect shut-outs. And the one he's watching is heading that way. It makes no sense. She's not throwing like a girl. She's a glitch.

Sky finds he is drumming his fingers on his knee. He hears Duke's voice in his iBud: 'Do you have anything for us, Sky? We're seeing significant changes in your brain activity. Have you identified our target?'

Sky calculates quickly. This batch of data is from Northern California: Larkspur or thereabouts. There are things he knows about a house in Larkspur he doesn't want to think about now, not while Duke is watching the monitor, with men in dark suits alongside him. He thinks instead about the multitude of factors involved in throwing the perfect pitch; he feels his heart rate calm.

'Not sure,' he says. 'Looking again.' He watches the woman lining up to take another pitch. She's moving slowly and deliberately. He remembers standing in his backyard in Larkspur with his seven-year-old daughter as the dusk fell on a long hot summer day, throwing her a ball.

'Take your time, Tori,' he called to her back then. 'Don't be afraid to make 'em wait. It'll give you room to think.'

'Got it, Dada.'

How long can he give her now? How long before his brain behaviour gives her away? If she's in Larkspur, she won't be there for long. She would know that from the moment he had been arrested she would have to keep moving. No two nights in the same place.

He watches the woman in the baseball game. She's tossing the ball to someone else and jogging out to the outfield. He breathes deeply and focuses on the new pitcher coming in. Good girl.

It occurs to him only then that there may be a reason Duke has always asked him to focus on an area that includes California, his home state. Of all the people in the world, he is the one who knows Tori Markey the best. He would be the one to spot her in a crowd. His eyes would always find his daughter. Takes a thief to catch a thief. He didn't know how far she'd got with her projects. They'd agreed it was safer not to share details of their work, but he knew that a woman with her motivation and the skills he'd taught her – predicting and influencing mass behaviour, infiltrating and collapsing social networks, falsifying and successfully placing news collateral, resisting and recovering from cognitive interrogation, identifying and eliminating toxic obstacles, all that good stuff – would always be a target.

Duke's voice in his ear: 'Sky, we're having Cyan and Cobalt have a second look at the data you've got there. They're going to circle in now.'

'Sure thing,' he says. Relax, he tells himself. Watch the game. But he's agitated. His mind keeps flicking to and fro, between the past and present. His brain monitor's going to be spiking like a fucking porcupine. They'll be onto him any second now. And he knows, suddenly in a rush, that to save her, he must forget her. He must wipe her from his mind. Can he do that? He has to do that. It must be possible to undo what he has done. He must get rid of all the memories of her that he has from the full twenty-four years of her life: every thought, every image, every conversation, every hug, every swell of his heart. Everything he has packed into the basement of his mind and protected with all the tricks and techniques he has ever learnt. He must make her anonymous – just like she always wanted. And just as quickly, he knows that she must know this too. She would know that, wherever he went after he was arrested, he would have to forget her if he was going to keep her safe. She was always one step ahead of him. His clever girl.

Sky blinks. Takes a deep slow breath. Lets his mind spin through its Rolodex of Tori memories one last time. It's okay though. He knows that even when he lets her go, she will still hold onto something of him. Obviously, she will have already got rid of any memories of him teaching her – she'd have wiped clean all that easily accessed declarative memory years ago, and stored the lessons in her unconscious. But she's stubborn. She won't let it all go. Somewhere buried deep in her temporal cortex, tucked in behind how to open a bottle of beer on a park bench, she will retain something of her father, an untraceable, unidentifiable memory – maybe how much they laughed that time they swam together in a freezing lake, just the sound of it echoing up into the air, nothing that anyone could ever link back to him, or maybe how he would rub her back with his big footballer's hands when she had nightmares, yes, maybe that – so a little fragment of him will continue to exist at a flickering, cellular level. A little spark. *James Malcolm Markey. Dada.*

For a second, he wonders if he can hold onto something of her, but he knows it's impossible. He's a man who can't be trusted; that's why they've got him in here, strapped up to a machine, hunting down his daughter.

Well, now.

Sky shakes his head and focuses on the new batsman stepping up to the plate. He checks his stats, runs some numbers, thinks about the weather. He doesn't look at the skinny girl crouched out on the boundary, the small figure in his peripheral vision who is slowly disappearing in the fading evening sunlight.

Sky watches the game.

Sky concentrates.

Sky tries to forget.

Afterword:

We've Got Your Numbers

Dr James Dyke
University of Southampton

IN THE TIME it takes you to read this sentence, about 100,000,000,000,000 bytes of information will flow around the internet. That is many, many billion times more information than you will transmit via all the words you speak over your entire lifetime.

This flood of data comes from an ever-increasing range of sources as more and more previously 'dumb' devices are becoming plugged into the global information system in a phenomena that has come to be known as the 'Internet of Things'. In the near future, your fridge will communicate how much cheese and milk you have to a local grocery store. Your car will augment satellite GPS information with connections to the world wide web in order to get traffic information while an insurance supplied black box will record your speed, acceleration, braking and other driving parameters. You will monitor the temperature of your house using your phone while at work. Your watch will silently upload your location to a range of online servers that will record your proximity to systems of interests such as advertising hoardings or shopping centres.

What is all this data for? Many companies are keen to gain access to more data as this can give them a competitive edge. If an insurer can assess your driving style, then it will be able to offer lower cost insurance to safer drivers. If your fridge communicates to directly to a store, then products can be sold quickly and efficiently. As well as increasing immediate opportunities to sell products, the mass of data that is generated when we shop, drive, fly, walk, etc., allows companies to build profiles of consumer behaviour. You will be represented by a detailed dataset that will seek to not only record what you do, but allow others to understand why you do these things and what actions you may perform in the future. You live in an end of terrace house, in a particular postcode. You drive a five-year-old diesel people carrier. You drink a lot of goats milk and your favourite website is Reddit.

This data can be aggregated into *metadata*. Metadata is data about data. A common example of metadata is the ordering system in a library. Letters and numbers (data) are used to order books and periodicals (another type of data). You already have a significant virtual online presence via metadata that has been collected about you. This metadata is analysed, mined and bought and sold in order to better understand your behaviour and by inference the behaviour of other people that are like you in certain respects. It is also increasingly used by security agencies in their anti-terrorism operations.

Since 2007, the United States National Security Agency (NSA) has been monitoring and collecting increasing amounts of information that is sent around the internet via the *PRISM* program. Information is intercepted from corporations such as Microsoft, Yahoo!, Google, Facebook, Paltalk, YouTube, AOL, Skype and Apple. An individual's emails, video calls, purchase details, internet browsing history, social media posts and online documents can be intercepted and stored in bulk for future analysis.

The United States is not the only major actor in this area. A significant proportion of internet traffic is routed through the territory of the United Kingdom as a consequence of the main trans-Atlantic fibre optic cables reaching land in the southwest of England. Since 2011, the UK Government Communications Headquarters (GCHQ) has been collecting 1-2 billion records a day from internet traffic via probes that have been connected directly to these cables as part of the *TEMPORA* program. Other programs such as DISHFIRE run jointly by the NSA and GCHQ store approximately 200 million text messages a day and add further to the collection of intercepted data.

Analysts have the ability, for example, to read emails, listen to telephone conversations or watch video chat calls of suspects. NSA analysists are also able to perform the same level of scrutiny for people who have, at some point in the past, communicated with people who have, at some point in the past, communicated with terrorist suspects. Three degrees of separation. However, it is impossible for analysts to read any significant fraction of individual emails or watch more than a few minutes of video calls. So it is the analysis of metadata that has proved to be the most important and challenging aspect of the analysis of intercepted data.

These surveillance programs generate very large amounts of metadata. Initially, data that relates to known suspects will be highlighted. Next, keywords that relate to things such as people, places, technology, political factions, ideas and ideology will then trigger further rounds of analysis. The overall challenge is to see the wood for the trees – to see the structure in the data. What patterns emerge and how those patterns change over time. Sophisticated algorithms have been developed that deploy a wide range of information theory and statistical analysis tools and techniques.

One approach to seeking sense in large amounts of data is to build Artificial Neural Networks (ANNs). These are essentially computer simulations of very simple representations of biological brains. While original research into ANNs in the 1940s was inspired by the brains of animals, modern implementations do not seek to understand real world brains but rather develop effective machine learning techniques. ANNs will be fed data which will be routed between virtual neurons via virtual synapse connections. Algorithms then adjust the strength of synaptic connections between the neurons in order to find underlying patterns in the data. In this way, ANNs can learn to spot trends in house prices, detect the onset of epilepsy or identify a person from their handwriting.

When run on large, powerful computers, ANNs can perform tasks extraordinarily quickly. However, they remain limited to the applications of problems with relatively simple structure to the data. Any ANN will be limited in terms of the amount of information that can be stored within the configuration of its nodes and synapses. A typical ANN will have tens or hundreds of virtual neurons.

The human brain has approximately 100 billion neurons with trillions of synaptic connections. Homo sapiens evolved their large brains in a recent burst of adaptation over several million years. But the ground work to the emergence of consciousness on planet Earth stretches back to the dawn of life some 3.5 billion years ago. Countless generations of organisms have twitched, swam, crawled, run or flown before us. Each in their own way exploring the vast space of evolution and its possible forms of life.

The neural network of a human brain is a prodigious pattern recogniser. Lying on your back watching clouds gives a clue as to how readily you can identify faces in otherwise random shapes. Humans can easily see faces in burnt toast, coastal features or the mountains of Mars. One attempt to harness some of the pattern-recognition capacity of the human brain is to build a molecular-level simulation. This is the aim of the ten-year, billion-euro, Human Brain project. Another route would be to work directly with real brains and seek to combine them with computing and information hardware to get our billions of neurons to participate in specific pattern-matching and data-processing tasks.

This would produce a cyborg – short for cybernetic organism – which the story you have just read proposes. Sky is a union of the biological and mechanical. The virtual world in which he inhabits affords him the capacity to perform prodigious feats of data analysis and pattern recognition. In Joanna's story, Sky has to sacrifice that which he holds most dear in order to protect it – and in doing so moves further away from the human towards the machine. Whether a machine would ever make such a sacrifice is open to question. A question that is as hard to answer as whether a machine could ever love.

Bruno Wins!

Frank Cottrell-Boyce

— *SINCE THE TIME of the Babylonians men have tried to predict the future — searching for it among the stars, in the entrails of birds, or in their own imaginations...*

'This is interesting,' said Russell.

'This is obvious,' said Maya.

— *You have imagined futures for yourself, for your children, for the World.*

'This is true.'

'Pass the sugar.'

— *When you imagined a future of instant sharing and Bespoke coffee, did you ever even consider just how much of that Future you would spend hoovering the stairs?*

Maya was always pressuring Russell to upgrade their BespokeCoffee subscription so they wouldn't be bothered by questions like this anymore. But Russell liked the questions. They made him think. 'The mental stimulation of the question,' he said, 'perfectly compliments the chemical stimulation of the BespokeCoffee.'

'You really think that?' said Maya.

'It's nice to be prompted to think about the Future. The Future of this world and also the future of Russell and Maya.'

'I'm thinking about that very thing right now,' said Maya. 'Unprompted by the coffee machine.'

— *When you imagined a Future^{TM} of perfect coffee for a perfect start to your day - did you ever dream that the rest of the day might* *be spent up a ladder removing potentially bio-hazardous dust from the light fittings?*

'See, Maya? I bet you never thought about the fact that the dust on the light fittings might be bad for our health? And the health of our potential children.'

'I'm leaving,' said Maya.

Which she did.

'You can keep the dog,' were her parting words.

So it was a comfort to Russell that he had not upgraded to ad-free membership or there would be no human voice to start the day with, just perfect silence to compliment the perfect coffee.

— When you imagined a Future where EveryCup just hit the spot, didn't you just wish there was a single household appliance that would clean floors, walls, under the bed, behind your toilet and just about anywhere you can name?

'You know what that would be?' said Russell. 'That would be the opposite of Bruno.' It was the first time he had spoken to the BespokeCoffee machine out loud. Except on matters of coffee.

— Bruno is the Newfoundland who you have owned for eighty one weeks and who has made five trips to the vet in that time?' said the Bespoke.

'Bruno is the single organism that can get hair just about anywhere you could name. I sneezed the other day and a clutch of his hairs came up in my mucus. Think about it – that dog even managed to deposit some of his hairs inside my lungs.'

The thought struck Russell that maybe it was Bruno that had driven Maya away. Maybe he left hairs in her lungs too and maybe she hadn't liked that.

'I try to keep the place clean but Bruno always wins.'

— Let's take a look.

BespokeCoffee pulled together a series of clips from other appliances around the house and shuffled them into an amusing sequence. It showed Russell hoovering carpets and cushions and the space down the back of the couch in a forlorn attempt to control a blizzard of dog hairs. It intercut them with shots of Bruno lolloping about the house, eyes moist with the untroubled expectation of love, tongue lolling with an exuberant ignorance of his own unceasing moult, while Russell followed him round sighing, 'Bruno! Oh, Bruno.'

BespokeCoffee shared the collage with 'all' BespokeCoffee members.

Every one of them liked it.

Most of them shared it with people from beyond the BespokeCoffee community even.

'Bruno! Oh Bruno' became a catch phrase.

So eat that, Maya. Now the World is listening to me.

Well-wishers sent sympathy and hints, also anti-moulting tonics though Russell was too cautious about interfering with Bruno's metabolism to use them. Then someone sent him a link to The Flock.

'Coming soon – The Flock, the ultimate cleaning system.'

That's it.

No information.

But plenty of speculation.

Everyone who liked The Flock was excited. Everyone seemed certain that it would be a 'flock' of tiny robots – or why would it be called Flock? The robots would probably swarm together to clean your carpet but then peel off into teams to do those smaller, hard-to-get-to jobs, licking away the sticky stuff from behind the sink or sucking up pools of gloop from the bottom of the dustbin below the bin liner. They would be tireless, enthusiastic, and thorough.

Russell announced that the Flock could probably clean anything. Individual flockees might be tiny enough to get into every nook and cranny and pipe. They would probably do away with the bio-hazardous dust on the light fittings hanging from your ceiling and maybe even get between your teeth and clean there too. The Flock was the Future and the

Future was finally here. 'All my life,' said Russell, 'I've been waiting for various Futures. Futures involving teleportation, adjustable gravity, truly immersive games, driverless cars. They never arrived! Those Futures were flaky but the Flock is for real.'

Because Russell was the 'Bruno! Oh, Bruno' guy, his enthusiasm was shared and repeated until it became cold fact. Even when the Flock people refused to confirm that the Flock really could clean between your teeth, everyone dismissed it. 'We all have teething troubles,' said Russell – a joke that was shared globally.

Everyone wanted to be the first to own a Flock. Flock fans flew to Flock HQ and queued all night. 'They flocked to Flocktown,' wrote the commentators. Fans shared their moment of purchase and the opening of their Flock boxes. Russell's box of Flock was delivered 40 hours after official release. He could not have been happier with it. He lounged in his big chair, Bruno's head resting on his lap, and watched as the Flock nibbled across the carpet, identifying and digesting every last one of Bruno's hairs. When they had finished, they parked themselves in front of Bruno, humming tunefully in sleep mode, their sensors rippling colour, ready for the moment when the dog might shed another hair.

What you're missing here, Maya, he thought, *is the Future.* Then he wondered if she might be tempted back now that the whole Bruno hair thing had been resolved.

The Flock had its drawbacks.

In order to learn your priorities it first had to observe your actions. The tiny robots couldn't clean the light fittings until Russell had got out a ladder and cleaned them once himself. Once was enough. They would see to it from now on. But climbing off the ladder, Russell twisted his ankle when Bruno barged against it. Bruno had been restless and clumsy ever since the Flock arrived. The Flock had identified him as the main source of dirt and assigned a small detachment of flockees to follow him everywhere. Most of the day the dog stayed still as death, hoping that they would go away. Then he would make a sudden break for it, hoping to shake them off. Since he took no trouble to plan them, these escape attempts usually ended with him braining himself against a wall, or in this case the ladder. At night Russell, lulled to sleep by the sound of flockees grazing on the muck under his bed, would be woken by the sudden crash of a coffee table or the clatter of a waste basket. He would turn over, relishing the knowledge that the Flock would take care of the spillages.

Then Bruno vanished. His designated Flock attendants patrolled the locked door in confusion, like hounds who had lost the scent.

Bruno was a smart dog. He wouldn't wander the streets, looking for scraps. He would go straight to a place where he knew that he would be fed and offered bedding and attention. Namely that bitch Maya's place. Russell was straight over there.

She wouldn't even open the door properly. She stood with her head peeping around it, barking at him. 'Yes he's here. Take him if he'll come with you. The dear Lord knows I don't want him – dropping hairs everywhere and knocking stuff over.'

Bruno's head appeared below hers. The dog didn't bark but looked anxiously off down the path, worried that Russell might have brought the Flock with him.

'The dog's a nervous wreck.'

'It's the Flock...'

'No it's not the Flock. It's the fact that you allow the Flock to take care of everything while you sit on your wide lardy backside. Your entire life is mediated via social household appliances. Which is why we couldn't have children together! You can't even care for your dog.'

A thought occurred to him. 'Are you... pregnant?' Is that why she was hiding behind the door?

'None of your dam beeswax. Take the dog and go. Or leave him here and I'll have him put down anyway. I can't afford to feed him.'

She opened the door a bit wider to let the dog out. Bruno just whined and slipped back inside. Even under threat of execution he wasn't coming home. Russell left alone.

Maya's HomeSecure system liked and shared the doorstep humiliation incident with the whole HomeSecure community.

The fact that the 'Bruno! Oh, Bruno' guy had lost Bruno looked bad on Flock's profile. People began to share their other Flock-related gripes and disappointments. 'Flock sucks', 'They said it would clean teeth', 'Flock just doesn't know when to stop!' Russell liked all of these but the way his Flock trailed after him when he came in, like a row of trusting ducklings, made him feel bad about turning them off. So they wandered the floors and walls while he sat motionless in his chair. Twenty-four hours later they arranged themselves in a curved, twinkly rug around his feet. He leaned forward and snarled, 'I hate you. You've erased every trace of the dog I love. Was it too much to ask to leave a few hairs or a pawprint to remind me of him?! I hate you and whoever invented you. You and all the other flaky futures that never came to pass. I'm sick of disappointment. If I ever find the man who invented you I will cut him into pieces and say – this cut is for the jet pack I never got, and this one is for the glasses that tell you who you're talking to, which I also never got, and here's one for the driverless car and one for the silent airplane and then I'll stake you out on the carpet and let the Flock nibble you to death.'

The Flock's default is total privacy. It would never have shared Russell's outburst. But the incident was witnessed by BespokeCoffee and went public that way. It was the end for the Flock. Special areas were set aside in the municipal recycling centres, just for Flocks. There the Flocks would busy themselves removing rust and flaky paint from the sides of the echoey skips in which they were stored. Sometimes several flocks would join together into a superflock and roam the recycling facility, pointlessly sorting things.

Everyone ordered the BespokeCleaner. It was nowhere near as sophisticated as Flock. It couldn't learn behaviour. The advantage of that was that you didn't have to teach it. It was so obvious. Who wants an organic, growing relationship with a cleaning appliance? What you want is an on–off switch.

It was also the end for Russell-the-Oh-Bruno guy. It was his enthusiasm that had led everyone to waste time with The Flock in the first place. Also his need to chop people up was disturbing. No one liked him. No one shared him. Even the BespokeCoffee machine seemed to ask him fewer questions.

Then the doorbell rang.

It was someone he didn't know. A woman. It had been a lot of years since someone had just turned up on the doorstep unannounced, let alone a female someone. He wasn't sure of the etiquette. 'Hi,' he said, 'would you like to...'

She strode past him into the house and deactivated his Flock. Whatever the ettiquette was, he was sure it wasn't that. She also disabled the BespokeCoffee machine. 'Got any other blabbermouth Bespoke appliances?'

'Hmmm... the fridge maybe?'

She turned off the fridge. 'I'm the person,' she said, 'who invented the Flock. So chop me up and feed me to your household cleaning appliance.' Normally Russell was a man of his word but on this occasion he hesitated. 'But before you do it,' she hissed, 'I want to know why you killed my baby.'

'What baby? I love babies. Why would I kill...'

'The Flock. I worked for years getting those robots to swarm, to communicate, to learn – then you came along...'

'Excuse me. I was the one who called them The Future! They would still be sitting on the shelves if it wasn't for me.'

'They are sitting in skips thanks to you. You created an atmosphere of unrealistic expectations – cleaning teeth for Heaven's sake! Can't you clean your own teeth! This is exactly why the future keeps not happening. 3-D printing. Wearable tech. Teleportation. We imagine. We predict. We get excited. Then we get way way too excited so that when when they arrive we're disappointed.'

'I got a little excited but...'

'The Flock was brilliant. My little robots could have solved a million problems for mankind but now... now they're a failure. Now no one will fund me. No one will fund robots. You have plunged the world into robot winter.'

'But I love the Future. I've been waiting for the Future all my life.'

'You don't wait for the Future. You make it. Or in your case, break it.'

'I didn't mean...'

'Someone has to pay for science. You get them to pay for it by telling them you're doing something useful. But really – who knows what's going to be useful? You come up with something, thinking this is great... robots that swarm and learn. But you have to come up with a function for it or no one is going to pay. So I said – domestic cleaning. But who knows, once it's out there maybe people will find a million other uses for them. You tell the kids you're going to buy ice cream...'

'What if you don't have kids?'

'It's a metaphor. You tell these metaphorical kids you're going to buy ice cream but the ice cream is just the bait. It's the walk that matters. On the way maybe they're going to meet someone, or see something. Forests and oceans or amazing people or whatever. The ice cream promise is just to keep them walking. As long as you keep walking, something might happen. As long as I kept working on these robots, maybe more and more functions would come. Maybe they would save the World as long as I kept them walking. But you, you shot them in the legs.' Russell winced. Some metaphors were just too vivid. 'Where did you even hear about The Flock? We were so careful to avoid hype.'

'BespokeCoffee gave me a link.'

'Bespoke told you? You weren't even a little bit suspicious that a rival company shared my baby?'

'Why would I be suspicious of my own coffee machine?'

'What do people buy now instead of Flock?'

'BespokeCleaners.'

She stared at him. It seemed like the conversation was over. It had been so long since he had one face to face. It was kind of tiring what with all the extra data to take on board from such things as the way she looked at him, the way she twisted her hair, her perfume and now the way she was jabbing a bitten fingernail at him and demanding a pen and some paper.

'I'm not sure... my phone has DrawPad on it.'

'I think we've got something here. A pattern. Look... here's how it goes...'

She began to draw a graph. Russell tried to keep up with what she was saying but it soon became clear that she was talking mostly to herself. The only pause was when he stood up. 'Do. Not. Turn on. The coffee machine,' she warned. 'Look at this.'

The line on the graph began with a fairly steep climb. 'This axis is expectation. This is people excited about stuff as it develops and word gets out.' Then the line fell off a cliff, plunging towards zero. 'This peak here, this is the peak of inflated expectations. This trough is the trough of disillusionment. Where all the great ideas get smashed to pieces on this zero here... the zero of no-funding. This shape... like a rocket going up and coming down again... that's human creativity and hope being burned up and crashed by people like you. There goes 3-D printing and wearable tech and driverless cars. It happens every time.'

'But I liked all those things.'

'But look at all those things! What do they have in common? Bespoke have cheap commercial versions of them all. What if Bespoke were actually fuelling expectations? Making people excited about other people's products? So that when they come, they come with disappointment guaranteed? What if they're doing this deliberately?'

'You mean my coffee dispenser lied to me? That it manipulated me?'

But she was still talking to herself, not him.

'But look... look at all this space this side of the graph. What's here?'

'You just said – space.'

'Time. This axis is Time. Over here is the Future. Over on the left where ideas are being born, Time is accelerated by pressure from money and rumour. But over here, beyond the trough of disillusinment, beyond failure, look – acres of time and space, no pressure. Maybe this is a place where baby robots can grow at their own pace and find some purpose. Maybe the line will climb again, slowly, up the gradient of enlightenment onto the plateau of usefulness...'

Russell stared at the graph. 'Is it like that for people?' he wondered.

'What are you talking about?'

Russell bit his lip. He hadn't realised he had wondered out loud. 'Maybe the same is true for people. Maybe they think they're useful for something – for instance being with someone and having children with them and building a future – but then bang! that doesn't work out. Maybe that person could find another use for themselves and not be useless forever?'

'Well someone sure found a use for you,' said Flock Woman. 'You were a crucial node in the spread of disinformation. You tried to crush me but you've inadvertently given me hope.'

'I honestly did not try to crush you.'

'Maybe the most important things we do are all inadvertent. Now you can make some coffee.'

He switched on the Bespoke and asked her what kind she wanted but she had gone. The house was silent for a few seconds while the coffee machine booted up. When it greeted him, its voice - marinaded in betrayal - filled him with nausea.

So Russell left.

There was no one else in his house, so he walked out on himself. And his household appliances, of course – his cheating, two-faced, cynical, manipulative household appliances. The fridge, the coffee maker, the blender, the cooker – they had all treated him as a node.

He walked out and kept walking. And walking. And walking. Down the avenues, along the dual carriageway and out into the open country, beyond the reach of the traffic control cameras. HomeSecure picked up the sight of him stumbling out of the house. Traffic cameras watched him standing clueless at corners, hesitating at intersections, striding along the bypass and finally, hauntingly, disappearing over a grassy rise into the unfilmed country beyond.

They shared these things but they were lost in the tide of general sharing.

With no one in the house, there was nothing to share.

One by one, his appliances powered down.

Only the Flock maintained its restless vigil, searching under chairs, scrabbling in the backs of cupboards, rooting through bins. Until it organised itself into a tower, and unfastened the front door and left, leaving the door open behind it.

HomeSecure shared this.

A lot of people liked it, amused by what they took to be another hilarious Flock malfunction.

They unliked Russell's open front door, swinging slightly in the breeze. It made the house look like a body from which the soul had fled. They shared old clips of the 'Oh Bruno' guy to try and shake the feeling of unutterable loss that his absence created in them. But they only served to make the feeling more intense.

HomeSecure shared clips of Russell's Flock crawling over Maya's lawn and lying in wait. Thousands commented about how the poor dog was going to howl with despair when it saw its old tormentor had tracked it down. 'Run, Bruno, run' was the most liked comment. But when Maya did come to the door, the Flock seemed to graze her toes for a moment, then go. Then, amazingly, Bruno followed it out towards the by-pass, under the gaze of the traffic cameras.

They watched as Flock gathered itself at the kerbs, crossing in a tightly packed formation before dispersing like starlings on the other side.

They saw superflocks from the recycling centres answer Russell's Flock's inaudible call and stream out into the road.

Flock was learning new skills. It communicated, organised, did road safety, seemed to remember where it had been. All the way along it collected little piles of rubbish and passed it round its myriad self, sorting and dumping.

Then it passed beyond the traffic cameras. Vast now and shimmering it swarmed up the side of a hill and into the unfilmed country, with the dog trotting along after it.

That's when they realised.

The Flock was looking for Russell.

The end of its quest could not be seen on camera. You had to go there. And they did. People came in their cars and slogged up the hills, following the flicker of the Flock. Because all at once it seemed that finding that one lost soul was the most important thing on Earth. They had all shared his thoughts, liked them or unliked them. Without him they were all diminished. They had to find him to restore themselves.

He was crouched under a hawthorn, shivering, half-starved and bewildered when the first of the Flock found him. He lifted his head. A carpet of Flock, like bluebells covered the grass. And up beyond them, people. People who cheered when he got to his feet. Bowling towards him down the hill came Bruno. The dog did not jump up on him, as if it knew that he was too weak for that. Instead it crouched at his feet the way it used to do. Someone wrapped a blanket round him. Someone else gave him a hot chocolate. Maybe it was Maya but for now he was too weary to check. For now he was content to let the Flock lead him home.

Afterword:

The Hope Cycle

Prof Andrew Vardy
Memorial University of Newfoundland

'BRUNO WINS!' REFLECTS on the cycle of hype and disappointment that accompanies all new technology. Russell, while living amidst appliances intelligent enough to converse with, bemoans the promised technology that never came to be (e.g. jet packs and driverless cars). And his subsequent rant – witnessed by a world of social media followers – steers one particular product from inflated expectation to the dumpster.

Gartner's hype cycle[1] is a graphical tool that depicts how new technologies develop amidst an initial wave of expectation and hype culminating in the 'peak of inflated expectations.' If a product fails to meet these inflated expectations then it will fall into the 'trough of disillusionment,' climbing out only if early adopters begin to see its promise and push the product towards the 'plateau of productivity.' This evocative language reflects the dramatic impact that the success or failure of these technologies can have on the companies involved, as well as the consumers. We learn later in the story that the wave of hype for the Flock was actually instigated by a competing company that subsequently takes over the robotic cleaning market with a much less innovative product. This is an example of raising expectations in a destructive way. On the other hand, downplaying expectations is a strategy practised by major movie studios so that the open box office returns of a new film can be seen to 'beat industry predictions,' as opposed to falling short[2].

1. Gartner Incorporated, *Gartner Hype Cycle*.
 http://www.gartner.com/technology/research/hype-cycles/.
2. Goldstein, P., *'Star Trek' and the Real Art of Movie Marketing: Managing Expectations*, in *Los Angeles Times*. 2009.

The hype cycle is merely one organisation's attempt to interpret the rise, fall, and slow climb of new technologies. One thing it fails to capture is that technologies morph and flex in various unpredictable ways. The transistor revolutionized electronics and dealt a near fatal blow to the vacuum tube. But tubes survive even today, nestled in the amplifiers of guitarists who swear by their 'warmer' sound. In the story, the Flock learn and change. They form a larger collective and they seek out the missing Russell – perhaps to 'sort out' his life.

GARTNER'S HYPE CYCLE

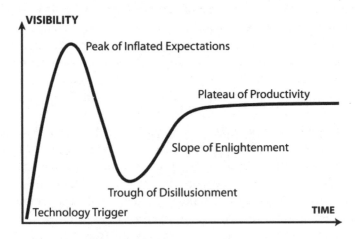

The technology of the Flock is an extrapolation from recent developments in swarm robotics. Swarm robotics is a technique for designing multi-robot systems that takes inspiration primarily from the social insects: bees, ants, wasps, and termites[3]. The key idea is that simple individual robot behaviours can lead to useful collective behaviour. In my own research group we developed an algorithm which allowed a set of simple robots to sort coloured pucks perceived through on-board cameras[4]. One of the most

3. Brambilla, M., et al., *Swarm robotics: A review from the swarm engineering perspective.* Swarm Intelligence, 2013. **7**(1): p. 1-41.
4. Vardy, A., G. Vorobyev, and W. Banzhaf, *Cache Consensus: Rapid Object Sorting by a Robotic Swarm.* Swarm Intelligence, 2014. **8**(1): p. 61-87.

interesting aspects of this work is that the robots self-organize and mutually agree upon locations where the pucks of each colour are to be deposited. The Flock are clearly much more powerful, but they inherit this notion of bringing order to the environment through collective action.

In addition to concepts from swarm robotics, there are other ideas that might be crucial in developing a real-world Flock. How could the bodies of such tiny robots be constructed? An exciting new trend in robotics research is to consider the fabrication of robots as a whole, not as disparate components linked together. A team of researchers from Harvard University have developed a new type of robot called the RoboBee which is built at the scale of actual bees[5]. A RoboBee is composed of layers of carbon fibre and soft polymers with gaps that allow the three-dimensional robot to 'pop out' of its two-dimensional template, much like a children's pop-up book. Another collaborative project between Harvard and MIT has seen the development of a robot that is born out of a flat sheet of specially prepared materials which can actually unfold and walk away without any further human intervention[6]. With regard to their visual systems, we envisioned flat robots with a top layer covered with compound eye facets, similar to an insect's. Although, in this case, the overall eye shape is flexible, which means that the robots can focus on particular regions of space by deforming so as to direct more individual eye facets towards those regions. This design is inspired by the CURVACE project, which resulted in the development of a curved artificial compound eye[7]. Compound eyes appear iridescent, so we imagined that the robots would shimmer: '...their sensors rippling colour.'

Of course, for such technologies to flourish and find useful application, they have to be nurtured and developed. This requires

5. Wood, R., R. Nagpal, and G.-Y. Wei, 'Flight of the RoboBees'. *Scientific American,* 2013. 308(3).

6. Felton, S., et al., 'A Method for Building Self-Folding Machines'. *Science,* 2014. 345(6197): p. 644-646.

7. Floreano, D., et al., 'Miniature Curved Artificial Compound Eyes'. *Proceedings of the National Academy of Sciences,* 2013. 110(23): p. 9267-9272.

time and money. In the story, the inventor of the Flock accuses Russell of plunging 'the world into robot winter.' This term is borrowed from 'AI winter', a dark period in AI research when the mismatch between expectations and results led to a crash in funding and interest[8]. The cycle of hype and disappointment probably plays a role in most areas of innovation, whether it is technology development, research, or science. So it is perhaps wise to be mindful of the slim one-character divide between hope and hype.

8. Russell, S.& P. Norvig, *Artificial Intelligence: A Modern Approach*. 3rd ed. 2009: Prentice Hall.

A Brief History of Transience

Toby Litt

THIS IS PERHAPS what didn't happen, although to us it feels like it probably was within the similar if not upon the exact. What is always was, because there has been no alteration of the given givens. If we tunnel down, below strings and things, to where the absolute is all, where all is all, we come to us coming towards us. It's not exactly a meeting, because there can't have been separation; it's not a recognition, because we know we always really knew; it's acknowledgement in the too-bright whiteness of *yes*. At the glare of this, vision is not even a possibility, but it universally works backwards instead; the *what* seen elsewhere everywhere is due to an absence of obliteration. So, although there never was division, we must begin in one tributary *I* – and I am delegated to pretend to have been that I – (this unparticular part of *we* that could never amount to *me*) – and I am wordgifted by miracle and English-plonked by luck. Seemingly, I was immediately split into two born eyes, two round blues that looked a human life from leaning nurse to tent of mother-hair to dark father-swoop to silver of scale to mini–yes and whoop of solid weep to slope of initial sleep. Then we – as I for we – jump to maturity, because you can assume growth through the conventional developmental stages – rage to cynicism, hope to shrug – and fasten ourselves there within a chair. I was watching television, sitting back in my comfortable chair, yes, I was there. If I were to say that I remembered, I would say that I remembered this – the screen was green. Either green of jungle or grass or helicoptered-over fields. I may have been male or female or other and I may have been young or

367

advanced in years or middling. More importantly, my vision
was better and more permanent than my eyes. Yes, there was
flesh around them and thick bone above them and thin bone
behind them. Yes, jelly and cornea and iris and created
shadowplay. Yes, rods-cones. But what I say I saw was what
was apparent there, which was green TV until time passed
away from it. To my right was a window with curtains and to
my left was a wall with all we'll see fall apart, because also in
front of me – behind the TV – was a similar wall. This green
moment is the one we issue from, for now I, as I, die. The
heart stops, the head drops, but the vision remains what it was
– parallel to the horizon. A lifted head is implied above a neck
so flopped that air could not pass through it. The TV is still
seen and, behind it, the pale wallpaper upon a wall that once
was painted blue. I die, and time does not speed up – time is
what it always was – but I do have a great deal more of it; and
sometimes, it seems, I start to lose focus upon minutes and
rejoin myself as if a quantum and another quantum have gone
by. The hours begin to jerk, light through the window is a
flash and lurch and twilight-into-darkness-into-dawn. This
diurnal to nocturnal swoosh is something with which I will
become extremely familiar. It seems there was a stop, not just
specific to me but, for want of a better, planetary. So no-one
came for the slumped body below the two viewpoints. It was
to remain there, in all its future states – and some particles of
it must still remain hereabouts. The screen continued for a
while, there was activity some of which was pink and
centralized. Fewer bright reds appeared, more pales of what
might have been sky and grays of what might have been
rubble. Then the screen was on but blank but capable of all-
over glow; then it was back to a mirroring black that dust
made less and less reflective. To begin with, I could see myself.
This was an intense time, before jerky perception had become
usual. The haired head slumped forward onto a body
beginning to do various things, including dancing, that
should not have been possible. I know now what must have
entered the room, or been there on the lightshade or

windowsill. To attract them from outside there'd have been plenty of juicy odour, maybe even of shit. And for a while the mind's eye saw dotty activity, a fleck of presence here that flicked to there. In a while, there was a growing density of darknesses, and some of them rang with blue. It seemed, soon after, that I was beginning to move and grow and get funky. My head lifted as my chest pushed up at it, my hands flexed straight and purple, the seams of my clothing withstood what was dough rising, or very like dough rising. Then at the skin-point where chin touched chest, the breakthrough occurred, and suddenly I was a disco of emergences and spewings forth from the middle of spewing forth. Here was a bolus of interested nutrition, spaghetting as the maggots moved too fast to be individually perceived. From thigh down to knees went one peristalsis, beneath cloth. And grandly the stomach burst and acid had its effect on what it fell upon, including chair. Robotic ripples went down the arms, as sinews kept movements fluid and seemingly cultural but gravity always brought small, sudden collapses. Scalp appeared beneath hair, and bone beneath sliding scalp – but that happened later than the rise of white clumps into black clouds. The TV screen became brief home to some of these, and gathering dust softened the edges of what was seen – though, by this stage, it had few enough sharps. Bones rose up through the skin, and what had been a bloat of balloon became a tent of rib. Throughout this, the sight was also taking in the moving areas of dark and light upon the wall. Where the dominant shadows high-pointed began to mark season change and then, when the body-business was over, season after season. The light had – now – water inside of it, now glitter, now song, now death. From where it reached the ceiling, the wallpaper began – different strips at different paces – its slow lowly unpeel. This was when the blue paint was revealed. There to be seen behind the TV screen, all the wall as a bigger screen. Storms brought lightning flashes that were memorable even though they had no retina to wow. And with wind and pummelling of rain, hail, then weight of snow, rooftiles must have split and skidded off. Water made its debut in the room, gamechanger, and all of a sudden things happened all of a sudden. Between me and the TV, the carpet became its own gentle ecosystem of moss. The plaster beneath the blue paint beneath the glue left by the wallpaper began to perform its own less spectacular bloat and blow. A beautiful civilization of black stipple overtook it, top left to bottom right. I had no sense of years – I had lost count before I even thought of counting, but chunks of off-white began to topple from the top, revealing brick. The TV was remarkable in not collapsing until the floorboards beneath its stand were too softened to support what had been an only slightly-pushing-forwards weight. My comfortable chair had subsided long, long before the oblong screen, itself, in an instant, failed as part of the composition. Always there had been an oblong, front centre, and now it had flicked to a slice of still fairly dark grey. The TV stand was metal and glass, and almost as robust as the oblong itself. A nest appeared there and I saw traces of grey flimming in and out. There was a hairy red repetition of my own decomposition as a trapped fox went big then flat after streaking back and forth along the far wall. The windows did not crack until the ceiling had begun to fall in, beam by beam. I should have mentioned the heroic persistence of the curtains. I should have mentioned the curtains, patterned with thin diagonal stripes. Even when there seemed no plaster left to which to cling, their supporting screws kept faith with the bricks. Apart from one absurd chunk of plaster, shaped like Greenland, the whole wall facing me was now back to brick. Rainwater washed down the verticals and swished away at the horizontals. One falling beam left a gash, where attrition happened faster. On the right-hand side, I saw the hint of the join beginning to unzip, and years before it happened, I knew the behind-TV-wall would fall outwards. It was not exactly a relief more a culmination when this happened. The sight of what was now beyond changed things: it was another wall of another house, the next along, and although it was half-collapsed, it still blocked my sight of the wall – or whatever – behind it. I saw more sky, and the familiar darkening and brightening of surfaces – puddle and evaporation – could now be linked to whipping clouds and snapping mists. Increasingly, predictably, there were whiteouts and glistening thaws – bottoming out the floorboards with rot. The next wall fell and after that the wall four walls away, and then the houses were down to foundations. It takes so much for brick to remain on brick with all these swirling forces. And I saw no skeletons. By now I had done a great deal of tunneling though time, towards what tunneled back in my direction. I had not been alone in terms of the animal, sensual – nests continued to blur brownly whilst there still was a height of safety to the walls. After the ground rose up through the blobs of the bricks, I saw molehills bubble like boiling mudpools, and the pock-pock-pock of a warren. There were still flecks of blue paint on the earth, strings of fabric, even after the biggest whiteout rose and fell, but all human-fashioned forms were gone. I could not expect to see another oblong, and the ground level was higher – if I had been bodily there, I would have been half-buried. So what I saw now was a closer-up coming and going of smaller tracks. Holes I'd not have been able to pay attention to before seemed clearer than they should have been, as if I were nearer than I should have been. It was as if I were coming out of them, and encountering my own lack of absence with something beginning to approach acknowledgement. Because, after all, I hadn't not been present. The level of this here bump or that there bump was made from inside. Matter was not disorganized within my field of vision. Further off, there were hills which the white and grey had scraped flatter. The brown around me still darkened with wet and pinked with dry, but I began to sense this as also cold and heat. Somehow this was now the point at which my incorporation began to become irresistible. I had not been attempting to reside in a particular *I* – although I had known the shape of Greenland, I suppose, and the form of spaghetti, the fact of cones in eyes, disco. We only see our own sights, I suppose. I slowly realised that in watching the fall of the house, I had been watching nothing inordinately alien. Its deformation, following my own deformation, was not significant but it was signal – it was in obedience to laws and subject to organisms not irrelevant to me, or separable from me. After a while, I could no longer resist my own self-colonization. At this point, it becomes a failure of exactness to keep the *I*, so we can let it go as unimportant – apart from a few more tunneled words: We saw ourselves looking back at ourselves in a moment of infinite witnessing, our feelers felt feelers, and that's that.

Afterword:

Where am I?

Prof J. Mark Bishop
Golsmiths, University of London

IN TOBY LITT'S account, *A brief history of transience*, Toby poses multiple questions of mind (*res-cogitans*; consciousness) and its relation to organism (*res-extensa*; super-organism); and of life and death, and all our carryings-on during and after; skirting only the before. For it is an age-old problem in the cognitive sciences, just where the 'I' in I resides. You see, as I am thinking, typing and responding to Toby's story, just where is it, what is it and how is it, that *witch,* which conjures all this thinking, typing and responding to be brought forth?

Certainly, these things we call fingers are now moving and typing, but what controls these fingers? Of course signals from my motor neurons enervate the muscles which control movement, but what controls the neuronal behaviour: outputs of other neurons; the sensory inputs from the environment (via my eyes, ears, mouth, skin and nose).

So wherein lies this 'I' that now decides to type: the 'I' in a maze of twisty little passages, all alike?

Many stories have been told about this magik; the magic eye, my magic I. But let's pause a moment to examine one of the best known; an account from the Nobel Laureate and co-discoverer of the structure of DNA molecule, *Francis Crick*. The man who in 1994, in his book *The Astonishing Hypothesis*, the scientific search for the soul, famously wrote:

> You, your joys and your sorrows, your memories and your ambitions, your sense of personal identity and free will, are in fact no more than the behaviour of a vast assembly of nerve cells and their associated molecules. As Lewis Carroll's Alice might have phrased, You're nothing but a pack of neurons. This hypothesis

is so alien to the ideas of most people today that it can truly be called astonishing. [p3]

Although for a few people Crick's hypothesis on consciousness verges on the heretical these days, as the eminent philosopher John Searle eloquently remarked in *The Mystery of Consciousness*, for most – especially those working in the neurosciences – it rarely generates even the mildest surprise. Indeed Crick's core insight – the 'temporal synchronisation' of neural firings – has now effectively become a new orthodoxy used to explain the dynamic organizing principle in more and more types of cognitive activities.

Perhaps this transition to orthodoxy is partly because Crick recounts a simple, fundamentally physicalist tale of 'the visual pathway' and visual experience; describing how light first *falls* onto photoreceptors on the retina, passing signals from the rods and cones, via horizontal cells, bipolar cells and amacrine cells, to the retinal ganglion cells. From here, electrical signals pass via the optic nerve across the chiasm and onto the lateral geniculate nucleus, before finally innervating neurons in the *visual cortex*; a brain structure located at the back of the head (which in turn has multiple feedback pathways back to the lateral geniculate nucleus).

But there is nothing particularly special about the neurons that make up the visual cortex; nothing to suggest that they might somehow *bring forth* this mystery of consciousness and the magic of sight. Indeed, a neuron is 'merely' a cell like any other; it has a cell membrane, a cell body and a cell nucleus. But where neurons differ from other cells is that, in addition, they also have a long, thread–like, structure growing out of one side of their cell body – the axon – and bushy branches of spiny structures attached to the other – *dendrites* – which collectively form the cell's *dendritic tree*.

Input signals are received by the neuron on its dendritic tree and processed in its cell body; *output signals* are passed along its axon for subsequent processing by other cells. Unlike the chips in an electronic computer, however, neuronal cells are not directly physically connected to each other. Instead, at the point at which the axon of one neuron connects to the dendrite of another, there is a small *synaptic* gap. Signals cross this gap only by the action of chemical neurotransmitters such as acetylcholine, dopamine, serotonin, etc.

Thus an electrical signal along the axon causes the release of a neurotransmitter into the synaptic cleft. These chemicals contact receptors at the post-synaptic dendritic side of the synapse, causing charged ions to flow in or out of the dendritic side and thus altering its electrical charge; hence synapses can be excitatory or inhibitory. Broadly speaking, if the sum of such electrical charge exceeds a particular threshold the cell will fire; otherwise it remains quiescent. In this manner, as generations of music lovers in the 60s, 70s, 80s and 90s illicitly (re)discovered, subtle modifications to the balance of such neurotransmitters in the brain (via the ingestion of cannabis, LSD, amphetamine and most recently 3,4-methylenedioxy-N-methylamphetamine) can have *profound* effects on conscious experience...

So Crick asserts that, although much simplified, this mere story of signal transformations across populations of brain neurons is the story of our entire mental life. For example, the suggestion is that our memories are formed by the alteration of synaptic connections strengths between neurons. And yet, as even Crick himself remarks:

> ... on balance it is hard to believe that our vivid picture
> of the world really depends entirely on the activities of
> neurons that are so noisy and so difficult to observe.
> [ibid, p246]

For example, how does the brain associate the multiple parts and different modalities of a sensory experience together so we can perceive them all at the same time? E.g. The colour, smell, sounds, feelings, etc. as triggered by seeing your child amongst a raucous crowd of other children.

Crick's now well-publicised solution is that coherent

oscillations, pitched between 35-75Hz (but most often around 40Hz) between groups of neurons across the cortex, is the 'binding mechanism' deployed by the brain that gives rise to the 'neural correllates' of our conscious experience. Thus in Crick's story – and something along the broad lines of Crick's story has informed the conventional neuro-scientific view for many years now – our consciousness is formed when coherent 40Hz oscillations build up in groups of neurons in our cortex.

It is not the time or place to criticise Crick's work here, although the astute reader might wonder what is so special about '40Hz' or, indeed, why synchronised firings of neurons should give rise to anything much, never mind consciousness. And yet, even for 'the most hard-nosed scientific materialist', at the heart of Crick's thesis there remains a deep mystery: '*as on one level, ever since classical times, the brain has been perceived as the seat of thinking; but on another level, "contra", say the heart and the circulatory system, "one hundred billion neurons don't suggest the most obvious design for a thinking machine"'*.

An alternative account of consciousness comes from recent embodied, enactive, embedded and ecological accounts; the 4Es, defining the so-called radical cognitive science. In this view, I, the mind and consciousness stem from complex physical interactions between neuron and brain, brain and body, and finally body and world/society. Taken together, these feedback loops described one complex, collective, dynamic system where the precise location of the boundary between I and world is merely a projection of the observer.

And it is in this feature of *consciousness leaking into the world* that we find overlap between the theories of radical cognitive science and the ideas that spring forth from Toby's graceful imaginings.

For in Toby's account we also find an attraction to the notion of a richly interconnected *I*; an I emerging as some collective property of the myriad complex interactions between *all the cells in the body-as-a-whole* and their local 'society' and 'environment'.

Indeed, Toby deconstructs much deeper by speculating that as his *dead viewer's* body is gradually consumed by moulds, ants, and other creatures of decay, elements of the viewer's body in turn pass through these creatures' digestion (and thus become, in part, incorporated into their bodies); and that by this mechanism residual elements of his, the viewer's, conscious-self persist beyond his conventionally perceived 'death', through their continued disparate, collective activities. A residual consciousness that dims only as they, in their turn, become ever more physically thinned, separated and dispersed into the world. Ultimately following which *the voice* - the distinct perspective of *the viewer* - in becoming seamlessly merged throughout the wider environment, finally fades.

And in this context we may recall that, as humans, we each carry three to five pounds of bacteria with us as we go about our daily lives - our *microbiome* - and that such bacteria are fundamentally *part of us*; what makes me, me and you, you. And the microbiome outnumber human cells in our bodies ten to one; there are more of them than us. Furthermore, as John Cryan, Professor of anatomy and neuroscience at University College Cork, recently suggested: *there are several different ways that messages can be sent from gut microbiome to brain (and vice versa): by hormones or immune cells via the bloodstream, or by impulses along the vagus nerve, which stretches from the brain to intertwine closely with the gut. Through these pathways, actions in one organ produce effects in the other such that, for example, we see gut microbiome diversity greatly diminished in 'stressed out' mice.*

So if our human consciousness is a property of the lived body-as-a-whole and bacterial cells outnumber the human cells whilst the human body lives, is it really so fanciful to speculate that after the death of their human host, as the human body decays and is transformed and these micro organisms consume and continue their own broader environmental life cycles - much as they did whilst the human host was alive, but now interacting with the local physical environment and not just their human host - that some, residual, component of the human-host-self *lives on* in the surrounding flora and fauna of decay and rebirth?

And so the *I* that was *I*, reflects on life: as neuron-in-brain, brain-in-body, gut-in-body, shit-in-gut, bacteria-in-shit, fungus-in-bacteria, fungus-in-earth, earth-in-water, water-in-cloud, cloud-in-rock, rock-in-planet and planet-in-stardust:

... at this point, it becomes a failure of exactness to keep the I, so we can let it go as unimportant apart from a few more tunneled words: We saw ourselves looking back at ourselves in a moment of infinite witnessing, our feelers felt feelers, and that's that.

About the Authors

Dinesh Allirajah is a Liverpool-based short story writer, poet, creative writing lecturer (UCLan and Edge Hill University), author of the Real Time Short Stories blog, chair of National Black Artists Alliance and a director of Comma Press. Previous work includes the short story publications *A Manner Of Speaking* (Spike 2004) and *The Prisoners/Overnight* (Flax #023, 2011), as well as work in numerous anthologies, including Comma's *The Book Of Liverpool* and *ReBerth* anthologies.

Martyn Bedford is the author of five novels for adults which, between them, have been translated into thirteen languages. His first, *Acts of Revision* (Bantam Press/Black Swan 1996) won the Yorkshire Post Best First Work Award. His novels since are *Exit, Orange & Red*, *The Houdini Girl*, *Black Cat*, and *The Island of Lost Souls*. He is also the author of a novel for young adults, *Flip*, which was shortlisted for the Costa Children's Book Award, longlisted for the Carnegie Medal and named as a Red House Children's Book Awards Pick of the Year title, as well as winning four regional prizes.

Lucy Caldwell was born in Belfast in 1981 and lives in London. She read English at Queen's College, Cambridge and is a graduate of Goldsmith's MA in Creative & Life Writing. She has published two novels, *Where They Were Missed* (2006) and *The Meeting Point* (2011), and her third, *All the Beggars Riding*, will be published in January 2013. *The Meeting Point* featured on BBC Radio 4's Book at Bedtime and was awarded the 2011 Dylan Thomas Prize. She is also a playwright whose stage plays (*Leaves, Guardians,Notes to Future Self*) and radio dramas (*Girl from Mars, Avenues of Eternal Peace, Witch Week*) have won numerous awards including the George Divine Award and the Imison Award. In 2011, Lucy was awarded the prestigious Rooney Prize for Irish Literature for her body of work to date. Her short story 'Escape Routes' was shortlisted for the 2012 BBC International Short Story Award.

Frank Cottrell-Boyce is an award-winning screenwriter and children's novelist. His film credits include *Welcome to Sarajevo, Hilary and Jackie, Code 46, 24 Hour Party People, A Cock and Bull Story*, and most recently *The Railway Man*. In 2004, his debut novel, *Millions*, won the Carnegie Medal and was shortlisted for The Guardian Children's Fiction Award, and was followed by *Framed* (later adapted into a film by the BBC), *The Unforgotten Coat*, and three installments of the *Chitty Chitty Bang Bang* series. Frank also writes for the theatre and was the author of the highly acclaimed BBC film *God on Trial*. He has previously contributed stories to Comma's anthologies *Phobic, The Book of Liverpool, The New Uncanny, When It Changed,* and *Litmus* and is currently working on a full collection for Comma, *Triple Word Score*. He also wrote the script for the opening ceremony of the 2012 London Olympics.

Claire Dean's stories have been published in *The Best British Short Stories, Murmurations: An Anthology of Uncanny Stories About Birds, Still, Shadows & Tall Trees* and elsewhere. *Marionettes* and *Into the Penny Arcade* are published as chapbooks by Nightjar Press. A collection of Claire's new fairy tales was published by Unsettling Wonder in 2014. She lives in Lancashire with her two young sons.

Stuart Evers was born in Macclesfield, Cheshire in 1976. His first book, *Ten Stories About Smoking* was published by Picador in 2011 and won The London Book Award. His short fiction has appeared in Prospect, The Best British Short Stories 2012 and 3:AM, and he regularly writes about books for The Guardian, The Independent, The New Statesman and

Time Out. He at one point read with musical accompaniment from Fighting Kites. *If This is Home* – his debut novel – was published by Picador in July 2012

Julian Gough was born in London and grew up in Ireland. He now lives in Berlin. He won the BBC National Short Story Prize in 2007 with 'The Orphan and the Mob', which later became the prologue for *Jude: Level 1*, a novel short-listed for the 2008 Wodehouse Prize for Comic Fiction. Julian's first novel, *Juno and Juliet*, was published in 2001, followed by *Jude in Ireland* in 2007. *Jude in London*, his most recent novel, was published in 2011 and was short-listed for the Bollinger Everyman Wodehouse Prize. In 2010, Salmon Poetry released his first poetry collection, *Free Sex Chocolate*. Julian Gough has also written columns and opinion pieces for various newspapers and magazines, including the *Guardian, Prospect Magazine* and *A Public Space*.

Andy Hedgecock is a freelance writer, researcher and trainer. His earliest reviews, essays and interviews were published in the anarchist press in the 1980s. Since then he has written for publications such as *The Spectator, Time Out, Penguin City Guides, The Oxford Companion to English Literature, Interzone, The Third Alternative, The Breaking Windows Anthology* and *Foundation*. Since 2006, Andrew has been co-editor (fiction) of *Interzone*, Britain's longest-running British sf magazine and 2013 winner of the British Fantasy Society Award for Best Magazine/Periodical. This is his first piece of fiction.

Annie Kirby is a storyteller, short story writer, novelist and writing tutor. Her stories have appeared in various anthologies, including Comma Press's *Bracket* and *Bio-Punk*. Her Asham Award winning short story 'The Wing' was published in *Don't Know A Good Thing* (Bloomsbury) and adapted for audio download by Spoken Ink. Her stories have been selected for new writer showcases including Radio 4's *Writers to Watch* and the *Portsmouth 2012 Bookfest* anthology. She lives in Portsmouth and has recently completed her first novel.

Zoe Lambert's first collection, *The War Tour* was published by Comma in 2011. A graduate of the UAE Creative Writing MA, she is currently a lecturer in Creative Writing at the University of Bolton, and has previously published stories in *Bracket, Ellipsis 2,* and *Litmus* (all Comma).

Toby Litt is the author of eight novels – *Beatniks: An English Road Movie, Corpsing, Deadkidsongs, Finding Myself, Ghost Story, Hospital, Journey into Space* and *King Death* – as well as three collections of short stories: *Adventures in Capitalism, Exhibitionism* and *I Play the Drums in a Band Called Okay.* In 2003 Toby Litt was nominated by Granta magazine as one of the 20 'Best of Young British Novelists'. His short story 'Call it 'The Bug' Because I Have No Time to Think of a Better Title' was specially commissioned for Comma's *Bio-Punk* anthology and was shortlisted for the 2013 Sunday Times EFG Private Bank Short Story Prize.

Adam Marek is an award-winning short story writer. He won the 2011 Arts Foundation Short Story Fellowship, and was shortlisted for the inaugural Sunday Times EFG Short Story Award. His first story collection Instruction Manual for Swallowing (Comma, 2007) was nominated for the Frank O'Connor Prize. His stories have appeared in many magazines, including: Prospect and The Sunday Times Magazine, and in many anthologies including Lemistry, Litmus and The New Uncanny from Comma Press, The New Hero from Stoneskin Press, and The Best British Short Stories 2011. His second collection, The Stone Thrower, was published earlier this year. To subscribe to Adam's blog, Twitter and Facebook updates, visit www.adammarek.co.uk

Sean O'Brien is Professor of Creative Writing at Newcastle University and has published seven poetry collections, including *The Drowned Book* which won both the Forward and TS Eliot prizes, and *November*. His *Collected Poems* was published in 2012. His translations include Dante's *Inferno*, Aristophanes' *Birds* and Zamyatin's *We*. He has also published a collection of essays, *The Deregulated Muse*, and a novel, *Afterlife*. He is a regular writer for the *TLS* and makes occasional contributions to the *Guardian* and *The Independent*. Sean's first full collection of short stories, *The Silence Room* was published by Comma in 2008. Short stories have since appeared in *Litmus*, *Lemistry*, and *Bio-Punk*, and an essay on Poe in *Morphologies* (all Comma).

K. J. Orr was born in London. Her short fiction has been broadcast on BBC Radio 4, and published by The Dublin Review, The White Review, Lighthouse, Daunt Books and The Sunday Times Magazine online, among others. She has been shortlisted for awards including the BBC National Short Story Award, the Bridport, and the Asham. She is currently completing her debut collection of stories, and an Arts & Humanities Research Council funded PhD on the short story form.

Adam Roberts was born in London two thirds of the way through the last century. He is a writer and academic, and lives a little way west of the city of his birth – fifteen miles or so. His latest books are *Jack Glass* (Gollancz 2012) and *Twenty Trillion Leagues Under the Sea* (Gollancz 2014). His short story collection *Adam Robots* was published in 2013. He has previously contributed to Comma's *Lemistry* and *Morphologies* projects.

Sarah Schofield is a new writer whose recent prizes include the Writers Inc Short Story Competition and the Calderdale Short Story Competition. She was shortlisted for the Bridport Prize in 2010 and was runner up in The Guardian Travel Writing Competition. Her story 'Traces Remain' appeared in *Lemistry: A Celebration of the Life of Stanislaw Lem*, 'Shake Me and I Rattle' in *Bio-Punk: Stories from the Far Side of Research*, 'All About You' and 'The Tiniest Atom' are to appear in Comma's forthcoming *Reveal* and *Thought X* anthologies.

Joanna Quinn is studying for a PhD in Creative Writing at Goldsmiths, University of London. Her work has been published in the *New Welsh Review* and the *Bridport Prize* anthology. She was one of four writers short-listed for the Arts Foundation Fellowship in Short Stories. She lives in Dorset.

Margaret Wilkinson is a short story, stage and radio writer and a senior lecturer in creative writing at Newcastle University. Her most recent radio play for BBC Radio 4, Nocturne, merged mothers, daughters and Chopin. In all her writing she is deeply interested in, and inspired by, character and the sound, tone and rhythm of voice.

Robin Yassin-Kassab is the author of *The Road From Damascus*, a novel published by Hamish Hamilton. He co-edits and writes essays for the Critical Muslim, a quarterly magazine that looks like a book. His book reviews and political analysis have appeared in *the Guardian, the Times, the New Statesman, the National, al-Jazeera* and elsewhere.

About the Scientists

Martyn Amos is Professor of Novel Computation at Manchester Metropolitan University, and the author of *Genesis Machines: The New Science of Biocomputing* (Atlantic, 2007). His research interests include complexity theory, artificial life, synthetic biology and natural computing. He has previously contributed to Comma's *Litmus* and *Bio-Punk* anthologies.

J. Mark Bishop is Professor of Cognitive Computing at Goldsmiths, where his research in Radical Cognitive Science explores how interactions between 'neuron and brain'; 'brain and body' and 'body, society and world' form and shape consciousness. He was president of the UK society for the study of AI, the AISB, between [2010-2014] and currently serves on the organising committee of ICRAC: the International Committee for Robot Arms Control.

After studying cognitive science and gaining a PhD in evolutionary simulation modelling at the University of Sussex, **Seth Bullock** had spells working in Berlin and at the University of Leeds, where he founded the Biosystems research group. He is Professor of Computer Science at the University of Southampton where he is Director of the Institute for Complex Systems Simulation. He has a history of interdisciplinary research into a wide range of different systems problems, and has core interests in modelling methodology, complexity science, evolution and artificial life.

Dr James Dyke is a researcher at the Institute for Complex Systems Simulation at the University of Southampton. Prior to that he was a research scientist at the Max Planck Institute for Biogeochemistry, and prior to that he attained a DPhil in the Centre for Computational Neuroscience & Robotics, building on a MSc in the Evolutionary & Adaptive Systems research group (both at the University of Sussex).

Christian Jantzen PhD, is full professor in Experience Design and Cultural Analysis at Aalborg University (Denmark). His fields of research are consumer research, market communication, media studies, cultural studies and experience design. He has published research in these areas in Danish as well as internationally.

Francesco Mondada is professor at the Ecole Polytechnique Fédérale de Lausanne (EPFL), Switzerland. After a master and a PhD received at EPFL, he led the design of many miniature mobile robots, commercialized and used worldwide in thousands of schools and universities. He co-founded several companies selling these robots or other educational tools. He is author of more than hundred publications in the field of robot design. He received several awards, including the *Swiss Latsis University prize*, as best young researcher at EPFL and the *Credit Suisse Award for Best Teaching* as best teacher at EPFL.

James D. O'Shea is a senior lecturer in computer science at Manchester Metropolitan University. He received the B.Sc. (Hons.) degree in chemistry from Imperial College in 1976 and the Ph.D. (Short Text Semantic Similarity) degree from Manchester Metropolitan University in 2010. He was general chair of the KES-AMSTA conference in Manchester in 2011 and curator of the MMU Alan Turing Centenary Celebrations. His other scientific work covers semantic similarity, including the recent publication 'A new benchmark dataset with production methodology for short text semantic similarity algorithms' in ACM Transactions on Speech and Language Processing.

Andrew Philippides is a Reader in the Department of Informatics at the University of Sussex. He is a member of the Sussex Insect Navigation Group and Sussex Neuroscience and co-director of the Centre for Computational Neuroscience and Robotics. His research combines biological experiments with robotic and computational modelling to understand biological systems. Two projects relevant to this article are: visual navigation in ants, bees and robots; mechanisms of neural learning. The latter includes the EU-funded INSIGHT project which is attempting to demonstrate causal learning by interfacing cultured neurons to a computer through a micro-electrode array.

Lenka Pitonakova is a PhD student at the Southampton University Doctoral Training Centre in Complex Systems Simulation, where she studies biologically inspired swarm intelligence with application to robotics. Her main interest is in discovering general rules for engineering of collective systems capable of performing autonomous tasks such as exploration and item retrieval. Her previous work on a self-configuring, ultrastable neuroendocrine robot controller was published in *Adaptive Behaviour* in 2013.

Steen Rasmussen, Professor Physics, Center Director, University of Southern Denmark & External Research Professor, Santa Fe Institute, USA. Previous 20 years research leader at Los Alamos National Laboratory, USA. Honors include P. Gorm-Petersens Mindelegat in the presence of Her Majesty the Queen, Magrethe II of Denmark (1988) & World Technology Network Reward, USA (2005). Won $35+ million in research grants to home institutions and consortia. Published 100+ peer reviewed papers, edited five books, 200+ invited presentations, 100+ media interviews including Wall Street Journal and New York Times. Three adult children. Lives at a farm by the sea.

Thomas S. Ray is professor of Biology and Computer Science at the University of Oklahoma 1998 to present. Assistant and associate professor in School of Life and Health Sciences University of Delaware 1981 to 1998. BS in Biology and Chemistry Florida State University; MS and Ph.D. in tropical plant ecology Harvard University. External Faculty of Santa Fe Institute 1993-2003. Invited researcher ATR Kyoto Japan 1993-1998. AAAS Fellow. Research in ecology and evolution of rain forest organisms 1974 to 1989. Research in artificial life 1990 to 2001. Research in the human mind 2001 to present.

Micah Rosenkind is currently employed as a researcher and lecturer at the University of Brighton's school of Computing Engineering and Mathematics. His previous research includes publications on believable artificial intelligence for games and biologically inspired agent architectures for virtual characters. His currently researching the role of emotions in human computer interfaces.

James Snowdon conducted his PhD research at the University of Southampton, UK, modelling transport systems and the effects of variable traffic control within computer simulation. He currently works in transport planning outside of academia, creating forecasts and conducting appraisals of proposed highway and public transport schemes. He has published academic papers in a variety of areas including driver diversion behaviour, automated CCTV monitoring and smart 'learning' traffic light control systems which was featured on BBC Television's 'The One Show'.

Susan Stepney is Professor of Computer Science at the University of York, and Director of the York Centre for Complex Systems Analysis. Her main research areas are in Unconventional Computation, in simulating Complex Systems, and in Artificial Chemistries. Her current research is into computational systems that can generate unbounded novelty. Two research projects in this area are: the EvoEvo (Evolution of Evolution) EU FET project, developing novel evolutionary algorithms based on inspiration from bacterial and virus evolution; Subsymbolic Artificial Chemistries, developing novel complex computational systems based on inspiration from molecular chemistry.

Dr Germán Terrazas is a research scientist at the University of Nottingham. He has expertise in artificial intelligence, optimisation, stochastic simulation, explorative data mining, complex systems and nanomolecular design. After working for more than a decade in computer science, Germán has recently moved to engineering to focus on the research and development of innovative computing applied to the UK manufacturing sector. His scientific interests comprise unconventional computing, crowdsourcing, bio-inspired architectures, internet of things, virtualisation and data analysis. German's professional career is demonstrated by his track record of publications some of which awarded by IEEE, the organisation of international conferences and the edition of books and journals.

Andrew Vardy is an Associate Professor of Computer Science and Computer Engineering at Memorial University of Newfoundland in St. John's, Canada. His research interests include biologically-inspired robotics, swarm robotics, and navigation. In general, he studies simple mechanisms for robot autonomy. Current projects include distributed object sorting, terrain reshaping for underwater construction, and route following by autonomous underwater vehicles. Andrew is a proud owner of a Newfoundland / Labrador cross named Bruno who provided inspiration, as well as the use of his name, for 'Bruno Wins.'

Alan Winfield is Professor of Electronic Engineering and Director of the Science Communication Unit at the University of the West of England (UWE), Bristol, UK, and Visiting Professor at the University of York. Alan co-founded the Bristol Robotics Laboratory, where his research is focussed on robot intelligence. Alan led UK public engagement project Walking with Robots, awarded the 2010 Royal Academy of Engineering Rooke medal for public promotion of engineering. His book 'Robotics: A Very Short Introduction' was published by Oxford University Press in September 2012.